Fondly from us all

Christmas 1985

The Roberts

A Treasury of
NEW ENGLAND
SHORT STORIES

A Treasury of
NEW ENGLAND
SHORT STORIES

from *Yankee* Magazine

Published by Yankee, Inc., Dublin, New Hampshire 03444

Editors: Laurie Hillyer and Clarissa M. Silitch
Art Director: Carl F. Kirkpatrick

FIRST EDITION

Contents

Foreword

As a writer who lives in New England, loves New England and has written many short stories about New England, helping edit this book about Yankees has been indeed a labor of love.

The stories have all appeared in *Yankee* Magazine. In the woodshed days (*Yankee* started, as many New England ventures have, in a woodshed), letters were mailed out, requesting, with all possible charm, submission of fiction. Now, 39 years later, with twenty short stories arriving at the magazine in a single week, and only twelve stories being published in a single year, times have changed indeed.

The stories that come to my desk are divided into three parts—the largest number, obviously, receiving rejection slips; the second largest comprise "possible" stories which will be distributed among members of the staff for reading and discussion; the third type story—the smallest by far—is brought to staff meeting with the ringing jubilant cry, "Here is one we simply must have!" From this category all the stories in this book have been drawn.

Without magazines the short story could never have attained its present literary distinction and importance. The stories here have a wide and fascinating range of subject but each and every one of them is laid in that proud and happy land to which *Yankee* is indubitably dedicated—New England.

More important than the setting, of course, as all writers know, are the characters out of which the plot, to make it credible, must spring. If the word "Yankee" conjures up a certain type in your mind, let it go. In this book are farmers and professors, saints and snobs, grandmothers, lovers, heroes, murderers, little boys (we hope you like them, we do), devils, writers, lawyers, fliers, priests. They might live on that stern and rockbound coast or near the bridge that arched the flood or next door to the barefoot boy with cheek of tan.

Some of the stories, but not all, could have happened only in New England. Harvey Snow and his pa and grandpa ("How Harvey Snow Got Religion") are as Vermont (but not as sugary) as maple syrup. One immediately associates the dowager in "Mrs. Van Dusen and the

Myrtilles" with Beacon Hill. Some of the derisive letters in "The Collaborators" were knocked out on the famous Concord turnpike but might have been written anywhere. The village described in the gentle "Gunther's Song" is a New England village, but the place is not important.

"The Magic Hat" is, amazingly, the author's first published story. It is an unforgettable and beautifully written story. The hero returning from the war hotfoots it away from the welcoming home-town band, tagged by his questioning small brother, and tries—fast—to bury his war memories with his military gear. But memories, like wars, cannot be buried.

There is a saying "Once a Yankee, always a Yankee." It reminds me, as I write it, of my Vermont grandfather, an adventurer, who went west to help start the wheels rolling on the Atchison, Topeka and Santa Fe. He lived out his days in Topeka, Kansas, but he and my grandmother are buried on a green hillside above the Connecticut River, in Vermont.

Laurie Hillyer

The Line Fence

by Curtis K. Stadtfeld

They had shared a line fence for over forty years. One hundred and sixty rods long, half a mile, it stretched back from the road to the woods where it just sort of petered out, as they used to say, down in a swamp where the cows didn't go anyway. The fence wasn't maintained there even in the years when they both ran a lot of cattle. Paul farmed eighty acres on the east side of the fence. His farm was in a conventional shape, a quarter mile wide by half a mile long, eighty rods by a hundred and sixty. George was on the west side, and he had a hundred and twenty acres, in an L shape, so he shared line fences with three other farmers. But the line he shared with Paul was the longest, and the most important. The men who owned the other farms lived in houses separated by roads or woods from George's farm, so Paul was his closest neighbor, all those years.

They worked in each other's sight most of the time. The land lay on a great slope, with Paul's farm above George's. Paul could look down on the other farm while he worked, keep an eye on things, almost as though he were in an airplane. Once in a while he would get in his car, drive around on the road, come to tell George that cows were out or someone's cattle were in his corn, something like that. If they had not been friendly, George might have thought of him as a snoop, a spy, the way he could look at things. But no unfriendliness could outlast forty years of sharing a line fence. In any case, they had been boys together, had been friends in the cautious way that farm neighbors are friends. Their work had kept them together, and they had never fought over the fence.

There was bound to be a little friction, with a fence that long shared for so many years, bound to be a little irritation once in a while when livestock broke through. But that had happened no more than half a dozen times in nearly half a century, and it was nothing at all compared to the many times they had shared help, worked on the fence together, talked over it about the crops or cattle, given each other a hand with one chore or another.

The fence had pretty well fallen down in recent years. Neither of them had kept a head of cattle on his land for more than a decade. There was no need any more to keep up the fence. Most of the posts were rotted just about off at ground level. Several of them had fallen, broken off by an animal or a child or the wind or just simply with the gravity of time. Where the other posts were still good, the broken ones would lean over, still held off the ground but swaying in the wind, pulling at the wires. There were four barbed strands—"bob wire" they called it, in their slightly flat accents—and they were rusting, breaking, settling into the grass, growing into the trees that stood here and there in the fence row, substituting for posts. And of course the grass, untended by horse or cow, had grown up, season after season, had matured and fallen down, tangled with the weeds, built up the fertility for the little wild cherry brush that was making a comeback now that no one pruned it.

The first thirty years of the neighborness, the fences had been important. Paul kept Holsteins, rough rangy animals, always with a little extra touch of wildness in them because Paul had little compassion for his cattle. He was one of the few farmers around who numbered his cows rather than naming them. He never groomed them, never spoke to them, let the bull run loose with them in the late summer for breeding. In the early years, he had kept horses, too, three or four, wild and unattended as the cows.

George kept Durhams for a long time, big red and roan cows, shaggy and shy. But he switched to Guernseys, dairy cows, smaller, higher bred, more delicate by nature than the Holsteins, more domesticated because they were cared for by George's swarm of children, who named them and petted them and brushed and combed them and showed them at local fairs—who made friends of them.

So the herds had to be kept apart by the line fence because George's children did not want the big rough Holsteins upsetting the Guernseys, and George did not want to take a chance of having one of his cows bred by the Holstein bull.

Also, there was usually a piece of corn along the line, or potatoes, and the fence kept the cows out of that.

By tradition—both men believed it to be common law, though neither had ever checked—a man was responsible for the half of the line fence that was on his right as he faced his neighbor's land. So if the cows got out, it was easy to tell whose fence had been broken through. If much crop was destroyed, there might have been damages to pay besides fixing the fence. So it was a good idea to keep your half of the line in good repair.

It was Paul's end that drifted down into the woods; George's was straight except for a place where a sink hole pocked the line and all year, except in the late summer, the fence there was under water, at least for the bottom wire or so.

The custom had become a tradition with them. Sometime in the spring, George would walk out of his house, up to where his section of the fence came to an end near the road, and begin to walk along, carrying a scythe or corn knife, a hammer in the loop on his overalls and a pair of fence pliers in his pocket, lugging a little bag of staples. He would trim back the weeds and grass, kick at the posts to see if any was shaky, replace staples if they were coming loose. If more than one or two posts needed replacement, it would be a job marked for a morning when the fields were too wet to work, or for a Saturday, when the boys were home from school to help.

Paul's wife, who was not a busybody but for other reasons had plenty of time to watch out the window, would tell her husband that George was checking the fence. Paul would gather up his own tools and staples, and start walking the line from his end.

Through the years, neither of them had ever made any attempt to mark the center post that divided George's half of the line fence from Paul's. Some years, they might meet two-thirds of the way to one end, another year, toward the other end, depending on which section weathered the winter best. But they never divided it up sharply; it was their line fence, and they kept it together, and they never quarreled over it.

George would point out to his sons that the fence was an example of how things evened out in the world, if a man just did what he was supposed to do without worrying too much about whether he was doing too much. Paul's big cows, and especially the bull, were harder on the fence than the Guernseys, George would explain, so you might think that Paul should take a bigger share of the responsibility for keeping up the fence. But on the other lines, no one ever ran cattle at all, and the other owners had to keep up their half of the fence for George's cattle. That's the way the world was, he would explain— just follow the rules and things will even out sooner or later.

There were some good stories about the line fence to be told in the winter. There was the day that George and his sons were dumping trash into the pothole, and Paul's big bull was tearing at the fence, pawing the ground, scaring hell out of everyone. George had recently come by a rat terrier, a tiny tense little whirlwind of a dog, and the dog was eyeing the bull with considerable interest. When it seemed that the fence was about to yield, George pointed to the bull and told the dog to "sic'em."

The terrier, too fast to know fear, darted down and nipped the bull on the nose. The bull was startled and turned to dispatch the little nuisance. The terrier pulled one of his favorite tricks, a little thing he used to do to cows to show them he meant business. He would jump, grab the tail up high near the top, and slide down it, keeping his teeth gripped and letting his weight pull him along the tail. Once was usually enough to convince a cow that the dog was to be obeyed. It got the bull's attention, too, and he spun to find his tormentor. The terrier was very quick; he could run down a squirrel in a wood lot, and a Holstein bull is much slower than a squirrel. The dog bit the bull on the ear, then ran around, took a nip or two at the scrotum. The bull capitulated, ran bellowing toward the barn, the dog nipping along happily and biting at every tender part he could reach.

That night, after the chores were done, Paul drove down in his Hudson. "What did you do to my bull? He won't even come out of the barnyard. Every once in a while, he goes up and peeks over the hill and bellers and runs back to hide under the overchute." He and George had a good laugh about such a little dog putting such a big bull in his place.

And there was the time the Canadian thistles began to spread in a big circular patch with its center at the line fence. George waited all summer until the moon was in the right sign and the thistles' round purple flowers were full, and then took a scythe and gave another to his son, who was in high school at the time, studying agriculture, and who did not believe in the sign of the moon as it related to crops. But to humor his father, he went out with him and they cut the thistles, right up to the line fence. For years, Paul's thicket of thistles flourished, but the patch ended abruptly at the fence and it never reestablished itself on George's farm. There was no logical reason for this, but there it was, and it made for much story-telling and head-shaking.

Those times were long past, and the fence had fallen in. George's family had grown and gone, no one staying with him on the land, working instead in factories and offices in distant cities. He had sold the cattle when the last of his boys left, and Paul had sold his when arthritis cramped his hands so he could not milk or handle a hay fork in comfort. Paul and his wife had no children. She was a mental invalid, sometimes sitting at a window for weeks staring out without comment, sometimes playing her piano, now and then feeling well enough to go for a ride with Paul in the Hudson. She spent some years in an institution; her last few at home. She died in the winter, one cold afternoon, after she had awakened from a nap and seemed bright and whole again. They had about an hour, and then she died.

George's wife, weary from the hard years and the work of raising eight children in the harshness of a farm home, had died the winter before.

Both men took money from the government now.

Yet the habits had taken deep roots over the years. And one spring day, George walked out, up the road to where the line fence began, and started along it. As he reached the top of the first hill, he stopped and looked up at Paul's farm, and saw his neighbor walking stiffly down the lane toward his own half of the line fence.

George found that he could not walk the line as he once did. The matted grass and weeds had grown too thick, the puzzle of fallen posts and wire too tangled. He wanted, though, to cut out the cherry brush that was invading. He had brought along his jackknife, sharpened the night before. He came to the first wild cherry shrub, and stopped. It was no shrub. The little sapling trunk that George had planned to slash with his jackknife was nearly four inches in diameter, the tree some twenty feet high—big enough to shade four or five cows.

He stood before the tree for a little while, and finally folded the knife and dropped it back in his pocket. He turned and looked down toward the barn, where the brush was growing up around the fences since the cattle had stopped bothering it. Some of it was as big as this tree, George saw. He hadn't realized how big it was, it had grown up so slowly. Gradually, year by year, slipping in when a man's back was turned, taking over again. And no one there to help him, no cows to pen in the barnyard overnight once in a while so they would chew back the brush, no one to get out an ax and take down the trees.

He had a good ax, although it might need sharpening. He had hung it up in the garage last fall, there by the door. Or was it the fall before. It seemed that he had spent much more time in recent years hanging things up for the last time. In earlier years, when he and the farm were young, he had hung things up with a flourish when he knew he was through with them.

He had hung up the corn planter one day, because he had a tractor and he could afford an automatic two-row planter. He had hung up the hand grain-broadcaster when he bought the old Superior nine-hole drill. He had hung up the milk stool when the milker was working, and he had hung up the crosscut saw when he got his first chain saw.

He walked along the line fence again, toward Paul, who was making a little better time. Maybe he didn't notice the cherries, George thought. Or maybe he just didn't care.

Every posthole, George had dug, or he had supervised the digging. With shovels, later a posthole digger, hard work even where the soil was soft, brutal in dry clay or if you hit a big stone two feet down and had to start the hole over somewhere else.

My God, how many postholes had he dug! Four hundred eighty rods of line fence alone, a post every rod. Two rows of fence along the lane, full length of the eighty and across to the back forty. Cross fences at least seven or eight of them, eighty rods long each. Average life of a cedar post, five or six years. He gave up trying to figure it out, but he could count them all in the muscles of his back and shoulders, all those postholes; all the posts, too—he had cut many of them from his own cedar swamp, cut and peeled and cured them and then planted them and put the wire on them and braced them in the corners. His shoulders remembered them all.

They met near a place where a fence had once crossed George's land. His oldest son had taken the fence row out fifteen years ago to make room for strips, longer, more efficient. God, it was good to see those fences go. But then his son had gone too, and George had neither fence nor son. "How's it look?" he asked Paul.

The other man snorted. "Like hell. Take two younger men a week to get it in shape. Goddam thing couldn't hold a sick sheep.

Now, of course, if they wanted to replace the fence, they would put an auger on the back of the tractor, dig the postholes by power, twenty or thirty an hour, or simply put in steel posts. Nothing to it, except strength and money. And a reason for doing it.

"George, I've wanted to come down and talk with you since Velda died." Good God, what a name for a farm wife! But she had been so beautiful and strong when they were married, and she could sing like an angel. She and Paul used to walk down the road to the church on Sunday and sing together in the choir and the priest would speak the mass softly so everyone could listen. She had not looked frail at all.

"I went to the funeral."

"I know, George, I know. Did I ever tell you that when we had that little time, those few minutes before she died, that she asked for you and Mary? How you were? I don't think she remembered that you'd had children. She asked how you were, the two of you."

"I'm proud that she asked. We always thought a lot of her, you know."

"I told her you were fine, both of you. I didn't tell her that Mary had died. We just talked about people and places and things for a while, the first time in thirty years she had more than just a minute or two. Most of the people she wanted to talk about are dead, and I've forgotten where some of the places are." He looked up toward the big unpainted house, almost hidden among the untrimmed trees in the overgrown yard.

After a minute, he turned back, brushing his eyes with a glove. "But I wanted you to know something else. I've thought about it a lot, how lonely you must be since Mary died and the kids all gone. I see they come up sometimes on a weekend, but it's not the same, I know."

Not the same. These two men had gone to school together, hunted watermelons in the dark of fall evenings from Model T Fords. They had filled each other's silos thirty falls, helped in each other's fields in emergencies. There had been eight children for George, only one had died. From the time the first was born until the last left home was over thirty years. There were two dozen grandchildren, some of them he hardly knew, and his wife was dead a year and a half. The big house, so noisy for so long, was quiet now. No, it wasn't the same.

"Well," Paul said, "I want you to know it's the same for me. You'd think that after all these years, caring for her and worrying and wondering and all, that it would have been a relief, finally. I almost thought it would be. There were times, George, years ago, when I looked forward to it, God help me. But now she's gone and, by God, George, I miss her as much as you miss your Mary. I just wanted you to know."

Their eyes did not meet again. But they stood for a few minutes, looking past each other at the empty fields. Then Paul lurched away, and hobbled up the lane.

That was in the spring—and now it was a week before Christmas and George decided to mention something to Paul—something he'd had on his mind since Mary had died, and especially since they had buried Velda. If Paul's house had a light at the side that faced George's house, George could check it at night before he went to bed. He could come out on his back porch and look up the long slope and see if things were all right with Paul, see if the light was on. It would be nice if Paul would put a light back there. After all, George thought, Paul has been up there all these years with my lights to check. It probably hasn't occurred to him that I'd like his house to have a light that I can see, too.

George decided that he'd drive up later and mention it to Paul. The light might help a little, make it less lonely while they watched.   END

The Case of the Mortgaged Pig

by Philip B. Buzzell

Fond as Jonathan Blanchard was of his sister's johnny-cake, the remark she had just made stopped him short in the act of conveying a generously buttered slab of it to his mouth.

"Do you have to bring up Lem Peavey's troubles while I'm trying to enjoy my breakfast?" he inquired resignedly. The question was in fact purely rhetorical. The Squire knew perfectly well that Sophrenia, the self-appointed keeper of his legal conscience, was not to be diverted when she had made up her mind that some unfortunate was entitled to his services, usually on a charity basis.

"Simeon Gudgell ought to be ashamed of himself," his sister sputtered. "Grinding down the faces of the poor!"

"Seems to me Lem Peavey's face could stand a little mite of grinding down," the Squire interjected dryly. "Might improve it quite a bit, specially his nose. What's Sim done to him, besides grinding his face, that is?"

Sophrenia dismissed his levity with an expressive sniff. "Dragged him into court to collect a measly fifty dollars, that's what he's done," she explained indignantly. "Wouldn't you just know that nasty little Toothaker would take a case like that?"

"Oh come now, Phreenie," her brother objected good-naturedly, "Milton Wordsworth's not such a bad fellow. How do you know but what Lem really owes the money?"

"Because I know Sim Gudgell," Sophrenia retorted tartly. "And Martha Peavey's sure there's some skulduggery mixed up in it. I told her you'd see Lem this morning and straighten it all out."

The Squire recalled that the Ladies Benevolent Society had met at his house the previous afternoon. He had learned to accept more or less philosophically his sister's habit of making unexpected appointments for him following such meetings, at which one or another of her less fortunate friends was apt to confide some hard-luck story to her sympathetic ear. After all, it was not such a heavy price to pay for having his house kept in apple-pie order, and mouth-watering meals appearing three times a day on his table. Few bachelors, he reflected, were so fortunate as to have a widowed sister who was universally acknowledged to be the best cook and housekeeper in town.

He finished his second cup of coffee in the leisurely fashion made possible by the fact that to reach his office he had only to step across the hall from the dining room. Some years before, a doctor newly settled in town had suggested to him that he ought to take some mild regular exercise, and had been temporarily impressed by the Squire's assurance that he walked to and from his office every day, "rain or shine."

"What time'll Lem show up, think likely?" he inquired as he pushed back his chair. "Yes, I know," he answered his own question, "When he gets good and ready. Pretty busy fellow, Lem is."

With this mild parting shot he disappeared into his office, which had its own outside door opening onto a side porch, where his weathered shingle, "Jonathan Blanchard, Justice of the Peace, Attorney and Counsellor at Law", was readily visible from the street.

Contrary to his prediction, Lem Peavey made his appearance almost as soon as the Squire had seated himself at his cluttered roll-top desk. Lem was a lanky, horse-faced individual who had long ago decided that the world and all that was in it was agin him, thus rendering any effort on his part a useless waste of energy. His overalls were amateurishly patched, his shirt far from clean, and he kept turning an old straw hat with a badly abraded brim around and around in his hands as he talked on and on in a high, whining voice. As the old lawyer watched him, he was thinking that Martha Peavey might with profit have spent more time on her housework and less on the affairs of the Ladies Benevolent Society. A few minutes of listening to Lem's rambling discourse convinced the Squire that unless he brought his client to the point with a few pertinent questions the interview was likely to waste the entire morning.

"So Sim Gudgell's had a writ served on you," he broke in, at Lem's first nearly imperceptible pause for breath. "What's he claiming?"

"Says I owe him a bonus for some money he loaned me a while back," Lem answered.

"Bonus, you say?" the Squire persisted. "How about the loan itself?"

"Paid that all back, with six percent interest on top of it," Lem asserted.

"Got any receipts?"

To the lawyer's very real surprise, Peavey produced a half dozen grimy, dog-eared forms from a printed receipt book which indeed appeared to show the payment of one-hundred and fifty dollars in installments of twenty-five dollars each, with six percent interest added to each installment. All the receipts bore Gudgell's signature, with which the Squire was familiar. He began to take a little more interest in his unwelcome client's dilemma.

"What about this bonus?" he asked. "Did you ever agree to it, and how much was it supposed to be?"

"Never heard nothing about it till I paid the last installment," Peavey told him. "Gudgell claims it's fifty dollars for makin' the loan."

"Did you sign anything when you borrowed the money?"

"Yup, some kind of a paper, note, I guess you call it." Lem admitted. "Didn't read it, so I don't know what was in it."

The Squire shook his head. "Why folks will sign papers they don't read is beyond me," he complained. "I wouldn't doubt but what the paper you signed had an agreement in it to pay the bonus. Did Sim do anything to keep you from reading it? Hold his hand over— it or anything?" he suggested hopefully.

"Nope," Lem admitted. "Could have read it if I'd wanted to, I guess."

"Chances are, then," the Squire told him, "if Sim shows up in court with a paper you signed agreeing to the bonus, he'll get a judgment all right enough. Not much point in my putting in an appearance," he added, hopefully.

Lem's mournful features took on an even more hopeless look, impossible as that might have seemed.

"Martha said Sophreeny was sure you could do something for me," he lamented.

The last thing the old lawyer wanted was to discourage the belief in his omniscience which he well knew to be generally held throughout the town.

"Even if Sim does get a judgment," he suggested, "the question still is, how's he going to collect it?"

"Can't he have me put in jail if I don't pay?" Lem wanted to know.

"Not if you don't have any property that can be taken on execution," the Squire assured him.

"*Execution?*" repeated Lem in a quavering voice. "What's that mean?"

Keeping his face as straight as possible, the Squire hastened to explain that the word in this context implied no threat of capital punishment.

"It's just a paper the court gives the sheriff so he can go and grab property to satisfy the judgment—if he can find any, that is," the old lawyer concluded.

"Question is," he added, "whether you've got anything that isn't exempt from being taken under the statute. Let's see, you don't own the place where you live, do you?"

Lem shook his head. "Just rent," he said. "Never got enough ahead to buy a place."

"No bank accounts or investments?" the Squire continued hopefully. His client's disclaimer of any such embarrassing encumbrances was gratifyingly prompt and positive.

"Never try to remember what's in a statute without looking at it again," the old lawyer admonished himself after a moment's reflection. Turning to the bookshelves back of his desk he pulled down a bulky volume entitled "Public Statutes". Locating the section he was looking for he ran through it to the accompaniment of a muttered running commentary.

"H-m-m, following articles exempt from execution—necessary wearing apparel—household furniture not exceeding three hundred dollars in value—no worry there, Lem, I guess—h-m-m—Bible, school books and library not exceeding fifty dollars in value—safe enough there —one cow, six sheep, one swine, and two tons of hay—how about that, Lem—got any livestock?"

"Nothing but one pretty fair pig," Lem allowed, "might dress out better'n three hundred, come fall."

"That seems all right, long as there's only one," the Squire said.

"Come to think of it, though, I have got one little runt besides the big one," Lem added. "Almost forgot it. Cy Perkins just give it to me day or two ago."

Jonathan started as though a bee had stung him.

"Isn't Cy Perkins some kin of Sim Gudgell's?" he inquired. "How'd he come to make you a present of a pig?"

"Don't rightly know," Lem admitted. "Just said he didn't want to bother feeding it. Kind of unpromising looking runt, anyhow."

"*Timeo Danaos*," the Squire muttered. Ignoring Lem's puzzled "What say?" he turned again to the bookshelves and took down a volume of Supreme Court reports. Presently, he gave a grunt of satisfaction. "I'll bet I know what Sim Gudgell, Cy Perkins and Company are up to," he concluded, "and what's more, I know how to put a spoke in their wheel. You wouldn't mind giving me a little mortgage on the runt, would you, to cover my fee?"

"Runt ain't wuth much of anything," Lem protested. "Better put the mortgage on the big one, hadn't you? That's the one Sim'll try to grab."

"No," said Jonathan cheerfully. "You just leave it to me, Lem. A mortgage on the runt will suit me first rate. Just tell me what he looks like so we don't get the two of them mixed up."

Condensing Lem's rambling description into a few words, the Squire filled in a printed form of chattel mortgage to cover "one four-weeks-old pig with black and white markings," along with a note for fifteen dollars as "retainer for legal services."

Since he was himself the town clerk, Jonathan then proceeded to stamp and file the instrument as duly recorded. By repeatedly assuring Lem that he would be in court to lend him at least moral support at the trial, he finally managed to ease his client out of the office.

On the following Monday, true to his promise, Jonathan strolled into the dingy courtroom on the second floor of the Masonic Building, where Judge Peters, a contemporary and long-time friend of his, was meting out summary justice to a procession of drunk and disorderly defendants, preparatory to calling the civil list. With a reassuring nod to Lem, who was sitting on the edge of the rearmost spectators' bench as though poised for instant flight, he took his seat in the cramped bar enclosure, noting as he did so that Milton Wordsworth Toothaker, the young lawyer who represented Gudgell, and who had only recently been admitted to the bar, looked almost as pale and apprehensive as Lem himself. Even after forty years of practice the memory of the butterflies in his own stomach when he had tried his first case was still acute enough so that he tried to put a little extra touch of friendliness in his whispered greeting to his young colleague.

When the clerk finally called the case of Gudgell versus Peavey and the Squire arose and announced that he was appearing for the defendant, he caught a gleam of amused surprise in the old judge's eyes. It was a rare occasion indeed when Jonathan Blanchard, recognized as one of the leaders of the county bar, appeared in the police court. Sweating and stammering, young Toothaker managed to have his client sworn and called to the stand, where he identified the note, and confirmed that the bonus it called for had not been paid. The Squire asked no questions, but merely examined the note to make sure that it did indeed provide for a bonus for making the loan, and that it bore Lem's scrawled signature.

The judge's grizzled eyebrows rose even higher when Jonathan announced that he had no evidence or argument to offer. The look of relief on young Toothaker's face was almost comic when he realized that his formidable adversary was apparently surrendering.

After another quizzical look at the old lawyer, and a pause to make sure that he had nothing further to offer, Judge Peters announced his finding for the plaintiff in the sum of fifty dollars, as demanded. Thereupon Jonathan again arose and addressed the court.

"If Your Honor please," he began, "there are certain aspects of this case which in the interests of justice should be called to the attention of the Court—as well as to the attention of my young friend. I would suggest, if Your Honor will permit, that for several reasons which will be made to appear, this could best be done in chambers."

The judge's curiosity had evidently been aroused, and he got to his feet with some alacrity. "The list for the day is concluded," he announced, "so, Mr. Clerk, you may adjourn the sitting until tomorrow. Meanwhile, gentlemen, I shall be most happy if you will join me in my sanctum."

After the judge had peeled off his black robe and seated himself in shirt-sleeved comfort behind his desk, he packed and lighted a blackened corncob pipe. "Make yourselves comfortable, gentlemen," he invited. "Smoke, of course, if you like. Now, Jonathan, let's hear what's on your mind."

Out of the tail of his eye the Squire noted a renewed look of apprehension on young Toothaker's face. "This is, perhaps, a little irregular," he began, "but I have a notion that my young friend here is planning to have certain property of my client seized on execution to satisfy his judgment, and I thought it would save him embarrassment, and save me the necessity of suing my good friend the sheriff, if I called certain matters to his attention in Your Honor's presence. It occurred to me that Your Honor might be good enough to relieve Brother Toothaker's mind by confirming for his benefit what I am about to say."

Judge Peters gave vent to a throaty chuckle. "Chances are I'll confirm it all right if you say it's so, Jonathan," he nodded. "If I'd been half the lawyer you are, I'd have been on the Supreme Court by now."

"May I say in reply to your generous exaggeration of my abilities, Tom, that in my humble opinion you should long since have been gracing that bench," the Squire told him.

Young Toothaker was looking more bewildered than ever. This friendly informality between bench and bar was evidently quite a revelation to him.

"Seriously, though," the Squire continued, "I don't want to be compelled to bring an action of trover or replevin against the sheriff, who as I have said is my good friend, or even against Brother Toothaker's client, for whom I must admit I entertain somewhat less fondness, but I shall have to do so if my client's sole asset which might be thought not exempt should ill-advisedly be seized on execution. I refer, Your Honor, to his very fine fat pig which will be ready for butchering in another month or so."

"But his pig's exempt under the statute—that is, if he's only got one," the judge objected.

"Quite so, Your Honor," the old lawyer replied, reverting to his more formal manner. "By a most extraordinary coincidence, however, namely an unsolicited gift from a cousin of the plaintiff Gudgell, my client received a present of another pig—a runt of small intrinsic value, I might add—just before this action was brought. Of course I would not for a moment suggest that this gift was prompted by an ulterior motive, but the effect of it might be thought to expose the more valuable animal to seizure on execution—at least by anyone not familiar with our Supreme Court's decision in the case of Tryon v. Mansir, Volume 2 of Allen's Reports, Page 214."

Turning to the shelves behind his desk, Judge Peters pulled down the calfbound volume in question and turned to the citation. As he read, his face broke into a broad grin. "Substitute 'pig' for 'cow' and I guess it's on the nail right enough," he chuckled. "I suppose you're going to tell me there's a mortgage on the—ah—runt, eh, Jonathan?"

"Exactly, Your Honor," the old lawyer replied solemnly. "A mortgage which I hold to cover my retainer in this case."

"I don't blame you for looking a little bewildered," said Judge Peters, addressing the fledgling barrister. "No doubt you never heard of this case till this minute, any more than I did myself. But let me read you a little extract from the opinion, written back in 1861 by Chief Justice Bigelow: 'By Rev. St. c.97, s.22, one cow, the property of a debtor, is exempt from execution. Giving to this provision such a construction as will make it operate beneficially to debtors, and secure to them the full advantage of the exemptions contemplated by the legislature, we are of opinion that it must be held to mean, that a debtor has the right to the sole, exclusive and absolute ownership of one cow, which his creditors cannot seize and apply in satisfaction of their debts. In other words, it is not a mere partial interest or right of redemption only in the animal which is intended by the statute to be secured to the debtor and his family. The case at bar affords an illustration of the inequality in the operation of the statute to which a different interpretation would lead. The plaintiff was in possession of two cows, one of which was subject to a mortgage. If his creditor could lawfully seize on execution the one which was subject to no lien or encumbrance, it is obvious that the plaintiff would be left in a worse condition than a debtor who was the absolute owner of only one cow. The former would be permitted to hold exempted from seizure nothing but a right of redemption in a cow, while the latter could retain to his own use the entire beneficial interest in the animal. Nor is this the only result which might follow. The exemption would be ineffectual and useless to the debtor, in case the amount of the debt secured by the mortgage was equal to the value of the cow. Without determining therefore whether, on the facts proved, the mortgage given by the plaintiff had been foreclosed, we are of opinion that the officer, under the circumstances of this case, had no right to seize on execution the cow which was not subject to the mortgage."

"Sounds pretty conclusive, doesn't it, Brother Toothaker?" the old judge commented, not unsympathetically, as he closed the volume and returned it to the shelf. "Of course, it leaves your client perfectly free to have the sheriff seize the runt on execution, assuming of course that he's ready and willing to pay off the Squire's mortgage."

"But the mortgage is for fifteen dollars and the runt isn't worth five," Toothaker protested.

"No doubt," the judge agreed, "but that's the way the judicial ball sometimes bounces. Incidentally, I think you owe a vote of thanks to Squire Blanchard for warning you against action which might have resulted in serious liability for your client and consequent embarrassment for you."

After a moment's hesitation, Milton Wordsworth got up and shook the Squire's extended hand. The latter quickly interrupted the young man's stammered thanks. "We're brothers at the bar, and that means we ought to act like brothers," he declared. "And incidentally, if there's any lingering thought in your mind that Lem Peavey might have any non-exempt assets—outside the runt of course— you can rest assured that he hasn't and furthermore, if I'm any kind of a prophet, he never will."

"I've known Lem for a good many years, and I'll say amen to that prophecy," Judge Peters affirmed. "And I'm delighted to see such a fine brotherly spirit between the members of the Middlesex Bar."

On his way out of the courtroom, Squire Blanchard paused briefly to assure Lem that the sheriff would not be coming around to seize his fat pig, and to remind him not to acquire any other non-exempt assets—an admonition to which his client fervently assented.

At dinner that day, a meal which, according to old country custom, he and Sophrenia always had at noon, Jonathan recounted the morning's events. "Of course, Phreenie," he concluded, "you'll have to take charge of the runt. You found the client, so by rights you've earned the fee. It's just a matter of slopping him, night and morning. He ought to get along mostly on our scraps, with a little skim milk now and then."

Sophrenia, with an indignant sniff, said she guessed she wasn't going to be a nursemaid to any old pig.

"Well, in that case we'll just have to let Lem take care of him for us," the Squire conceded.

"What happens when Lem butchers the big pig?" his sister wanted to know. "He won't be a 'swine' then, will he?"

"Nope," Jonathan cheerfully agreed. "Then he'll be 'provision'— and that's exempt under the statute too."   END

Governor of the Whole State of New Hampshire

by Lael J. Littke

When Miss Willis told us one morning that our school was going to have a visitor that afternoon, four of the boys and Geraldine LaPlante sneaked away at noon and didn't come back. The rest of us would have done the same had we possessed the courage, for the only visitor who ever came to our small country school besides the county school superintendent, who had already been there to give us achievement tests, was the doctor who came to jab his vaccination needles into our quivering flesh. The very thought of the doctor standing there in the Principal's office, relentless and impassive, clutching his dripping hypodermic syringe, was enough to make even the teachers blanch.

I didn't blame Geraldine LaPlante for going home. The last time the doctor came, she fainted dead away just before he jabbed and then wet her pants while she didn't know what she was doing.

The fifth grade sat through early afternoon classes, pale and defeated, nervous eyes straying from books to the big windows. Trapped and hopeless, we watched two long black cars pull into the muddy schoolyard.

"Well," said Miss Willis brightly, "here we are."

Collectively we hated her, a beloved shepherdess delivering her flock gaily to the slaughter.

"Children," she said in a low confidential voice. "Guess who our visitor is. The GOVERNOR."

The Governor! We sat stunned. Our fear was replaced by a nameless apprehension. Why would the Governor come to our little school? Something worse than a vaccination must surely lie ahead.

Silently we got our coats and lined up outside with the rest of the school. Wordlessly we stared at the group of men who stood chatting with the Principal. We tried to pick out the Governor. What could he be like? Would he glow faintly, surrounded by a soft diffused light like the pictures of angels we had seen? Would he wear a scarlet suit like the high school drum major, with perhaps "N.H." emblazoned on it in gold letters? We shivered in the chilly April air.

"People," the Principal bellowed to the assembled teachers and children, "we have in our midst today a very distinguished personage." He smiled benignly at the group of men beside him.

Where was the Governor? Were they keeping him in the car, to pop out amidst a fanfare of trumpets like the trapeze star we had seen in a circus?

While the Principal spoke at length, my eye was snagged by a movement in the ranks of the second grade. My sister Tootie was furtively sneaking into the shrubs behind us. Hoping the Governor was not watching me from some secluded peephole, I slid silently into the bushes myself and startled Tootie by grabbing her pigtail.

"Tootie," I whispered fiercely, "you stay here."

"I got to go, " she said.

"It's not the doctor," I whispered. "It's the Governor of the whole State of New Hampshire."

Tootie shrugged as if she had met a Governor every day of her life. "Phoebe needs me,"she said.

"Phoebe?" I said.

"She's going to have her babies today."

"Well, wait until after the Governor goes." I looked around, feeling somehow that the Governor, like God, must be omnipresent and would strike down little Tootie for not wanting to stay to meet him.

"How do you know Phoebe will have them today?"

"I just know," Tootie insisted. She yanked her hair from my grasp and ran off into the trees. I watched her go, then slipped stealthily back into my place. The Principal saw me. He paused. I smiled beautifully, trying to convey to him an impression of the call of nature being too strong to resist, but that everything was all right now. He went on with his speech. He explained that the Governor was on a highway inspection tour and now that he saw how bad our roads were we would soon have a nice oiled highway. He said something about "His Excellency, Donald Barnett," and a slight, gray-haired man stepped forward from the group of men. He said a few words, none of which I heard.

Could that be the Governor? A plain, faded little man, no more impressive than Lafe Turner, our sometimes hired man? What was there to fear about a man who looked like Lafe Turner?

After the Governor's speech, our high school band marched and played a sour rendition of "The Trumpeter." I watched my brother Tom strut proudly and self-consciously past. He acted as if the Governor were watching him, personally, every minute. His face was red with the effort of playing his tuba.

Then the Governor came down the lines of children, shaking hands with each one, and I had a chance to look deeply into his dark eyes. They flashed and glittered like a half hidden star. The sun shone on his silvery head and I could almost make out a glow around him. My heart beat fast as his firm fingers grasped my limp ones. Suddenly all the day's tensions were climaxed by an overwhelming feeling of shame, shame that I should be standing there in front of that exalted being in my shabby brown coat, shame that the Principal and the teachers were such drab individuals who could not say something brilliant and witty to make this great man laugh away some of the worried lines from his face, shame that the Governor of the whole State of New Hampshire had to wallow ankle deep in the muddy schoolyard to shake hands with a bunch of back-country clods like us. My only hope was that he would lift his eyes to the beautiful mountains in the background and draw strength therefrom to withstand the indignities he was being subjected to.

After we were dismissed, Tom and I walked home in a state of euphoria.

"I'm going to vote for him," Tom offered at one point.

"You're too young. You can't vote."

"If I could vote, I would vote for him. He even shook hands with ME." His tone implied that he was the very least of all creations.

We moved out of the muddy highway to let one car of the Governor's party slosh past us. A few moments later the car carrying His Excellency himself came by. I felt I should throw myself into one of the mudholes in order to spare him a jolt or two. How could we subject him to such things when he came to our town, he who was used to the even streets and expansive green lawns of the capital city? What must he think of us?

When we came around the bend just beyond the long lane that led to our house, we saw the Governor's sleek black car sunk hub-deep in the mire. Its wheels spun helplessly. Dad, in his faded bib overalls and shabby chore jacket, was heading up the lane. He just couldn't be walking up to the Governor like that! If only he knew who it was he would surely go back and stay out of sight. I wanted to turn and hide myself, but the Governor and a companion, who were standing beside the car while the chauffeur spun the wheels, had already seen us.

"Hello," said the Governor. "I think I just saw you at the school, didn't I?"

Tom and I nodded numbly. I wondered if my face was dirty or something, that he should remember me. Dad came slogging through the mud, saving us from further conversation.

"Having trouble?" he asked cheerfully.

"Seems that way," said the Governor.

"These roads are a hell of a mess," said Dad. I wished that I could sink right into the mud.

"Yes," agreed the Governor.

"Maybe I can help," Dad said. "Name's Adam Colton."

He stuck out his big, chapped, calloused hand and the Governor grasped it in his own well-kept one. I shivered as I recalled the touch of those firm fingers. My cheeks burned in embarrassment for my father standing there in his rough farm clothes, shaking hands with the immaculate Governor of our state.

"I'm Donald Barnett," said the Governor. "I'm happy to meet you, Mr. Colton."

Mr. Colton! The Governor called my father Mr. Colton, just as if he were the Principal or the Mayor or Somebody. Everyone else called my father "Ad."

"Glad to know you, Governor," said Dad.

Fierce pride shot through me. My Dad knew who Donald Barnett was. And he stood there looking him right in the eye, not fawning like the Principal or simpering like Miss Willis. My Dad just stood there shaking his hand and smiling friendly-like, as if the Governor were just a next-door neighbor. My Dad WAS Somebody.

Tom and I were in too much of a fog to know just what took place. But eventually the car was out of the mud. It was discovered, however, that something had torn loose, and the chauffeur was going to go into town with a neighbor who came by in a rut-jumping pickup truck to get a replacement part. The other man was going, too, because he had to catch up with the other car which was full of county officials. Everyone, including Dad, assured the Governor that he would be better off resting at our house until the chauffeur came back.

I had always regarded our frame farmhouse as a cozy, comfortable place to live, but as we approached it with the Governor I saw it with new, critical eyes. It needed paint. The back porch sagged. The barns were too close, and we could smell the pungent odor of the animals. Mother had washed earlier, and long lines of overalls and underwear flapped in the April breeze.

Dad made one concession to the unbelievable fact that the Governor was coming to our house. He took him to the practically unused front door rather than through the back porch which was always filled with manure-encrusted boots and eggs that had been gathered but not yet cleaned.

"Bessie," Dad called to Mother as we all trooped through the front door. "Governor Barnett is here."

"Well, tell the old boy to wipe the mud off his feet and come on in," Mother called cheerfully from the kitchen in the back of the house.

Tom and I sagged limply. Tom's eyes looked twice as big as his face. Could there be such a thing as capital punishment for speaking disrespectfully to a Governor? What would he do to Mother, good, kind Mother who evidently thought Dad was bringing a neighbor and was playing one of his little jokes.

The Governor grinned. "Now that's the kind of woman I admire," he commented. He dutifully wiped the mud off his feet and stepped into our threadbare but spotless living room. He sat down on the lumpy sofa.

Dad laughed. "Oh, Bessie's the salt of the earth. But I've got an idea she's going to have a little surprise."

Mother came briskly through the door from the kitchen, drying her hands on her apron. A bright welcoming smile lit her face. She looked at our visitor, and the smile sagged and dripped off her face like a snowball thrown against the house and warmed by the sun.

The Governor leaped to his feet. "How do you do, Mrs. Colton," he said, extending his hand.

Mother seeemed to have lost her hands somewhere in the apron. After a few moments of fumbling she brought one forth and laid it inertly in the Governor's palm.

"I'm fine thanks," she said weakly. "You look just like your pictures."

Suddenly she turned on Tom and me where we stood transfixed, still clutching our schoolbooks.

"Get back out there and clean the mud off your feet," she said fiercely, before walking unsteadily back to the kitchen.

We cleaned our feet, then went around to the back porch and into the kitchen. Mother was slamming pans around.

"Always dragging Governors and everything home," she muttered. "He might give me a word of warning."

Aunt Sadie, hearing the commotion, came downstairs. She was a frail little bird, an aunt of Dad's who lived with us when her visions indicated that she should.

"Who's here?" she inquired.

"The Governor," Mother said shortly. "He could have given me a chance to vacuum the living room and throw a cover on that sofa."

"The Governor," said Aunt Sadie. "He's come for me. I had a vision that he would ask me to be the Commissioner of Agriculture."

Aunt Sadie was too harmless to lock up.

The old lady slipped past Mother and tottered into the living room. Tom and I watched, peering around the door frame.

"Why not?" Mother was saying to herself. "Might as well know this is a complete madhouse."

"Glad you finally came, Governor Spencer," Aunt Sadie said. "I'm ready to go any time you are."

I admired the way the Governor's face didn't change its polite expression. He stood up and bowed graciously to Aunt Sadie.

"This is Governor Barnett," Dad told her.

Aunt Sadie's brow furrowed. "Oh, I thought Governor Spencer was coming."

"Governor Spencer is dead," Dad said gently.

"No!" said Aunt Sadie, "When'd it happen?"

"Oh," said Dad, "about sixteen years ago."

Aunt Sadie looked thoughtful. "Sure sorry I missed his funeral," she said.

"Governor Barnett is inspecting our road," said Dad. "We'll probably get an oiled highway through here any day now."

"Well, now isn't that fine," said Aunt Sadie. "I had a vision about Greyhound buses whizzing through town. Hundreds of Greyhound buses. Couldn't figure how they'd do it on these muddy roads." She sat down, but jumped right up again. "Oh," she squeaked, "I think I'll go see Minnie Ames. Stop the 5:15 Greyhound when it comes by, will you, Oscar?"

"I'm Adam," said Dad.

Aunt Sadie peered at him. "So you are," she said. "It's nice you could come visit Oscar while I'm here."Smiling softly, she wandered from the room.

Dad cleared his throat.

"What were you saying about the school taxes, Mr. Colton?" the Governor inquired placidly.

Before Dad could reply, Mother pushed Tom and me out of the doorway and walked into the living room. She had recovered her aplomb.

"Governor," she said, "we'd be mighty pleased if you'd stay for supper."

"I'd be happy to," said the Governor.

"It'll take a while," said Mother. "The steaks have to thaw."

"Pshaw," said Dad, "let's have bread and milk like we always do, Mother. And some of your good strawberry jam. She baked new bread today," he told the Governor.

"Adam!" gasped Mother. "That's not a fit meal for a Governor."

The Governor interrupted. "Mrs. Colton, I'm a farm boy myself and

I haven't had a bread-and-milk supper for thirty-five years. I'd rather have that than anything you can name."

Mother was flustered again.

"Where's Tootie," she demanded of me. "Why didn't she come home with you and Tom?"

"She came home by herself," I stammered, not wanting to say right out that she didn't care to meet the Governor.

"Well, go find her and we'll have supper." Mother went back to the kitchen and dug out her snowiest tablecloth and put it on our oilcloth-covered kitchen table.

"Governor," said Dad, "I've got a couple chores to do before I eat. Mind if I leave you here with the kids?"

"Not at all, Mr. Colton. Not at all."

After Dad left, Tom and I edged ourselves into the room and onto some chairs facing the Governor. Tom cleared his throat. The Governor and I waited expectantly. Tom coughed. He evidently decided this was the best way to avoid conversation. He had a regular coughing fit.

The Governor looked at me. "What grade are you in?"

"The fifth," I whispered.

We sat in silence until Tom recovered from his spasm. Then the Governor said, "Young man, I wonder if you'd show me where the bathroom is. I would like to wash my hands."

Tom pointed dumbly down a short hall leading from the living room, and the Governor followed his directions. He returned in a minute.

"There doesn't seem to be any water in the fixtures," he said.

Tom glowed a brilliant scarlet.

"It isn't hooked up yet," I whispered. "We just put it in. You can wash your hands in the kitchen sink."

"Fine," said the Governor. "And where do you go when . . . "

I could feel my face redden. *Dear Lord*, I prayed, *I'll never miss Sunday School again if You'll just hook up that bathroom long enough for the Governor to go.*

". . . you know," finished the Governor.

Blindly Tom got to his feet. "Come on," he said and led His Excellency outside and down the path.

After the Governor had washed at the kitchen sink, things didn't seem so bad. He sat at the table and chatted amiably with Mother. Tom even opened up under the Governor's questions and admitted he liked algebra although, he hurriedly amended, he preferred civics, of course.

"Did you find Tootie?" Mother asked. As if in answer, Tootie burst into the kitchen.

"Mama," she cried, "Phoebe just had a baby out in the barn and there's another one coming."

The Governor paled. "Good Lord," he whispered.

Mother, impressed by Tootie's wild-eyed urgency, hurried from the kitchen, followed by the Governor. Tom and I brought up the rear.

Tootie led us recklessly through the barnyard and into an old shed that sometimes housed new calves.

"There," she said dramatically, pointing to her straining mother cat and one slimy, new-born kitten.

"Great Scott," breathed the Governor, "somehow I thought, I thought . . ."

Mother grinned for the first time since he had come. "You can expect anything around here, Mr. Barnett.".

"Here," said the Governor, "let's see if we can help."

He knelt down in the straw beside the cat and gently stroked her side. Phoebe, apprehensive at first, gradually relaxed and produced her second kitten, which lay motionless after she had cleaned it.

"Something wrong with this one," murmured the Governor. He picked the tiny body up and slowly bent the head into the crotch of the back legs, then straightened it out. He repeated the process until the kitten emitted a weak "Mew."

"Artificial respiration," he explained, putting the kitten down to assist Phoebe with her third baby.

Somehow it seemed perfectly natural that the Governor should be kneeling there in his expensive clothes, giving artificial respiration to a new kitten.

Five kittens later, we all sat back and relaxed, except Phoebe who seemed a little overwhelmed by her large family of seven. Tootie was enchanted. "Seven kittens," she whispered. "Seven darling kittens." She patted Phoebe affectionately.

Although the chauffeur had returned when we got back to the house, the Governor insisted on having his meal of home-made bread, milk, and strawberry jam. The chauffeur, a city-bred boy, had a cheese sandwich and a glass of milk, although he acted as if he were sure he'd be poisoned and get Bang's disease. We didn't care. After all, he was only a chauffeur.

When the Governor finally departed, he insisted that he hadn't had such a pleasant day and so delicious a meal in years and years. He said, a little wistfully, I thought, that he'd like to come back again.

"Anytime, Governor. Anytime," said Dad. We all knew he would never be back. It made me feel a little sad.

Later that night Dad sat and read his newspaper as if nothing had happened. I looked at him through new eyes. My Dad had talked to a Governor as if he were nothing more than one of the neighbors! And he had brought him into our shabby house as if it were the Governor's Mansion itself. I looked at Tom and thought he could someday be Governor. Tom. My own brother. The Governor said he had been a farm boy. It was almost too much to contain.

Mother was sewing. "Next time you go bringing Governors home, will you please be kind enough to warn me?" she complained.

Dad grunted.

"So I can at least vacuum the living room. And fix my hair a little." Mother resented the fact that the Governor had not seen her at her best.

Aunt Sadie meditated. "Governor Spencer is sending a Greyhound bus, just for me," she said.

"The kids will never believe me," I mused. "The Governor himself sat right here." I patted the lumpy sofa beside me, then leaned back. It had been an exhausting day.

"Huh," said Tom. "He's not so great. He has to go to the bathroom just like anyone else." Was he, too, perhaps realizing the potential of even a humble farm boy?

Tootie was in a pink reverie.

"I can't believe it," she whispered.

"I can't either," I said. "Imagine, the Governor of the whole State of New Hampshire!"

Tootie sighed. "I can't believe it," she repeated. "Seven! Phoebe had seven kittens."

END

The Unreal Never Changes

by Kenneth Andler

When the class of 1926 was graduated from Dartmouth College, we had a splendid yearbook called *The Aegis* containing individual photographs of all members of the class. For example, on page 123 appears a picture of George Ulysses Lenson, smooth-shaven and neat as was the custom in those days, dark hair combed smoothly back and parted in the middle, well-dressed, wearing a bow tie and peering steadfastly into the alumni future he was about to enter.

Lenson apparently had not been terribly active in college, as the brief description beside his photo does not show any fraternities, extra-curricular activities or honors. But there certainly was nothing unusual, about that—this was the case with a great many of the class, men who went out into the world and became useful citizens, sometimes well-known ones.

The brief caption with the photo simply gives his name, his nickname, "Gully," his address, 203 Troy Road, Ellenston, New York, and his educational background: Ellenston Free Academy and Columbia University. This latter indicates that he had transferred from Columbia, and surely no Dartmouth man would blame him for that.

In the years between 1926 and 1960 I would, from time to time, consult *The Aegis* to see about some class member who had cropped up in the news and then I would glance through the whole roster of photos. It never struck me as particularly odd that I didn't know Lenson because I never knew a majority of the class anyway. But then in 1960 Lenson popped up out of his apparently comfortable obscurity and became something of a *cause célèbre*. The class newsletter, appropriately entitled, given Dartmouth's Indian background, "Smoke Signals," announced that Lenson did not really exist, had never existed as such (despite his very real-life photo) and had never therefore been a member of the Class of 1926 or even attended Dartmouth College.

Great consternation in the class! Smoke signals rising from every hill and mountain! The hoax was discovered when one of our members, Ken Weeks, and his colleague in the Alumni Records Office, Charlotte Morrison, were preparing the 1960 Alumni Directory and could find no record of Lenson. The anguish of losing the first file ever on any man to matriculate at Dartmouth drove them into doing their utmost in detective work, all to no avail. At this desperate point they appealed for further information to the man who as a student had been the editor of *The Aegis* in 1926, and he then "confessed." That undoubtedly is too harsh a term; let's just say he told what had happened and not judge lest we, too, be judged.

He expained that the heeler who had arranged the pages alphabetically had, through an error, prepared only four names and pictures for page 123 in the Ls instead of five as elsewhere. Consequently, that plate and all others clear through to Z, would have had to be remade to keep the proper sequence. This would have been such a time-consuming job that the publishing company said it could not guarantee delivery by Commencement. So, obtaining consent from a Columbia man for the use of his photo (this chap had originally wanted to go to Dartmouth anyway), the editor and his colleagues invented another classmate for this defective L plate, and only that plate needed to be done over. The day was saved and George Ulysses Lenson was born.

Lenson therefore was just a necessary figment of the imagination and that was all there was to it, according to the class officials, editors and Alumni Records Office. Maybe! But, as a humble member of the class and one who never made much more of a stir in college than Lenson did, I believe I should tell you a strange experience I had at Hanover, of all places, and let you decide if there isn't a little more to it than that.

In the late fall of 1960, I went to Hanover to see Bob Monahan, the College Forester, about some timber land. (I am a lawyer in Newport, New Hampshire, only 30 miles south of Hanover.) By some miscalculation of the time, the reason for which I have since forgotten, I arrived at the campus an hour sooner than I should have. With this suddenly granted leisure, I joined a small group of sidewalk superintendents overseeing construction of the Hopkins Center just then under way. The day was fair and cool; the campus elms were bare.

Peering over the protective board fence by the construction shack, I looked out upon a scene alive with bulldozers snorting about and workmen in hard hats swarming all over the enormous excavation as busy as ants. There is something very relaxing about being a sidewalk superintendent; perhaps this comes from watching the other fellow work. Anyway, I felt lazy and rested. I basked in the unusual prospect of an idle hour and became increasingly absorbed in the bustling scene.

Before long I fell into conversation with the man next to me, and I could soon tell that he had been in college about my time. I introduced myself. I detected a sudden slight hesitation in his manner, I thought, but he said, "My name's Lenson."

"What class?" I asked, beginning to feel an uneasiness creep into my relaxed mood.

"Twenty-six," he replied, a little belligerently, it seemed to me.

I looked at him more closely. He was a middle-aged, apparently successful business man, probably bald beneath his gray felt hat. He looked about like an average Twenty-sixer. Ordinarily rather congenial perhaps, he appeared somewhat defiant just now.

"What's your first name?" I asked.

"George," he said.

My vague uneasiness turned to a chill foreboding. "Your middle name doesn't happen to be Ulysses?" I inquired nervously.

"Yes, it does," he snapped. "I am George Ulysses Lenson."

I felt wobbly about the knees. But then a sudden thought struck me—this fellow is a superb practical joker, some classmate who apparently knew me although I didn't recognize him.

"Oh, come off it!" I laughed. "You must be kidding."

"I am not!" he insisted, obviously offended. "You've been reading this stuff in 'Smoke Signals' about how I don't really exist and was only dreamed up by the editor of *The Aegis* back in 1926 to fill a blank space.

"But, really, Mr. Lenson . . . " I began.

"Look," he interrupted, quite vehemently, "it's some kind of a prank."

I leaned rather weakly against the construction shack. "What do you say we go into the Inn for a short drink?" I suggested, feeling the need for one.

"Okay," said Mr. Lenson. "Call me Gully," he added, with tacit apology for his outburst.

When we walked through the Inn lobby, out of habit I glanced over the bulletin board on the wall, the one headed "Dartmouth In Town Again," which always contains, in a sort of rack, neat white cards showing the hand-printed names and class numerals of those alumni staying at the Inn. As I recall it, there were about eight cards all told. I ran my eye over the names of alumni of incredibly recent vintage in the '40s and '50s, and I came to the conclusion that none of my college generation was about.

But then I saw it. I still see it in my sleep and it wakes me up—the neatly lettered name, "Gully Lenson, '26."

My companion, observing my startled appearance, simply confirmed the presence of the card with an easy nod of his head and a casual motion of his hand, as much as to say, "Let them try to get around that."

As we drifted into the cocktail lounge I said, "You know, Gully, I think it's too darned bad, this trick they're playing on you."

"Well, it's an uncomfortable feeling. They are trying to make me an unperson. I don't know why they picked on *me*."

We took seats at a corner table. There were no other customers

there and just one waiter. We ordered martinis, increasingly admired
them and the Paul Sample mural of the ski jumper. I questioned him
cautiously as to who his friends were in college. He named a number of
them, all bona fide Twenty-sixers, I am sure, because I have heard their
names for years although I cannot recall knowing them any more than
I had known George Ulysses Lenson.

As we sat there over our drinks in the congenial atmosphere of the
Inn, I developed a considerable liking for Gully, which name he said with
some forcefulness was not derived from the word "gullible" or the
verb "to gull" but of course from his initials.

"And your work?" I inquired.

"Salesman for North Country Skis. I cover northern New England
and upstate New York—still live in Ellenston, as a matter of fact.
Married and have three kids."

"Are you staying here tonight?"

"No. Actually I'm all checked out and I guess they haven't got around
to taking down my card. I'm leaving for Stowe, Vermont, very shortly.
By the way, if you see any of the fellows, tell 'em not to believe everything they read and that I'm still going strong."

"I sure will," I promised.

We sipped on our drinks in easy companionship, silent for a moment
or so.

Gully suddenly spoke up, eyeing me shrewdly, "Now look here, I
just happened to think—these jokers that claim I don't exist, what do
they say about whose picture that is in *The Aegis*? If it isn't me, who
is it?"

"That's right, too," I said. "It's a photo of a real guy all right. He's
got to be somewhere! Of course, they said he was a Columbia man, but
I wonder who he was?"

"Why, damn it, man, you're talking to him!" Gully burst out, ex-
asperated. "I'm him!"

I felt embarrassed. "Why of course you are," I apologized. "This
martini must be a lot stronger than I thought. I'm not used to drinking
in the afternoon. I guess I got mixed up for a minute there."

"That's okay," Gully said, mollified. "I can understand that. It's
hard to adjust one's thinking to any drastic change of conditions."

We were silent a while. I felt rather uneasy at having been momentarily confused. I knew well enough it wasn't the drink but that had
made a good excuse just the same. Gully appeared to be concentrating on something as he crunched on some pretzels.

"You know," he said seriously at last, "I've given this whole matter a lot of thought, and I like to believe I'm something of a philosopher. Do you remember Mr. Naylor?"

"The history prof?"

"Sure. That's the one. He loved Napoleon. I think I learned this from Naylor, what Napoleon said: 'History is a fable agreed upon.' "

"Say, that's great!" I exclaimed. The quote really struck me. I go for quotes like that.

"Well, see how true it is in my case," Gully went on. "Suppose for the sake of argument this really had been a hoax and there was no such person as myself. Okay? So I was a fable agreed upon for years, photo in *The Aegis,* one of the alumni, and all that. Everyone believed in me. That made me real. Then these editors pronounce me a hoax, there's no such person, and they get everyone to agree to that. Now the fable agreed upon is that I don't exist, never did, and I'm not real any more."

"If I follow you," I said, gazing at the olive in my almost empty glass, "you are dealing with the fundamental nature of reality—what is finally and truly real, or to reverse the phrase, really true."

"I believe you can say that," Gully agreed, nodding his head thoughtfully. "Shouldn't we have another drink?"

I glanced at my watch. "Gosh, I'd like to," I replied—we were hitting it off real well together now—"but time's marching on here and I've got that appointment."

"Probably just as well," Gully said. "I want to see customers at Stowe today."

We made no move to go, however. We both hated to leave.

Gully went on, "Napoleon should have added something to that saying. It should be 'History is a fable agreed upon *by the victors.*' If the Germans had won the war, for instance, just what kind of history would we be reading now? And if I were to write up my version of this *Aegis* affair, don't you think it would be some different from the version they've been handing you?"

"You really do think things through, Gully," I said admiringly.

Gully resumed, taking a different tack. "Consider the case of classmates who have died and you've never seen them since graduation. You still visualize them as they were then. But they weren't that way finally at all, different people really. When you see classmates now at reunion, do you recognize them?"

"Well, people change a lot in thirty or forty years—if you haven't been seeing them right along," I replied. "I see some resemblance between you and your picture though."

Gully laughed and rubbed his bald head. "My hair line was receding some even in college as you'll notice by the photo." He popped the olive into his mouth and munched on it.

"You know," he resumed, serious again, "we were talking about what is real. When people are nervously overwrought about something, their surroundings begin to seem unreal to them. Do you know why that is?"

"Why, no, I can't say that I do."

"A doctor told me the reason for it once. It's simple. You get just as much reality out of your surroundings as you put into them. So if your thoughts are all turned inward, you are not putting reality into the things around you and consequently you don't get any back. It's a matter of degree, of course."

"Gully," I said, "you are a pretty knowledgeable fellow." I was becoming more impressed with him all the time. But nevertheless I was listening to both of us with my mental ear, as it were, to see if I heard alcohol speaking. I didn't, I am glad to say.

"Now," Gully went on, "about visualizing people as always young— you wouldn't regard Cal Coolidge as a very fanciful guy, would you?"

"No, but I don't get your drift . . . " I began.

"You will," Gully replied. "You know Dick's House, the college infirmary— given to the college by Ed Hall, Class of '92 or thereabouts? Well, Mr. Hall gave it in memory of his son Dick who died, I think, while in college. And President Coolidge was in the White House. Coolidge wrote Ed Hall an inscription in a book—I think they have it up there at Dick's House, or used to—it goes something like this: 'To Edward K. Hall/In recollection of his son and my son who have the privilege by the grace of God to be boys through all eternity.' "

"I recall that now," I said. I noticed that Gully actually had tears in his eyes. He was apparently quite an emotional fellow.

"The point is," Gully resumed, "Coolidge apparently found some comfort in thinking of things that way. So even if I was a hoaxed-up nonperson as they claim, I suppose a lot of people would like to go on thinking I was kind of real and just a young fellow that never aged."

"Well you certainly are real enough to me, Gully," I assured him.

"Thanks, Ken," he replied warmly. "It's done me good to talk with you."

He rose. I insisted on paying for the drinks, telling Gully I regarded it as a privilege. We strolled out into the lobby, put on our hats and coats and walked out the front door. We stood there quietly, gazing across the campus at Old Dartmouth Row gleaming white in the sunlight of an autumn afternoon.

"*There's* something that's real!" I exclaimed, moved by the beauty of it.

"You bet!" Gully agreed wholeheartedly. "I sure hope they leave it that way. You know, they're going to remodel the Inn here and you see all that hullabaloo over there at the Hopkins Center site. And they may even go coed! What kind of reality is it that won't stay put?"

We shook hands at the corner of the Inn and I watched him walk south on Main Street to get his car at the garage. As there weren't very many people on the street, I was rather surprised to lose sight of him between the drug store and bank, but I guessed he must have gone into Tanzi's.

A rather interesting idea struck me and I went back into the Inn. I asked the tall, gentlemanly clerk at the desk if I could have Lenson's card from the bulletin board.

"What name did you say?" he asked.

"Gully Lenson '26," I replied.

"We don't have anyone registered by that name," he reported, glancing through his registry file.

"Well, he just checked out," I insisted.

The clerk looked again through his file. "Hasn't been anyone here by that name and I've gone back for a month."

"Then how come you have a card here in the rack?" I was getting a little peeved. I took the card down and handed it to him.

He looked at it closely and gave it back to me. "That's not my lettering," he said. "Who is this man anyway? Name sounds familiar."

I hesitated, beginning to feel a little awkward. (Hotel clerks often make me feel either sore or awkward, sometimes both.) "He's the fellow in the Class of '26 that's supposed to be a hoax—but he's not, I can tell you that!" I hastened to add.

"Oh, that guy!" the clerk laughed. "I think we've had his name up here before—when some '26 men were staying here. Let's see," and he went through his register. "Yes, sir," he announced, "there were two of them here just the first of the week," and he told me their names.

"As far as these cards go," he added, "when the alumni boys are really feeling their oats, anything can crop up. Daniel Webster is the most common."

"But confound it, man!" I exclaimed. "I was just having a drink with this fellow!"

The clerk gave me a level, cool look. Rather shaken, I backed off from the desk and found my way out the front door. In something of a daze I wandered back to the construction shack by the excavation site.

Gradually, as I watched the bulldozers, I began to pull myself together. Had I been to the Inn at all? I reached into my pocket and drew out the lettered card. Good, at least I'd been to the hotel! I concluded shakily that an idle hour is something you have to practice with to know how to handle.

The Baker chimes sounding the hour startled me with the message that I'd be about five minutes late for my appointment and I must tear myself away from there. As I walked across the campus, I found myself planning to write Gully at Ellenston, New York, but then an unsettling thought suddenly plagued me—hadn't *The Aegis* editor said in his explanation that Ellenston existed only by virtue of his wishing to honor a girl by the name of Ellen?

Taking deep breaths as I walked along and concentrating on the legal business in hand, I tried with real determination to put Gully out of my mind. I more or less succeeded, too. I didn't want to be Walter Mittying all day and I couldn't afford to have Gully around all the time à la Harvey with Elwood P. Dowd.

But the very deuce of it is that I keep running into Gully both at home and in the swank surroundings of the new Inn and the splendor of the Hopkins Center. On these occasions he makes all sorts of observations about reality versus unreality; the phony versus the genuine; the elusive nature of truth, its advantages and possible disadvantages; what, if anything, we can believe of "history." In fact he delivers, on a variety of subjects, some of the most outrageously unorthodox opinions and also some of the most startling orthodox ones that I am sure he would confide to no one but me. Sometimes I think that he is "really" and "actually" only a figment of the imagination, but whether he is or not, he's a comfort just the same, for I find that only the unreal never changes.   END

A Husband out of the Blue

by Harriet Crowley

Kate Cummings lived with her mother on a small island off the coast of Rhode Island and deplored the fact that day by day her life became more predictable. Every day her mother found some new reason to beg her to give up flying and pay more attention to the young men on the Island—"while there are still a few eligible ones around," she always said. Every day Kate pointed out that she knew them all and had for years and wasn't interested and that she stood a far better chance of meeting the man who would make her mother happy by getting out in the world and not staying cooped up on the island.

As a pilot for a charter service, Kate certainly did get off the island, but the job which had been a dream-come-true when she first took it was rapidly becoming dullsville—nothing but taking some extremely unexciting types back and forth to Logan Airport, or perhaps Hartford. She would have given anything for a customer who wanted to be deposited on an Arctic ice floe or the nether reaches of the Amazon.

One winter day everyone around the airport was talking about a pilot who had had to land on the island and be taken to the hospital instead of continuing to ferry a small new plane from the factory where it had been made to the person in France who had bought it. Kate fell in love with the little plane, a single-engine one with a blue and white leather interior, a special order for the woman in France who awaited its delivery.

It was one of those days when Kate felt that all the adventure in her life was behind her and that at twenty-four she was doomed to spend the rest of her days flying the crowded air corridors of the Atlantic coast. Without giving it a second thought, she volunteered to substitute for the stricken pilot. There were telephone calls to the mainland plant where the plane was made. Everybody vouched for Kate's ability as a pilot, and since the manufacturers were concerned about getting the plane to Orly Airfield on the date promised—but mainly since no one else was even slightly interested in the job—Kate was hired.

Kate didn't tell her mother until the last minute and then there were certain details that she left unmentioned—such as the fact that, for pilots of low-flying craft like hers, weather reports were inadequate, to say the least, since most of the aircraft traveling the route flew at high altitudes; that the ocean hop would start at St. Pierre, one of the three tiny islands off Newfoundland which flew the French tricolor (all that was left of France's once vast empire in the New World), because it maintained a more relaxed attitude than the American authorities toward clearing "one-fan jobs;" and that she would share the cockpit with auxiliary fuel tanks which would literally come up around her ears.

It was a warm February morning when Kate took off, feeling like some Arctic bird migrating north a bit ahead of schedule. There was no snow on the ground until she had left Boston and its island-strewn harbor. Kate wore a red wool suit which she would have to wear until she got home. Space was the primary concern. When the auxiliary tanks were filled at St. Pierre, there would be scarcely room for her small overnight case, pocketbook, short fur jacket, food, and thermos of coffee. The cockpit was warm and cozy, a sort of flying boudoir, and she could fly as well in a skirt as in regulation flying gear; and if she plunged into the North Atlantic, she might as well perish quickly in a becoming suit as prolong the agony a few minutes with insulated clothing.

She flew over tiny islands covered with snow; on some of them she could make out little shacks and barns, which gave her pangs of loneliness as her own, far more complete isolation in the vast sky didn't.

When she landed on tiny St. Pierre, Kate, who had never been in France nor in an Esquimau village, felt as if she were in both at once. There were dog teams drawing children through the streets, and buildings crowded together looking as though they might have built in the old country and brought on barges across the sea.

What she wanted was a quick dinner and to go to bed immediately—but that was not to be. The dining room in the hotel was packed with islanders who spent most of their waking hours there waiting for someone, or anything, to relieve the winter's monotony. Kate kept hearing that she was the best thing that had happened to St. Pierre since "le whiskey," which she finally learned was what they called the great days of Prohibition when the island had enjoyed an unprecedented prosperity as a rum-running center. Her new friends kept her up late and were reluctant to let her go to bed at all. Many of them stayed up all night and were on hand to see her off in the morning.

It was still dark and cold when she was back at the air strip. The temperature was 24° above zero, but the forecast was for clear sky and a warming trend when the sun was up. With the weather reports so sketchy for planes like hers, Kate knew it didn't necessarily mean anything. Still, it was better than learning that things were bad all over. She watched as the auxiliary fuel tanks were filled, turning them from flat piles of plastic in the bottom of the cockpit into huge obese dragons. One of the men advised Kate not even to carry cigarettes with her, for recently, he said, a pilot with auxiliary tanks in his cockpit had absentmindedly pulled a cigarette out of his pocket, lighted it, and taken a puff before remembering where he was. He put it out so fast then that he burned the palm of his hand. Kate laughed and said not to worry. She didn't smoke.

When it was beginning to be light, Kate taxied out on the runway, waving goodbye to the people who were standing together, some laughing and some looking grave. She was so excited that at the end of the runway, while she revved up the motor, she told herself to calm down and take some deep, relaxing breaths.

The wind was from the southwest. After takeoff, she eased the plane towards the great fiery ball of the rising sun, climbed to her assigned altitude of 3000 feet and leveled off on her easterly course, with the sun on the southeast horizon. With the added weight of the fuel in the auxiliary tanks, the plane was less responsive than on the day before and her airspeed, 130 knots, was lower but would increase to a maximum of 180 knots as the fuel load grew lighter. She switched on the radio to Gander. The lights on the little island behind her grew tinier and disappeared altogether, and she was completely alone in the empty sky with the streaks of red along the horizon fading to a pale pink and the sun slowly turning from red to gold. One huge planet dimmed and disappeared.

She had never looked forward so eagerly to a day. She felt that of all the people in the world she would know this day more fully than anyone. In her tiny perch above the ocean, it was hers alone. She would see every phase and facet of it, every step in the sun's ascent and descent until its ultimate disappearance below the horizon. She felt closeness to the sun that she had never felt before. It would also be a shorter day than any she had ever lived through, since she and the sun were sailing along in opposite directions.

The voice at Gander wanted to know if she knew that she was the only idiot flying a single-engine plane across the Atlantic that day. Kate talked to him every half hour, pinpointing her positions and reporting weather conditions—bright sunshine and occasionally scattered clouds below her. At one o'clock, when she had covered more distance than she had anticipated because of the favorable tail wind, she ate the cold chicken and buttered French bread they had given her at St. Pierre, and drank a cup of hot coffee. She felt as if she should give some as a peace offering to the plastic creatures looming behind and beside her. She was always aware of those huge auxiliary tanks. Her head touched the one behind her when she leaned too far back. The one beside her seemed from the corner of her eye like some menacing, misshapen human form that wanted to crowd her out of her seat. To prove to herself that she still had some room, she flexed her toes, moved her legs, and stretched her arms.

The day passed too quickly. When it would have been four in the afternoon at home, with the sun still shining, up in her flying boudoir its last rays were fading and what looked like a bank of intensely black clouds was ahead of her. The light, what little was left of it, was deceiving. She had been handed over from Gander Air Frequency to Orly, where a voice told her that no unfavorable weather conditions had been reported. She reported a shift in the wind, a headwind of considerable velocity—enough to counteract the picking up of speed expected with the lighter fuel load.

Within a short time she was in clouds. The change was as abrupt as opening a door and passing from a placid front hall into a raging storm. The plane bucked and lurched, and hail bombarded it. It was like sitting in a metal can while people threw rocks at it. Or like being locked in an automatic washer. A fine sheet of ice formed on the windshield, and for the first time in her life Kate knew what it was like to suffer from claustrophobia. It seemed to bring the windshield closer to her and make the auxiliary tanks snuggle nearer. There didn't seem to be enough air to breathe.

Ice was also forming on the wings. She switched on the de-icing pumps. After a long wait, the ice was thicker still. She was forced to face the fact that the pumps weren't working. The little plane flew like a huge overloaded truck. She reported to Orly and asked clearance to climb above the turbulence and ice. There was such a long silence that Kate feared she had lost contact.

"I'm handing you over to KCS at the Azores," the voice said at last. "They may have more information on your weather. Switch to 3023 point 5."

It was the Overseas Distress Station, as she knew. It took all her nerve to go from the known to the unknown on the radio dial, and the limbo between the two stations seemed to stretch out forever. Finally a voice came through. It was a distinctly New England voice! He already knew about Kate from Orly. He sounded calm and reasonable and capable and reassuring, and Kate was so relieved that she sobbed and giggled at once.

There was a note of alarm in the Azores voice as he asked if she was all right.

"Not really, but for a second it seemed that way," Kate replied.

"You want clearance to climb above the mess you're in? Better off going down."

Kate knew that there were two ways to melt ice when the pumps wouldn't—to climb above the clouds and let the clear air evaporate it or to fly close to the water hoping that the warmer temperature would melt it. Kate wanted to go up and said so.

"I can't see to go down," she said.

"What's your altimeter for?" he asked.

She nosed the plane down as gently as she could, hating every second of it and having to reason with herself that the opaque windshield made no difference since in the dark she wouldn't have been able to see anything anyway. Air speed, of course, picked up. She kept her eyes glued to the altimeter. She had to have blind faith in its accuracy.

At two hundred feet she began to level off. At one hundred and fifty she leveled off completely and opened the window beside her. She was still in the clouds. Did she dare try for one hundred feet? Did the clouds extend all the way to the water? She had to take the chance and continued the descent with her heart in her mouth and flying the plane as if it were a runaway elephant bent on destruction. She managed to level it off at one hundred feet. She took her first deep breath in a long time when she discovered that she was *not* in the water and was below the clouds. The plane, still heavy and lumbering, flew along more smoothly even though hail still pelted it.

Although she couldn't see the surface of the water, she had a mental picture of its black presence and of the plane barely missing the wave tops and she kept her eyes on the altimeter. The icy blast that blew in through the open window made it hard to believe in the de-icing capacity of the North Atlantic, but something was helping. The plane was recovering some of its maneuverability, and Kate thought that the ice on the windshield was less thick. She dared to hope that the de-icing pumps had started to work. When she had flown at that perilously low altitude for a long time and was gaining enough confidence to put her mind to her other problems, she switched on the radio and, to her relief, heard the insistent voice at the Azores calling her. There were still no reports from other pilots or from weather stations of the conditions that Kate was experiencing, which led the Azores station to the belief that it was limited to a comparatively small area and that Kate had probably seen the worst of it. The air was a lot smoother at the moment and she decided to climb back to her assigned altitude of 3000 feet. Within minutes she would have to switch to her last tank of fuel—the plastic ogre behind her had already collapsed, leaving only the one beside her—and Kate wanted to make the switch to give herself more room and less worry.

As she climbed, there were only intermittent crashes against the windshield, which she recognized as hunks of ice dislodging themselves from the engine cowling. Suddenly there was a clear space on the windshield. It lifted a great weight from her shoulders and somehow made it easier to breathe.

The bad weather was behind her. She was eight hundred miles from her destination. She no longer had a headwind, and her air speed had picked up to 170 knots. In less than five hours she should touch down at Orly. The outlook had gone from bleak to extremely favorable so fast that she felt lightheaded with relief and happiness.

She switched over to the last tank.

There was an interim of perhaps only a few seconds—but it seemed much longer—during which Kate groped for a logical explanation for the odor assailing her nostrils. It had to be expected occasionally, she told herself, that in a gas-burning mechanism you would smell gas.

But the fumes were overpowering! Gas was running into the cockpit! As automatically as a wounded person tries to stop the flow of blood, Kate reached under the overhang of the tank to a valve and gropingly found where it was escaping. The cotter key had fallen out of the valve, allowing it to become unseated. She could hold it together and reduce the escaping gas to a trickle, but she couldn't fly one-handed and leaning to the right for eight hundred miles. And she couldn't afford to lose any gas.

She couldn't get to the voice at the Azores quick enough.

"Listen to me as carefully as you can," he told her as soon as he knew of the escaping gas. "I'm going to talk fast, and the minute I'm through you're going to turn off the radio and all other electrical equipment. Rule number one when gas escapes.

"Concentrate on the problem at hand and you'll forget to be scared.

"Feel around quickly for the cotter key. If you can't find it, use some sort of makeshift. Got a pocketbook?"

Kate said she had.

"You've got something in it to fill the bill. Women always do. Now switch off all electricity. Good luck!"

Kate switched off the radio, leaned to the floor, groped and searched in the dark, sloshing her hand through the puddle of gas in the most awkward position she had ever been in. Panic was trying to surface but she held it down by reviewing the things she had in her pocketbook. She had put things in it and taken things out with great care because she didn't want to get out of the plane in Paris, of all places, looking a mess. She'd planned it minutely to have everything at hand with which to spruce up before landing. On the other hand, she hadn't wanted to descend on the fashion capital of the world with a pocketbook bulging like a mechanic's tool kit. So she knew every item in it and its exact location down to the last bobby pin.

Bobby pin! It might work! She stopped groping for the cotter key and reached for her pocketbook instead. Getting it in her left hand, she carefully opened it. The bobby pins were in a side pocket and quickly found.

It was tight quarters to work in. If her hand had been the slightest bit larger she couldn't even have attempted it. It was like threading a needle one-handed in the dark. When it was done, she gingerly released her grip. The bobby pin stayed, and there was no more leak.

With both hands back on the wheel, she took a cold, hard look at her predicament. She was sure that the acrobatics during the turbulence had shaken the cotter key loose. It would take much less to dislodge the bobby pin, but for the present, at least, the plane flew smoothly. She could only hope that it would continue to and that the amount of gas lost wasn't crucial. More than anything else she longed to turn on the radio and hear the voice in the Azores. She told herself that it was well worth the risk, that hearing him would give a lift to her confidence that might mean the difference between life and death. But she remembered his warning about radio silence. He had meant it.

She knew he would have sent out an order for search planes. Maybe they would spot her, but it wasn't very likely.

When the sky in the east began to turn red and on the horizon she saw land, she had no way of knowing what part of France it was—nor even for certain that it was France. It took all her will power to keep her hands off the radio control. She wanted to explain to him that she was too tired to think clearly, that she should have gone to bed earlier in St. Pierre (which now seemed like a place she had visited years ago), and that she was afraid of making some fatal mistake because she couldn't concentrate.

She felt certain that he would have been able to tell her what the biggish town was over to her left. What looked like a big church rose in the middle of it.

It seemed to take her ages to realize there was no reason she couldn't fly closer and have a good look at it all on her own. Not that she expected to learn much, but she flew nearer. There was something familiar about the church: its two tall spires didn't match—one was ornate, the other starkly simple. She remembered the cathedrals she had had to identify in an art course and this one had been the easiest of all to remember because of those mismatched steeples. It had to be Chartres! She reached for a map. She found that Paris was forty-five miles northeast, so Orly, on the city's southeast perimeter, was even closer.

She opened her pocketbook and took out her comb and lipstick.

When she brought the plane to a full stop on the runway, a large crowd surged towards her. Out in front there was one person, with arms stretched out and a broad grin on his face, who outstepped the others with every long stride.

Kate was to tell him later—and for years to come—that she knew who he was even before he swung her off her feet and that back-home voice was in her ear asking what miracle she had fished out of her pocketbook.   END

Whale!

by Eleanor Sterling

On an afternoon in mid-August, a very large gray whale appeared up out of Casco Bay and swam between the rock ledges off Harpswell Island, scattering the perched seagulls to the winds, and washed ashore finally in little Dingley Cove; there it lay on its side like a stone half in and half out of the water, blowing lazily and dreamily through the opening in its head.

Now a great many things had come ashore at Dingley in the past: strips of old linoleum, spars, wooden crates and kegs, broken lobster pots, buoy markers, plastic bleach bottles, dead fish of all kinds, and once even a dead seal pup all fat and spotted, but never before a whale. Harley Perkins, who'd been fishing the incoming tide just off the ledges, immediately rowed for Harpswell Harbor and told the news that he'd seen a whale wash over. In fifteen minutes the Coast Guard at Seguin had been alerted, and half the Island was down to watch the whale die, for undoubtedly that was what it had come for.

The boy, Willan, was up-Island picking blueberries. He saw people driving down the dirt road to Dingley in an awful hurry, pick-ups and cars and a couple of jeeps, and he thought that maybe someone almost drowned. He was an Island boy and in his ways he was as laconic as his ancestors' crayon portraits. As far as he was concerned someone was always and forever "almost drowning," especially summer people; his Mam told him that summer people could almost drown in a teacup.

Mam had the roadside Square Deal Restaurant on the Island. It was because she wanted to put blueberry pie on the menu early that Willan was out there picking, though not too many berries were ripe yet. Still, had he gone swimming or fishing he would have missed that whole thing about the whale altogether. As it was, the rush of people down toward Dingley finally poked at his curiosity enough to make him set his buckets aside and hurry down through the bay bushes to the cove too.

The first men into the cove had been the Quinn brothers, who'd been out that way site-ing for a new wharf and actually saw the whale float in. They'd slid down the rocky slope to the beach with caution; the whale was heaving its sides up and down, gleaming like wet

slate with a slice of corrugated white on its underside. When the
Quinns got down quite close, the whale suddenly snorted and spouted,
a great spray rising up, and it watched them coming with the one eye
on its side that lay upward out of the water.

Then more people arrived; the whale's eye rolled about, trying to
watch them all coming from separate directions: Perley Doughty and
his boy Phil, Marge Hapgood from the general store, the Moody
boys home early from fishing, and the Coffins from the gas station.
The whale's eyeball rolled and rolled. By the time Willan finally saw
the whale, its huge head was surrounded by a bunch of ladies in pink
raffia sunhats and high-heeled sandals, who were snapping pictures
with their cameras and laughing pleasurably, and men with fat stomachs
and walker-shorts and clean sneakers, who stood by helplessly, watching the ceremony of a whale's dying with all the involvement and
compassion that might have accompanied any other afternoon's activity.

"Well, will you looka there at ol' Moby Dick!" someone was
hollering. "He sick or somethin'? What's he doin' hea'?"

Nobody said anything. They were all watching the whale, fascinated by its mammoth size. Once again the whale blew lazily, a
white spray rising sideways out of its head and blowing a hole into
the place at the water's edge where the gravel began. People moved back,
silent.

"Now who ever seed a whale hereabouts?" asked an old man in
overalls of nobody in particular. "Who ever *seed* sich a thing?"
he asked again, incredulously looking into the faces around him.
Nobody met his old eyes, rheumy and shocked, and he began to circle
through the crowd asking over and over, "Who ever *seed* sich a thing?"

The whale, about forty feet long, seemed to fill the small cove.
It appeared to reach from one end of the gravel crescent to the other,
its hulk gleaming smooth and slippery-dark, rising slightly on the
incoming tide, the spade-shaped tail moving easily and powerfully
back and forth in the low water. From the curve of its mouth and the
way the mouth reached back along the whale's side some people
thought the great creature was grinning, but it soon became clear that
the whale was not grinning—was, indeed, wounded or sick to the
death, and in great suffering. Once it seemed to scream; the mouth
opened slightly at the front and a sound came out, thin and piercing,
and then the mouth closed down again and the whale rolled ever
more to one side, spouting weakly.

"'E's a right whale, not a sperm," Thomas Quinn was announcing
just as Willan scrambled to the scene.

"How come *you* know the difference?" Perley Doughty wanted to know. Along the Maine coast there had been few whalers, and knowledge of whales was not in the Harpswell Islanders' tradition. Other fish, yes; not whales.

"The head, see the head, how it's shaped? Now a sperm's got a big blunt head, but this fella's kind of flat-shaped and low to the front."

Nobody argued; nobody knew.

"We're going to have to nudge him down with a jeep and tow him out," said Mr. Coffin. "He dies here and it'll be a smell they'll know in Portland, ayeh."

Willan just stared. An artist was kneeling on the beach, sketching the whale in charcoal. A lot of little kids were there, and bigger ones who hadn't jobs that summer, and housewives in faded cotton aprons, men in hip-high boots, and lobstermen with faces as long and creased as bark, all just standing impassively there and watching.

Willan remembered Mam and the blueberries; Mam had to have them in time for the afternoon baking. Mam had taken care of Willan since his mother died the winter before; though Mam was good at being patient with a boy, and Mam was good at questions and answers, she hadn't even tried to give Willan the answer to why his mother was gone so soon. Willan had stopped his grievous asking. Instead they played the game that Willan was really Mam's own little boy. All they had in the world to be responsible to was each other and the Square Deal Restaurant; Mam did the cooking and the baking and whenever Willan could help, Mam pushed him into it, like gathering apples and slicing them for turnovers, and picking blueberries for pie. It was the blueberries that were really nudging Willan's mind just then.

He took one more look at the dying whale and the crowd of Islanders and Summer People watching it. Then he climbed back to where he'd left his buckets, going the long way to avoid the tumblestone edge of the Island cemetery where his mother and father both lay out of sight of the sea.

The buckets were full enough. He took them up to Mam in the Square Deal kitchen and she gave him a jelly sandwich. Mam had already heard about the big whale in Dingley Cove. She said she'd like to get down and see it but there was no time, what with the baking to finish. Then she said it was a crying shame, but what could they do except have the Coast Guard come and haul the big fish away?

"You wanta go back down and watch?" she asked, without turning from her pie dough. "Go now and I'll ask Billy to come for you later."

Billy was Mam's kitchen helper. He was Island and you had to "ask" him, you couldn't "tell" him anything; a paid salary would never alter that.

So Willan went back to Dingley, scuffing his sneakers down the long dirt road, and got there just as the small white Coast Guard cutter came in carefully between the ledges, its motor chugging and rumbling. Everyone in the cove and sitting up in the bushes on the rocky bank stood up and cheered when the cutter came about; their shouts made the whale rise up terribly and flail the water with flukes and fins until its body was enveloped in sea foam. It spouted, and a thin spray of blood came through.

Coming as rocking-close to the shore as they could, the Coast Guardsmen tried heaving ropes around the whale's mammoth body. Each line fell short or flicked right off the whale's skin, which looked to be as smooth as a piece of silk. The cutter lolled sideways in the trough of the waves.

Then Willan, looking almost idly out to where the rock ledges broke the sea, saw the whale's calf. It was swimming in a long, frantic ellipse, rapidly back and around and forward.

"A baby!" he shouted in spite of himself. People looked and saw and Phil Doughty said, "Well, I be damned, he ain't a bull-whale, he's a mother!"—which made a lot of them laugh. The whale, as though knowing her calf was coming dangerously close, increased her dying struggles. With repeated strokes of her flukes she worked her way a little off-shore, and then the ropes fell true and she was rapidly lassoed and secured. Again the watchers on the shore shouted. Willan noticed the whale's ears were little and lay far back on her sides. He wondered if she could hear her baby calf over the shouting and the beat of the cutter's engines and the crashing little waves that were running into the cove.

The whale was pulled slowly, slowly, farther from the beach. Willan kept one eye on the calf swimming near the ledges. It looked no bigger than Willan himself, pale as its mother was dark, and suddenly it turned and rapidly swam away; Willan lost sight of it completely, but there were other things to watch right then, for the ropes slipped and the whale cow wallowed back into the cove again, blowing weakly. The watchers groaned at the failure, and the cutter came in again slowly and lay off for another try.

Then Billy, Mam's kitchen helper, shouted "Willan!" Looking up, Willan saw Billy at the top of the cove waving a dishtowel, and he knew he had to come away. Dingley Cove was so jammed up by then that Willan thought there were more people than he'd ever seen on Harpswell

Island, and the dirt road was parked solidly with cars and trucks, like a supermarket lot in town.

Billy was even older than Mam, too old and too long on the Island and too worried about getting Mam's dishes done to really care about the dying whale and her calf, so Willan walked silently with him. But as they went in the back way of the Square Deal, Billy spoke suddenly. "I saved you th' cherries from th' fruit salad," and gave Willan a grizzled, toothless smile; it was all right with folks like Billy, Willan thought, they understood.

That evening a lot of strangers came into the Square Deal, and Billy and Mam were kept on the hustle from kitchen to counter and back, with plates of lobster salad and fried clams and pie; most people had come over to see the whale and got hungry just standing there, so Mam said laughingly that maybe the whale was a good thing since business had been slow; when she saw Willan's face she changed her mind. No, she said, it wasn't a good thing. She was sorry for that poor big old Mam and her baby but for Willan not to worry; the baby would get on by itself, for that was the way it was with whales, she was sure.

Later, when the rush was over, Marge Hapgood came down from the store for a cup of coffee. She said the whale was still down there in the dark, higher up than ever now that the tide was on its way out. Willan wanted to know about the calf; was it still out there? he asked carefully. Marge didn't know, but she said she thought all the people had gone since it was too dark to see anything.

Willan waited and thought awhile, sitting under the electric light and listening to Billy's radio in the kitchen and the clash of dishes. Then he went out alone, picked a lantern off the shed door and lit it, turned the wick down, and started back to Dingley once more. He had to be careful on the road because he'd forgotten his sneakers and he wondered all the while that he was going at all; the night was black and silent and hung over the Island without a moon or a star, and the damp night wind was cold.

As Willan came down in the lantern-light through the trampled baybushes they lent their fragance to the wind, tarry and wild, but when Willan got to the beach where the whale cow lay high and dark the air was troubled by a strong, oily smell; the whale herself, Willan knew, and she was surely dead.

Nobody else was there. Raising the lantern wick he went up close, walking carefully on the wet, cold gravel, and the whale was so huge, so dark, and so terrible! He put his hand on the whale and she was fat-soft and icy, with crusts of barnacles along her fat lips.

Willan had once read that whales died heading into the sun, but this one had died in the night facing north, landward, and stirred up the beach for yards around it. The oily smell was thick in Willan's throat. He dropped his hand off the whale and, raising his lantern higher, he saw the calf, as he supposed he knew he would, lying half-submerged in the black shallows as close as it could get to its dead cow, pale and shining and desperate in the lantern-light.

"Go away, baby," Willan called out softly, and the calf-whale stirred. "Go on, scram, git!" he called more loudly, swinging his lantern high in an arc, and his voice echoed back from the corners of the empty cove—go away, scram, git, scram git, scramgit.

Willan didn't know *why* he wanted the calf to go away. Partly it was because they'd made him go away in the wintertime, when Mam had come and gotten him and taken him with her too soon, before. . . But it was too late here already, for this child had been there and known when it happened, had been with her all the time.

Willan began to cry silently. He set his lantern down and cried for the question that Mam couldn't answer; and when the crying was all done he let his face dry and stiffen in the wind. He picked up his lantern again and looked out at the whale-calf; it was there, Willan's terrible, sorrowing kin, and he whistled and called out softly to it, "All right you there, stay now, but you go later," and the calf stirred again in the dark water, spouting softly like a clear bell ringing in the lantern-light.

"It's all right, I say, but you take care in the morning, hear?" He swung the lantern toward the open sea. "You better go then, I'm telling you! Hear me?"

And there was one more thing, perhaps the thing he'd really come for.

"And listen," he cried out to the calf in the water, "there *ain't* no real reason, you hear? No real reason at all, not in the whole world, so don't you go asking questions!"

Then Willan was more satisfied. Dimly he sensed that his whale-calf kin had already been a part of a death larger and greater than most of the Islanders would ever, could ever, know. And when that calf-baby finally swam away, Willan thought to himself, then for him it would be all over. He lowered the lantern and started back, tired, up the dirt road to Mam.   END

How Harvey Snow Got Religion

by David G. Snow

Down in Vermont just after the turn of the century there were no church sermons about the varying shades of grey—how a person isn't all black or all white; not all good or all bad, but some shade of grey in between. Then, nobody was coddled into thinking there was some good in him just the way he was, and that with a little straightening out he'd make it on into heaven. He was told in no uncertain terms that sinners were going straight to hell, and no two ways about it.

Whether they were sinners or not was left up to them to decide, but folks always looked mighty relieved after the last "Amen," sitting through the sermon wearing their seats shiny on the hard wooden pews. And the preacher never lacked for invitations to Sunday dinner, either. Heaven wasn't *denied* to anybody, but the congregation just knew time was getting shorter every Sunday, and that they'd better start cutting back on earth and start storing up those treasures in heaven.

To some folks this tough-minded religion came easy, as if it were a shelter from the storm. To others it came hard, as if it were the very storm itself. To Harvey Snow, it came hard.

Harve was eight years old when his mother died, leaving him and his pa all alone on the farm. At thirteen he was full of piss and vinegar—the boy who didn't show up for school on the opening day of trout season; the kid who led the snowball attack on the town policeman; and who rat-a-tatted on Parker Royce's window so loud on Halloween that the poor old man tipped over backwards in his rocker. It didn't hurt him, except where the cat sleeping in his lap dug into his leg.

Harve wasn't like Tuttle Snow, his father, at all. His pa was the very picture of a sober-sided, humorless New England Yankee, and the whole town looked up to him. He was first selectman of the town, and deacon in the church; a big man with a stern face and striking eye. And a striking big hand too, which he used to good advantage on Harve now and again when it looked like Harve was becoming too much like his grandfather, on his mother's side. That was old Ephraim Greene, a hell-raiser around Chittenden County that gave the men who gathered at the blacksmith's shop on rainy days plenty of fodder. Nobody could figure out where else Harve could have got his contrariness from. They say blood will tell, and folks speculated Harve was a throwback to his grandpa. Old Eph sure was a hell-raiser of note. He was a boozer and lady's man, and they say when he was young he regular tore up the Rutland Fair every fall. Some say his wife's dying young like she did had soured him on life early, but his son-in-law thought of him as something more than sour. Pickled, more likely. To give the devil his due, Eph had a big heart. Would give the shirt off his back when needed, and all the kids and dogs in town loved him. That is, when he did come into town. Mostly he stayed out at his farm, coming into town (barefoot in summer) only when he needed something from the general store. Swore worse than any man in the county. Tom Snell, who was also a deacon in the church, said he was passing by Eph's place one day when he heard the worst language he ever did hear coming from mortal man. He said it kind of drew him on as if he were being pulled by some unseen evil force, the evil force having the foresight to pull Tom sneaky-like around the corner of the barn where he wouldn't be seen. There was Eph, naked to the waist with his overall straps hanging loose by his sides, sweating and swearing over a gigantic old elm stump that had been plaguing the place ever since Eph's own pa had cleared it. He had his team hitched to it, and he'd shovel, and chop, and holler some more, swearing all the time when he had the breath,'til the shovel broke, the head flew off the ax, and the team popped the traces. Then Tom said he howled. Stood there with his fists doubled, looking up at the sky and howling like a demon. Then he started in to cuss. He started with the shovel and worked his way right through the whole state of Vermont, and Tom said he was horrible shocked at the language and just had to leave; but before he could tear himself away he saw the stump sort of quiver right down to the roots, and then just give up and tumble over.

True story or not, it is well known that Eph could cuss, and that was particularly hard for Harve's old man to take, being a deacon in the church. He was a mite hard with Harve at times, wanting him to grow up right. When he brought Harve to church on Sunday, he was clean and slicked up just like his mother was still living, and wearing a cap with a button on the top that his pa always made him wear to church. It was the same color and material that his britches and coat were made of. It's understandable how that could go against a fellow's grain, especially since none of the other boys had to wear a cap.

One of Harve's school chums made the mistake of just mentioning that cap. Not *meaning* anything, but just how "cute" that little button looked on top. Harve knew he wasn't supposed to fight, but

he had a fast temper and a slow memory, and by the time he remembered
he wasn't supposed to fight he had already pounded the ticking out
of that poor lad. Harve had been told to wait in the buggy while his
pa and the preacher were in the parsonage after meeting, counting
the offering and wondering why the Lord kept the pious folk so
poor. When Harve's pa heard the ruckus he came running, just in
time to see Harve dusting himself off. He pitched in and helped
Harve along with that task, vigorously. The preacher came right along
too, and told Harve a young Christian shouldn't be fighting like
that, and if he did it again he'd just have to take one of Harve's
silver stars off the blue card all the kids had for attendance, and that
would be one more week further away from winning his own Bible.
Harve's eyes started to water over at this news, and you could tell he
was hurt clear to the bottom, which was the part he was most concerned with when his pa planked him back on that oak buggy seat
for the longest ride home he ever had. "Now you listen to me," that
preacher had said before they left, "I know what's wrong with you,
the devil's in you, that's what, and you let him out there for a spell
when those children taunted you. Well, Jesus was taunted too, and
he didn't strike out. He turned the other cheek. So you start acting like
Jesus, and show them what a good Christian you are. The next time
you're taunted, boy, you turn the other cheek." Harve at the time was
an impressionable young boy, especially after the shaking up he'd
just got, and he took the preacher's words to heart.

The next day in the school yard he came face to face with the kid
he'd drubbed the day before. The kid wanted to know why Harve
hadn't worn his Sunday cap again to school, and if maybe he didn't
want some pink ribbon for it. This piece of wit was of course not lost
on the rest of the kids standing around, and they tittered appreciative-
ly. Ordinarily, the kid's question would have been like asking Harve
if he didn't feel lucky again that day, but Harve remembered the
preacher's words, and as the kid took a step backwards and put up
his dukes, Harve initiated the attack by just standing there, grinning!
The kid could have taken insults, or a puffy lip maybe, but to have
his opponent stand there and grin like Harve knew something he
didn't was more than he could bear. Especially knowing Harve as he
did, he probably thought it was some new trick. He advanced cautiously
to the grinning Harve, afraid of what sucker trap he was about to get
caught in. As he got closer he danced around a little and threw a couple
of feints while the rest of the fry alternately urged on the kid and asked
Harve if he hadn't maybe lost his mind. Finally the temptation of
that unguarded mug got the best of the kid, and Harve's trick to hell,

he had to throw a punch. He caught Harve a good one on the side of his head that must have given Harve a moment of dark thought, but he stood his ground and turned the other cheek! That evil kid was about to smite Harve again when he realized Harve was just standing there with his face all screwed up and his eyes closed—not even looking at him! That must have been too much, and *was* very unlike Harve.

"What the hell's the matter with you?" the kid asked him.

"I'm turning the other cheek," said Harve.

"Well, you damn fool," said the kid, "supposing I hit you again?"

"Go ahead," said Harve, "the Lord's eye is on the sparrow."

You never saw anybody look more like one of those cherubs in those dark pictures that people hang on their parlor walls than Harve did as he imagined himself standing there in a beam of light direct to the Lord's eye. But the next thing Harve knew there was a blinding flash of light in his own eye, and he found himself flat on his back looking up at the treetops leaning against the blue sky. That's where faith breaks down: when the rules are applied but they don't work out to what is expected. The preacher's words went flying around in Harve's head, but what got through to him was the smart in his eye. "Why goddam you," he hollered, and jumped up and fetched that kid a crack that left a tooth hanging through his upper lip. Harve wasn't any child fighting then; he was a man disenchanted. There's no telling what he might have done, but a heavy hand was laid on his neck, and he was jerked off the ground and face up to the preacher, who had happened by the school yard. "Fighting again," said the preacher, "and you a deacon's son! Your father will certainly hear of this."

"You goggle-eyed bastard," Harve shouted, twisting in the preacher's grasp. "You turn loose of me." That wasn't just exactly what the preacher was used to hearing from one of his Sunday School pupils, and shortly after Harve recovered from the tanning he got he was sitting up beside the preacher on another oak buggy seat on the way home to face the prospect of yet another tanning. All the while the preacher told him over and over that the devil was in him. It must have occurred to Harve more than once on the way home that there should be an easier way of getting the devil out of him than by applying the palm of the hand to the seat of the trousers. At the time, Harve was really sorry for his many grievous sins.

They found Harve's pa at work in the barn, and while the preacher was in telling the story, Harve was standing outside with his head hanging, waiting. Some people think the preacher left out the part about the whipping, because if Harve's pa had of known he probably wouldn't have laid it to him the way he did. When Harve's pa and the preacher came out of the barn his pa didn't say a word, but went straight to get an old piece of harness strap and went at it. Harve would have got off a lot easier if he'd raised more fuss, but he took it real funny and quiet. He was pretty occupied with thinking over the preacher's words as that piece of harness cut welt after welt on his behind and legs. "Now you get in the house," his pa said, "and wait for me there. We're going to have a little talk, you and me."

Harve wasn't much in the mood for talking. He'd heard enough words. It appears that the preacher and Harve's pa, instead of beating the devil *out* of him, they packed the devil *in* even more tightly, because when they next went looking for Harve he was sitting out in back of the barn on top of the manure pile.

"Harvey," his old man yelled, "what in Tophet are you doing on top of that manure pile?"

"I'm making me a preacher," hollered back Harve, "and if I've got enough left over I'm going to make me a church!"

Harve never did get to finish his preacher. His pa let out a bellow like a strangled steam calliope with all the stops out, and charged the manure pile. He got to the top just in time to see Harve jump the stone wall at the far end of the pasture and disappear into the woods. His pa floundered around hunting for Harve until it got dark, and then went home. He sat up all night, waiting, but Harve didn't come. He had lit out cross-country for his grandpa's place.

In the past five years since his mother had died, Harve was allowed to spend every other Saturday afternoon with his grandfather. Grudgingly. Harve's pa didn't think that Eph would be exerting much of a good influence on him. But on those Saturday afternoons Harve enjoyed something that he didn't get any of at home. Fun and laughter. So it was no wonder that in his hour of need Harve went directly to his grandfather's place. And even at thirteen he was already too much of a New England Yankee to go to some friend's house and let everybody know that things were not going so good between him and his pa. He got there just as Eph was setting out his solitary plate for supper.

Harve slipped around back of the house and walked in to the kitchen without knocking. He stood there breathing in great gulps of air from his run, right on the verge of tears but a little too grown-up to let them out. "I guess you'll be hungry," said Eph, and got another plate from the cupboard. The two of them ate in silence, Harve showing very little appetite. Finally, Eph thought he'd better say something, or the little clam might sit there all night. "I wasn't expecting you 'til Saturday," he said. "I figured maybe we'd take a walk and plan a trap line for this winter. Been plenty of fox sign around."

Harve didn't hear the words, but apparently the sound of another voice reminded him he could talk. He pushed a boiled potato around for another minute, then looked at Eph and asked, "Why does my pa hate me? I try to be good so he'll like me, but I know he hates me." With that, the tears couldn't be held back another instant. Eph let him cry a spell until the worst of it was over, and then leaned across the table and said,"He doesn't hate you, boy. He just wants a lot from you, maybe too much. He's a pretty important man in this town, and I think he probably worries a lot about what folks think. I'm sure, deep down, he loves you very much." Harve mulled this over for a while, and when he stopped crying he said, "Well, if he loves me so much, I sure wish he'd find another way of showing it." Then he blurted out the whole story, starting from Sunday. Eph listened to it judiciously, managing only by the hardest to keep from laughing about the manure pile incident. He might even have taken Harve home to his pa that night, until he saw the welts and cuts on Harve's legs. That's when he decided he'd let his son-in-law cool off overnight. He got some Bag Balm from the barn, rubbed it on Harve's legs, and put him to bed in what had been Harve's mother's room. "Maybe tomorrow I'll ask your pa if you can't stay on here a spell and give the two of you a little time to think things out." Harve allowed it would be fine with him if he never went home. He was afraid of what his father had in store for him if he ever caught him again.

When Harve didn't come home that night his pa figured he must have gone to his grandfather's. The thought of that had tormented him all night, as he sat nodding in his chair. The next morning he was out at dawn and on the way to fetch Harve home. Instead of driving into the yard, he left the buggy out on the road hitched to the fence, by way of letting Eph know he had not come for a social visit. He walked the rest of the way in and clomped up on the front porch and pounded on the door, just as Harve and Eph were getting dressed.

The door opened with a great deal of reluctance, creaking and crack- ing from disuse. Front doors were never used except for weddings and funerals, and this one hadn't been opened since Tuttle Snow walked out of it with Mary Greene as his bride. As the door groaned fully open Eph moved in and pretty well filled the space, standing there bearded and silent, the straps on his overalls let out so the crotch hung halfway to his knees. He always said that he liked plenty of room for action. Eph was not an unreasonable man, and even though he was mad about the treatment Tuttle had given Harve, he could understand how Tuttle felt. More than once after his own escapades his daughter had asked tearfully how she could be expected to hold up her head in town after what he'd done. He was ready to talk.

"Morning, Tut," he said. But Tuttle was feeling his own grievances too much to catch the significance of that opening statement. The double humiliation his son had caused him, first in front of the preacher and then preferring to run to his grandfather than come home to him, was all that was on Tut Snow's mind.

"I've come for my son," announced Tuttle in a very no-nonsense tone of voice, as if he expected this approach would stampede Eph.

"I guess he'll go when he gets ready," replied Eph. This was not the answer the single-minded Tut wanted.

"I said I've come for my son," he answered, "and I mean for him to come home with me. I'll go in and get him if I have to."

Tuttle should have known Eph well enough to bring an ax handle with him if he was going to take that approach, and lay it on his skull the minute the door opened. Unfortunately for him, this method of negotiating a difficult situation probably hadn't occurred to the gently disposed Tuttle. Maybe he even thought Eph was about to give in without any trouble when he sort of hung back in the door to give the kick he planted in the middle of Tut's chest some extra force. Tut sailed off the porch and lit flat on his back, and before he had time to even take one breath of air Eph was on him.

Eph only knew one way to fight, and that was to win the best way he could, never mind how he did it. His tactic was to keep the other fellow on the ground while he battered him with his fists, elbows and knees, and butted him with his head. They rolled over and over and tore up a good piece of ground before Tut finally got loose and on to his feet. Eph got up too, and charged in, head lowered, like a bull. He didn't quite make it. Tut poled him on top of his head with a huge fist that dropped him in his tracks. As Tut moved in to finish the job, Eph grabbed him around the ankles and down Tut went again with Eph on top. Tut was younger, and maybe at that time stronger, but Eph was crafty and still a stout man, and when the two men finally rolled apart again Tut didn't move for a minute. Then he slowly drew himself up to his hands and knees, crawled, then painfully got to his feet and staggered out to his buggy with never a word or look behind. Eph crawled over to a tree and sat with his back against it, eyes closed, sucking in air through his open mouth with a noise like the bellows made in Pearly King's blacksmith shop. When he could finally talk he said, "Goddam."

Harve had watched the whole fight from the open door, and when it was over he came out and sat on the porch with his chin resting in his hands while the tears rolled freely down his cheeks and onto the top step, making big splotches where they soaked into the unpainted wood. His grandpa heard him snuffle, and opened his eyes.

"Come on over here, boy," he said. Harve went and sat down beside his grandfather, who put a big arm around him. "I guess you're caught in the middle, boy, and I don't envy you none," he said. "Maybe you'd better go back to your pa."

"Do I have to?" asked Harve.

"No, you don't *have* to, but I think you'd be better off there."

"No! I'm scared he'd really whip me now."

"I don't think he will. I think he'd just be glad to have his boy back."

"Well, I guess I'll go with him the next time he says he wants me."

"All right then. You stay as long as you want."

Eph grinned through a split lip, which cracked and started to bleed fresh. He licked at the blood, spat on the ground, wiped his mouth with a dirty sleeve and said, "Whew! For a deacon and a man that don't hold with fighting, your old man sure gave good account of himself. I thought for a while there he had this old billy goat's ass." Eph let go of Harve and hunched himself more upright against the tree, grunting with the effort. "I must be getting old," he said, more to himself than to Harve. "I've got a bottle of whiskey in under the commode in the kitchen. How about bringing it out here for me. I feel like I need a little taste to get me started today."

Harve stayed a good deal longer with his grandpa than expected. Tuttle never did send for him. He was waiting for Harve to come home. And Harve never went. He was waiting to be asked. Eph could have taken the boy home, and probably given them both a fresh start, but he liked having the boy around. Nobody really likes living alone, given the right companion. Eph stood by silent and let two stubborn people pretend the other didn't exist, when all along, if the truth be known, they missed each other like hell. Harve did for a while, and then he didn't think about his pa much any more. He was growing up and learning new things.

He learned how to work hard. Not that he hadn't had plenty of chores to do at home, but now he learned to do a man's work. Although Eph never aimed to get rich, he had never aimed to owe anybody anything either. He had done just enough work to make do for his needs, not working his place or keeping it up any more than was necessary. But with Harve there it was different. Then he had someone to leave the place to who might need it. Harve quit right after grammar school,

and he and Eph worked side by side to turn the neglected dairy farm into a going concern. He learned other things from Eph too, some not so
industrious or admirable. He learned how to swear properly, and how
to make home brew and hard cider. He learned how to catch the wary
native eastern brook trout, and how to poach deer in the winter. He
learned how to chase around the woods half the night listening to his
'coon hounds bay, and how to play the fiddle and the hearts of young
ladies. He learned that last part right smart too, because Harve grew up
to be a fine-looking young man with a big smile and devilish, flattering
tongue.

The town was divided sort of equally between those who went to
church and those who didn't. Eph and Harve didn't and since the two
groups had little in common, Harve seldom ever saw his father;
and if either of them saw the other coming in town, they'd turn some
other way to avoid getting too close. During all those years they never
spoke to or about each other. Harve even went over to the next town
to get his hair cut to make sure he wouldn't run into his pa while
trapped in the barber chair, and when Tuttle got himself married
again, Harve's only comment was to take a bottle of Eph's store whiskey
and his fiddle and disappear out to the barn. Eph heard him out there
playing "Here Comes the Bride" to the cows. Harve was sixteen then,
and Eph let him go because he didn't know how to tell him not to.
It worried Eph sometimes, the example he set. When Harve didn't have
much of an appetite the next morning, Eph recognized the symptoms
and worked him unmercifully hard that day. Not a word was said about
the whiskey but Harve got the point.

Harve grew up with a sunny nature, which was a good thing because
he also had a little bit of a wild streak in him, and a great capacity
for whooping it up on Saturday night. He was building quite a legend
for himself around those parts just when Mr. Ford's kidney buster was
becoming less of a rarity. Harve bought one with his share of the farm's
profits, and that's when the expression "hell on wheels" came about.
Harve and a couple of his friends would load up the Ford on a Saturday
night with a few quarts of Philadelphia Old Stock beer and their instruments and go play for a square dance somewhere in one of the surrounding towns. "Try and keep that thing between the ditches," Eph would
say as Harve was leaving.

Harve never did pay particular attention to any one girl. He said he
liked them all. So it was in his twenty-third year that he met Nathan
Gallup's daughter, Naomi. She liked to come to the Saturday night
dances, and she and Harve had struck up a speaking acquaintance
which they had carried on for a couple of years. It was usually about

music, and what and how he was playing. But that was all there was to it. She always came in a group of several couples, with different fellows from the churchgoing half of the town, and wouldn't have gone with Harve if he had asked her. Not with his reputation. And Harve wouldn't have asked *her* either, because her reputation didn't interest him one bit.

One Saturday night Harve and Naomi were dancing in the same set, not together of course, and Harve in his usual exuberant Saturday night mood was cutting up on the floor, causing general confusion among the serious dancers. As a result, one of the fellows got his feet all bollixed up, and in trying to catch his balance swung a wild hand that landed full and square on Naomi's bouncing behind. Naomi spun on her heel just as Harve danced by, innocent of any wrongdoing for perhaps the first time in his life. But there was no doubt in her mind that Harve was the culprit that had got fresh with her as she open-handed him across the face with a crack that stopped the music. In a quivering voice that carried the whole dance floor she delivered that time-honored line of righteous female indignation, "How *dare* you, Harvey Snow!"

Before the stunned Harve could get his mouth closed enough to make any kind of reply, the guilty fellow came between them and stammered out an apology to Naomi. Poor girl, she blushed from her hairline down to where her neck disappeared into her collar. Harve, by this time, recovered, made a mock little bow and turned his face to offer the other cheek. "Here," he said, his voice oily with sarcasm. "You left one side out."

About this time Naomi saw her beau coming across the floor with a look on his face that showed he was coming to defend the honor of his lady fair, although he didn't appear to be in any too much of a hurry. To avert further embarrassment, and certain mayhem, Naomi raised up on her toes and kissed Harve a chaste little peck on the proffered cheek, smiled sweetly at the caller, tapped her heel twice, and, as the music started, whirled Harve away at a pace that left him dizzy for the rest of his life.

By the time the dance ended he was in love up to his eyeballs. "By Godfrey," he thought, "It took ten years, but there's something in what the preacher said about turning the other cheek after all!" Over a glass of sweet cider, Harve apologized for his sarcastic and rude reply and Naomi admitted the whole thing was all her fault and Harve insisted it was his and Naomi said how embarrassed she was for her unwarranted snap judgment of him and Harve said it was probably justified and she said it wasn't and how could he ever forgive her and ·he said he'd already done that; and then they didn't have anything to say so Harve asked her if he might call at her house Wednesday evening. She said that would be nice.

The ride home that night was a lot less hairy than usual, as Harve had a lot on his mind. Or rather, one thought that kept repeating itself. He had turned his other cheek, and instead of what he expected to happen, the best thing ever in his life had happened instead. The image of Naomi's demure sweetness at the cider bowl flashed across his brainpan, and his cheek flamed anew. The side on which he got kissed. The other side was long forgotten. "My old man was right about one thing at least," he thought,"the Lord sure works in mysterious ways." Harve's addled brain had worked it all out that it must have been the Lord that sent Naomi, because he knew damn well that no nice girl in town would have come on her own.

Harve spent a restless night, and next morning was up early and had all the Sunday chores done by the time Eph was up and stirring around in the house. It being that Harve was not exactly an eager riser on Sunday mornings, when he came in from the barn and announced to Eph that the chores were through it caught the old man by surprise. "What in tunket's got into you?" he asked.

"I'm in love!" blurted Harve. Eph's reply was a noncommittal grunt. Harve hadn't expected a gush of ooohs and aaahs from his taciturn old grandfather, but he did think that this most important piece of news in all the world deserved more than a grunt. "And on top of that," said Harve, put out by Eph's grunt, "I've been thinking maybe I'll ask the girl to marry me, too, goddam it!" Eph grunted again, but this time showing a little surprise.

"Don't you even want to know who she is?" asked Harve.

"Ehyah," said Eph. "I would be curious to know what woman could get you to thinking about marriage."

"Her name is Naomi Gallup."

"That wouldn't be *Nathan* Gallup's girl, now would it?"

"Yep!"

"Met her folks yet?"

"Nope!"

"Unh-hunh. And her? Met her last night, did you?"

"Yes, I *did* indeed!"

"Umnph. Then I take it you've not set the date yet." Harve blushed under Eph's gentle needling. "Well, I didn't say I was going to rush into anything, did I?"

"No, you didn't. And there's no rushing it, anyway, I can promise you." Eph turned away from Harve to poke around in the stove, hiding the faint trace of a smile that softened his face as it stole down from the corners of his eyes. "I guess you'd better be getting cleaned up and ready for church."

"Church!" Harve exploded out of his chair, cracking his knee on the kitchen table. Pain, and fear, made a tremolo of his voice. "What do you mean, church?" He hopped about on one leg, holding his injured knee. "Who said anything about going to church?"

"You did. That *was* you saying you were in love and thinking about getting married, wasn't it?"

"Yes."

"Well, do you want to marry her or not?"

Harve forgot about his injured knee. "Yes, by damn. I know it was meant to be!"

"Then you'd best be getting ready for church. That is, if you're wanting to marry Nathan Gallup's daughter." With that Harve reached over and pulled Eph's beard, something he hadn't done since before he'd come to live there.

Harve had bought a new suit just before he took the train to Burlington to buy the Ford, and he put it on for the second time that Sunday. When he didn't see Eph down in the kitchen to say goodbye, he climbed back up the stairs and tapped at his door. "I'll be going now," he said.

"Come in here a minute," came from inside, and Harve stepped in to see his grandfather tucking his gold watch and penknife into his vest pockets. Harve hadn't seen Eph in a suit since he was baptized, and the sight struck him dumb.

"Don't just stand there with your mouth hanging open," said Eph, "or we'll be late for church."

"You mean you're coming with me?" asked Harve, incredulously.

"Of course I am," said Eph. "I couldn't let a man face an ordeal like this alone. Besides, I was thinking maybe I ought to take you by the doc's to see if you're not running a fever."

Harve and Eph sat in the Ford until they were sure the last straggler was in, then slipped in and sat in the last pew. Nobody turned around then to see who it was that came in late, but when the plate was passed for the offering the collection men also passed along the astounding information that Eph Green and Tuttle Snow's boy, Harvey, were sitting in the back. As each person handed the plate on to his neighbor, a whisper went with it, and a head would turn around to see if it was really true. Harve tried to look somewhere above everybody, straight to the front of the church. His ears burned red. When the plate reached his pa, way up front with his new family, Harve waited a tense moment to see if he would turn around too. He didn't, much to Harvey's relief. Eph, wiser in the ways of his fellowman, sat there as if he owned part of the place and looked every person he could right in the eye as they turned around, nodding and smiling like *he* was the shepherd of the flock. When the collection was over, Reverend Burch launched into his sermon about the prodigal son. Harve started twitching and fidgeting somewhere along into the second half hour, and after the sermon had passed the hour mark he slid close to Eph and gave him a gentle elbow in the ribs. "I forgot to leave some milk for the cat this morning," he whispered. "Don't you think we'd ought to get back and feed the poor thing?" Eph's reply was a stoic stare. However, after he himself had secretly looked at his watch for the third time, he leaned closed to Harve and whispered back, "I think you're right about that cat."

They rode the six miles back home in silence, Harve intent on the snowy road and Eph occupied with his own thoughts. While Harve backed the Ford into the shed, Eph went in the house and straight down cellar. He emerged carrying two quarts of home brew just as Harve entered. Harve got the pitcher, and held it up to the light from the window so Eph could see to pour, the object being to decant the bottles into the pitcher so that none of the yeast that had settled in the bottom of the bottle ran out into the pitcher. Harve then poured out two glasses, which they drank sitting at the kitchen table. When he finally got up to take off his overcoat, with a guilty grin on his face he poured out a saucer of milk for the cat. As he downed his second glass of brew Harve said, reflectively, "It's going to be a hard pull." Eph raised his glass, tilted it slightly in Harve's direction, and said, "A-men."

And a hard pull it was. Wednesday evening after the milking, Harve scrubbed himself up and shaved, put on his suit and presented himself in town at Nathan Gallup's house. Naomi opened the door and Harve's brain went dizzy again at the sight and smell of her. She led him in like a puppy on a leash to introduce her parents. "Haven't seen you since you were a little tad," Nathan said to Harve, "but I see your *father* at least every Sunday. Heard you were there yourself last week." Then he stuck his nose back in the Burlington Sunday paper, which had only arrived the day before. If Harve had been thinking, he'd have caught the barb in Nathan's greeting and got an inkling of the conversation that had transpired between father and daughter when she told him who was coming to call on her. But of course Harve was in no condition to think. He said, "Yes, sir, a pleasure to meet you, sir, uh, again," Naomi's mother recollected how she and Harve's mother had been little girls together, and Harve said, "Yes, sir," to her too. After that Naomi took Harve into the parlor, taking care to leave the door open to the room where her parents were, of course, where she sat upright in a straight-backed chair with her hands folded in her lap. They rehashed the events of the previous Saturday night until they got to the part about Naomi's behind, when Harve tactfully changed the subject and started to tell her about his trap line. "Fox are a lot smarter than skunk," he said authoritatively. "We bait the skunk traps with chicken guts, and then save the skunk musk to smear on our boots and clothes to disguise how we smell when we go to tend the fox traps." Being the thorough person that he was, he went into greater detail than was absolutely necessary for Naomi, who excused herself to get them some homemade doughnuts and coffee. After Harve had wolfed down a good half dozen doughnuts they played two of the coyest games of checkers on record, each trying to be polite and lose without being too obvious about it. Then Harve pulled out Eph's watch, made some inane comment about how time flew, and took his leave. Before he left, though, he made a date for more of the same the next Wednesday. On the way home Harve wondered how such a dull evening could be so exciting.

More Wednesday nights were followed by daytime social functions such as traverse sledding down Poker Hill, followed by properly chaperoned nighttime do's like the church supper and the sugaring-off party they attended. With two other skeptical couples that Naomi arranged for, they even went square dancing twice that winter, Harve being careful to pick the dances away from his old stomping grounds. It had all started in October, and by April he and Naomi were going off by themselves on Sunday afternoons. In July he asked her to marry him, and they set an October date. Hallelujah! All because he turned the other cheek!

After Naomi said yes, Harve's enlightened heart decided enough was enough. He wanted his pa at his wedding. He talked it over with Eph, who said that was the best thing Harve ever thought of. They even decided Tuttle ought to be best man to show the town the hatchet was buried.

Harve went to see his pa. He set off on foot, cross-country the way he'd left ten years before. He got there right at milking time in the morning, and found Tuttle alone in the barn. His pa was just moving from one cow to another as Harve let himself in. Tuttle heard the noise of the door sliding and turned, and then just stood there with his pail in one hand and stool in the other. Harvey walked to within three feet of his father, took a deep breath, and said, "Morning, Pa."

"Hello Harvey."

"Pa, I'm getting married in October to Naomi Gallup."

"I heard."

"I'd be proud for you to be my best man."

"I'd be proud to do it."

Harvey was surprised that he was tall enough to look directly into his father's eyes. He was a man grown.

"Pa, I'm sorry I ran off."

"I am too, son."

Harve shuffled his feet. "Well, I'd best be getting back to help Eph with the milking."

"Yes, he'll be needing some help."

"I guess."

"Harvey, maybe you and Naomi could stop after church on Sunday for dinner."

"We'd be pleased to come."

"Good enough." Tuttle nodded one affirmative bob of his head, as if signaling enough talk.

"Take care, Pa."

"You too, Harvey."

Harve turned to go, but before he reached the door his father called after him. "Harvey," he said. "I've got two fine boys now, and I want you to know I've never laid a hand to either."

At this, Harve turned and ran back to his father, jumping up to grab him around the neck like he used to do when he was a little kid. Over they both went and down on the barn floor, and up in the air went the pail of milk, splashing all over them. Never had two grown men laughed so hard over a little spilled milk.

Harve and Eph worked industriously to get the place fixed up in time for Naomi to move in, Eph grumbling all the while about the imminent changes to occur with a woman in the house, but he had made her a curly maple vanity table for a wedding present.

The wedding went off with never a hitch, although some of the townspeople wondered if it would last, Harve and Naomi courting for only a year. It was referred to as a "whirlwind courtship." After the ceremony, Harve slipped the preacher a five-dollar bill, and at the time it happened nobody knew about Harve's final piece of devilment except Harve and the Reverend Burch—and you've got to give the Reverend credit for Spartan courage (or wanting to hold on to that five-dollar bill awful bad) because when Harve shook that preacher's hand he grinned right in the Reverend Burch's face—and cracked his damned knuckles for him!   END

We Gather Together

by Lilli and John Wahtera

By the family's standards, Aunt Zanya was a success. It wasn't that she was rich, for her husband was a farm-implement sales-man. It was that she lived in New Hampshire among green hills and lakes. To the family back on Ansonia Street, where the only green thing was the streetcar rattling by, New Hampshire seemed as far away as Kiev and as beautiful as Switzerland.

"Kiev is closer!" my grandmother said grimly, coming home to Boston from a visit to Aunt Zanya.

My Uncle Ben and I were sent to North Station to meet her. The train was early, and we found my grandmother at the gate surround-ed by brown shopping bags of green vegetables, jars of honey and maple syrup, her battered suitcase, and a redcap who had labored to carry all this off the train. We found my grandmother considering him with frank bewilderment as he lingered on, shuffling around her parcels.

"He wants a tip, Ma," whispered Uncle Ben.

"What is this, a tip?" she queried loudly.

"A little money, for carrying your bags," Uncle Ben explained.

My grandmother thought this over for a moment and gave the man a coin. "You should pardon me," she said. "I thought it was included free with the ticket."

When the redcap left and we were loaded up with her bundles, Uncle Ben asked, "How much did you give him, Ma?" since the man had not seemed pleased.

"A nickel."

"Oh, God!" groaned Ben. "Even Uncle Morris would have given him a dime."

"God and Uncle Morris can afford it more than me," replied his mother.

Before we could leave, she inventoried each bag and took away from Ben one containing small green tomatoes and cucumbers. "Look. For pickles," she said smiling. They were as gold to her, and she held the bag herself all the long hot streetcar ride back to Ansonia Street.

Sauerkraut, pickled green tomatoes and cucumbers were the special-ty of my grandmother's house. She made them in the cool, dark, back hallway in great stone crocks of brine. It was rare that they ever finished pickling for, although my grandmother guarded them, there was no one in her large household with the moral fibre to let them pickle in peace. Especially my grandfather and I, who, on our way to the cellar to check his wine-making efforts, would stand in the dark, holding a handful of sauerkraut, the fragant juice running down to our elbows. "Ah, Naomi," he might say softly, biting into a pickle, "God lightens my burdens with pleasures like this!" We learned to be careful, for the rumble of a wooden cover being replaced on a crock was certain to bring a shriek from the kitchen.

My grandfather was a paper hanger. And the first thing I learned when my mother brought my sister Marilyn and me to my grandparents to live—my father having turned out to be something of a disappointment—was the difference between a butt and a lap. Also, no matter which way you hung it, it was a poor living for a soft touch like grandfather. It was 1934, and around Ansonia Street, if you papered a room, it was because a son or daughter had married and the Depression was making them come home to live. My grandfather received many compensations, sometimes even cash.

"What is that!" cried my grandmother, setting down her bag of green tomatoes.

"From the Bellingham job," said my pleased grandfather.

In the room which should have been a parlor, but which we called "The Store" because its walls were lined with rolls of wallpaper, sat a Victorian chaise longue on which you could stretch out and also bounce up and down. It was covered in faded mauve velvet and ringed with gold tassels. Even Marilyn and I sensed it was wicked. To my grandmother it was as welcome a sight as a final notice from the gas company.

"Victor, is money out of style?" asked his wife.

"Ida," he shrugged, "is something better than nothing?"

"So? We starve in comfort!" she snapped and took her tomatoes to the kitchen.

It was a telling point for she had eight mouths to feed every day, and food was always uppermost in her mind. Life had filled the house with dependents, and her husband was filling it with *antiques*. Aunt Rose was a stenographer who was so picky that the family had despaired of her finding a husband. My mother had found a husband, but he had gone away. She spent her days in her room at the top of the brownstone, becoming almost a ghost, appearing only for meals. Uncle Ben was our hope for the future. He went nights to the University, but a law student isn't a lawyer. He couldn't find a steady job, but he did what he could, even running errands for the drugstore. So it was Aunt Zanya we held up to the light, seeing through her as through a prism the promise of better days, if only the Depression would end the way President Roosevelt was assuring us it would.

"Does Aunt Zanya have a farm?" I asked my grandmother as I helped her wash the green tomatoes.

"Is three rooms and a bath a farm?"

"Then where did you get the vegetables?"

"Vegetables Zanya has," replied my grandmother. "If the farmers have no money, they give Zanya's husband vegetables, or what they can spare."

My grandmother had been tired by her visit to Zanya, but it was not until the tomatoes and cucumbers rested in their crocks of brine in the back hall and the cabbages were shredded into sauerkraut that she paused.

The day after Labor Day a letter came from Zanya. A surprise for the family was coming, it said, by Railway Express.

The rest of the household was curious but not excited; they expected something to eat. Something to eat was a second-rate surprise, and Marilyn and I expected something more glamorous. We hurried home after school each day, rushing past the open doors of Charlie-the-Chinaman and the printer, Mr. Pasternak. We usually haunted Charlie, who saved us stamps from China, and Mr. Pasternak, who gave us his odds and ends of paper. We never felt richer than when we carried home a dragon stamp and a ream of bond paper with a misspelled, downtown letterhead on one side.

The surprise was so long in coming that the family seemed to have forgotten it; even Marilyn and I had stopped rushing home. But one afternoon, as we sat at the kitchen table covering sheets of Mr. Pasternak's paper with beautiful women in beautiful gardens, the doorbell rang.

"Who do we owe?" My grandmother sighed and put aside the *Daily Forward*.

There was the sound of the front door opening, followed by quarreling voices. One of them was Grandmother's.

"The wrong house!" she cried.

"It's 345 Ansonia, ain't it?" a man replied. "Sign here."

"Naomi!" she shrieked. "Come here! Read me what this man's paper says!"

"Come on, lady," the fellow insisted. "You don't want it, I don't want it, but this is 345 Ansonia Street. Sign here."

"What does it say?" she asked, thrusting the man's bill of lading into my hands.

"It's from Zanya," she echoed in disbelief, watching the Railway Express man push a huge crate into her hall.

"You sign it, kid," he said, handing me a pencil and rubbing his forearm across his face.

My grandmother nodded silently, and I did as he asked.

"Watch out," he offered as he left. "It bites."

When he slammed the door behind him, an enormous turkey's head appeared through the slats of the crate. It looked around with large piercing eyes, not in the least pleased to find its long journey had ended in our hallway.

Marilyn and I were struck dumb by this ornithological wonder. We had never seen a live turkey before, hardly anything except pigeons and the dusty sparrows of Ansonia Street. When it suddenly fluffed itself out to twice its size and lifted its head in a deafening, yet perfectly enunciated gobble-gobble-gobble, Marilyn and I trembled with joy and fear.

"It looks like Uncle Morris," whispered Marilyn.

"For shame," said my grandmother.

Uncle Morris was Grandmother's brother, who appeared once a year at Thanksgiving, carrying a two-pound box of chocolates made in his candy factory. We knew these cherry chocolates were seconds because the liquid centers had leaked out and the cherries rattled around like shriveled seeds in a pod. Uncle Morris only stayed as long as he felt he had to, and long enough for us to wonder why he came. His great virtue was that he was rich; his great fault was that he gave nothing, not of himself nor of his riches. His cold eyes, missing only pince-nez, now stared back at us from the turkey. If the bird had said: "Rose, you ain't got a husband, yet?" or, "You still hanging yourself with wallpaper, Victor?" or, "The world is already full of lawyers, Ben," we wouldn't have been surprised. Uncle Morris the bird certainly was, and Uncle Morris he remained.

Uncle Morris came to us a full-blown misanthrope whose luggage was a large bag of feed. Marilyn and I dragged his feed into the back hall, but Morris remained in the front hall, almost in the dark since it was lit only by the dim stained-glass panels of the front door. Grandmother went back to her *Daily Forward*, but we knew she wasn't reading because the pages didn't turn. Marilyn and I took fresh paper and began to draw Pilgrims and turkeys.

At precisely quarter to six, the front door slammed and Aunt Rose

called into the kitchen, "I'm exhausted. I'm lying down and I don't
want any noise. Ma, there's a terrible smell in the hallway." When Aunt
Rose wasn't lying down exhausted, she was smelling terrible smells.
But that night she was probably right.

Perhaps because he was startled or maybe offended, Uncle Morris
retaliated by bringing his beak down on her ankle. Aunt Rose let out
a screech that must have shocked even Uncle Morris and should have
brought the police from Precinct No. 10, at the other end of our block.

"I'm stabbed!" Rose howled, rushing into the kitchen. "And look
at my stocking!" Marilyn and I were trying not to giggle. "It's not
funny!" she snapped at us, and to my grandmother, "And it's smelling
up the whole house."

"It's a turkey," shrugged my grandmother. "Should it smell like a
daisy?"

"It doesn't belong in the house," complained Aunt Rose, who was
now considering the damage to her stocking more serious than that
to her leg.

"You don't want it, I don't want it, but this is 345 Ansonia Street,"
replied Grandmother, quoting the delivery man.

"Zanya's surprise?" Rose asked.

"Zanya," sighed my grandmother.

"I don't know why she didn't send a cow while she was at it," sniffed
Aunt Rose.

Uncle Ben was noncommittal about the turkey, though he did raise
his eyebrows when we told him its name was Uncle Morris. "That's
grounds for slander," he said solemnly, in his best professional manner,
"but I'm not sure who's the injured party."

My grandfather was delighted with Zanya's gift. "Ah, what a wonderful Thanksgiving we'll have," he said, "and in such hard times. Are
the Vanderbilts better off?"

Ben and he carried Uncle Morris—who protested all the way—through
the house to the back porch and set him next to the iron picket fence
which separated our tiny garden from the alley leading to the public bath
house next door. Uncle Morris seemed to consider this location worse
than the front hall, and while we ate our supper in the kitchen, his head
poked through the iron railings as he complained bitterly to the parade
of workingmen who came in the evenings to have their showers.

It was a warm evening, and while it was light, Uncle Morris would
gobble to any passerby who would listen. But when the darkness came,
he settled down quietly.

In the middle of the night a sudden commotion in the house awakened Marilyn and me. On the porch below, we heard Uncle Morris gobbling with alarm.

"I see you! I see you!" shrieked my grandmother out the window. "Victor! Victor! Wake up!"

"I'll get him, Pa!" yelled Ben, and he ran downstairs.

Marilyn and I got to the window in time to see a man's shape vault the iron fence and disappear into the alleyway.

In a moment the family had congregated on the back porch. Though his kidnapping had been averted, Uncle Morris would not be calmed.

"Oh," said Aunt Rose, who arrived bleary-eyed and last, "if only they had got him!"

"Hard times," said my grandfather who always took it upon himself to make excuses to one-half of the world for the behavior of the other half. "If a man is hungry, he steals."

"But not from us," injected my grandmother, ever the realist. "Put Morris in the back hall."

So Ben and Grandfather dragged the crate into the back hall next to the pickling cucumbers and tomatoes.

In the days that followed, Uncle Morris became a fixture of the back hallway as much as the huge pottery crocks. In fact, much to my grandmother's delight, he became positively possessive about the crocks. No one could lift a cover, however stealthily, without his setting up a fuss which would bring Grandmother rushing in from the kitchen. For the first time, she had some hope of her pickling efforts coming to fruition.

Morris was not only a watchdog. When he was not alarmed for his own safety, or that of the pickles in his charge, he was a better-than-average listener. He cocked his head attentively and did not interrupt to interject problems of his own into the conversation.

October was hot that year. On long golden evenings the neighborhood spilled out onto the stoops, the men talking quietly of who was hiring and who was laying off. On the back porch, my grandfather smoked his pipe, Aunt Rose endlessly manicured her nails, while Ben studied and Grandmother sewed until the light failed. Usually, Uncle Morris was brought out for some fresh air. He had become a neighborhood favorite, and his gobblings often brought people over to check on his progress. When they found him fattening up nicely, Marilyn and I looked at one another with shared apprehension.

In November our group was not much different except that we had moved from the porch to the kitchen, into which Morris was again carried.

"I think it must be bad for his eyes to spend so much time in that dark place," reasoned my grandmother.

"What difference does it make?" asked Ben, looking up from *Cases on the Law of Trusts*. "In a week he'll be on a platter."

The family was aghast at Ben's callous remark, but Uncle Morris seemed unaffected by this ominous reference to his destiny. No one had mentioned Thanksgiving in Morris' presence since the day he arrived. Marilyn began to wail since it was she who gave him his ration of corn each day.

"We can't eat a friend," I said angrily, being far too old to cry, and suggested, "Let's send him back to Aunt Zanya."

"No," said my grandmother firmly. "Zanya sent us a turkey only so we should have a nice Thanksgiving, not an Uncle Morris. If the Pilgrims filled the woods with Uncle Morrises they would have starved. We wouldn't be sitting in America now. You will never know Chidniv, where the Czar—may he rest in peace—sent pogroms to us, not turkeys. Wipe your face, Marilyn," she said not unkindly, and glanced at my grandfather who scarcely looked more cheerful than Marilyn.

On the Tuesday before Thanksgiving, preparations began. My grandmother loved this holiday best of all the New World's celebrations, and had constructed a mythology about the Pilgrims' virtues all out of proportion to those possessed by the Plymouth adventurers. They had fled persecution; she had fled persecution. They had sought a better life; she had sought a better life. All had known hardship. Some of the dishes that turned up on her table would have seemed curious to the Pilgrims but, on the other hand, some of them would have seemed curious to the village of Chidniv. They all took much time and effort.

On Wednesday morning she said to my grandfather, "Today, Victor, you take Morris up to Bluestein's."

Bluestein was the kosher butcher and my grandfather became visibly uneasy at the thought of it. "I can't, he said evasively. "I have to finish the Slotniks' dining room. They got fancy relatives coming from Long Island."

"Fancy relatives I don't have," said my grandmother, "but I have a dinner still walking around with its feathers on. Who's going to take him to Bluestein's?"

"Ben," membled my grandfather, guiltily, and then left after half a cup of coffee.

A few minutes later, Ben came down to breakfast his whistling stopping abruptly at my grandmother's announcement: "Your father says you'll take the turkey to Bluestein's. Go early so you won't have to wait."

"Me? Why me?" Ben queried. "I have a job at Estes' Market for the day!"

"A job?" asked my grandmother, who had not heard of it before.

"If I get there early," Ben hedged, looking not unlike his father had. "If I'm one of the first ten."

When he, too, had gulped his breakfast and left, my grandmother stood looking at the empty doorway, shaking her head. "They got hearts like lions, your uncle and your grandfather," she observed to Marilyn and me. Sighing, she lifted off her apron and smoothed her hair at the kitchen mirror, frowning at her own image as though expecting it, too, would have some pressing reason why it could not go with Uncle Morris to Bluestein's.

The butcher was not more than a half mile farther up Ansonia Street, but getting Morris there was not merely a matter of distance. In the ten weeks he had lived with us, he had had little to do but gorge himself, and by that morning, he had fattened to a truly impressive weight. He could barely turn around in his crate. Taking the crate on a streetcar was out of the question, and so with Marilyn and me on one end, my grandmother on the other, we dragged Morris out to the sidewalk to wait for the only other alternative—a taxi.

The first two cabs passing slowed and turned to the curb at my grandmother's fluttering handkerchief; but, before they had quite stopped, they had seen the crate and speedily nosed back into the traffic. Since Morris was not to be considered a choice fare, we dragged his crate a little into the alley beside the house. Marilyn and I stayed with him, comforting him for he was complaining loudly, allowing my grandmother to return to the curb and snare the next unsuspecting taxi.

The driver was very fat and wore a chauffeur's cap, under which were stuck several pencils. With obvious exertion he eased himself out and opened the door for my grandmother with a weary compliance to his sense of duty. He had already decided with the wisdom of his tribe that her tip, if any, would be small.

My grandmother stepped off the curb but stood squarely in front of the door, smiling. "I have a little bundle," she said sweetly, "if you would be so kind," nodding towards Marilyn and me, who were laboriously dragging the crate from the alley.

"You call that a little bundle?" he asked, glowering at the crate but making no attempt to help us. "Lady, this is a cab, not a moving van. What else you got? A piano?"

"A canary I could carry myself," she shrugged. "In here," she said.

"Not in the trunk?" he asked sourly.

"In here," she repeated.

There was a moment of indecision—on his part, not on my grand-mother's. She stood immovable in front of his open door. He could not have shut the door, nor could he have driven off without sweeping her into the gutter. "What else?" he grumbled to no one in particu-lar. "Yesterday, a dog who bites my ear. Today a turkey. God forbid a millionaire should ever get in my cab!"

Triumphant, my grandmother slid into the taxi. Wheezing from his exertion, the driver jostled the bulky crate into the back seat beside her.

As the taxi pulled away, Uncle Morris' head stretched far out the taxi window, declaiming to Marilyn and me and the world that he was being kidnapped.

"Will he go to Heaven?" Marilyn asked me tearfully.

"If he's tender," I replied, trying to be brave.

On Thanksgiving Day, before we sat down for dinner, Aunt Zanya called us long distance to wish us a happy holiday. It seemed to us the most unheard of extravagance.

"They got money to burn?" asked the real Uncle Morris disap-provingly. "I should give up the candy business and go into farm machinery." From the looks of the chocolates he had brought, no one around the table would have disagreed.

We were each allotted a few seconds to thank Zanya for the turkey, and Zanya told us each in turn that she would like nothing better than to join us.

The phone was near the kitchen door on a Victorian rosewood buffet, Grandfather's pay for some papered hall or living room. The smells from the kitchen were overpowering. Boiled onions, of course, squash, and over it all, roast turkey. What a pity, everyone agreed, that Zanya wasn't here to appreciate it.

My grandmother appeared in the kitchen doorway announcing, "Al-most ready. One minute more. Marilyn, Naomi, sing one nice song for Uncle Morris."

Although Uncle Morris had yet to contribute a dollar to Ben's educa-tion, there was a family fiction that if Marilyn and I pleased him, he would some day send us both to Smith or Radcliffe. So, with Aunt Rose at the piano, we began a self-conscious rendition of, "We gather to-gether to ask the Lord's blessing." While the Lord "hastened and chastened his will to make known," I looked carefully at Uncle Morris and deduced from his pained expression that if I ever entered the gates of Radcliffe it would be on my own.

During the song, my grandmother had rushed back and forth bearing bowls of vegetables. Now she shouted from the kitchen, "I'm ready!" and carried into the room a platter on which there was the most splendid turkey ever to be seen on Ansonia Street. It was our good luck that it bore little resemblance to anyone we knew. She set the platter down in front of my grandfather and took her seat at the other end of the table.

My grandfather rose. We watched, silently expectant, as he looked down the table at his wife, then laid aside the carving tools to pick up his wine glass. "A turkey or a poet is born to a hard life," he philosophized, "but we thank God for both."

"Victor," said my grandmother gently, for his eyes strayed wistfully down to the bird, "a goose, a chicken and a turkey shouldn't have to die of old age like us."

No one would have disagreed; yet, with the deeper wisdom of the heart, although I think each of us reserved a little sadness, we were Pilgrims, hungry and thankful for this moment, free of want.

"I ask you," said my grandfather, picking up the carving tools purposefully and with better cheer, "are the Vanderbilts better off?" END

Silhouette of a Wedding

by Laurie Hillyer

It had come, it was the day of it, Pen Frazier thought opening her eyes to the October morning. The world had not ended, no bombs had been dropped on Harbor Crest, Alison had not come running in, crying, as she had so often cried when she was small, "Mummie, I've changed my mind." At that moment, the first sound in the quiet house, Pen heard Alison singing; it had been one of the charming things about Alison, always, the way she went singing upstairs and down. She was singing now, for no reason at all, "The bear came over the mountain."

She had sung in the dark when she was a little girl because, although she was afraid of the dark, she was determined not to show it, determined to be brave. Was that why she was singing now, her mother wondered, because she was afraid and determined not to show it?

Pen felt her tears rising and glanced in apprehension at the parallel bed. If Jim saw her crying this morning, all would be lost. It was only by holding their personal emotions in check, together, that they could get through this terrifying day. He was awake but he did not fail her, he gave no sign. "Hullo, dear," he said, "it looks like a fine bright morning."

She remembered over again what Jim had said at one of the endless family conclaves, "We are not going to lose hope until the final words are spoken."

She smiled back at him. "Yes," she said, "it's a fine bright morning."

The announcement of the engagement had sounded like any other announcement. Pen had, in fact, written a note to each social editor, asking that the announcement be printed exactly as sent: *Mr. and Mrs. James Bartlett Frazier of Harbor Crest, Connecticut, announce the engagement of their daughter, Alison Bartlett, to Mr. Charles Lincoln Johnson of Worcester, Massachusetts—Miss Frazier was graduated from Barnard last June and has been studying this winter at the Sorbonne. Her fiancé is a graduate of Columbia. An October wedding is planned.*

There was no mention of forbears—as frequently, if they were worth mentioning. Most of Alison's forbears, Pen knew, preferred to be left out. And Charles, so to speak, had none.

Pen had read the announcement with a sinking heart. Say what you will about not believing a thing you see in the paper, she thought, there is, still, a potency in the printed word. Reading it there, in small neat black type, she said to herself, *It's true, it's really true.* Until then she had never quite believed it.

At one time she and Jim had worried there might never be an announcement. Alison had seemed in love with learning rather than with boys. The friends Ted, her older brother, had brought to the house had excited her less, it seemed, than her college courses. Her father had now and then looked speculatively at Ted, lying on the couch, feet higher than his head, reading the sports page, pleased with everything as it was, and at Alison, feet tucked under her in the wing chair, reading French, seeking, seeking, determined to seek. If Ted had been born with more brains and Alison with less, their father thought, it might have been just as well.

Then her last year in college, she had begun to change. There had gathered about her that loveliness, that bloom that comes only to the girl in love. She fell in love with herself as well, which is a part of falling in love. Her blond swinging hair, the tilt of her nose, the shade of her lipstick, the color of her stockings, all were of discoverable importance. She spent hours in a dreamlike trance before the triple mirror on her dressing table. And the name *Charles* began cropping up in her conversation. Ted asked amiably, " 'Oo the 'ell is Charles?"

" 'E's a 'istory major," said Alison who was painting her nails with the tenderness of an artist. "He's writing a thesis on French colonialism in Africa. He's crazy about French like me."

"Quel chic," said Ted.

"Oh my," said Alison, "the way they teach French at Yale. Charles is the most brilliant man I have ever known in my life, ever."

"He certainly sounds interesting, darling," said Pen. "Wouldn't he like to come out some time for Sunday lunch?"

"He'd love to," said Alison. She seemed about to qualify this but when her mother glanced at her expectantly, she only smiled back, a loving and confident smile.

A date was set and Alison went singing upstairs and down. *The bear came over the mountain.* "What are we going to have for lunch, Mummie?" she asked.

"Well, what would you like to have?"

"Oh, could we have that sophisticated thing with shrimps and mushrooms and sour cream? And, Mummie—"

"Yes?"

There was an instant's silence. Then, "I *know* you'll like him," Alison said.

"Oh, I know I will. Tell me a little more about him, though, so I'll know what he likes to talk about. Does he come from New York?"

"No, Worcester. You don't need to worry about what to talk about with *Charles*. He's interested in everything, he can talk about *anything*. Well, let's see— his father is dead, he was killed in the war, and his mother is a teacher, a high school teacher. Charles is going to be a teacher, too, a professor, I mean. He's already had one or two very good offers, he may stay at Columbia. He's an only child."

"He sounds wonderful," Pen said, smiling at her daughter on whom at that moment a shaft of sunlight fell. Her hair which swung to her shoulders and turned under was silvered by the sun. Her shining hair, her skin lightly tanned by the salt air, her jonquil-yellow sweater, all were part of the blondness of Alison. I hope Charles is tall, dark and handsome, her mother thought, even her name, Alison, is a *blond* name. "Do you like your name, darling?" she suddenly asked.

"Alison? Oh yes," Alison said, "I love it."

When Alison returned from the New Haven Station, a few Sundays later, where she had driven to meet Charles, her mother watched their arrival from a window near the front door. Alison and a young man stepped out of the car. But who under the sun is that, her mother thought, and where under the sun is Charles?

Alison and her passenger came laughing up the gravel path together. They were talking with eagerness, the two faces alight with laughter, as if each one of them lighted up the other. And Penelope Frazier realized that this *was* Charles.

She gathered her forces, determined not to fail her beloved child. But thank God, she thought, I saw him first, I have this one minute—.

She opened the door with a welcoming smile, hoping in the depths of her, though it was a faint hope, there might be some mistake.

"Mother," Alison said, "this is Charles," Her voice was full of happiness and pride.

The hand of Charles met the hand of Penelope. *This is the first time in my life*, she thought, *I have shaken hands with a Negro.* Well, she thought wryly, I seem to have survived.

His handclasp was firm, he was a handsome boy. Only slightly taller than Alison, he carried himself so well he seemed taller than he was. He had the thoughtful face of a scholar, the face accentuated by eyebrows shaped like two sharply pointed roofs. It was only on second glance that one noticed the melancholy of the eyes. His thick black hair was clipped close to his well shaped skull and he was dressed exactly as Ted Frazier would dress if he were lunching out—a little better, really, a little more shined up—in a gray suit, a shirt as fresh as snow, striped tie, brown loafers. And he was as black as the ace of spades.

"Come in," Penelope said, "we always breathe a sigh of relief, Charles, when the New Haven Railroad safely delivers our friends. What do you think of it?"

"It was quite good exercise," said Charles, "I thoroughly enjoyed it, though." He smiled at Alison.

She ran her hand lightly through his arm, drawing him toward the living room. "We think the railroad is maligned, Mummie," she said. "Come in here, Charles, and meet Daddy and the boys."

"I think they're out in the garage, Alison," Pen said, "I'll go and round them up in a few minutes." But she did not hurry away, lest the reason for her haste be all too apparent. Everything must be natural, must be *easy*, as easy as she could make it.

Charles and Alison sat down on the couch and Pen sat facing them, in the wing chair, where Alison liked to sit and read.

"Charles, I'm so glad to meet you." Pen said. "Alison has given you a tremendous build-up in the family. She says you can talk on absolutely any subject under the sun."

Charles and Alison burst out laughing.

"He can," said Alison.

"With one or two exceptions," said Charles.

"Name them."

"Well: who settled Connecticut, I had to ask you that. Alison has told me, Mrs. Frazier, that you are an authority on lemon meringue pie and the poems of Emily Dickinson."

"I said you were a well rounded woman, Mummie."

"Heavens," said Pen, "that's so unfashionable, darling. Will you excuse me a moment, Charles, while I go find the rest of the family?"

James Frazier was in the pantry, contemplating bonded bourbon and amontillado. He had martinis in the pitcher and now reached for a bottle of white dubonnet. He had decided to go all out for Charles. Pen let the door swing shut. "Jim."

"Hullo. Anything the matter?"

"Jim: Charles is here, he just came, he's—"

"A beatnik?"

"Oh no. Not that."

"Long hair?"

"He's a Negro."

"*What?*"

"Yes. He is."

"It can't be Charles or she would have told us. Is this supposed to be a joke?"

"I'm sure it's Charles and I'm sure it's not a joke. I think Alison adores him."

"Adores him! Of course, she doesn't." He gave his martinis a stir, emptied in too many ice cubes and said, "*Damn.* Why didn't she tell us?" He glared at his martinis.

"I simply don't know. Go and warn the boys, will you, Jim? Tell them there mustn't be a *sign*, not one, of anything unusual—especially tell Bates. Charles is our guest, he's Alison's friend—tell them you'll *beat* them—"

"I'll tell them. Don't worry." He patted her shoulder, handed her a swallow of neat bourbon and poured a martini for himself.

Alison was showing Charles her photograph album when Pen returned to the living room. The record player, at pianissimo, was playing Bach. Alison turned it off as the three Frazier males trooped in—her father said he couldn't understand Bach.

Bates, who was thirteen, had not changed for lunch; he wore torn blue jeans and a loud strange shirt like a madman's dream of Hawaii—gamboge pineapples and orange hula dancers. He shook hands solemnly with Charles and dropped on the edge of a chair and, avoiding his mother's indignant eyebrows, sat and stared, holding a large glass of tomato juice in his hands. James Frazier and his older son, however, were all that one could ask in the way of hosts.

"How do you like Connecticut, Charles?" asked Jim.

"It's my first visit to the Connecticut shore," Charles answered, "but I think I like any place that's near the sea."

"So do I," said Ted heartily, "why don't we take Charles for a walk along the shore after lunch, Alison? Tell him all about the Land of Steady Habits—that's Connecticut, Charles." He dropped on the floor beside Charles' chair, took a sip of his martini, set it on the rug and clasped his hands around his knees.

Bates turned his gaze, a betrayed gaze, toward his brother. *Don't take him on any walks*—his eyes said—*what will people think? You keep him out of sight.*

Charles was a tactful guest. At lunch he mentioned having seen "Raisin in the Sun," dispelling any anxiety about touchy subjects that ought to be shunned. He sipped his soup from the side of his spoon which disappointed Bates who was always being reminded how a gentleman eats his soup and had hoped Charles wouldn't know. His courteous *savoir faire* seemed effortless but Penelope noticed his left hand was frequently clenched into a fist so tense the fingers could scarcely have been pried away from the palm.

Why didn't you warn us, Alison?" her father asked, after the day was over.

She was instantly and blazingly defensive. "Warn you about what?"

"That your friend was a Negro."

"Why should I *warn* you? If it had been Kippy Gibson, would I have warned you he had red hair?"

"It's scarcely the same, is it?"

"It's *exactly* the same. A matter of pigmentation. As a matter of fact, Daddy, I thought of telling you but I decided Charles could stand on his own merits. If you can't judge a man on his merits, Daddy I've nothing more to say."

Her head was high, she turned and walked without haste out of the living room.

Pen followed her into the hall and put her arms around her. There must be no antagonism, none, it would react frighteningly, she was sure. "Alison dear, be reasonable. We both thought Charles was charm-ing, he is—but you know perfectly well what your father meant. We live by certain standards—" the minute she had spoken, she knew she had chosen the wrong word.

"Standards!" echoed Alison, backing away, "not if the standards are *false*, I don't. You know the time is coming, Mummie, don't you conceivably *know*, when ideas like yours will be absolutely *dead*? People will marry whom they please without thinking about the color of their *skin*."

"Marry!" echoed Pen.

"Yes," said Alison, "*marry*. Charles and I are going to be married. In October. We're in *love*."

She ran upstairs. Her mother could hear her door shut and the key turn in the lock. She returned to the living room and she and Jim sat in silence, too shaken even to talk.

"Jim," Pen said at last, dully, "this is the tragedy—if he had been white, we might have fallen in love with him, too."

"White! He is not white and this is going to be stopped," said Alison's father.

But it could not be stopped. All they could accomplish was a com-promise, hard won. Charles and Alison agreed to wait a year, spending it apart. Alison was to be sent to Paris where she had always wanted to go—and now did not want to go—to the Sorbonne. Charles, living up to the tact he had shown at every encounter, was to disappear into French Equatorial Africa; he had been awarded a fellowhip for research on his thesis. "But it is a whole year out of our lives, Daddy," Alison said, "one whole lost year, that is what you are asking, Daddy, of Charles and of me."

"And it's not much to ask," her father said grimly, "in a decision involving all your lifetime, and ours."

"It's only Charles' and my lifetime, really, not yours—you're just taking part in it. His mother didn't want it, either, at first, but now she understands we must make our own decision, the way a person should."

"His mother didn't want it?"

"No, she didn't. She thinks it will interfere with his career. It won't, it will *help* it. She looked stonily at her father. "At the end of the year, you won't interfere in any way?"

"We'll try not to," he said, "if you still feel the way you do now. Which your mother and I pray you won't, Alison."

Alison did not answer.

Paris was full of young Americans and all the Frazier family and all the Frazier friends wrote to their friends in France to look after Alison. She was invited out, her little calendar was written over with engagements, she wrote home about all her parties. And she never mentioned Charles. And the family, after one courteous note from him before he left for Africa, had no sign of his existence. They began to build up fantastic hopes—*had* he ever existed? Had the fantastic thing that had seemed to be happening to them ever really happened? And then came Alison's letter, a reminder indeed of the existence of Charles. She wrote that the long year would soon be over and that she and Charles were going to be married in October—"October 18 is the best day for me," she wrote calmly, "and we would love to be married in the church at home but if you would rather not, we can be married here in Paris. So in your next letter, Mother and Daddy, please let us know."

Jim wanted to fly to Paris at once, but Pen restrained him. "Darling, there's no *use*, you'll only make things worse. If there were an atom of hope, I'd implore you to go. We promised we wouldn't interfere, they have kept their part of the promise and we have to keep ours. And I think we should tell the boys and the family at once. And write to Alison—you and I both—that we want the wedding here."

"Oh God. This will kill mother and dad," said Jim, "to have the Frazier line carried on by a Negro."

"No, it won't kill them. And it won't be the Frazier line," said Pen, "it will be the Johnson line. The boys will carry on the Frazier line." Upon which, without warning, she laid her head on his shoulder and bitterly cried.

The shock to the family was all, and more, than they had feared. Jim's father had a heart attack and was told to remain in bed until after the wedding; he would never—he told Jim—recover, he would never acknowledge Charles as a member of his family.

The only champion for Alison and Charles was Penelope's sister, Alison Hunt, for whom young Alison had been named. There had always been a bond of sympathy between the two Alisons.

"It's awful," Alison Hunt agreed. She leaned forward, patted her sister's knee and sat smoking a cigaret in a long holder and looking at Pen, compassion in her eyes. "I'm sorry it's Alison, Penny, but there are going to be a lot more Alisons as time goes on. It's in the air. In the future, races are going to be intermarrying as a matter of course, white with black, black with yellow, yellow with white. Maybe it will lead to a better world, God knows we need one. Alison is a pioneer, actually. I'm proud of her courage, Jim."

"Being proud of her courage has nothing to do with the case," said Alison's father. "The question is—what is this going to *do* to her? Alison is living in the present, not the future, and the present is going to tear her to shreds. She'll be insulted, kept out of places where she has every right to go—clubs, hotels, any number of places. She can never move without being conspicuous, she'll hate that. She'll be pilloried. Her children, if she has any, will be mavericks, ostracized. And she is *ours*."

Alison's brothers were miserable, each in his own way. "I'd like to poison Charles," said Bates. "I'd like to kidnap him, I'd like to get him compromised with a prostitute, I'd like to—"

"Oh, cut it out," said Ted wearily. He had had, at one time, such high hopes for his sister. "Hear this, Batesey—Charles is going to be our brother-in-law, we've got to *accept* him. He's going to be Alison's *husband*."

"Oh God, God," said Bates, "don't *let* him be. *Do* something. What's Kenny Foster going to think, I want to know, me having a brother-in-law that's a Negro?"

"He's going to think you have a brother-in-law that's a Negro. And if he weren't a Negro, he'd think he was a helluva nice guy. And he *is* a helluva nice guy."

"I'm going to kill him," said Bates.

James Frazier determined to make two more appeals, two more tries.

He went up to Alison's room, which was a litter of clothes and books, and flowers from the garden, and little bottles of perfume she had brought back from France as gifts. He knocked. "May I come in, Alison?"

"Of course, Daddy. I'll find you a place to sit." She lifted a pile of French paperbacks from the seat of a chair. They talked for a few minutes about France, agreeing on what they liked and did not like about Paris.

"Alison?"

"Yes?" She lifted an eyebrow in his direction. "Out with it, Daddy."

"There it is in a nutshell, Alison. You know what I'm thinking— and I know what you're thinking. There's a bond between us, there always has been, and this is what I'm asking you with all the strength that's in me. Don't, for God's sake, destroy that bond."

"How *could* I?"

"You know the answer."

Alison who had been moving about among her things sat down on the edge of a chair and studied her father as if he were a curiosity. Tears rose to her eyes, her lip quivered. "Daddy," she said, "you promised. Don't *you* destroy the bond."

All the things he had planned to say, all the arguments he had intended to rally, crumbled away. He saw her on the edge of a precipice, blind, about to leap *joyfully* to destruction, rejecting the wisdom, the safety of his impeding hand.

"There is not one single thing you could possibly, possibly say, Daddy," she went on, her voice trembling, "that would make us change our minds."

"I don't *want* to 'make you change your mind,' Alison. I want you to change it yourself because you see things as they are."

"It's you who don't see things as they are. Do you remember how when I was a kid I used always to be reading the *Rubaiyat*? Do you remember the lines: *A hair, perhaps, divides the false and true/Yes, and a single alif were the clue/Could you but find it . . . ?*"

"No," he said unhappily, without interest, "I only remember the 'jug of wine' thing. What's an alif?"

"It's the first letter of the Arabic alphabet. Well, I'll give you the alif, Daddy. Please don't think of Charles as a Negro any more than you think of me as a Caucasian. This is the alif in five words: *Think of Charles as Charles.*"

His first appeal had failed, was denied, had accomplished nothing.

He asked Charles to lunch at his New Haven Club, having first checked with the Club office. "Have we any rules about admitting Negroes?" he asked.

"Not that I know of, sir. I don't think the question has ever come up."

"Reserve me a table for two, then, please—one o'clock on Thursday. Thank you."

He gave Charles a dry martini and English mutton chops, the club's specialty. They talked about the President—Cuba—an editorial in the *Times*—the African experiences of Charles. Charles listened attentively to what James had to say, as if the opinions of Alison's father were important for him to know but he held to his own views and lucidly explained his reasons. James Frazier realized that he was enjoying this talk and would like to prolong it. He was, he thought, remembering Alison's alif, accepting Charles as Charles. He was forgetting that Charles intended to marry his daughter and that—the fact emphasized by the whiteness of the cloth—he was as black as the ace of spades. He was *black*.

The pleasure of the lunch, briefly felt, was gone. In the lounge, over cigarets and coffee, he brought the conversation to the point. "Charles," he said, "we have more personal problems to discuss than Africa and Cuba. A problem of transcendent importance to both of us— the happiness of Alison. Having seen a little of our family, you must know there is not much in the world as important to me as that. And I think you are planning to destroy it. You must know the tragic, the humiliating situations you and she, if this marriage goes through, are sure to face."

Charles listened courteously, his dark, mournful eyes, which were always mournful, even when he was merry, studying the really agonized face of Alison's father. Charles had gone so far in his own thoughts beyond these expressed thoughts of James Frazier that he felt a depth of pity for anyone so untried. He knew quite well why he had been invited to lunch—it was no welcoming and traditional gesture from the father of the bride to the groom. He had determined beforehand to keep inviolate his relationship with Alison, so personal, so sacred—to share none of it, nor any of himself, with Alison's obstructive father. He felt no more drawn to James Frazier than James Frazier did to him. But the obvious and helpless suffering of his host, which he was unable to hide although he, too, wished to give none of himself away, stirred in Charles the sympathy he had not wished to express, or even feel.

"Mr. Frazier," he said, "I am sorry you feel the way you do. It is the same way my mother felt. And there is not a single thing that you have said—or, I imagine, thought—that I have not thought of long ago—"

"Then how can you bring yourself to ask of my daughter what you are asking of her?"

"—I was going to tell you. You say there is not much in the world as important to you as Alison's happiness. But there is *nothing* in the world as important to me as Alison's happiness. And I think she will be happier with me, in spite of the calculated risks, than without me. And that is why I am asking her what I *am* asking her."

"Why do you think she will be happier with you? What can you give her? What was your life before she came into it? What is the life you are asking her to share? Tell me. I want to know."

He had checked only on Charles' ability to support Alison, which had seemed, much to his surprise, adequate. He had not wanted to hear about the personal life of Charles because he had not wanted to imagine Alison in it. Now he felt he had to know.

Charles hesitated, deciding what to give, what to withold. He said, slowly, "It was a lonely life before Alison came into it. We kept meeting in the French section of the library, we discovered we had many similar tastes and we began to enjoy talking about them. We both like Camus but not Sartre. We think there is no language as beautiful as the language of France. We have a passion for the music of Bach. And for the spiritual quality in jazz. We laugh at the same things—and people. We like to walk better than to ride in cars. We think that the days—and the nights—are not long enough to learn all there is waiting for us to learn . . . These are some of the things we share and want, all our lives, to go on sharing."

He paused. Alison's father waited.

"We want to share each other's backgrounds, too, different as they are. My great-grandparents were slaves. They could read and they could write, they were owned by a family kinder than most. My grandfather was born in freedom. In Worcester. He was a janitor, he read and studied at night, he was determined that his son should have a real education. His whole life was dedicated to that—and the life of my grandmother, too. Their son was my father. He went to high school and to college and he planned to study law but instead he was sent to war and he was killed. His death killed my grandparents—they continued to live but they were dead. My mother took care of them—and of herself—and of me. She saw to it that I developed a love for the miracle of learning.

"That is the proud history of my family," he said, "my great-grandfather was a good slave, my grandfather was a good janitor, my father would have been a good lawyer and I shall be a good teacher. In spite of what my family at first considered an insuperable obstacle—my marriage to Alison."

"What did you say?"

Charles answered quietly, "Your apprehension is less than the original apprehension of my mother. She felt that my future—which was to be a vindication of our family's past—would be jeopardized, even destroyed by a black-white marriage. She implored me, 'Keep our race pure.' She threatened to destroy herself, even. Then I took Alison to see her."

This Alison had never mentioned—had it been too terrible to mention? Jim waited. Charles paused, remembering that day—a roaring March day, over a year ago, when dust and cigaret butts and bits of paper and filth were spiraling and swirling about the non-segregated Worcester street. Alison had got a speck of dust in her eye. The area railing at his house was broken, the bell did not ring. Alison had shown no slightest sign of distaste but when they entered the first-floor flat, his mother's and his, he had known her relief. It was another country—clean, with big shabby comfortable chairs, old books, a record player, prints on the wall, new books, even a fire of splintered wooden crates burning on a queer little hearth behind an iron screen. "Each, I think," said Charles, briefly, "found the other better than she had expected." Now he had said all that he was going to say, he was not going to say anything more, nothing could induce him. He and Alison had been beaten down from all sides, they had survived so far.

Jim did not know what to say. The fact that remained uppermost was that Alison, this fellow said, wanted to share the background of a slave. He was also aware that Charles Johnson was more of a man than he had first supposed.

Charles stood up. "Thank you for the lunch, sir," he said, "and for hearing me out. I must be getting along. Try not to worry too much about Alison and me. Could you trust us?"

James rose and shook hands with him. "Thank you for telling me all this," he said. "I'll try."

When Charles had gone, Jim walked to the window and stood staring out of it, his hands deep in his pockets as if his hands were ferreting out the safety of the known. He shook his head. He almost groaned. "God damn it," he thought, "why couldn't he have been born *white*?" Even if he trusted Charles, and trusted Alison, he could not trust what the world would do to them.

They met downstairs, Alison and her mother, on the day of the wedding. Alison in jonquil-yellow shorts and a white shirt, looking about thirteen, was wandering through the rooms which had been put in exquisite order for the wedding breakfast. Her eyes were rapt. She turned toward her mother an instant before Pen had had time to adjust her tired face to a quick smile. Immediately Alison's face clouded over. "Oh Mummie," she said, "smile! I know what you are thinking, dear—I've thought all those thoughts and forgotten them long ago. About hotels and all that. About being kept out of places—don't you see, I couldn't be kept out of any place when I'm with Charles; he's my place and I'm *there*."

Penelope put her arms around her—she seemed always to be wanting to put her arms around her. Alison was so small, so soft, so untried, she smelled so sweet, she was so vulnerable and did not realize how vulnerable she was. Her hair was like threads of sun. "Of course," Pen said, "you and Charles always have a place here, too, darling— don't forget that."

Hand-in-hand, they walked about, admiring the chrysanthemums and autumn leaves, admiring the way everything was picked up and polished and shined. Presently the caterers would arrive and take over the kitchen. The breakfast was to be family only, but the wedding in the church would be the size, if everybody came, of any "small" Frazier wedding. ("What if nobody comes," Penelope had said to Jim, "I have nightmares about it." "Don't worry," he had said, dryly, "the church will be full.")

It was Bates who, later in the morning, caught sight of Charles coming toward the house. He was not supposed to come, he was not supposed to see the bride on the day of the wedding until he saw her coming down the aisle. This was tradition. Bates watched like a hunter who hopes wildly that what is coming toward him is his unexpected prey. He thought he would wait and make Charles ring the bell, then he decided the bell would alert the household and he himself wanted to know, first of anyone, what was up.

"Hi, Charles," he said, opening the screen door.

"Hi, Bates," said Charles, scarcely recognizing Bates as Bates but only as someone who had opened the door. "May I speak to Alison, please?"

At that moment Alison, who was everywhere that morning, skimmed lightly down the stairs and ran to him. "Charles! I was just starting to get dressed! You shouldn't *be* here! Didn't you *know?*"

"Could we talk a minute?"

Her eyes widened. "Of course."

Charles glanced desperately toward a small, book-lined room to the left of the front door. Alison, seeing the look, stepped inside and Charles followed, his hand on the knob. Neither of them paid any attention to Bates—and scarcely to Penelope who now appeared from the dining room.

She turned forlornly to her second son. "What's happened?" she asked him.

He shook his head from side to side and a look passed between them of dismay and a shred of latent hope.

Alison knew why Charles had come. He had come to say once more what he had been saying over and over again when despair overcame him, the despair that was his heritage in the land of the free and the home of the brave; the despair against which he fought and from which he wished to save Alison. He had come to ask her, once again, before it was too late—he would say—if she did not want to change her mind. It was the only thing Alison feared—the despair of Charles—and, beginning with this morning, she must never let him feel it again. When two are together, she had been saying to herself, there is no need of despair. Two is an army, the strongest in the world.

The minute he closed the door, she threw herself into his arms, then leaned back, cupped his tragic face in both her hands and looked into his eyes. "I'm so glad you came, darling," she said, "even if you shouldn't. I wanted to see you—it's been so long since last night. I kept waking up and missing you. And now you're here."

He said: "Alison—"

She shook her head and laid a hand over his mouth. "Not today, darling—not today and not ever, ever again."

"Yes," he said, taking her hand away and holding it between both his own, "I have to speak, Alison. I walked the streets all night, thinking how I was going to hurt you, as your father says. We must face it once again before it is irrevocable. No matter how much I love you, no matter if I devote every fibre in my being to making you happy, no matter if we seem made for each other, as we are—how can I give you happiness, how can I do it, how can I guarantee it, against such awful odds?"

"All right," said Alison. She withdrew her hand from between his two hands. "Goodbye. I'm tired imploring you to marry me. I never never never will again."

Their eyes met and clashed. Slowly the antagonism drained. He said, "I love you," and bent his head to hers.

"I love you," said Alison.

"Seat plenty of our friends on the groom's side, Bates," his father had told Bates who was an usher. To have a color line would be catastrophic. Two of the four ushers were Negroes, college friends of

Charles. Ted was the best man. Alison's white brother and Alison's white best friend, her only attendant, would walk out of the church together, looking the way Connecticut expected its best man and its maid of honor to look.

The church, as Jim had prophesied, was full. Only Alison's Frazier grandparents were not there. Charles' mother had arrived, looking—except for her eyebrows—very like her son.

The guests rose with the wedding march, the traditional march, although tradition was being thrown to the winds. Charles Johnson, the bridegroom, and Ted Frazier, the best man, took their places by the chancel steps. Preceded by the maid of honor, whose bouquet was shaking in her hands, Alison and her father came down the aisle. Her hand was on his arm and his other hand covered it, as if he would never let it go.

Charles watched her coming to him, pale, fragile, and very blond, under the flowing veil. When they stood together, side by side, his shoulder touched hers.

"Dearly beloved, we are gathered together . . .

"If any man can show just cause, why they may not lawfully be joined together, let him now speak or else hereafter forever hold his peace."

The church was silent. Remained silent. Unbroken silence. Not a movement, not the rustling of a page.

This is the final moment. James Frazier thought, *this is the moment when I speak out or forever hold my peace.* And he could not say a word. Bates heard in his imagination an outraged voice—his own—ring out, crying *Stop!* but not a word was spoken.

"Those whom God hath joined together, let no man put asunder."

Borne by the Mendelssohn march, Charles and Alison started down the aisle together, swiftly, as on wings. Alison flashed toward her parents a smile of complete happiness and love, and was gone, her veil streaming behind her.

And Penelope, seeing them together, one so dark and one so fair, had the last thought in the world she had ever expected to have. They were the two dissimilar component parts that make the harmonious whole. They were the most beautiful wedding couple she had ever seen.

In the minute before Bates came to give her his arm and take her down the aisle, she turned to Bates' father. "Jim," she said in a low voice, "don't you think they are beautiful?" Alison's father smiled without acquiescence. *Still, there is one of us, one of us at least,* she thought, *who sees this as I hope it is.*   END

The Ghost with the Bursting Bustle

by Jane H. Shwedo

The day they start giving out prizes for cussedness at the County Fair, my Aunt Emma will be a "shoo-in" for first. She once fought the income-tax people tooth and claw over a fifteen-dollar difference of opinion. By the time she finished with him, that poor tax collector was worn down to a quivering mass of frustration. You could hear him shouting clear to Putnam!

"All right, all right! So it's a legitimate deduction, God help me! *Uncle Sam* help me! We'll send you a check! Just *go away* and leave me alone!"

My grandpa had left some money to Aunt Emma years ago, and it had been sitting in the bank, accumulating interest and waiting for an "emergency." When Aunt Emma heard about the new shopping center going up right next to their property, she figured that was it.

I could see her wanting to buy a new home. But the *Thornton Place!* It sat up high on a hill, peeking down into Hampton Valley, sort of like a poor relation, eying the town from the outside. The house was all gray and ramshackle, with what few shutters were left hanging all dejected and flopping in the breeze like dead bat wings.

When I was little, I used to sneak up there sometimes with the boys. We'd throw rocks at the windows and pretend that there were Indians holed up in there that we were trying to drive out.

Aunt Emma finally bought the place, making out like she was doing Ed Thornton a big favor by taking it off his hands. She bought it so cheap that she still had a good bit of money left over. Pretty soon there were carpenters and painters (and Uncle Jess and me) swarming over the place like ants on a salami sandwich. Uncle Jess had found the rest of the old shutters in the barn. We painted them black and hooked them on good and tight.

Ed Thornton could be heard groaning all over town. Everyone said that the old tightwad had finally met his match in Aunt Emma. Ed just grumbled some more and said we'd have to wait and see who really got the best of the deal.

"There've been a lot of funny stories about that place. If you ask me, only a fool would buy it."

Aunt Emma said he was just "chewing sour sassafras."

The day we moved in, Aunt Emma had me and Uncle Jess hopping, but by the time we had supper, Uncle Jess had built a fire in the kitchen fireplace, the red curtains were up, and the fire was just crackling away to beat the band. My black cat was curled up next to the hearth, while Uncle Jess and Aunt Emma rocked in their chairs next to the fire, just as though they had lived there all their lives. Then a queer thing happened.

I had just opened my mouth to ask if I could pop some popcorn, when we heard the sound of the front door opening and someone walking across the parlor floor and up the stairs. I could feel the little hairs on the back of my neck lift in a ripple that went up and over the top of my head, tickling as it went.

"What in blazes?" Uncle Jess jumped up and opened the door to the parlor. Aunt Emma and I followed him, and the three of us stared through the door at the living room, which was empty except for the packing cases that stood around the room. The front door was wide open. Nothing was disturbed in the room. The only thing different was the hay. Across the floor and heading up the stairs was a wobbly little trail of hay.

We looked at the hay, then at each other. Suddenly Aunt Emma grabbed a broom that was leaning against the wall and started up the stairs, holding the broom like a bayonet.

"If you're trying to make trouble in my house, Ed Thornton, you'll be sorry!" She charged up the stairs, the gray bun at the back of her head bouncing with every step. Uncle Jess and I stood there for about a second and a half watching that little woman go, then we bounded up after her. Ed Thornton wasn't up there. No one was. There was just the little trail of hay leading to the spare room and ending in a small pile near the bed.

Aunt Emma looked puzzled for a moment, then her common-sense latched hold of her like a vise. "The wind must have blown that door open and all this fool hay into the house." She started sweeping violently with the broom.

The next night, Aunt Emma had fixed clam chowder and biscuits for supper. I was just tucking into my second helping when the lights in the kitchen went out. It was as dark as Main Street after nine.

"There goes a fuse!" Uncle Jess scraped back his chair. "Get the flashlight, Tom, and come on down cellar with me." By the light of the flashlight we had made our way half way across the parlor when the front door bounced open with a thump, and a chill colder than spilt lemon ice went through me. The lights came back on by themselves just in time for me to see hay being dropped, deliberately, all across the floor and up the stairs. The only trouble was there was no hand doing the dropping, just hay coming from out of nowhere and falling on the floor.

The chill disappeared as quickly as it had come, but before my spine could thaw out, something new took its place. From the upstairs, in the area of the spare room, came the sound of someone crying.

Aunt Emma came into the parlor from the kitchen, took one look at the hay and said, "I thought I told you to sweep up the barn, Tom!"

"Ssh, Aunt Emma," I said, "I cleaned up the barn, but there's no hay out there. Ssh! Listen!"

Just then Aunt Emma caught the sound of the whiny weeping, which was more of a prolonged snivel than anything else. Her eyebrows rose as though they would pop right off her forehead. We went upstairs, but there wasn't anything to be seen in the spare room except for the pile of hay near the bed.

Aunt Emma stooped over and picked up some hay, letting it slip through her fingers. She just stood there by the bed with her mouth opening and closing like a guppy breathing hard. It was a ghost. It had to be. There was just no disputing it. Uncle Jess gave Aunt Emma an "I told you so" look.

"Maybe somebody killed a horse and the *horse* is haunting us!" I said.

"The worst thing that ever happened in this house," said Aunt Emma emphatically, "was when Colonel Allen got drunk before Stony Point, fell off his horse and broke his leg. No insanity, no scandals . . . not one thing!"

"How about Ed Thornton's aunt?" Uncle Jess asked. "Wasn't she a little peculiar?"

"That dried up, prissy old maid? She never had the gumption to burp, let alone haunt a house!" That just shows you even Aunt Emma can be wrong once in a while.

I went to my room early that night. When I kicked my shoes under the bed, they hit the box of books I'd hauled from the barn that day. It seemed like a good time to look through them.

They turned out to be mostly old Tom Swifts, Horatio Algers and some pretty bad romances. They were wormy and dirty, and I was going to take them out back to go to the dump when, in a corner at the very bottom of the box, wrapped up in an old smelly cloth, I found a book covered in worn blue velvet.

As I opened it, something dropped out of one of the pages and landed on my rug. It was a small piece of hay.

I picked up the hay and stood wondering at it. Then I opened the book. On the first page, in fading brownish ink the words peered out at me: "Hannah Thornton, her diary—Anno Domini 1882." I glanced through the book. It was pretty dull stuff until I hit October. I laughed.

"Aunt Emma, come quick! I've found your ghost!" Aunt Emma came stumbling into my room, tying her red wrapper around her middle, her hair loose and hanging like gray spaghetti around her face.

"Where?" she asked, blinking her eyes as she got her glasses in place.

"Right here, in this old diary!"

She took it from me and read aloud where I pointed out:

"October 14, 1882: *Mr. St. James has asked me to accompany him to the church social next Saturday evening. I think he will propose. I will be a* St. James *of Philadelphia! Papa must let me buy a bustle. Everyone will be wearing one!*

"October 18, 1882: *How can Papa be so cruel? I am the only girl in town who does not have a bustle. He says I can sit down at the Social and no one will know the difference. I shall be mortified. I will not go. I shall stay home and waste away.*"

Aunt Emma said, "I guess Ed takes after his Grandpa all right! Both tight as ticks. But where's the Ghost?"

"Keep on reading!"

"October 19, 1882: *Papa will still not relent, but I have found a way. Since he will not allow me to buy one, I will make my own. I made a pattern from Elizabeth Owen's bustle. With the bustle in my dress I will look outstanding!*"

"Ha!" said Aunt Emma. "She was outstanding all right! Homeliest old maid I ever saw! Stuck out like a sore thumb!" She leafed over until she found the next entry.

"October 30, 1882. *The ways of men are cruel and unkind. I am glad I found out in time. I know now that I will never marry, and I hope never to have to speak to a male again. Thank God no one knows of my mortification! Mr. St. James has left town and may he never return! The night of the social is burned into my memory.*

"*I looked so grand in my new bustle. After I filled it with sweet hay, it was as plump and puffy as any of the ones in Flood's Store.*"

"Hay!" Aunt Emma fairly shouted, looking up so quickly that her glasses slid down her nose. She read on:

"*We rode to the social in Mr. St. James' green phaeton. He tied his horse up outside the front of the Inn, and as we strolled around I knew that I was the object of many an envious glance, and I must admit (in all modesty) that everyone took note of my figure!*

"Mr. St. James suggested that we take a moonlight drive down near the river. I felt that the time had come when he was about to ask for my hand. We walked over to where his horse was tied, and sheltered by the shadow of the Inn, he leaned down, and I allowed him to kiss me. Oh shame!

"In the middle of that kiss, I heard a dreadful, tearing sound and felt myself half lifted up off my feet. I was shaken half out of my wits and dumped down on the ground half naked! That horrid man's sinful horse had bitten clear through my bustle and was chewing on the hay! My dress was ruined and hay was pouring out all over. Somehow I managed to wrap my dress around me and run as fast as I could towards home, but that was not the worst part of what I suffered. That idiot man laughed! I saw him bent in half next to the horse laughing his fool head off. I could still hear him all the way to the top of the hill."

"Well, I'll be . . ." Aunt Emma looked up. "Of all the silly reasons for a person to shut themselves up in a house the way Ed Thornton's aunt did . . . and then to *haunt* it!" It sort of hit Aunt Emma all at once. "And her dropping hay all over *my* house!" As she tucked the diary under her arm and started out of my room, she had a nasty little smile on her face which boded no good for Miss Hannah Thornton, Ghost.

The next day, when I got home from school, the dishes were still sitting on the breakfast table, Uncle Jess's newspaper and shoes were still at ease in the parlor where he'd left them the night before, and the beds were unmade. Aunt Emma's old Remington with the crooked E was out on her desk, but she was nowhere to be seen.

"Aunt Emma, I'm home!" I called, my voice bouncing off the walls. She answered me from the cellar and a few minutes later emerged from the stairway, her big work apron dabbled with red and black paint. A smear of green went diagonally across her nose.

"What've you been doing?" I asked.

"Oh, just a little *home improvement*," she answered and chuckled sadistically.

At supper, the table was set for two. "I'm just not very hungry," Aunt Emma said with that queer little smile. She went upstairs while Uncle Jess and I sat down to eat.

We had hardly tasted our food when the front door popped open. We looked at each other for a moment, then walked quietly into the parlor. The hay was there all right, but instead of weeping, from upstairs all you could hear was the sound of Aunt Emma's voice. Sometimes soft, but more often pretty loud.

A few minutes later, as Uncle Jess and I stood peering up the stairway, a chill breeze came hurrying down past us, sweeping before it the trail of hay. Right across the parlor it blew in nervous little motions, piling up before the door. Quickly the door opened again, and the hay blew out into the night with the soft sound of eager escape.

"Emma! Are you all right?" Uncle Jess was bounding up the stairs. We found her sitting on the Hitchcock rocker in the spare room with a pleased smile on her face, surrounded by big, bright, black, red and green placards.

"What in the Sam Hill is all this?" asked Uncle Jess.

"Just a little friendly persuasion," said Aunt Emma, sweeter than maple sugar in March.

"After I read that diary last night, I figured anyone who was as silly as she was over that business with the horse just had to be the world's vainest woman. Well, I figured she probably hadn't changed too much the other side of the vale, so I told her that if she didn't get out of this house and stay out I'd just have to advertise and open the house as a tourist attraction."

I looked at the signs:

"Haunted House . . . See the Ghost with the Bursting Bustle . . . Open to the Public . . . 50¢ admission.

"Ghost House . . . Old Maid Returns Nightly . . . The Whole Story told in Informative Souvenir Leaflet . . . $1.50."

"Guided Tours Afternoons to Site of Bustle Biting . . . $2.00."

Aunt Emma had typed up a sample leaflet with the entire story told inside, complete with excerpts from the diary. I looked at it. It was pretty funny. Aunt Emma, who's always had an artistic flare, had done some illustrations with it showing Miss Hannah Thornton being bitten on the derriere, then running to the house holding her dignity together. I thought they were great.

It worked all right. Things were a lot quieter in our house after that. But I sometimes wonder if Aunt Emma is completely happy with the way things worked out.

The other day I heard her say to Uncle Jess, "You know, we'd of been able to make a good bit of money come summers . . ."   END

The Man Who Saw the Elephant

by Avram Davidson

The story is short, and quickly told.

There was a man of the people called Quakers whose name was Ezra Simmons, and he and his wife had a farm in the hills behind Harperville. Esther Simmons was a woman who never rested during the hours she was awake, and the hours of her slumbers were few. It is recalled that she did once go down to the main road and sit on the stone fence there to see John Q. Adams go by, the year he became President. It is also recalled that she took her spinning along to keep her hands busy. "Waste not, want not," was a common word with her, and another such was, "Whatsoever thy hands find to do, do it with all thy might."

In short, she was one of those of whom the Scriptures speak, saying, "A woman of virtue, who can find, for her price is far above pearls. The heart of her husband doth trust in her . . ." There was good reason for Ezra Simmons to trust in her, for had he trusted in himself the cattle often as not would have gone unfed, the sheep unshorn, and the meadow unmowed. It was not that Friend Simmons was a lazy man. The summer of Eighteen Hundred and Froze to Death, as some light-tongued folk called it (it would have been the year Sixteen, give or take a year or two), he toiled late and early on an engine he intended should make shoe-pegs. It never did make enough to fit his own shoes, and meanwhile his kine and his swine alike should have laid stark and cold, had not his good wife Esther tended to them. Snow and hail in July! Truly, a heavy judgment upon a nation overgiven to vanities; but that is neither here nor there.

Simmons Farm was neat and trim enough, and so was Ezra Simmons's grey coat, but his grey eyes looked beyond his farm. They looked beyond his native hills, and, as he confessed, beyond his native country as well.

"Suppose," he said once to his wife, "suppose a Friend had a concern. He might go and preach unto those lost in darkness, and even now groaning beneath the spiritual tyranny of the Muscovite Caesar or the Grand Bashaw of High Barbary."

"Suppose a Friend had a concern," Esther answered, tartly, "he might pick up his scythe and commence on the home acre."

Too, Ezra had a great interest in curious and foreign beasts, and this, too, he voiced to his wife, from whom he concealed nothing.

"Does thee suppose, Esther," he would ask her, "that the Bengal tiger, for an instance, is striped merely as our Tabby, in grey and darker grey? Or is it indeed striped in yellow-gold and black, as Captain Piggott says?"

Esther, for her whole answer, would hand him the milk-bucket—and point to the barn. In truth, she was not over fond of Captain Piggott, considering him and his tales an unsettling influence on Ezra. "How large would thee say the whale-fish is, Captain Piggott?" her husband asked him once, when he came a-visiting. "As large as the farmhouse?"

"As large as the meeting house!" the old mariner declared.

Ezra exclaimed in wonder, but Esther was unimpressed. "It is no affair of ours, John Piggott," she said, "if the whale-fish is as large as the meeting house or as large as two meeting houses. When was the last time thee was inside the meeting house, John Piggott?"

John Piggott coughed behind his hand, and shortly afterwards he took his leave.

It was, accordingly, with no great surprise—and, for that matter, with no great attention—that Esther heard Ezra say to her one afternoon, after returning in the shay from Harperville, "There was a broadside given out in town, Esther, telling of a travelling show which will make a visitation to the county seat come next Second Day."

Esther was at her churn, and the day was hot, and she spoke in a sharp voice without much heeding her words.

"Must thee be forever a-gadding after vanities, Ezra Simmons?"

He stood a moment, silent and taken aback, then turned and took up his axe. She heard him splitting firewood for a good long while, and then, scarcely giving time for the echo to die away, he was in the springhouse before her, as she paddled the roll of new-made butter. "Does thee do well to rebuke me, Esther?" he asked.

She looked up, surprised, for she had clean forgotten the matter. "In what way have I rebuked thee, Ezra?"

"Is it a vanity to look upon the great beast which the Lord hath made? Can it be that He hath made it for nought? I doubt not that the showman is one of the world's people, but can the great beast be less a marvel for that?"

Esther dabbled her fingers in the shallow pool fed by the spring, and touched them, absently, to her face. "I do not understand thee," she said. "What marvel and what great beast is it of which thee speaks?"

"The elephant, Esther Simmons! The elephant!"

There was buttermilk to be put in crocks, and the crocks to be put in the well; potatoes to be peeled and the peels fed to the hogs and the potatoes to be put up for supper. There was a dried-apple pie to be baked, and linen to be spread in the sun against yellowing and mildew. There was a labor of work, and scarce daylight to do it in, and Esther said, "I have lived in this world five-and-forty years, Friend Husband, and I have never seen the elephant, nor have I ever been moved by the Spirit to see him, yet."

Ezra stood before her, his head bowed, his broadbrim dusty from the wood he had been splitting, his hands folded on the handle of the axe. He stood there, thus, for quite some moments, and then, in a low voice, he said, "I have lived in this world for nine-and-forty years, Friend Wife, I have lived in this world for a jubilee of years, thee can reckon. I have never seen the elephant either, but I tell thee, Friend Wife, that I feel moved by the Spirit to see him now, for I truly believe that else I do I shall never have chance to see him again."

There was hay in the meadow, ripe for the mowing, and shingle trees in the yard needing to be split for the roof of the barn. A cart-load of corn stood as it had stood for two days—unloaded. Esther did not hesitate.

"Thee feels moved by the Spirit to see this elephant?"

"They say it is the great beast Behemoth of the Scriptures."

"Thee feels moved by the Spirit to see this elephant?"

"I do."

"Thee has a concern to see this elephant?"

"I have."

"Then thee must see him," she said.

She rose before dawn on Second Day and baked fresh bread and put it in his wallet. She put in a roll of butter wrapped in green ferns, and sliced meat, and three apples, and a jug of water and one of buttermilk. She paused to reflect if she had forgotten anything. It occurred to her that the world's people took money for preaching the Word of the Lord, and, this being the case, might also require to take money for showing the Lord's creatures. She took a brick out of the fireplace and, reaching in her hand, pulled out a sock. From the sock's scanty store she selected a Spanish milled dollar, and she put this in her husband's wallet, too.

He led out the horse and harnessed it. "Will thee not come with me, Esther Simmons?" he asked.

Again, she shook her head, and again she made the same reply.

"I have not been moved by the Spirit to see this elephant, nor am I moved to see him now."

The old shay rolled down the lane, and she turned to her work. And, to his work, too.

Ezra drove down the white, dusty country roads. He rode past fields ripe with grain and past orchards heavy with fruit. People called out to him, but he did not pause to talk. He rode over rattling bridges and beside mudflats covered with eelgrass and salt hay, and turned inland again, through granite hills. He stopped at times to water the horse, and then he drove on again. The sun was on the decline when he arrived at the county seat, and he drew up and called out to a man afoot, "Friend, can thee tell me where the showman is, who has the foreign beast to see?"

"Showman? There hain't no showman here."

Ezra lifted his hat slightly. The evening breeze cooled his head. "There was a broadside given out to Harperville," he said, "which related that such a person was to be here, come Second Day."

"Showbill, ah. I recollect, now. Someone did arrive in a caravan, all painted in outlandish colors, yes. A foreign-looking man, as you say. But the Selectmen wouldn't give him leave to stay, so he went on. Who knows what mischief he might be up to?"

Ezra set his hat down. "How old of a man would thee say he was, Friend?" he asked.

The townfellow scratched his head. "Hard to say. Might 'a' been thirty. Might 'a' been forty. Why?"

"Thirty or forty. The Lord has given him leave to tarry in this world for thirty or forty years, and thee would not give him leave to tarry in this town for so much as a day." He shook up the reins and drove on, leaving the townsman with mouth agape.

The sun set, the sweet smell of the earth rose into the night air. The moon came up, broad and yellow. "Thee sees how it is, Friend Horse," Ezra said, to the plodding animal. "It was not the Lord's will, it seems, that I should look upon the countenance of His great beast Behemoth, which men call the elephant. So be it. I have dwelt all my days within the circle of these hills, and if at times I have felt it to be a somewhat smaller circle than I could wish, still, I have never wished to go against His will."

The horse whinnied, and then it shied. Startled, but not so much so as to forget the account of Balaam and the ass, Ezra Simmons peered into the silvery road ahead. He saw no angel there, he saw a wagon painted over with strange devices, drawn over to the side of the road.

Horses tethered to a tree raised their heads and nickered. A curtain at the back of the caravan parted and a man appeared. In his hand was a lamp. Rings glittered in his ears.

"Is thee the person called a showman?" asked Ezra.

"I am that very one, Reuben."

"My name is not Reuben, Friend. It is Ezra. I have come to see your great beast."

The man gestured Ezra inside. There was a bright quilt on the wagon bed, and a woman sat on it, with a child at her breast. Her legs and arms were bare, and so, though she smiled at him, he turned aside his head. The man led him to a door in a partition, and held out his hand.

"There was no money at all in the last town," he said. "And no bread grows by the sides of the road."

"What money is the fee?"

The showman shrugged. "I take any money that will pass muster. York shillings, United States gold and silver, fips and thrips and picayunes. I take paper notes of all New England states, as well as New York and Pennsylvany. Virginny and Caroliny, I take at a discount, but as for the wildcat currency of Tennessee and Missouri, them I do not take at all."

Ezra felt in his wallet. "I have nought but one old piece of eight," he said.

"I take them, too. Come along."

It smelled musty in the large space beyond the partition. It smelled odd and wild, it smelled of strange places and strange things, and it smelled most of all of strange beasts. Shadows danced and something rustled in the soiled hay, something made an odd sound. The showman held out his lamp. "There he be," he said. "Have you ever seen the like before?"

"Nay, Friend," said Ezra. "I never have. And never will again. Hold the lamp steady." He looked into the eyes of the strange beast, and the strange beast looked into his own eyes. There was silence. "Thee has a canny look about thy face," Ezra observed. "I believe that thee would laugh, if thee but could. So. And this is the Behemoth of the Scriptures."

The showman took out a piece of pigtail tobacco and thrust it into his mouth. "Now, as to that, I cannot say. On that subject I am coy."

"The elephant, then."

The showman mumbled his chew. "Hmm," he said. "Hmm, hmm."

"This is the only foreign beast thee has? Thee has no other?"

After spitting a brown stream into the straw and wiping his mouth on the back of his hand, the showman shook his head. "*Had* another one. It died. Over a week ago. A great loss, believe me."

Ezra took another look at the beast, and the beast at him. Then, tentatively, he reached out his hand and touched it. The creature nuzzled at his hand, then sniffled his pockets. "Would thee eat an apple? I believe thee would." He watched it eat the apple. Then it turned away. "Thee is right," Ezra said. "It is time I was gone."

At the door, foot on the step, he turned around. "If thee has by chance a likeness of the beast . . . ?" he asked. "But I have no more money with me."

The showman waved his hand, rummaged in a box, produced a sheet of paper with a woodcut on it—the precise likeness of the beast. "No need to mention money. Take it. My compliments. You're the only gent I met today." He stooped, grunted, took out a demijohn, gurgled it. "Splice the mainbrace?"

"Nay, Friend. I thank thee. But I must be getting back to Esther Simmons." He peered at the paper, lips moving slowly. "What is the meaning of this strange word?" he asked.

The jug gurgled again. The showman lowered it a bit. "Oh, that. Why, commodore, that there is the animal's name in its native language."

Ezra's lips moved again. "The Hebrew is a sacred tongue. How full of awe its syllables be. *Kan-ga-roo.* There. I have it now." He took the showman's hand. "Friend, I thank thee," he said. "With all my heart. Thee little knows what thee has done for me. My soul is now at rest within me, like a weaned child."

Earrings glittering, wet mouth smiling, the man said, "Don't mention it. But, say. Like to take a look, scot-free, at the very hat Old Boney wore at St. Helen's Island? Or a parmacetty-tooth? Hey ? Do."

Ezra shook his head. His eyes were grey, and very gentle. "What care I for such things, Friend? I have seen the elephant. What more is there for me to see?"   END

The Day Mama Wept

by Lael J. Littke

Tom noticed as soon as we got off the schoolbus that there was no smoke coming from the chimney of our house. That was unusual, but we didn't stop to worry about it. Probably Mama and Tootie had gone to visit Aunt Maude and just forgot the time.

Reaching the house, the three of us trooped inside—Marcie, the eldest, Tom, and I—stomping the snow from our feet and filling the kitchen with our lingering odors of paste and pencils and stale classrooms since there was no welcoming aroma of boiling soup or baking potatoes to over-power them.

Mama sat at the kitchen table, but not cheerfully peeling apples or cracking nuts as she frequently did there. She was all hunched over with her head buried in her arms. Her shoulders shook as her indrawn breaths made moist, ugly sounds in the otherwise still room. Tootie, too young to go to school, stood at her side, reaching one short little arm up to pat her gently on the back, her tear-streaked face close to Mama's head.

The three of us stood in suspended animation, staring into the dim room, gloomy in the winter afternoon because no one had switched on the light. Tom had removed one overshoe, but Marcie and I stood still fully dressed for the freezing weather outside. We all clutched our school-books as if to cling to something familiar in a world suddenly become threatening and strange.

"Mama's crying," Tom whispered.

"She's weeping," Marcie said softly, and that did seem the right word.

None of us moved. We had never seen Mama weep before. Even on the day two years before when she told us our father was dead, she had been dry-eyed. She had been a solid pillar of strength, standing between us and a world where death lurked to snatch away the unpro-tected. It was all right, Mama said. Daddy had gone to Heaven, but wasn't that a fine place to go what with seeing Grandpa and Grandma Barton and our tiny sister who had lived only four hours, and Pete Hansen who was sure to have a joke for him, to say nothing of Amos Peabody and Margie Anderson, and even Kenny Wells, who would be lonesome to see someone he knew since all of his relatives lived such long lives that none of them Kenny knew were up there in Heaven yet. It sounded like a regular picnic, and when Mama finished describing it we were a little envious of Daddy. All it took was Tootie piping, "Oh, Mama, can I go, too?" to make us burst into laughter which had ended quickly since after all it was a solemn occasion.

But there Mama was now, those silent sobs making her shoulders shake.

Tom was the first to move. He tiptoed to the table as if heavy footsteps would cause Mama further anguish.

"Mama," he whispered. "What's the matter? Is somebody dead?"

Mama didn't answer, except to draw in another of those terrible, deep breaths. The sound of Tom's voice broke me from my spell.

"Mama," I cried, running to her side. "Mama, what's the matter?"

Marcie tried to pull Tootie away to question her, but Tootie clung to Mama, continuing to pat her back and peer anxiously at her bowed head.

"Tootie," Marcie whispered. "Tootie, what happened?"

Tootie's chin trembled as she shook her head.

Tom tiptoed over to switch on the light. The large bare bulb, hanging from the ceiling directly over the table, only made things worse. In the bright light Marcie, Tom, and I, still clutching our school books and wearing our steaming coats, looked from Mama to each other and back to Mama. What does one do when a pillar crumbles, when a mighty oak falls? What does one say when faced suddenly with the fact that the strong have weaknesses, that the invulnerable are vulnerable, that Mama cannot really hold at bay lightning and tornadoes and the evil things of the world which crouched beyond the walls of our house? The fire in the stove was out and the bright light from the overhead bulb hurt our eyes as we realized there is no Santa Claus, no Easter bunny, no fairy Godmother; that frogs do not turn into princes; that our freckles and straight hair would not one day miraculously turn into creamy skin and curls.

Marcie took a giant step in that moment.

"Tom," she said, and her voice had a new note, very similar to Mama's brisk tones. "Tom, go get some wood. The fire is out."

Tom turned to go, and it was only when he went to open the door that he remembered he still carried his schoolbooks. He came back to drop them on the table.

"Put on your other overshoe," Marcie said. When he had gone out, she removed her coat and told me to take off my things.

"We'll fix something to eat," she said.

"What will we fix?" I whispered.

Marcie's tone was positive.

"There's plenty. I'll boil some potatoes and open a jar of peas. You get some apples from the back porch for dessert."

It wasn't until the potatoes were bubbling over a cheery fire and the baking apples were filling the kitchen with their sweet aroma that Mama got up. She had long since stopped those awful, silent sobs, but she hadn't moved. She didn't look at us. She just rose and went into the bathroom. Tootie stumbled along at her heels, but Marcie grabbed her arm and kept her in the kitchen. She tried to put her to work setting the table, but Tootie camped outside the bathroom door and waited.

When Mama came out we had everything ready to eat. Marcie had put out the best dishes, the ones which weren't too chipped and cracked, and had fixed a bowl of apples as a centerpiece.

Mama smiled as she came into the kitchen, and we couldn't see any signs of the weeping except for the puffiness around her eyes.

"My goodness," she said, looking at the table. "Isn't that the prettiest sight you ever laid eyes on? And dinner all ready?"

"It isn't much of a dinner," said Marcie. "Just potatoes and peas."

"And apples," I said.

"Just boiled potatoes," Marcie said.

"I baked the apples," I said.

"It's not much of anything," Marcie said modestly.

Mama put an arm around Tootie, who was clinging to her skirt. "Why, it's the nicest dinner I ever saw," she said. "And the fire so cheerful and all."

Importantly, Tom walked to the stove and poked energetically at the burning wood.

"Sit down, Mama," Marcie said, guiding her to her chair.

"I feel like a queen," Mama said. "I never saw such good little fixers."

We all sat down, hitching our chairs around to be as close to Mama as possible. Tootie practically sat in her lap.

"After we finish," Mama said, "we'll pop some popcorn and I'll read *Snowflake*. How's that? It'll be like a regular party."

We all laughed breathless little laughs and our faces felt stretched from grinning so wide. Everything was all right now. The pillar was righted, the oak firmly rooted again. The lightning and tornadoes were checked and Mama was in command, but we shivered just a little there in the warm kitchen.   END

The Sort of Thing Hector Heath Would Do

by Eric Cameron

Arthur Wickson stood at the ivy-fringed window of his office overlooking the velvet-smooth lawns of the school grounds. The flagstone walks were bordered by stately elms, now rooted in pools of shadow that splashed over the neat flower beds. A kneeling gardener inched along like a pilgrim toward a shrine. Marlborough School *was* a shrine. Wickson reflected: an exclusive private shrine dedicated to wealth and privilege.

His eyes drifted to the clock tower and he noted the time, checking it against his wristwatch. Then he stared intently at the watch, fascinated by the steady, relentless sweep of the second hand. It was twelve years old, a graduation gift from his father, whose death that year had brought an abrupt end to Arthur's plans for post-graduate studies in Europe. Because the estate had not even provided enough to support his mother, Arthur had had to find work. At the time, teaching had seemed a logical choice; he had believed that he would be working in an environment where it would be easier to excel in the things he enjoyed doing. So much for wishful thinking, he concluded with a lethargic lack of bitterness. He recognized that a moss of indifference had spread over his most sensitive areas of awareness . . . a cloak of cynicism had become his daily apparel.

Then he saw Gordon Powell moving through the pools of shadow on the walk leading to the administration building. Wickson hurriedly crossed to the clothes closet, where a mirror on the inside of the door enabled him to check the knot in his tie and the part in his thinning brown hair.

Although the day was humid, he shrugged off his jacket and put on a dark gray suede vest with silver buttons, then put on the jacket again. The vest seemed to give him an aura of casual authority, which he felt he needed for the unpleasant interview with young Powell. He took the pupil's personal file from a drawer and scanned it as he filled his pipe.

The knock on the door was firm but not loud.

"Come in," Wickson called, deliberately making his voice deeper.

Powell edged into the room as if an invisible hand were prodding his reluctant back. He closed the door and stood stiffly, a frown indenting a vee between his black eyebrows. Wickson was reminded that the sensitive-looking youth in the dark blue blazer and gray flannels aroused a vague yet sympathetic interest. He wondered if he saw in Powell something of himself when he had been the same age, a subtle similarity of manner, perhaps. When he gestured with his pipe, Powell sat down carefully, his eyes on the Eskimo soapstone carving of a walrus that Wickson kept on his desk as a paperweight.

"Do you know why I sent for you?" Wickson asked.

Powell's dark head shook slightly, and he moistened his lips. Wickson struck a match and drew on his pipe, allowing the boy a few moments to marshal his defense against the accusation made against him by Hector Heath.

Wickson found himself wishing the boys' roles had been reversed; there would have been some satisfaction in seeing Heath squirm. He recalled the way Heath's pale blue eyes skittered over a person's face as he spoke to him. Probably something to do with nerves or glands, Wickson had concluded, but it gave him a shifty look. So it had been easy to believe that he could detect a trace of maliciousness in Heath's high-pitched nasal whine as he reported the disappearance of his expensive gold wristwatch from the gym locker he shared with Gordon Powell. He had made a point of establishing the value of the watch at two hundred and fifty dollars. It had been a birthday gift from his father, an investment broker whose influence with the school governors was something that the dean had been quick to impress upon Wickson when he had disciplined the youth for a misdemeanor.

In his contacts with the pimply, sallow-skinned Heath, Wickson found himself keeping a rein on his feelings. Powell, on the other hand, he had liked immediately because he was always polite, reserved, and obedient. According to his file, he was the only son of a widowed career soldier who had been killed in a plane crash. His uncle and guardian was an elderly civil servant who had no family of his own. The boy's tuition was paid from a modest trust fund established by his father's estate.

Tilting back in his armchair, Wickson felt in his vest pocket for another match. "Before we go into the matter . . ." he said, then paused, sighting carefully along the sentences the way he did along the rifle he used when coaching the school shooting team.

Powell straightened a little, and a ridge of muscle quivered along his jaw. Wickson noted that the nails of both small fingers had been gnawed to the quick.

"As a member of the faculty," Wickson resumed, "I have certain

duties other than those of scholastic instruction. Sometimes, it be-
comes my responsibility to investigate certain unpleasant situations,
and—should the circumstances warrant it—report my conclusions
to the dean. After that the decision for whatever action is taken rests
entirely with Dr. Martin. Do you understand?"

Powell frowned. "I'm not sure I do, sir."

Wickson sighed and leaned forward. "Hector Heath reported to me
this morning that his wristwatch had been taken from the locker
during gym."

"Yes, sir," Powell muttered, his frown deepening. "Hector never
said anything to *me* about his watch being gone when we dressed after
the session."

"Did you notice if he had it on when you left the gym?" Wickson
asked.

Powell shook his head. "I finished dressing before he did. Hector
was late for your class, sir."

"So he was," Wickson muttered, reflecting with distaste upon
Heath's eel-like way of slipping into a room. He looked at Powell's
hands for indications of tension.

"What time is it?" he abruptly asked.

The boy pulled back his sleeve and looked at his wristwatch
a plain and inexpensive model. "A quarter to two, sir."

Wickson toyed with the brass letter opener as he framed his next
sentence. "Do you like it here?"

Powell nodded, eyes on the letter opener, mouth tightened.

"Marlborough School is very proud of its high standards," Wickson continued, wondering if he sounded too pompous. "Any pupil
found guilty of taking property is expelled. And that sort of thing
could dog a person's career."

When Powell looked up, Wickson was disconcerted to see that the
boy's eyes were glistening with tears. He quickly looked away and
partly turned his chair, giving the youth an opportunity to get a grip
on his emotions. While he talked about the value of a good educational
background, his mind could not rid itself of the irritating suspicion
that Powell's display of emotion might be a silent admission of guilt.
The question mark became like a pebble in a shoe, hardening suspicion into conviction as his sentences limped along. Finally he swung
his chair around to find Powell dry-eyed and composed, listening with
a serious questioning expression. Wickson looked straight into the
unwavering dark eyes.

"Do you know anything at all about Hector Heath's watch?" he asked.

"Nothing, sir," Powell replied without hesitation.

Wickson relaxed with a sigh. "Very well. You may go."

The flash of relief that illuminated Powell's face made Wickson feel a twinge of guilt. He realized that the mere fact of being questioned must have made Powell feel threatened and insecure. Wickson sensed that the boy suffered from a feeling of inferiority that was exposed and rubbed raw every time Hector Heath flaunted his father's wealth.

"Don't let this worry you, Gordon," Wickson said, unconsciously using the boy's first name in a breach of the school custom. He wanted to let him know that the interview had been forced upon him, that he had never suspected him.

"I was quite certain that I was wasting my time," he explained. "But we do it just as a matter of routine. To clear the air, you might say," he concluded with a smile and stood up.

Powell smiled uncertainly, as if there might be a hidden trap waiting to snap shut. Then he nodded politely and left. Wilson crossed to the window and watched Powell hurry along the walk to the science labs. At the edge of a pool of shadow under an elm, the boy halted and reached into his pocket. His hand went up to his face and then came down with a casual flick of the wrist. Something glinted in the sunshine . . . something that dropped into the bed of closely-planted flowers. Then he hurried on his way.

No, it couldn't have been, Wickson told himself. He must have wanted to finish a piece of a chocolate bar, paused to put it in his mouth, then tossed aside the foil wrapper which had caught the sunlight.

Minutes later, Wickson used the same walk to get to his next lecture. He paused beside the flower bed, tempted to bend and peer in among the plants. The tower clock chimed a warning that he was five minutes late. Wickson strode away, trying to erase the question mark from his thoughts. After all, a gold watch would not reflect the sun as brightly as a crumpled piece of wrapping foil. His head began to throb as he thought of the coming interview with Dr. Martin. He would do his best to exonerate Gordon Powell, because Heath *could* have put the watch into the boy's blazer pocket. It was just the nasty sort of thing Hector Heath would do.   END

The Runaway Tractor

by John Wahtera

June had been so hot that hay dried golden in the Bowen fields almost as soon as it was cut, and along the unpaved roads dust lay over the apple trees, reminding the Heavens that a little rain would be appreciated.

Though it was only just past seven, the hot breath of the coming day was already invading the kitchen. Olive Bowen welcomed the coolness of the icebox where she chipped out an egg-sized lump of ice. She wrapped it in a napkin and placed it silently beside the old man who sat at the large kitchen table eating breakfast, remembering at the last minute to turn the pancakes she was tending. The old man was obliged to turn his head half around to see with his one good eye what she had put down. With a shaking hand he pushed the ice aside and grumbled, "I don't need that."

"You'll recover without it," Olive said cheerfully, "but it will certainly make your eye feel better and will take the swelling down. More pancakes?"

"One or two," he agreed, and decided to put the ice to his eye, after all.

"Who hit you this time?" Olive asked with friendly curiosity as she heaped his plate.

"How do *I* know who hit me?" he said irritably.

Olive poured herself coffee and sat down to keep him company. The old man worked busily at his breakfast, giving the impression he was too occupied to discuss his trangressions with this young woman. He knew very well the pretty face masked a mind wastefully clever in a woman. He seldom won an argument with her.

"Well, Angus," Olive said finally, thinking aloud, "if I'd provoked someone enough for them to black my eye, I'd at least remember who it was."

Angus laid down his fork and ran a hand over his thick gray hair which was ordinarily checked, inside the house or out, by an ancient felt hat. The hat presently rested on his suitcase nearby. He adjusted his necktie, a mangled butterfly at his neck, and glared at Olive with his good eye.

"Maybe it was someone provoked *me!*" he said. "Ever think of that?

I suppose I'm to pay for my breakfast with a temperance lecture."

"I've never lectured you," Olive replied. "Nate may lecture you, but I don't. The most I've done is wish for Prohibition, but now that it's here and hasn't stopped your drinking any, I'm ready to wish it out again. Besides, my cooking sherry is almost gone."

"I never touched it," Angus said indignantly.

Olive laughed and laid a hand on his arm. "Oh, Angus," she said. "I never even thought it!"

A flicker of humor passed over Angus' face but only this bare trace, for it wasn't in his plans to become conciliatory.

"An old man like me gets sensitive," he said sadly. "You give a family the best years of your life, you don't expect to be turned out of doors."

"No one's turning you out. No one wants you to go," Olive repeated mechanically, as she had done a hundred times before in the last few days.

"No one's *said* it, but it's clear to *me*," he replied airily. "But you needn't think I can't get along," he assured her in a tone which implied he quite probably would be dead in a ditch by the week's end. "I haven't just made up my mind where I'll go yet," he continued wistfully. "I may go to Florida and get out of these damp New England winters. I s'pose oranges have to picked, same's apples. But then again, I may drift up to Lawrence way and work in the mills. They pay damn-sight better wages than hiring out for a farm hand with no rights or privileges, and then be throwed out like a worn-out old chair that's no use to set on!"

He glanced up furtively to assess the effect of these remarks on Olive, but he found to his annoyance that she only smiled faintly into her coffee cup and played idly with her spoon. He guessed she's been listening to see if the baby was up and hadn't even heard him.

"To tell the truth," he continued, "after all these years in one place, I'll welcome a change. My only regret is I'd rather fancied to be buried here. There's a pretty ash tree at the foot of the Gravenstein orchard, just where the woods begin. I thought it would be nice to lie there under that pretty tree at the edge of an orchard I'd helped Nate to plant. In spring I thought the children might remember to put a few flowers on my grave. But I expect they wouldn't," he sighed.

"Oh, Angus!" Olive cried. "I swear I can't keep a straight face!" She got up and scooped his empty plate from under his nose. "We both know you aren't going anyplace."

"It's easy for the young to laugh," Angus replied. "But don't think because I haven't gone before, I won't go now."

With something in his stomach, Angus felt stronger. His hands were less shaky, and he filled his pipe, drawing on it with satisfaction. "Old Major," he speculated, "I expect Nate will pack him off to the glue factory now."

"Major will *never* go to the glue factory," Olive said firmly and with an edge of irritation in her voice. "Nate can't drown a kitten. If I want a chicken for Sunday dinner, I have to begin asking for it on Tuesday or maybe Wednesday so he'll work himself up to kill one. I don't even know where there is a glue factory."

"I'd offer to take him with me," Angus suggested, "but where's an old man to go with a worn-out work horse."

"A few days ago," Olive reminded him with malicious pleasure, "you said he had *plenty* of work left in him."

In the best of humors, Angus' hearing was apt to be selective, and he now chose to ignore the incongruity Olive pointed out to him. "You remember that horse when Nate bought him?" he reminisced. "Your husband knows apple growing but he don't know horses. It takes the wisdom and experience of age to know horses. It was a stroke of luck he didn't buy one with a broken leg. Old Major come here and no one could lay a hand on him. The first day here he kicked off a stable door and scared the cows half to death. They thought the devil himself was in that stall. But I broke him! I talked to him, give him apples and sugar lumps, made him know I cared for him. A man breaks an animal to a lifetime of hard work and he feels a responsibility to him."

"I'm sure that does you credit," Olive said kindly.

Angus rose from the table. "That was a nice breakfast, Olive," he said. He stooped for his old suitcase and Olive could see it was indeed full of clothes this time, not empty. For the first time since Angus' disagreement with Nate, it occurred to her Angus might leave them, after all.

"Angus," she said softly, not ashamed to plead, "go and put your clothes back in your bureau. And then go milk the cows. Nate hasn't done it. He expected you would. Please don't be foolish."

"I'll milk the cows," he agreed, "but I'll set my suitcase out on the porch. Nate oughtn't to mind taking me downtown so's I won't have to walk. I'm sure I don't want to stay to see him in bankruptcy over that damned tractor. Gasoline doesn't grow in the fields like hay. Gasoline costs dollars and dollars are scarce to come by around this place. He'll wake up to find he's bought himself a big iron hog swillin' down gasoline. And it ain't even *new*! If it's such a marvel as to halve a farmer's work, what's that fellow up in Andover gettin' rid of it for? Tell me that!"

"Nate's thought and figured it out," Olive argued. "Nate knows what he's doing."

"He knows what he's doing like that Calvin Coolidge knows what *he's* doing, and he's not doing *much!*" snorted Angus. "He could have bought himself another horse at a tenth the cost!"

"Horse or tractor, we never thought to get along without you," Olive said.

Angus opened the screen door to the porch. "When I can't pull my weight and need charity, I'll hike myself off to the Poor Farm. That's what it's for," he replied. "I'll milk the cows but that's all. When Nate gets back with the tractor, I'll thank him for three days wages and a ride downtown, if he won't be ashamed to sit behind a horse once more. I've dug in mines in Minnesota and worked in tanneries and cut timber in Canada. I've got skills I've hardly used yet, and some I can still learn. I'll get along."

Olive leaned against the kitchen doorjamb watching him walk to the barn. He was a tall, wiry man, not very stooped; the years had been good to him. He was in no hurry. Stopping at her front garden, he bent to pick a rose which he carefully put in his buttonhole, an action that caused Olive a sudden flood of tears.

She washed her face in cold water at the sink and felt better. She laughed at herself. Well, she supposed, that was the kind of morning she would have, treading on eggshells, seesawing between laughter and tears, overcome alternately with affection for the old man and annoyance at his pigheadedness.

Angus had originally come to them because Nate had broken his arm, and he had stayed beyond Nate's disability because they had come to like this hard-drinking drifter, and he, them. Through the years, Olive knew she and Nate had subtly "broken" him in a way not unlike the old man's taming of Major. Neither a settled life or the Eighteenth Amendment had stopped his drinking, but he drank much less. Olive could not believe a man would give up the only home and family he had over a tractor, a mechanical *thing!* But Olive also knew she was only saying to herself that *she* would not if *she* were he. A man's pride, like a woman's intuition, was not easily explained. She would have to wait for Nate. He would talk to Angus in a way she could not. Nate would be surprised. Angus had been threatening to leave for days but no one, of course, had believed him.

With her face cool from washing, Olive began to think what the day required of her. That's what she would give it, nothing more. She covered the remaining pancake batter and put it in the icebox. Nate and little Mark had rushed off without breakfast in their eagerness to get the tractor. They would want something when they got back from the Drury place. It occurred to Olive that the tractor would be brought back on the Drury truck and that perhaps Mr. Drury would have breakfast with them. Drury was a rich man, a gentleman farmer, and Olive considered setting a table in the dining room but then dismissed the idea as pretentious.

After a time, Angus brought the fresh milk wordlessly through the kitchen into the dairy, ran it through the separator, and then went out to sit on the shaded side of the porch steps, his hat tipped rakishly over his eyes, a blade of grass held between his teeth.

Olive knew she should be canning tomatoes but instead she made a pitcher of lemonade and brought Angus a glass which he drank straight down, remarking as he returned the glass to her, "Your flowers need water."

It was the middle of the morning when Olive heard the rumble of a lorry turning into the yard. Mr. Drury raised fine saddle horses and the lorry, Olive could see, was made to transport them. The tailgate folded down into a convenient ramp. The high wooden sides hid the tractor. Olive watched Mark jump from the cab of the truck and thought how tanned and full of life he seemed. Nate swung gracefully down after his son and Olive saw the same excitement on both their faces.

Mark ran the short distance to the porch, calling ahead to Angus. "Come on, Angus! Come and see it! Come on, Angus! Come on, Mama!"

"I expect I'll see it from here," Angus grunted. "Ask Mr. Drury if I could hitch a ride back to town when he goes."

Mark paid no attention. He hardly seemed to hear. "Come on, Mama!" he called into the house, full of impatience.

The commotion had awakened the baby upstairs. When Olive came out into the yard, holding the baby, the men had eased the tractor down the ramp and it stood alone, seeming gigantic to Olive and full of sleeping power. She could see that Nate and Mark were not in any mood to stop for breakfast.

"Ask Drury if I can have a ride to town with him," Angus growled as Olive passed by him.

"If you're in such a hurry, ask him yourself," Olive replied flippantly. But when Nate came to her, glistening with sweat, and said, "What do you think of my new toy?" Olive whispered, "Nate, you have to speak to Angus. He's really going this time."

Nate's face went blank for a moment and he glanced over at Angus, but then his smile returned. "He won't go, Olly," he reassured her. "He's a lot of talk." He tweaked the baby's nose playfully and turned to Drury, who had joined them.

"Good morning, Mrs. Bowen," the older man said, and touching the baby's arm said, "Ask your daddy to hitch his new tractor to a wagon and take you for a ride." He looked up at Nate and Olive. "I have seven grandchildren on the farm for the summer," he informed them with pride. "It's like having a tribe of Indians."

"*Can* we hitch it to the wagon, Papa?" Mark asked. "We can all take a ride."

"First I have to learn to drive it," Nate said.

"Oh, you'll soon get the hang of it," Drury promised. "Tremendously useful thing, a tractor," he assured Olive.

Nate had walked to the machine and stood admiring it. The spoked rear wheels stood as high as his chest. The metal seat was so high from the ground that Olive promptly discarded the vague idea she had had of learning to drive it herself.

"Start it up, Papa!" Mark urged. "Crank it!"

Nate shrugged happily. "I might as well," he said, and walked around to the front of it.

"You may have to adjust the spark," Drury suggested, pointing out a lever on the steering wheel. "I haven't driven this thing in a long time, but I daresay it will all come back to me."

"Angus!" Nate called. "Come sit on the seat and play with the spark while I crank."

"I wouldn't set on that thing for a hundred dollars," Angus snorted, but he did get up and wander over to stand looking at the machine as though it were a particularly inferior piece of horseflesh. "It looks mean to me," he informed them.

At Nate's look of exasperation, Olive bent and hid her laugh in the baby's hair. There was something comic in the scene, in the curious stares of the cows who lined the fence, waiting. The displaced Major stood beside his barnyard sisters, eyeing the goings-on with cold disdain, motionless except for an occasional haughty swish of his tail.

"I'll sit on it, Papa," Mark cried, and in a second was perched in the iron seat, his feet dangling. "What do these do?" he asked, pulling and pushing at every lever and knob within reach.

"Hey, don't touch anything," Nate said sharply. "Mr. Drury will show us. Just touch the spark when you're told."

"It's that lever on the steering wheel, Mark," Drury said. "Now, just move it a trifle to the right. If that doesn't do it, we move it a bit more." He nodded at Nate. "Crank away, my boy. Watch yourself. The crank's got a nasty kick."

Nate wiped his hands on the seat of his pants and bent over the crank. He moved it clockwise until it caught, and putting his shoulder to it, pulled upward with a grunt. The tractor made a genteel cough somewhat resembling a hiccup, and nothing else. Nate positioned the crank again and repeated the process twice. Still nothing happened.

Angus cleared his throat loudly, and though no words were spoken, the noise stated eloquently his satisfaction at the way things were going.

Olive looked at the rivulets of sweat pouring down Nate's face and half closed her eyes in concentration, willing with all her might for the beast to start.

"A little more spark," Drury advised.

Mark moved the lever an inch to the right. "Hurry up, Papa! Now try it," he said impatiently.

Nate drew his sleeve across his face, took a deep breath, positioned the crank once more and pulled up with all his strength. There was a horrendous BANG. A ring of fiery black smoke sailed up into the branches of an oak tree, and a surprised yelp of pain came from Nate as the crank whipped backward, striking his arm and throwing him to the ground. Olive screamed as the machine lurched suddenly forward toward Nate. But Nate rolled agilely aside, clutching his right arm. The tractor, carrying a terrified Mark, rolled irrevocably toward the pasture fence where the cows, with bouncing haunches and swinging udders, were absenting themselves with a speed Drury would have been pleased to see in his saddle horses.

"Jump, Mark! Jump, boy!" Nate yelled, but Mark was made of sterner stuff and tried valiantly to stop the machine by pulling on any knob or lever his flailing arms could reach.

Drury was hobbling vainly after them but it was Angus who closed in shouting, "Get off there, you little jackass! You'll be killed!"

As the fence loomed ahead, Mark turned and leaped off the rear of the tractor into space. Angus raced on past him, caught a grip on a fender and a toehold on the coupling, and swung himself in the seat in time to see the barrier of split rail fencing part before him as miraculously as the Red Sea parted for the Israelites. The tractor made a lasting impression on the fence but was not itself slowed or deterred by an inch. It roared on in pursuit of the hapless cows and Major.

"What the hell do I do?" Angus cried over his shoulder.

"Steer!" Drury cried after him feebly, but Angus could hardly have heard, for the front wheels struck a rock and the machine veered around the corner of the barn. In a moment it reappeared, traveling in the opposite direction and before anyone had the wit to appraise the situation, Angus, who now bore an expression partly outraged and partly grim determination, had disappeared through the farther end of the pasture and into the orchards.

Nate lay on the ground gritting his teeth and cradling his arm.

"Is it broken?" Olive asked, kneeling beside him.

"It's broken," he said.

It seemed hours to Olive since she first sat on the porch steps; it was perhaps two. She was alone except for the baby, who played nearby. in the shade of a maple tree. At intervals Olive was conscious of Mark crossing the barnyard, dragging a nervous, balky cow by the halter. He plodded back and forth with such an angry resignation that Olive's heart went out to her son. The disappointments of children were always deepest. Olive had lost count but she guessed he must have chased down nearly all the cows by now.

Mr. Drury had put Nate into the truck and driven him straight to the hospital. They hadn't returned and Olive could only sit and worry.

As if to remind Olive that what had happened had *really* happened and was not a dream from which she would awaken at any moment, there was the steady drone of the tractor motor. Whatever had happened to Angus, the tractor was still going, and she had to believe the tractor was not driving itself back and forth across the Bowen fields and orchards. The noise came first from one side, then the other. Sometimes it came quite close, once so close that Olive had run to the pasture fence to get a glimpse of it, but it had disappeared. Several times the motor stopped abruptly, then, after a time, it had started up again.

Olive finally went in to make dinner. Whatever calamities lay behind them or before them, men must eat.

When she heard Drury's truck, she dried her hands and from the window saw Nate stepping carefully down from it, his right forearm partly enclosed in a fresh white cast. Drury waved and drove off. Nate stood in the center of the yard glowering in the direction of the tractor's sound.

"Is it painful?" she asked when she reached him.

"No, not bad," he said wearily.

Olive put an arm around him and they began to cross the lawn. "Well, Olly, what do you think?" he asked soberly. "Are we turning in our faithful horse for a white elephant?" Then he stopped abruptly, for the sound of the tractor was certainly approaching. In a minute's time the tractor came careening around the corner of the barn. Steering with one hand, Angus tipped his hat to them, ran his iron charger once around the dooryard and slowed it expertly to a stop and killed the motor. In the sudden silence his voice came cheerfully across the yard. "Would you like a ride?" he asked.

At dinner, Angus was full of information. "Ain't so different from a horse," he chattered. "You tell a horse, 'Gee' and 'Whoa' and you tell this piece of machinery the same things by pulling this gadget or pushing on some other gadget. It minds quicker than a horse, though. I said to myself bouncing through that pasture, if you can break a horse, you can break this glorified alarm clock, and anyway, if I'd a jumped I'd likely have broken my leg. So, that machine and I set to it. We went 'round and 'round while I learned *it* and it learned *me*! I can tell you," he nodded sagely, "there's a good deal more to it than meets the eye. But I expect I'll be able to teach you, Nate, when you're up to it."

Nate looked up from his barely touched dinner and glared across the table.

"I should think," Angus continued animatedly, "if you was to hitch a chain to that thing and wrap the other end around a stump, that stump would come up quicker than pulling up a carrot. And you know something? You don't need half the space to turn it around as you need for a team of horses. I tell you, Nate, you set up there on that iron seat and you feel like you could go through brick walls and never feel it. You see what it done to the fence. The power in that machine is enough to make a man speechless."

"I'd never know it," Nate said softly.

"But that machine has squeaks and rattles in it, oughtn't to be there," Angus said critically. "If a finely made piece of machinery like that gives a man a day's work, it requires good care. I suppose once Drury made up his mind to sell it, he never wasted a drop of oil or dab of grease on it." He smiled sweetly and looked across the table at Nate. "Nate, there's no reason for you to look downcast. A decent man wouldn't go and leave you in a fix like this. I expect I could change my plans and stay if I was asked."

"You old soak!" Nate growled. "Whoever asked you to go?"

"Well, it ain't the politest invitation I've had," Angus chuckled. "But I accept. Mark," he said, his eyes twinkling, "Be a good boy and cut up your father's meat for him."

After dinner, as Nate and Angus sat on the porch steps smoking their pipes, the sound of their low voices gave Olive a feeling of warm well-being. She poured three small glasses of amber liquid and joined them.

"What's that?" Angus asked suspiciously.

"The last of the cooking sherry," Olive said. "Make a toast, Nate. Let's not waste it."

Nate raised the glass with his left hand and looked out at the tractor parked in the shade of the dooryard trees. "To three shrewd Yankees," he grinned, "living in an age of miracles."   END

Mrs. Van Dusen and the Myrtilles

by Axel Hornos

The mirror showed a tall woman in a blue-gray dress and gloves, wide-brimmed hat with matching bow, and raffia shoes.

"I could look worse," mused Cornelia MacKenzie Van Dusen as she studied her reflection critically. At fifty-eight her stately figure and long oval face with its arched nose still commanded attention. The general effect of majesty was heightened by the stern eyes.

She picked the invitation from the table and read again,

> *Mr. and Mrs. Andrew D. Fitzgibbons*
> *request the pleasure of your presence*
> *at a garden party to be held at*
> *The Oaks, Bar Harbor,*
> *in honor of*
> *Their Excellencies Baron and*
> *Baroness Saturnino de Olivares*
> *Saturday September 15th*
> *at four o'clock*

A few lines hastily scribbled on the back added, "Dearest Corny, please do come! You'll meet some of the choicest people. I'll have a room readied for you to stay overnight. See you on the 15th. Love, Maggie."

With a sigh she dropped the card into her purse. Oh well, better a garden party—the thought of the informality prevalent at those gatherings made her shudder—than nothing. Besides, she hadn't seen Andrew and Maggie Fitzgibbons for ages, and those cheeks of hers sure needed some fresh air. She smiled as she recalled that Phillip had uttered those same words many times during their thirty-four years together. "Cornelia Van Dusen," he used to say, "let's go out for a ride. Those cheeks of yours sure need some fresh air."

She began to descend the stately staircase, her hand sliding along the polished mahogany handrail in a gesture as instinctive to her as breathing. She raised her hand close to her eyes (she was coquettish enough to pretend she didn't need glasses) and looked disapprovingly at the faint traces of dust on her fingertips. She would have to tell

Benson that he should be more watchful of the new maid's cleaning.

She saw the girl then, darting across the hall below, a slight figure in a stiff apron and bonnet. Josephine was quick at her work, although not very thorough. She also had the annoying habit of prattling un-invited about her years on the family farm back in Vermont—the happy hustle and bustle at harvest time; the slap of wind on her face as she spurred one of her father's horses; her mother's mouth-watering pies with their crunchy crusts, which Josephine had learned to bake. "And they are pretty yummy too, Ma'am," she concluded, smacking her lips with a noise that gave Mrs. Van Dusen a painful start.

What impossible manners, she thought; but she had to admit that the girl had an unpolished charm all her own.

She noted in passing how the bonnet, precariously balanced over the bouffant hair, injected a touch of piquancy into the rather plain face. She felt like smiling but did not; Josephine might take undue advantage of the slightest sign of familiarity on her part. Better keep her in the place where she belonged.

Crossing the drawing room she headed for the back entrance. As she went past the servants' quarters she heard the baritone voice of Wil-liams, the chauffeur. He spoke in soft tones, but the words reached her distinctly: "Sorry, Jo. I wish I could say to hell with the garden party, but I can't. So tonight's dance is out. Bad luck, honey."

Mrs. Van Dusen's face hardened. So they were in the "honey" stage, those two, only three weeks after Josephine's hiring. My, my, how young people rushed things nowadays! To think that it had taken Phillip almost three years of persistent courting to earn her first kiss.

Since Williams was nowhere in sight when she emerged into the garden, she opened the door of the Bentley herself and sank into the deep leather seat, waiting.

After their marriage, Phillip had often come to her side as, standing in front of a mirror, she gave the final touches to her evening gown. "I'm waiting for that twinkle in your eyes," he used to say. "The girliest twinkle"—he had a knack for coining new words on the spur of the moment—"in the whole of Boston."

The twinkle in her eyes . . . She opened her purse and glanced at the small mirror inside. She saw a proud face, a mouth firmly set, two eyes which after years of careful grooming had acquired an unblinking fixity. Hastily she closed the purse. For a brief moment there was an ache inside her, then all was calm again.

She saw the chauffeur come out of the house at a run, buttoning his coat. As he placed her suitcase in the front seat, he muttered an apology for his tardiness. Without answering, she looked with annoyance at the gawky face. A typical product of the times, she reflected, not much sense of obligation toward his betters. Probably intent only on courting that little maid. And such language! What was it he had said? "To hell with the garden party!" A gross impropriety if there ever was one. And in her own house. Really, Benson was slipping.

The sights of Boston on a pleasant August morning restored her composure. Dear old Boston, with its tortuous streets, stingy houses and impossible weather. But where else did gracious living and solid common sense mingle so well? Where else would she find so many memories, carefully, lovingly nurtured? In Boston she had met Phillip and known her happiest years at his side. God willing, in Boston she would die. She leaned back and closed her eyes contentedly.

After an early luncheon in Portsmouth, time ran fast as they sped along the Maine Turnpike. Near Auburn frequent stretches of road construction forced them to decrease their speed. Several times they had to wait for traffic to go through from the opposite direction.

Made impatient by the delays, Mrs. Van Dusen finally called the chauffeur through the intercom.

"Williams," she said irritably, "let's leave the Turnpike and take less travelled roads."

Since as far back as she could remember she had enjoyed the gently rolling, violently contrasting landscapes of Maine, where barren, rock-bound areas alternate with fields of wild flowers and forests are mirrored on moody lakes. Only a few ramshackle farmhouses far apart from each other broke the emptiness of the road.

They were passing through some wooded hills when the motor started to cough and sputter, then it slowed down and died.

"What happened?" she asked.

There was a long silence before Williams turned his head. "It's . . . it's the gas, Ma'am."

"What about it?"

"It's gone. There is no more gas."

Mrs. Van Dusen's lips tightened. After passing dozens of service stations, he had forgotten to replenish the tank. And now they were stranded in a God-forsaken road in the middle of nowhere. And why? Because a scatterbrained youth, instead of concentrating on his work, had let his mind—if he had a mind—wander after a silly peasant girl who didn't even know how to dust a handrail properly.

She made an effort to recover her composure. "How could this happen?" she asked.

"I . . . I don't know, Ma'am," he replied, sheepishly. "I guess I kind of forgot."

He kind of forgot! She frowned, starting to boil. He forgot because of that ninny whom he had planned to take to some dance tonight.

"And just what are you going to do now?"

"We went by a gas pump a few minutes ago, Ma'am. I'll walk back and get some gas. It won't take more than an hour, I'm sure." He hesitated. "Perhaps you'd rather not stay alone on this road? I can wait for a car to . . ."

"No, no. You go now," she urged, impatiently waving a hand.

She sat for a long time, her eyes on the empty road ahead, trying not to let her ill humor get the best of her.

The wooded hill at her left looked inviting after the long seclusion in the car. Why not? She might as well take a walk.

She took a path which wandered upward among birch trees. The air was warm, the ascent strenuous. After a while she had to slow down. Orioles, catbirds and bobolinks rioted in the bushes around her. The summit was wide and strewn with boulders, and she noticed that it was covered in parts by clumps of small shrubs with light green leaves and bluish fruit. There was something familiar about them. How strange that the sight of blueberry bushes should suddenly put her in a reminiscent mood. Where had she seen them before? What were they saying to her? On an impulse she leaned forward and touched the round, smooth berries, half-hidden beneath the leaves and clouded over with a delicate patina of dust.

"Myrtilles!" she said wonderingly. "They are myrtilles!"

Long-lost memories came rushing in on her.

She saw herself in a small village near Chamonix at the foot of Mont Blanc. Her parents had rented a villa for the summer—a large, rambling structure with many terraces and fronted by a lawn where she and her two younger brothers played vociferous games of croquet. A tall, lanky girl of fifteen with long auburn braids and freckled face, she was given that summer to fits of unlady-like behavior which kept her mother in a state of permanent alarm. Left to herself, she would join her brothers in climbing trees, playing marbles, and throwing stones at the crows that infested the area. A rebel against all the social niceties expected of her age and sex.

At other times she was strangely quiet and uncommunicative and took long solitary walks in the neighboring country. During one of these expeditions she saw for the first time, as she strolled through some woods not far from the villa, the small shrubs with bluish fruit. She tried one, liked it, ate some more. The bitter-sweet taste lingered in her mouth. Taking off her sun hat, she had filled it with the berries which she brought back to the villa and showed to their gardener, asking him what they were.

The gardener, a stooped man with crossed eyes and a bristling mustache, said good-humoredly, "Why, mademoiselle, they are myrtilles. They grow in the woods. People around here pick them by the pailful to make pies. And what pies!" He rolled his eyes.

Her mother told her that myrtilles was simply the French word for blueberries. But they were myrtilles to Cornelia for a long time because the liquid sound of the word conveyed so well the very essence of the fruit.

That afternoon she borrowed a pail from the gardener and told her mother that she was going to fill it with myrtilles. Her mother looked apprehensive. "You won't go alone, will you?"

Cornelia's cheeks reddened with indignation. "Why, Mother, of course I will! Why shouldn't I? There are no wild beasts around here!"

"I know, darling, " her mother said, soothingly. "Still, I'll feel better if you don't go by yourself to those thick woods where you might easily lose your way. I'll ask Doug to join you."

"My darling kid brother!" exclaimed Cornelia with scorn. "Of what use could he be?"

"All right, then," conceded her mother, "you'll go with Doug and Emile, who knows the woods inside out.

Emile was the gardener's son. He was seventeen, and what could one expect from a boy of that age but a silly face, a tremulous, high-pitched voice and big, clumsy hands and feet? She was about to flare up again but thought better of it and shrugged her shoulders. After all, three pickers would collect a bigger harvest than one.

The woods vibrated with filtered light. A soft wind from the Alps rustled the leaves. Birds sang their heads off. Cornelia, eleven-year-old Doug and Emile worked feverishly, in silent, ruthless competition. They had one large pail each, and the berries, although plentiful, proved deceptively small.

Emile (funny how fast those clumsy fingers of his could move) was quickly way ahead of Doug and her. After a while Doug, who hadn't filled more than one-quarter of his pail, became restless. "There aren't enough berries around here," he complained, enviously eyeing the other pails. "I'll find myself a better place."

"Don't go too far," Cornelia called after him as he disappeared behind some tall bushes.

She and Emile continued their work, sometimes at a distance from each other, sometimes very near. They worked steadily, without talking; yet, perhaps because of their growing weariness or the torpor induced by the warm day, their pace began to slacken. Once or twice, as they picked the opposite sides of a shrub, their fingers touched. They withdrew them quickly, as from fire, but their eyes met, and Cornelia was furious at her blushing.

After what seemed a long time, the sound of leaves being crushed by feet startled them. It was Doug carrying his pail over a shoulder, a big grin on his face. "I've filled my pail!" he said in triumph. "I'm going home."

Cornelia and Emile went on picking berries, immersed in their troubled quietness, unaware that the light was declining and that the birds had fallen silent. She glanced at her companion furtively.

With surprise she noticed a slender body moving about with easy assurance, a fine manly face, two strong hands. Impulsively she cried, "Emile!" He looked up from behind a shrub and advanced towards her with hesitation. She was frightened but did not move. He bent and kissed her—an awkward kiss which barely touched the corner of her mouth. Lifting her heavy pail, she ran out of the woods and towards the villa. Despite the weight that pulled at her arm, she felt as light as a leaf, and her heart pounded deliciously.

She saw her mother coming towards her. "What happened, Cornelia?" she asked. "Why are you so late?"

"Oh, Mother! I guess we just forgot about the time!"

Cornelia Van Dusen was on her knees picking berries, filling her mouth with them. She had not realized how thirsty she was. Avidly her teeth broke into the fruit, crushing it, letting the cool tangy juice run free. Then she drew herself up and looked at her gloves, stained to an ugly purple. "Cornelia Van Dusen," she said aloud, "look at yourself! At your age! Aren't you ashamed?"

But she was not, and taking off her hat she began to fill it with blueberries, without haste, all the while humming old tunes that came back to her. Not for years had she felt so carefree and buoyant.

When the hat was full, she rested on a boulder. Far to the east the Atlantic glimmered in the sun. White clouds hovered high about it like guardian angels. She thought she could hear the sound of waves, but it was only the gentle rustling of leaves under the wind.

I must go back, she thought, and sighed. Regretfully she stood up and, holding the hatful of berries as if it were some precious thing, went down the path. The blueberries gave off a tantalizing aroma. At least, she mused, I can have a big pie made . . . with a fluffy crust. She remembered Josephine's claims as a pie-baker. She would let her handle the assignment. The idea pleased her, and she quickened her pace.

Vivacious Josephine in her stiff bonnet and apron—an unnatural combination if there ever was one, she thought suddenly. She had visions of Josephine galloping on her father's horse, of Josephine swirling on a dance floor, her eyes aglow with budding love.

When she reached the road, Williams was standing by the car, very smart in his uniform. How young he looks, she thought with a pang, and smiled.

He opened the door for her. She sat down and carefully laid the hat on her knees, holding it with both hands.

"We are still in plenty of time for the garden party, Ma'am," boomed the baritone voice.

She made up her mind. Surprising the life out of him, she said decidedly, "To hell with the garden party, Williams. Let's go home." END

Duck with Dressing

by Robert W. Wells

In the moment it took to boat the oars and crouch in the bow of the skiff, a twinge of doubt came over Rocky Schwantes. It had all seemed simple enough, talking it over with the others back at the Snug, but now he could see trouble ahead. He grasped the cold squares of the fence that was strung across the creek and peered over the top wire into the darkness of the headwater. But old Mike Harris, who'd been his father's partner and was now his, was handing him the shotgun and Rocky knew it was too late to turn back with dignity.

The flashlight beam stabbed out. The gun sent the echoes flying. There was a frenzied gabbling from the water and from the reedy banks, with the white feathers swirling and the limp bodies strewn, and Rocky was reloading, the gun was sounding again and then they were rowing hard, away from the fence and toward the bay, with Mike muttering joyfully.

"That'll learn her. That'll learn her to spoil our beds."

They caught a few hours sleep in the lean clapboard house lifted safely above even storm tides on weathered stilts sunk in the sand near the bay, and then they went out in their boat as usual. But when they came back in mid-afternoon with their harvest the deputy, Cal Higgins, was waiting on the dock. Rocky walked over, a lean, sea-weathered young man with a swing to his shoulders, and stood in his salt encrusted denims above the paunchy figure in the crumpled gray suit. The deputy held out a pudgy hand. A bedraggled duck feather was between the thumb and forefinger, and he twirled it, squinting at it.

"Twenty-two of Meg Campbell's ducks got themselves shot last night, Rocky."

"Suicide, maybe?"

"Very funny."

"I got six or eight guys'll tell you I spent last night at the Snug."

"All oystermen?"

"Who else goes there, Cal?"

The deputy sighed. He looked around at the worn dock, the freshly-painted oyster boat beside it, the lined, hostile face of Mike Harris peering from the tiny cabin.

"Listen, Rocky," he said, wearily, "I know the way an oysterman feels about anybody, man or woman, who buys up a headwater and starts raising ducks on it. Okay. You got to make a living and if the oyster beds you got staked out get polluted you don't make one. I been around oystermen all my life. I know about oysters—how they got nothing but trouble from the time they're spats to the day some sea-going farmer like you tongs them up. I know what dirty water can do to them. But ducks is private property, too, Rocky. And besides—."

"Besides what?"

"You got no call to pick on a woman."

Rocky frowned. His hands clenched. "She's got no call to spoil our beds."

The deputy's weariness seemed almost too heavy to be borne. He turned and started slowly off the dock towards his car. But then he stopped.

"Rocky," he said, "if there's any more duck shooting, I'll run you in. I know you. You're maybe the best oyster tonger in the bay like old Bob Schwantes was before you but you got your old man's bullheaded streak, too, and when trouble's being dealt you got to grab a hand. But why don't you get smart once, boy? Go talk it over with Meg Campbell."

Rocky turned away angrily. "I don't talk to duck farmers."

A slow grin made its difficult way over Cal's face, parting the heavy folds and rearranging the wrinkles. "You ain't seen this one, I guess. This is a duck farmer that don't look like no duck, boy."

Later, talking it over while supper was frying, Mike was for calling the deputy's bluff. But Rocky wasn't sure. Maybe guns and wire clippers weren't the way. They'd been tried other places, but they hadn't kept the duck raisers from buying up the headwaters of the streams, and they hadn't saved the oyster beds at the creek mouths.

"You're telling me somethin', mebbe," Mike exploded. "Wasn't it old Bob and me who had to move out after we'd stood by and seen one of the sweetest beds in Long Island Sound ruined? Once them farmers found out out you can fatten a duck for market two or three weeks faster on water than on land, there was no holdin' them. Look at what's happened to oyster fishing around that way. We let this thing get started here, it'll be just like it was on the island. I say cut the wire. There ain't a jury in the county'd convict an oysterman for protecting his natural rights."

But Rocky was stubborn. It couldn't do any harm to talk to Meg Campbell, could it? Especially if she was young and pretty. He'd talked to a lot of pretty women before now and, without bragging, he could say that he'd made a few of them get a new outlook on oyster fishing. Mike agreed, but reluctantly.

"Okay, boy," he said. "You got two things in your favor in life. You got a way with oysters. What's almost as important, you got a way with women. Go ahead. See what happens. But remember this. A woman who'd do what she's done'd stop at nothin'. Don't let her twist you around, boy."

Rocky changed into clean denims and hosed out the back of the pick-up truck to get rid of part of the oyster smell before he headed up the sandy ruts that led to the :nain road. When he pulled into the driveway next to the small white cottage that had been converted from a fisherman's shanty he saw her walking across the yard, a bucket in one hand. She was dressed in dungarees and her dark hair was tied up under a bandana, but she looked good, she looked mighty good and as he watched how she carried herself his hands tightened involuntarily on the steering wheel. She turned and regarded him and at once her expression became hostile. He climbed out of the truck and walked over to her.

"I'm Rocky Schwantes. Cal Higgins tell you about me?"

She came toward him quickly. He was a good eight inches taller and seventy pounds heavier, but the snap of her brown eyes made him take a step away from her.

"So you're the hero. So you're the one that came sneaking up the creek at night. Well, I want to tell you something. I bought myself a rifle this morning. I spent most of the day practicing with it and the next time you show up there'll be something besides ducks to deal with. The ducks can't shoot back but believe me, brother, I can."

Considering her size, the look of her threatening him was too much. He began to laugh, backing off from her, putting up his hands in mock defense. He circled away and his foot struck the bucket she'd been carrying. He stumbled and she was upon him, her palm swinging for his face, and the force of the blow combined with his uncertain footing sent him sprawling. She wheeled and ran into the house. He climbed to his feet, rubbing himself where he hurt most, and started after her but then he stopped and glanced guiltily around. If someone had seen him—someone who'd tell Mike or the boys at the Snug—. But no one had.

"I'll be back," he shouted. "Cool down, Meg, I'll be back."

The truck roared out of the driveway. At the stilt house he reported to Mike. "She's a wildcat, that gal. A real dish, too. This might turn out to be fun."

He went back again the next night. She wouldn't talk to him. And the next. She came to the door carrying the rifle, and he left abruptly. But on the fourth night he dressed up in his best suit instead of the denims and stopped by the village and picked up the biggest box of candy he could find, one with a red ribbon on it. He left the truck at the road and crept up behind the house until he saw her sitting in the kitchen near an open window. He tossed the box at her feet, and when she came storming outside he was sitting calmly on the narrow porch, his legs crossed, leaning against the railing. She waved the package under his nose.

"What's this supposed to be?"

"Bait."

"You think I'm an oyster?"

He stood up slowly. "There's things you don't know about oysters, Meg. Like the fact you don't use bait to catch 'em. I thought maybe you'd hold your fire long enough for us to have a talk."

"I'm not interested."

He moved quickly. His big hands grasped her arms firmly, pinning them to her side. She kicked at him, and he got the porch railing between them, but without losing his grip on her. She quit struggling.

"Okay, talk," she ordered. "But when you let me go you better run because thirty seconds after I come out of this house again I'm going to start shooting."

She meant it, too, this small, dark-haired bundle. He'd planned the words he would say, but when the words came they were different ones. He'd made a mistake, he found himself telling her. He hadn't realized how things were with her.

"So let's start fresh," he summed up. "You forget I might've been mixed up in a duck shoot and I'll forget your birds've been spoiling my oyster beds and—and I'll take you somewhere for supper. You could use a friend around here, maybe, things being like they are. And I got an idea any girl who'll fight for her livestock the way you been doing is entitled to her own opinion. Okay?"

"Let me go, Rocky."

He hesitated. Then he dropped his hands to his sides and stood looking down at her. She studied him carefully. A frown came and went and then there was something like amusement in her eyes.

"On one condition. I got a chore to do first. The condition is, you help me feed the ducks."

He swallowed and glanced around, the unreasonable fear on him again that Mike or the boys might be watching. "Okay," he said "You're a rough bargainer, but okay."

He considered taking her to the Snug for he would have enjoyed the nods and the soft comments paying tribute to his male prowess when he walked in—every oysterman on the bay knew of his campaign and there were plenty of bets on it. But he drove instead to a small restaurant on a side street of the village where they could be alone. They ate steak—she suggested roast duck, but Rocky said no, it was carrying the truce too far to expect him to eat them as well as feed them. Afterwards he took the truck down to the beach, and they walked on the sand and shied rocks into the softly lapping water, and then he brought her home and said good-night and drove off, with her watching him from behind the curtains. But whether she was watching because like him she was sorry the evening was over or whether she was waiting there to make sure he didn't circle back to her precious ducks was a matter that he felt was still in considerable doubt.

He developed the habit of dropping around each evening and helping her carry the mash to the swarming fowl in the headwater. It was, he told himself firmly, merely a way to gain her confidence so he could bring up the problem of the oysters. When she no longer had a chip on her shoulder maybe she could see what she was doing to him and the rest of the oystermen. But the first week went by and then several others and somehow the subject didn't come up. And with each succeeding day old Mike's patience wore thinner.

"You been shinin' around that gal long enough, Rocky," Harris told him finally. "Dancin' with her at the Point. Buying her steaks in town and walking her up the beach and who knows what all. And all the time those ducks fouling up the water, the oysters dying off. Next thing we know there'll be an inspector around to tell us we got to quit shipping them. Either you do something about it, boy, or I'm going to."

Rocky tried to make him see how it was. He hadn't turned traitor. But he could see now, he told Mike, that Meg had problems, too. She'd inherited a few thousand when her dad died. She'd quit her office job because she was tired of the city and tired of the boss and she wanted some fresh air and a chance to be on her own. She'd bought some books and studied up and then she'd sunk her last cent in the ducks and a down payment on the house and land. Raising them on water, she'd save on feed and show a profit. She'd lose her shirt if she quit now. Mike turned away in disgust.

"Okay, boy. You stick with that pants-wearing duck farmer if you want to, you marry her, even, if that's what you got in mind and the other boys and me can move on. Except there ain't no place left to move on to. But you won't care, with your ducks getting fat and a little woman to feed 'em for you. I'm glad old Bob Schwantes ain't here to see it."

The words stung. Rocky flung himself out of the stilt house and headed for the consolation of the Snug. But three of the oystermen got up and left when he came in. None of the rest would talk to him. The word had spread. If he'd been a little smaller there would have been a fight, but no one wanted to tangle with him. Instead, they looked the other way when he spoke or elaborately avoided him.

He stalked out and headed for the beach, wandering aimlessly along it, full of resentment. Well, he decided finally, okay, then. He wouldn't trade Meg for the whole crew of them, nor for every solitary oyster at the bottom of the bay. He ran back over the dunes and leaped into the pickup and gunned it out the familiar road to her cottage.

She suggested they eat at home. She asked him what he'd like and he told her: "Anything. Anything but duck. I won't eat duck." So she scrambled eggs and fried some bacon and when he came in from carrying the mash—it was almost automatic now, this chore—they ate together in the narrow kitchen. Then he fixed a fire in the fireplace, and they sat close together on the battered green-covered sofa in front of the flames as the darkness closed down outside and the night sounds came up from the marsh and the stream that led from it. He put his arm around her and she kissed him, but it was a duty kiss and he let her go.

"Meg," he said, "we got things to talk about."

"Like ducks, Rocky? Like oysters?"

She was needling him again. She was always needling him to see what he would do. His anger flared. He reached for her. This time it was not routine. Not for him certainly, but not for her, either.

"Like that," he said. "We got that to talk about."

They watched the fire flare up, the shadows flickering. Her voice was small in the dimness. "So talk, then, Rocky."

He held her at arms' length, frowning at her. "Listen. I came here at first figuring to argue you into killing off those lousy ducks or maybe keeping them on land—anything so you wouldn't drive me and Mike and the rest out of business. So what happens?"

"What, Rocky?"

He jumped to his feet and took a turn about the room, coming back to stand glaring down at her.

"So this," he shouted. "So I fall for you, that's what happens. Me, the best oyster tonger in the bay, falling for a duck farmer. Mike's sore at me. I'm as welcome at the Snug as a sting ray. My oysters that

I planted myself are dying. And you know what? I don't give a hang for the lot of them. I'll take you, ducks and all."

It was a ridiculous way to do it. He knew it and he knew that she knew it, but if she laughed—. But she didn't. She stood quickly and put her arms around him.

"Rocky, you big overgrown lug, I—." Then she stopped. She drew back. He heard it too. The ducks. They were sending up a wild clacking and something tightened around his chest.

"Mike," he thought. "That old fool Mike."

Meg was out the door at a run, the rifle in one hand, and he tore out after her, calling to her to stop, to let him handle it. But she ran on toward the creek, so he put his head down and lengthened his stride; he would have caught her except that he stumbled over a root in the darkness. He arrived breathless on the bank just as the moon broke through. Mike was in the skiff, rowing for his life. The fence was gaping open. The ducks were in wild confusion, many of them on the bay side of the wire. And Meg had the rifle to her shoulder, taking aim.

He lunged for it but she was too quick. The bullet sent up a spout inches ahead of the skiff. Mike swore mightily and stood up, the boat rocking, his hands in the air. Meg waved him to shore. Rocky grabbed her arm.

"Now look, baby, you better give me that gun before somebody gets hurt."

But she backed away quickly and swung the barrel to cover him, too. She was crying, the tears running down her cheeks unheeded, but her hands on the rifle were steady.

"Get over there with your pal. It almost worked, didn't it, Rocky? You almost kept me thinking about other things long enough for this dirty old man to finish his business."

"Meg—. Meg, I swear I didn't know—."

She wavered. She wanted to believe him, and he could see the doubt rising in her. But she bit her lips and fought it down and marched them both to the house, making them sit on the same green sofa before the same fire while she telephoned Cal Higgins. The deputy came. His disappointment with Rocky was genuine. He had, he pointed out, warned him what would happen.

"Come on," he said, "get in my car. You, too, Miss Campbell. You got to sign the complaint."

They drove, Mike riding beside Higgins in the front seat, Rocky and Meg in the back. No one spoke. Rocky sat dejectedly, his mind filled with the unfairness of it all.

Then Mike began to chuckle to himself. "Anyway," he said, "I done it. Jail'll be worth it. Them ducks'll be scattered from hell to breakfast by morning."

Rocky snapped out of his lethargy. He leaned forward and grabbed Higgins' shoulder. "Let me out, Cal. Jug me in the morning if you want, but right now Meg and I got to catch those ducks."

The deputy jammed a heavy foot on the brake pedal. He turned toward the back seat angrily. "What you trying to pull?"

"I'm pulling nothing. Meg'll lose every cent if those birds get away. I'm not sitting here and letting her go broke. Just because she's too dumb to know she's got me gaffed makes no difference." Then he grinned. "Besides, Cal, I wasted too much time carrying mash to those stupid ducks to let 'em get lost now."

He opened the car door and jumped out. Meg sat uncertainly. He turned back to her, his voice loud with impatience. "What you waiting for? We cut across the dunes here, we're at my boat in five minutes. We get one fish net. We string it across the creek mouth. That keeps them out of the bay. We take the other net. We move upstream with it and herd 'em back. Come on, girl, move the body."

The deputy was looking at the girl. "You going along with this wild oysterman, Miss Campbell?"

She leaned forward. "You think he means it?"

Higgins considered. Then he nodded his heavy head. "Any oyster tonger who'd go thrashing around in the middle of the night chasing ducks means it all right. You win, Miss Campbell. Like he says, you got him gaffed. You got him hooked solid."

Mike snorted as he watched the girl hurry off after Rocky into the darkness.

"If old Bob Schwantes—," he began. But Higgins silenced him. "Maybe you don't remember, you dried up old cod," he said, "but there's at least one thing in life more important than oysters."

When Meg caught up with Rocky's long strides she touched his arm and he slowed down. "It'll work out," she said. "I can go half way. The ducks don't have to live in the water, I guess. You help me, we can pen them on shore. Then Mike and the guys at the Snug won't hate you any more."

He turned and grasped her shoulders roughly. "I don't care about that. But I won't have you believing I'm playing games with you."

She touched his cheek with her fingers. "Rocky, where were we back at the cottage? Where was it we left off ?"

He showed her. There were no ducks to interrupt this time. For a while, in fact, while the moon shone hazily and the night noises enveloped them, there were no such creatures as ducks in the world—or for that matter, any oysters in the sea. But finally they walked on.

"Rocky," Meg said, musing, needling him a little again to see what he'd say, "am I wrong or do people sometimes eat roast duck with oyster dressing? I was just thinking. I could cook it for you sometime. What do you think?"

He lifted her off the ground and swung her around and put her gently down again. "Sounds mighty tasty, Meg. Sounds great. Sounds like a combination a guy could spend the rest of his life enjoying." END

The Devil and Father Grymes

by James F. Ryan

"This is the last straw," Father Conlon said, gingerly fingering the the bright enamel of the machine. "If the Bishop doesn't retire him now, he's as dotty as the old man himself." He lunged forward and kicked the rear tire of the snowblower.

"He said something about it being our social responsibility to keep the sidewalks clear," Father Burke said.

"Social responsibility? He wouldn't let me spend sixty bucks on drug-abuse booklets for the Confraternity classes. I'll bet that thing cost four hundred."

"Five-sixty-five."

"You knew about it?"

"He sent me to Boston to pick it up."

"And you *went*?"

"What else could I do?" Father Burke said, not looking at the younger priest. He stroked the chrome-plated headlight on the handlebar cross-piece. "Besides, Angelo's getting too old for shoveling."

Father Conlon snorted. "Angelo's got more sense. He wouldn't touch that thing."

"The old man intends to use it himself."

"That's just great. The suffering pastor. I can picture the scene now. 'Good morning, Father Grymes. And where are all those strapping young curates of yours this snowy dawn?' 'Sure, you shouldn't blame them, Mrs. O'Hara. They weren't brought up to it. Persian princes, you know.' "

"It's a beautiful machine, though," Father Burke said. He flipped the headlight switch back and forth.

"It doesn't even work, Denny." Father Burke looked up. "The headlight. It didn't go on."

"Grymes took the battery up to his room."

"Is he really afraid we're going to play with it?"

"He said he wanted to check it."

"I wish someone would check him. Preferably a psychiatrist." Father Conlon walked over to the side window of the garage. He gestured toward the empty parking lot behind the rectory. "It hasn't snowed since just after Christmas. Two crummy inches. And that melted before Angelo got over here."

"He says March storms are the worst."

"In the Yukon, maybe. Not in Quincy," Father Conlon said. He reached through the open window of his Volkswagen for a half-eaten candy bar stashed in a corner of the dashboard. "We're going to be the laughingstock of the diocese, you know."

"St. Patrick's has one too, I hear."

"With all their money, I'm surprised they don't have a payloader! That's not a parish. It's a Bostonian empire. But why us? What brought this on, anyway?"

"Don't know," Father Burke said. Then he snapped his fingers. "Hey . . . You think it could have been when Mrs. Gerity fell on the ice outside the rectory?"

"Ice? She was loaded."

"We don't know that for a fact."

"Maybe *you* don't. I picked her up."

"She said she was on medication."

"Sure. Extract of gin," Father Conlon averred. "I guess we can't afford to have our flock landing on its loyal duff, now can we?"

"Mike!"

"Oh, come off it, Denny."

Father Burke spoke the name again, this time through his teeth. Father Conlon looked around slowly and caught sight of the pastor's grinning face framed in one of the panes of the roll-up door. He smiled weakly and unlatched the side entrance for Father Grymes.

"Good afternoon, gentlemen," the pastor said. "How do you like my little red devil?" He unzipped his bomber jacket and used a sleeve to buff the machine's name plate. "Have to keep old Beelzebub's face clean."

"It looks more like an antelope." Father Conlon said.

Father Grymes was about to say something when Father Burke spoke. "How's the battery?"

"Fine. 1300 in each cell."

"1300 what?" Father Conlon inquired.

"Specific gravity, Father, specific gravity." The pastor eased the battery into its compartment and looked up at Father Conlon. "Would you hand me the socket wrench over there, please?" Father Conlon stooped over and grasped one of the tools on the floor. "The *socket* wrench." He dropped it and reached for the other one. "Thank you, Father."

"Is that the right terminal?" Father Burke asked the pastor.

"Don't worry. The red lead is always positive."

Father Conlon cleared his throat. "Speaking of colors, that thing wouldn't look out of place on a hook and ladder."

"You're thinking it's fire-engine red, Father. Actually, it's Chinese red. Nearly vermilion. Quite sacerdotal when you think about it." He pressed the starter button. The machine snarled to life. Father Conlon tripped backward and fell against his car. "Open the doors."

"What?"

"The garage doors. Open them." Father Conlon recovered and yanked the door pull upward. Tire chains clinking, the snow blower rolled out onto the blacktop driveway. "Want to try it?" Father Conlon shook his head. The pastor revved the engine several times, then let it die. He winked at Father Conlon. "The devil's work must truly be our own."

At dinner, the pastor sat behind the operating manual he had propped up on a bud vase. He ate without speaking, except for an occasional grunt of recognition. "There," he said finally, closing the booklet and looking up at his curates, "that should do it."

"I was wondering," Father Conlon interjected, "if we really need that machine." Father Burke coughed and looked away.

"How do you mean?" Father Grymes asked. "Angelo has as much as he can do shovelling the . . ."

"I'm not talking about Angelo."

". . . school sidewalks and the Church property corner. And why do you always interrupt people when they're speaking?"

"I'm sorry, but what I meant to say was that the teenagers in the parish would be only too happy to help with the . . ."

"And what makes you think that, Father?" The pastor tapped his fingers on the booklet. "Would you have been 'only too happy' at their age?"

"But it's just a matter of motivation," Father Conlon allowed. "They want to contribute. They want to feel a part of what's going on around here. They want to be asked."

"But not at five in the morning."

"I think you underestimate them."

"I think you overestimate yourself." The pastor raised his palm. "Now don't be offended. Nothing personal. We're all accustomed to having certain little things done for us. There's a long history of it. It's not entirely our fault we live like Persian princes."

Father Conlon pushed his chair back from the table and started to rise. "I don't feel much like a Persian prince."

.

"Oh? Have you ever washed a dish, Father?" Father Conlon sagged back onto his seat. "Father?"

"At summer camp once, I . . ."

After breakfast the next morning, the pastor led both his curates into the garage. "Not that I foresee such an eventuality, of course," he was saying, "but if I'm not around, I do want you gentlemen to know how to handle the machine."

"Why?" Father Conlon asked.

Father Grymes leaned his weight on the handlebars of the snow blower and stared at his young curate. "Father, I assure you I'll do my best to prevent the inclement weather we sometimes have from interfering with your pre-dawn meditations. But the machine is part of the parish plant now, and I think it's my obligation to familiarize you with its operation."

"That's not what I meant."

"I realize that. But you shouldn't be afraid of it. It's very simple."

"I'm *not* afraid of it."

Father Grymes stepped back. "All right then. Start it." Father Conlon slipped between the handlebars and moved his fingers across to the starter button. "No, Father. Try the pull cord. In case you ever found the battery dead." He hunched over the carburetor, his eyes searching frantically for something appropriate. He reached out for the small wooden toggle. "Choke, Father." He glared up at the pastor. "On the control panel." With the heel of his palm, Father Conlon slammed the black plastic ball forward. "Gently." This time he grasped the cord and pulled as hard as he could. Nothing happened. He yanked it again, then once more.

"Something must be wrong."

The pastor sniffed. "It's not a matter of brute strength. A snap of the wrist should do it. You try it, Father Burke." The other priest started the engine on his first attempt. "Good for you, Father," the pastor said. "Now the controls." He pointed to the two levers. "This one: forward speed—half and full. No reverse. This other is the blade clutch. Disengages the rotor. Always disengage before you change the position of the chute."

He guided the snow blower out of the garage and down the driveway, spraying loose gravel toward the grammar school. The eighth-graders already had their wide-eyed faces pressed to the window panes.

"Denny, I think I'm going to puke," Father Conlon said. "I'll bet he did something so it wouldn't start for me."

"Don't be paranoid."

"Look at the old fool."

Just then the school door opened. Out stepped the principal. She crunched her way across the lawn, kicking up divots with every step. "Father!" she screamed. "You're frightening the children." The pastor cupped his hand behind his ear. "The children!" He cut the engine.

"Father, what *is* that dreadful machine?" Sister Anise asked, dusting off her habit.

"A snow blower. For clearing the sidewalks."

"You mean it blows the snow away?"

The pastor chuckled. "Not exactly, Sister." He crouched down. "This rotary blade here throws the snow out the chute."

She bent over, level with him. "How clever! Archimedes' screw."

Behind Father Burke, Father Conlon muttered. "No, Conlon's." The other priest coughed.

"And such a lovely color, Father," Sister Anise exlaimed. "Though I must say the name chills me a bit."

"The root of a great Christian mystery, Sister," Father Grymes said, grinning. "Putting the devil to work for us."

"I'm sure you're right, Father. Well, I'll certainly have something to tell the children about, won't I?"

Father Grymes reached into the zippered pocket of his jacket and pulled out the operating manual. "This may be of some help there, Sister."

"Oh, yes. Thank you." She turned and stared up at the school windows. The children faded back to their desks. "Good morning, Fathers."

The pastor smiled at his curates and pointed toward the thin negligee of clouds lingering in the western sky. "That, gentlemen, could be the start of something big."

Not until late the following week did it finally snow. It must have begun in the middle of the night. Father Conlon woke to the alto growl of the little red devil shortly before five. He rolled over and listened more intently. Mostly slush, he decided, judging from the heavy splashing of the slop leaving the chute. More than likely it would all have disappeared before dawn, if left alone.

The engine stalled with a cough. Out of gas? Too much to hope for. He waited for the inevitable churning. A minute. Two. He climbed from bed and hopped across the cold hardwood flooring. More snow than he'd thought. Nickel-sized flakes ignited momentarily as they passed the headlamp of the snow blower. When his eyes adjusted to the glare, he saw Father Grymes lying on his side, both hands clutched to his chest? Heart? Father Conlon snatched up his robe and took the stairs by threes. A hem snagged on the bannister post. He released the robe and went through the front door in his shorts.

"Father!" he shouted from the top step.

The pastor was sitting up now. His eyes, creased with pain, popped open. "Go back! You've got no clothes on."

"Is it your heart?"

"Go back, Conlon. You're *naked!*"

"I'm not naked. I have underwear on. Is it your heart?"

"No," Father Grymes said weakly. "I forgot to disengage." He took his arms away from his chest. In his left hand he was holding at least half his right index and middle fingers.

"Oh my God!" Father Conlon said. "Put them back."

"What do you mean, put them *back*?"

"I mean . . . hold them back. Hold them in place." He stripped off his tee shirt and wrapped it around the pastor's hand.

"You'll catch pneumonia."

"Don't worry about me. You just sit here for a minute." He ran back into the rectory and pulled on the old dungarees and ski jacket he kept in the hall closet. While he was working his wet feet into a pair of loafers, Father Burke appeared at the head of the stairs.

"What's going on?"

"Grymes had an accident with the snow blower."

"Bad?"

"Yeah."

"I'll call an ambulance."

"Don't bother. I can get him there faster myself."

In the car, Father Grymes was silent for the first mile. When he spoke, he was strangely calm. "The devil won after all, didn't he, Father?" Father Conlon pretended to be preoccupied with signalling for a turn. "Of course, I asked for it. I lusted after that machine. Do you know I couldn't sleep the night I saw it advertised in the paper? I was awake almost till morning trying to justify it to myself when I knew it was only lust. Like a child with a toy he didn't deserve."

"Don't be silly, Father. It was just an accident. It could've happened to anyone."

"No," the pastor said.

The sleepy intern in the emergency room began unwinding the make-shift bandage on Father Grymes' hand with little more than moderate interest. When he got down to the last few turns, he called to a nurse in the hall. "Get Maddox," he ordered. "O. R. work." He turned back to Father Conlon. "He's going to need surgery, Father. Dr. Maddox is resident here, and he's a real expert with this kind of problem."

After they had transferred the pastor to an operating room cart, he and Father Conlon were left alone in the dim hallway by the elevator.

"Mike," Father Grymes said. "Never challenge the devil. Fight him when you have to, but never challenge him."

"I'll remember that, Father."

"He may lose battles, but he never loses challenges."

Father Conlon noted the beginnings of tears in the old man's eyes. "Is the pain very bad?" he asked softly.

The pastor shook his head. "I just realized . . . They won't let me say Mass anymore."

"What do you mean?"

"It's against Canon Law. You can't say Mass with mutilated hands."

"That canon must be a thousand years old."

"Still in effect, though." The tears, past his temples now, were racing towards his ears.

"You're forgetting about dispensations." The young priest's face brightened. "Remember? They dispensed Saint Isaac Jogues after the Indians cut his fingers off."

Father Grymes managed a smile. "That's the problem, Mike. I'm no Isaac Jogues." Two attendants wheeled his cart into the elevator.

It was still snowing when Father Conlon left the hospital. He drove home cautiously and left the car in the driveway. On his way to the rectory door, he noticed the snow blower sitting where they'd left it. He walked over and pressed the starter button. Nothing. The headlight was still on, its filament barely hot. "Damn you!" he exclaimed vehemently—then gave the pull cord a wrist snap and finished the sidewalk before breakfast.   END

The Lesson

by Sam C. Brown, Jr.

It seemed at the time as though it was all Harry's fault—that's my cousin, Harry—but in retrospect I have to admit that I was almost, if perhaps not quite, as much to blame as he was. I tended to blame him partly because he was older than I—nearly nineteen, while I was sixteen and a half—but also partly, I realize now, because I needed a scapegoat so as to keep my good intentions from seeming to pave the wrong road. But hell-bent they were, and I with them; and just because it was Harry's idea does not eradicate the keen pleasure I took in first following Harry, and then acting as his accomplice.

Poaching lobsters was what we were up to—I say "poaching" now, as I did then, not merely because it was technically that, but because it sounds more innocuous than "stealing" or "robbing." But robbery it was, in fact—larceny of the highest order—for we were depriving a man not merely of the fruits of his labor, but of the source of his entire income. A good analogy would be the theft or destruction of row after row of a wheat farmer's crop, irreplaceable until the next year's harvest. The enormity of our crime didn't occur to me, of course, at the time. I was a summer visitor who was exposed at home mostly to professional men, people like my lawyer father, whose sources of income were pretty much all in their heads. You can rob a lawyer of every bit of material worth he owns, and he can still practice law in a borrowed suit; but a lobsterman with consistently empty traps cannot earn his living.

But as I say, none of this was evident to Harry and me that summer; we were just caught up in the excitement of the theft, on open water (why, right in plain sight!), of those little creatures whose meat we found so succulent when boiled the next afternoon in our rocky grotto on the shore. Our fathers, who were brothers, had regularly brought their children to the Maine coast for a vacation which always included several lobster feeds. Ever since our folks had introduced us to the dish when we were ex-toddlers, we had both loved fresh lobster, boiled in salt water under seaweed, dunked in melted butter, and eaten on a barnacled rock above the swirling tide.

This summer, Harry's family had sent us up to their shore cottage a week before they came up for their August vacation, and we were to "open the place" and keep constructively busy in a "safe" environment. The week before, Harry had been picked up by the police along with several friends on charges, later dropped, of disturbing the peace, and he and his parents were ready for a temporary separation. My parents were receptive to their suggestion that I accompany Harry, principally, I think, because they did not much approve of the girl I was dating at the time, a moist-eyed, giggly gazelle I had taken quite a shine to. There was nothing at all wrong with her, but to parents I guess a teenager's girlfriend is generally either idiotic or slatternly, or both. And so we were sent to Maine as a way of keeping us off the streets. Ironically, we would probably have been into less real trouble in suburban Boston.

Our first day there together had been easy enough to kill, opening padlocked doors and shuttered windows, sweeping out minimal living space, de-mousing our sleeping quarters, and getting in a supply of food. But our adolescent interest in constructive projects was typically limited, though our energy was typically not; and after two nights of filling the silence with jokes about our school chums and arrogantly smoking cigarettes openly in the house (even Harry had not yet dared do so in front of his parents), we were bored.

"Hey, Mark." Harry that morning was sprawled indolently over a chair leaned up against the sunlit kitchen window. "Let's do something."

"Sure." I fumbled for a cigarette. "Feel like a swim or something?"

"Naw. 's too cold." Harry fingered a shade pull and looked out the window toward our rude boathouse. "We might get the dory out."

"Okay." I peered out the door toward the bay in the direction Harry was looking. Blinding bits of sunlight were bursting like continuous shrapnel from the surface of the water. It hurt to look. A bit to the left of this fiery display was a reef, an island really, partially exposed even at high tide, surrounded by a great many lobster buoys, tiny bobbing specks that trailed in kite-tail fashion off toward the eastern point of the mainland. Something larger bobbed evenly near the reef. "Hey, Harry," I said, "there's a lobster boat."

"Lobster!" Harry sat up. "Hey, that's for us." He got out of the chair expectantly. "Whaddya say, lobster feed tonight?"

"Good idea." I dragged on my cigarette, still looking out at the lobster boat with its tiny single helmsman, chugging now to a new buoy off the reef. The boat slowed, its stern heaving sluggishly, and the lobsterman hooked a buoy and began to haul in the line. "We'll have to drive over to Evans' Wharf to the lobster pound. Got any money?"

"Yeah. Some." Harry, too, watched as the distant lobsterman gracefully pulleyed the heavy trap to the gunwale, flipped open its lid, and began to toss back into the sea the many undersized lobsters which customarily were caught in it. Harry was silent for a moment. "You still want to work on the dory?" he asked.

"Sure. Nothin' else to do. But let's go get some lobsters first. And butter. And hey!" I squashed out my cigarette with slight nervous agitation. "Maybe we could get some beer!"

"Yeah." Harry obviously wasn't listening very closely. We both loved beer, but had never been able to get any except when our parents, mellowed by a vacation cocktail, had allowed us each a can. I was thinking now that we might drive around until we found an out-of-the-way grocery store where Harry's deep voice and mature height might pass for those of a twenty-one-year-old. Surely Harry would be interested. "Some beer, eh, Harry?"

"Wait a minute." He screwed up his eyes, peering at the distant boat. "Why don't we save our dough? *We* could do that."

"We could do what? Save dough on beer? How?"

"No, *we* could do *that*—" he gestured—"in the dory." He turned to me. "Pull some traps. He does it alone. There's two of us. *We* could do *that*."

"Pull traps?" I paused, reflective. "But we don't have any, Harry—?"

"Yeah, but *he* does."

"You mean, steal his lobsters?" I felt let down. "Aw, we can buy 'em."

"Look at him. He throws out most of all of 'em anyway. We wouldn't take the big ones. No problem. Hey, Mark?" Harry's eyes flickered. "Let's get at that dory."

I was not convinced. Theft did not particularly appeal to my moral sense, and I wasn't sure I'd know how to haul a trap. But those reasons could not be expressed publicly, of course; so I said, "I don't know, Harry. Suppose we get caught?"

"Caught? With what evidence? Anyone comes by, we just toss 'em back in the bay. And what lobsterman that you know of ever takes his boat out at night?"

"You mean we'll go out and pull traps in the dark?" I asked.

"Sure," Harry said. "Aw, we'll be able to see okay out on the open water. And there won't be any chance of being caught by a nosy lobster boat at *night*."

That pretty well did it. I was still uneasy about the idea of theft, but Harry had obliterated any argument I could, at that age and under those circumstances, effectively present. I almost (but not quite) wished that Mom and Dad were around so that I could protest that it would be impossible to pull it off without their knowledge. But what the hell, I thought; it sounded pretty darn exciting.

That afternoon, we lugged out the family dory, strenuously shoved it down the ramp into the water, marked the obvious leaks, hauled the boat out and caulked it, and lowered it in again to let it swell. It wouldn't really be tight for a couple of days and until we'd caulked it again, but it was not an old boat and would certainly serve us that night. Then, sweaty and happily absorbed in our project, we drove off to seek beer.

After we'd driven for about five miles, we saw a little grocery store on the left. MORRILL'S STORE, a sign said, and another sign proclaimed COLD BEER TO GO. We pulled in, got out of the car, and went into the store. I was jittery, so I let Harry lead the way.

A middle-aged man with wire-rimmed glasses jutted up behind the counter. "H'lo, fellas," he said. "What can I get you?"

Harry tried to look casual as he surveyed the glass-doored refrigeration compartment behind the counter with its army of assorted beers, ales, and soft drinks. "Hmm," he said. "Guess I'll take two six-packs of, uh, Miller's."

The man turned and procured the beer without a blink. He put it on the counter. "Anything else, fellas?" he asked brightly.

"No, thanks," Harry said, and paid for the beer. We walked out quickly, waiting until we were in the car again to cackle delightedly at each other. "You hot ticket!" I said. "Tut-tut," said Harry, "all in a day's work." We chuckled for several minutes. I felt exuberant; my last trace of uneasiness had disappeared. We were men! And we were going on a lobstering adventure!

We ate a regular supper that evening, figuring that we'd have our lobster feed the next afternoon after our midnight excursion. The time passed slowly until after dark; we had a can of beer each and played some cards, but were really too nervous to do anything well. We each lost a hand of gin rummy through pure carelessness, discarding the wrong cards, and ultimately we lost interest.

Finally, after looking out the windows for hours (forty-five minutes, perhaps), Harry decreed that it was dark enough to set out. We put on our jackets, climbed into the boat, and began to row stealthily out through the slightly choppy water. There was no moon; not a vessel was in sight on the bay. The perfect crime!

"Here's one." Harry was at the oars. "I'll back up to it. You grab it." The black water swirled around the stern as Harry maneuvered the boat toward the small bobbing buoy. The breeze gusted a bit, whipping cold droplets of water from the wet oars across my face. I shivered. Off to my left, a few lights glimmered on the point beyond our house; straight ahead was the faintly visible reef, and far beyond was the dark horizon. The buoy was far colder and heavier than I had imagined it would be, but I got it into the boat all right. I wondered if it was the beer that was making me a little shaky.

Harry shipped the oars. "Lemme give you a hand." Together we pulled the slimy potwarp up over the transom. The darned thing was bigger around than it looked lying in coils on the shore near Frank's Lobster Pound, and the slime made it hard to grip. But, with a few grunts and an occasional loss of balance, we got the line all the way up—and there came the trap: it emerged darkly, with a rush of water, and banged against the boat.

"Hey! Not so loud!" Harry said. I fumbled, and the trap slipped back a foot or so and submerged with a swish. "Sorry!" I whispered hoarsely. "Couldn't help it." "Well don't let it *slip*, for God's sake!" Harry's breath was hissing through his teeth now. It was hard work. We pulled together and got it lodged precariously over the gunwale, where it teetered and drained noisily.

Suddenly we heard a noise like a wet towel being snapped loudly several times—FWADASAPAPAP—and we practically lost the trap again. "What the hell was *that?*" I gasped. Then it dawned on us that it was a lobster, flapping his tail as he always does out of water in a vain attempt to propel himself back into the sea. We both broke into hoarsely voiceless laughter. "Damn lobster!" Harry said. From then on it was easier. We emptied the lobsters into the boat (they all seemed undersized to us) and let the trap gently—"Watch it now!" back into the water, smiling even as we panted, and occasionally imitating both the lobster's flapping noise and our own earlier fright, *"Fwadasapapap!"* and wheezed laughter. We were having a ball!

We worked for perhaps twenty-five minutes, pulling three traps, before we had what we thought would be an ample feed for the two of us: about eight rather small lobsters. To ease our consciences, we did leave two or three larger lobsters in the last two traps. "It's kinda funny," Harry remarked as he swished the lobsters around in the bilge, "there's so few of 'em in any one trap." I pulled on the oars. "Well, Har," I offered, "you don't get rich lobstering." We didn't say much else till we got to shore.

The next afternoon we built a fire in the shadow of a large overhanging rock near the high-water mark not far from the house. The horizon was misty, but the sun was out and our beer was cold and plentiful, and we felt pretty good. "Darn fine catch, captain!" Harry said as he cracked open his third claw. Butter dribbled randomly down my chin and the breeze ruffled my hair and T-shirt. Behind us, the fire cracked and smoked. I smiled broadly and took a quick pull at my beer. "You bet," I said.

"Hey, Harry, there he is again." Across the dancing sunlit ripples, we could see the lobsterman hauling his traps near the reef-island. Harry sloshed a chunk of lobster up and down in the can of melted butter and wiped his chin. "Seems to me I recognize that white buoy with the blue band," he said, and threw me a grin. "How 'bout you?"

"Can't recall. Does it go *fwadasapapap?*" We both roared. The lobsterman, we noticed, wasn't throwing out any undersized lobsters from these traps. "Guess we saved him some trouble." "Anything to help a fellow lobsterman," Harry said. We roared again, our laughter becoming the tear-producing giggles that leave one weak in the stomach and euphoric. Only in adolescence can this kind of gentle sadism be so amusing; I wonder, in retrospect, what had gotten into us.

The success and pleasure produced by our initial poaching experiment buoyed us for an inevitable second night of crime, and the confidence inspired by that success led to a third. Before we knew it, we had poached four nights running, becoming bolder each time, ultimately taking only the biggest lobsters and actually throwing the undersized ones back into the bay. This move was perhaps the unwisest of all, at least as far as escaping detection was concerned, for it left each trap completely empty at eleven p.m. and hence likely to be nearly empty when the owner pulled them next morning. Like all amateur criminals, especially those whose intent is far less malicious than the damage done, we did not give sufficient attention to the details which can lead to detection. We also failed to give enough credit to our unidentified victim, the lobsterman. He turned out to be far more wise, and we far more stupid, than we had imagined.

On the fifth night of poaching, Harry and I set out at about ten thirty, a little later than usual, after having a couple of beers each in the house. We were positively heady, not so much from the liquor as from an inflated sense of our own powers. We had hauled heavy traps, eaten free lobster, and drunk illegal brew for nearly five days straight without a hitch, and we were, I fear, more than a little wild-eyed and arrogant. The world, so to speak, was our lobster. And so we donned our light jackets and pushed off into the unusually still water of this particular night without even lowering our voices. Harry made an obscene noise from the stern seat, and I laughed so hard that I nearly dropped one oar into the water. Harry grabbed it with a great clatter, and we whooped a bit as the dory lurched awkwardly.

We were in the midst of hauling our third trap—giggling and joking about the heavy slime on the potwarp—when Harry suddenly bcame still and said, "Shsh!"

I stopped giggling and put one hand on the dripping gunwale. "What?" I whispered.

"Motor." I looked up and listened. From not too far off at all came a putt-putt-putt-putt. The lobster boat!

"Where is it?" I whispered.

"Can't see," Harry replied, tensing. "No lights?"

"Quick! Drop the trap!"

"No, don't drop it! Too loud! Lower it!"

We eased the trap into the water and hurriedly cast the line and buoy after it. "Let's get out of here," Harry said, and quickly put the oars in the water and began to row.

The putt-putt of the approaching vessel grew louder and clearer. No doubt about it, it was a lobster boat. But why no lights? I froze in the stern seat, my eyes darting around trying to see through the heavy moonless night. Suddenly the reef exploded in light. To the right of it, a powerful searchlight threw its beam onto the reef, then began knifing in other directions. *My God*, I thought. *The lobsters!*

In our haste we had completely forgotten that several lobsters lay partly submerged in the bilge of the dory. Absolute evidence! We'd be killed!

"Throw 'em out!" he whispered frantically, pulling at the oars as fast as he could without making a racket.

"Too many," I said. "Cover 'em!" I yanked off my jacket and bid Harry do likewise. He shook his head vigorously and kept rowing. I managed to get all the lobsters under my jacket (which became immediately soaked in bilgewater) just before the searchlight struck us. Straightening up from a crouch, I saw Harry's nervous face and awkwardly positioned body piercingly illuminated against an invisible background. Harry froze.

The searchlight bobbed a bit and pushed ahead until it was nearly upon us. The putt-putting died to a low rumble, and some smaller lights went on, revealing the dim outlines of a high prow, a long hull, and a stiff little cabin. The searchlight clicked off, and over its dying lens came a voice.

"Evenin', boys." Pause.

"H-hi," Harry stammered.

A flashlight clicked on and played on the two of us and the dory. The waves lapped at the hulls of both boats and seemed, impossibly, to drown the sound of the engine's muffled burbling. Harry moved the oars a bit in the water and tried to look relaxed.

"Out f'r a row, boys?" Pause.

"Yeah," Harry said. He gestured toward the shore. "We—we're in there. Our house." The flashlight beam caught his face and he turned his eyes toward me. "We kind of like to row. Good dory."

"Yes 'tis, boys," the faceless voice replied evenly, almost softly. The flashlight beam moved to me, then to the floor of the dory.

"You always leave your jacket in the bilge, son?"

I shivered. A small breeze rippled my T-shirt. "Warm night," I said weakly. It was warm, but not so warm as to make one discard a jacket carelessly in the bilge. He would catch us. I knew he would!

The pale beam of light slid around the edges of my jacket as it partly floated, partly lay over the lobsters. I held my breath; Harry and I stared in terror at it. What if one of the lobsters should crawl out? What if—

FWADASAPAPAP.

The jacket flapped; the flashlight clicked off. An enormous silence followed. I could hear nothing but the pounding in my ears.

FWADASAPAPAPapap.

"Boys." Pause.

"Boys, you row right over here." The voice had a new note of quiet but powerful urgency. Harry swallowed hard and backed the dory clumsily up to the side of the lobster boat.

I looked up from the stern and saw the gradually visible face of the lobsterman. He wore a small dark yachting cap pulled low over a large, sharp nose and hollow cheeks. His neck seemed too thick for the thin face; but his eyes quickly distracted me from the rest of him. He had the quietest, most unfathomable eyes I had ever seen. They could have been intensely angry or thoroughly benign; I could not tell. But they scared me to death.

"Boys," he said. "Someone's been pullin' my traps." He leaned over the gunwale and I noticed a slight tremor in his hands and face. "I make a living' on them traps. If they're empty, I got nothin'."

He paused for a moment, staring very deeply at Harry, who was transfixed, frozen to the oars. The lobsterman straightened up slightly and reached into his boat. When he leaned over again, one hand held a plank of wood, and the other a shotgun.

I was about to yell out, but the lobsterman began to talk in his quietly urgent way before I had a chance. I checked myself. "Boys," he said, "I want you to see what'll happen if I ketch them poachuhs."

With a sudden thrust he chucked the plank over the dory. My eyes followed it to where it splashed heavily into the water just beyond our gunwale. Before I could turn my gaze again toward the lobster boat, the silence was shattered with a deafening blast that caused me literally to jump off my seat and Harry to drop the oars into the dory with a clatter. There in the foaming water which rocked our boat bobbed the two halves of the former plank.

When I looked back, breathless and with heart pounding furiously, the lobsterman was putting his shotgun back into the boat. He settled himself down with hands on the gunwale again and looked at us, his jaws working.

"I don't shoot folks," he said. "But I don't mind shootin' a boat if I have to." He paused for emphasis and lowered his voice. "Mighty hard swimmin' ashore at night."

In another moment, he had straightened up, taken the helm, and revved up the engine. The lobster boat putt-putted to a deafening staccato, spun heavily away from us, and left the dory on a rising swell which made us lunge to keep our balance. Harry grabbed the oars.

"Holy God," I said. "Holy, holy God."

"Throw 'em out!" Harry fairly shouted. I grabbed my jacket and threw out the lobsters as fast as I could. Harry pulled at the oars and we headed for shore, both of us shaking rather badly.

As I reflected much later on our narrow escape, I realized that the lobsterman would have been perfectly justified in sinking our dory that night instead of merely shattering a plank. This fact has given me an enduring respect for the principle that no man is automatically entitled to the fruits of another's labor. But more important, I think, is the fact that he chose *not* to sink the dory; for he impressed our minds indelibly with a lesson about the efficacy of charity in matters of justice. He was a remarkably wise man.   END

Chicken-Soup Thursday

by Eileen M. James

When I was a little girl, the only folks who were sent off to Homes For The Aged came from either very poor families or very rich ones. Fortunately, ours was neither, so my grandmother, Louise Francine Redmond, lived with us. She slept on a small folding cot under the window in my room and everyone praised my cheerful unselfishness over the arrangement. The truth was I loved having her with me.

At night, when the house was dark (except for the gloomy hall light), she'd come to my bed (which for some strange reason was larger than hers even though I was smaller), sit guru style (before gurus were fashionable), and tell me ghost stories. They never scared me, but to make her happy I'd groan and shudder noisily, until she had to put her small white hand over my mouth lest my mother pad down the narrow corridor in her maroon felt slippers.

I wasn't one to make friends easily—at least friends my own age. I remember how, so often at breakfast (this was before my grandmother moved in with us), my mother would be daintily spooning out my soft boiled eggs and telling me I should bring a few of the children from school to our house occasionally for popcorn and cocoa. It was nice of her to be concerned, I admit . . . but the children from school were all so silly.

That's why when Grandmother Redmond came I stopped being lonely and difficult. We hung around together like pals, and although the neighbors and a few relatives thought it was rather unseemly, my parents didn't fuss. I guess they were glad in a way to have us both occupied and out of their hair.

Thursday was *her* day in the kitchen. Before she came to stay, my father had worked out an elaborate plan on paper so that things would go smoothly between his wife and mother. The Thursday-in-the-kitchen idea was part of this. Mama would take the twins (who were younger than I) to a kiddie movie, and I'd stay with Francine (which is what she wanted me to call her when it was us two alone).

Sometimes we made pecan fudge for my father, or sugar cookies for the twins, or cupcakes for mother's sewing club . . . but best of all was when we made chicken soup.

I say "we" truthfully. My grandmother believed that learning was doing. Not like Mama. Mama would let me watch her, or bring her the salt or flour and sometimes, if she were in a particularly good mood (usually on payday or if her quilt had won a prize), she'd let me stir. Francine let me do everything myself. She'd just lean against the door jamb and read the recipe aloud while I followed each direction with all the skill of a nine-and-a-half-year-old chef. Though occasionally I'd spill something or break a measuring cup, I never got burnt or scorched a pot. Still, my cooking was something we never told Mama about.

One of the reasons I liked chicken-soup Thursday so much was because the chicken soup wasn't for home. When it was finished my grandmother would pour it into thick green glass jars, let it cool a bit, and then fill a wicker basket up. We'd go visiting with the heavy load secure over her arm, leaving off one or two jars at each house.

Over the years, Francine had acquired an amazing assortment of friends.

There was Hildegard Flisk, a retired exotic dancer. She lived over a bawdy, sour-smelling tavern in a small, stained, yellow room with vasefuls of dusty plastic roses. Her clothes looked like old costumes remade with sequins and fringes strategically placed to camouflage the moth holes and grease marks. Since Hildegard weighed well over 200 pounds, it was difficult to imagine she had ever really danced.

Once, a stiff wooden chair she sat in had collapsed before our very eyes. I turned a sickly shade of blue, choking desperately on my suppressed giggles until Francine herself began to roar. Her laughter was so contagious that Hildegard, still a heap of splotched pink flesh and ugly gold taffeta on the floor, began to sputter giddily from her shiny red mouth, and I was at last released from my prison of good manners.

Hildegard would usually set up three bowls when we came and a plate of crackers. She made slurping sounds as she ate, and I knew that mother would never have sat at that table—slurping annoyed her terribly. But Grandmother and I didn't mind at all. After we had our fill of soup, Miss Flisk would heave herself up, go to a locked cabinet and get out a dish of gluey pink taffy. The stuff stuck to the roof of my mouth and went down my throat in a painful lump, but back then anything vaguely sweet was worth the trouble.

A few times Hildegard had beer in her window box—usually the day after the iceman came. On those afternoons she'd pour two foamy glassfuls and give one to my grandmother. It was the only time I saw her drink anything stronger than tea. We added that to the long list of things which had to be kept from my mother.

Another recipient of our succulent soup was Mr. Fiori, a pleasant gray-haired junk dealer with a bushy dark mustache. He owned a large shabby place in the business district. His "junk" was up front in two high-ceilinged rooms with patterned stains that widened after each rainfall. When we came, he put the "Closed" sign on the door and led us back through a curtain to the "house" part. While he and Grandmother reminisced (they had known each other forever, it seemed), I roamed freely through the furniture-stuffed rooms.

Quietly I peeked in closets thick with dust and heavy pieces of clothing, and in trunks—though a little hesitantly because I was sure that one day I'd have to find a body in one. (For the record, I never did.) Not that there was anything sinister about Mr. Fiori. He was warm and open and had a friendly booming voice . . . it was just all those Frankenstein movies I had seen.

Upstairs on the second floor, there was a huge mahogany piano, scratched a bit, keys chipped and discolored, that definitely needed a tuning. One day, more restless than usual, I pulled from the piano one of those piano scarfs with the fringe that used to be in vogue and amused myself by doing an exotic tango in front of the full-length mirror that was fastened to the door. When I got tired playing Ramona, I went to replace the cloth and noticed that the piano lid could be lifted. It was a wonder the keys had moved at all, because lying neatly within were several bottles of red wine. When I told Grandmother (in whispers of course) she just crinkled her eyes and smiled. Later she reminded me not to tell Mama.

I guess of all the people we visited Mr. Fiori was our all-time favorite. Francine blushed and cooed under his genuinely fond eyes. To him she had never gotten old but was the same girl he had known over fifty years ago.

My reason for liking him was a little more tangible—just before we'd leave, he'd remove the "Closed" sign from his door and open the cash register with a *brrrinng*. How I delighted at the sound. As though he were giving, and I receiving the Hope diamond—he'd place two shining quarters in my hand. To avoid explanations to Mama, I always spent it before we got home, usually on goodies from the bakery or candy shop. Francine and I would stuff ourselves.

Our Thursday pattern continued on to Mrs. Higgens' apartment on Front Street, facing a sluggish and dismal river. She was a pinched, hysterical woman who hated the mournful boat whistles that penetrated her walls day and night. When she found us at the door, her eyes grew wide and luminous like cold castle fires. She'd stretch her bony hands out to the ragged couch where the three of us would park in a formal row. Her non-stop whine recounted all the gory waterfront news. And then she would pull out a dirty handkerchief from her long

sleeve and cry that she couldn't stand the place another minute. Grandmother would pat her on the back and tell her better times were coming.
We used to have tea there—until I discovered a roach nest in the
kitchen. From then on, we shortened our visits at Mrs. Higgens'
place.

Freddie lived near the river too, but his room looked out on the city.
Freddie had no last name. He was a chalk-white skeleton of a man with
a saintly smile. I had to be quiet at Freddie's because Grandmother told
me he was dying. He was young. Younger even than my father, which
surprised me because I thought only very old people (near 100) died.
Once I started to ask him if he were scared about dying, but Francine
glared at me. The first, last and only time she ever did. From then on
I kept strict silence at Freddie's. While Grandmother spoon-fed him
and bathed his face with cold water and straightened up the room, I
stayed curled up on the window seat, watching the smoke rise from the
skyscrapers and thinking about what dying would be like. I'd close my
eyes and soak up the darkness and imagine God and Heaven and Hell
and Limbo and all those other places. When it got to be time to leave,
Freddie would tremble and shake. I'd run out and wait for Francine on
the street. It was usually a half hour before she came out. "Had to get
Freddie more blankets, and make sure that his medicine was right
next to the bed," she'd say, with deliberate nursing brightness. I knew
her well enough, though, to see that she was squeezing the tears
back inside.

Our last stop was usually Miss Cindy's fine brick house. She had
shiny furniture, crystal lamps, red velvet drapes, thick blue carpeting,
and a small terrier dog that I hated because he'd bark and sniff at my
stockings the whole time. I was curious why we had to visit Miss Cindy
at all, since she was (to my childish mind) as rich as Rockefeller.

"Just because a person has money doesn't mean that they stop needing
people"—Francine's wisdom.

For Grandmother's sake I really tried hard to like Miss Cindy, but
I never succeeded, perhaps because even though she had a full-to-brim-
ming cookie jar she'd only let me have two. However, I was extremely
well-behaved at Miss Cindy's, where I sat with my hands in my lap,
saying bad words under my breath to her pet but smiling politely at her.

For an always eternal twenty minutes, she talked to Francine about
the wretched hired girls who never did anything, and the old gardener's
daughter who had gotten into "trouble," or the tragedy of a valuable
porcelain plate breaking.

That visit over, we turned towards home. My mother and the twins would be waiting on the front porch if the weather were nice. Grand-mother would nod, then take her basket into the house, leaving me there to answer Mama's questions about the day.

Francine knew that I could be trusted to leave the right things out . . . Like I never told my mother that we went to see a dying man—she would have made us boil our clothes and take strong lye soap baths in steaming water. And I never told her about Hildegard Flisk's im-mense cleavage, or Mrs. Higgens' roach nest. And never a word about how Mr. Fiori would kiss Grandmother, sometimes on the mouth, when they thought I was upstairs rummaging.

And every night, right after prayers, when Mama would ask me with her self-assured smile whom I loved more than anybody else in the world (besides God and Jesus), I never said Grandmother. It was the one lie that bothered me.   **END**

Our Three Nazis

by Mary P. Sherwood

Regardless of ten-year-old Sammy's insatiable passion for mustard sandwiches, he was one popular youngster at our school's summer camp. Sammy was a Jewish refugee from Austria, whom we had acquired from the foreign legation that summer of 1939; a small, under-sized boy, whose fetching personality led us to contact the legation again.

"Sammy was such a nice experience," we wrote them, "we would like to offer a scholarship for our school to a refugee of high-school age." They telegraphed back, asking if we had room for two boys, guaranteeing a financial sponsor for the second boy. We were crowded, and had already turned away several well-to-do applicants, and many with high grades, from our own country. But we finally decided that refugees wouldn't mind a tight squeeze.

Came the day of arrival. Roger and Nancy, seniors with great pride in their mountain school, drove the horse and buggy the three miles down to the village. A car and a faculty driver were available, but Sammy had so loved a horse and buggy that everyone wanted the new refugees to be met that way. The new boys could have the fun of taking turns driving the horse up to their first American school.

Off the train onto the platform stepped three handsome young men. Not only were there three instead of two, but they were tall, mature-looking, immaculately attired, and exuded such perfect continental manners that Nancy and Roger dissolved into clumsy country hicks. In strongly accented, but correct, disdainful English, the three refugees ordered the students to put their baggage in the buggy and call a taxi for them.

A welcoming committee of two boys and two girls, all in jeans and barefooted, met the suave newcomers at the school door, for the taxi arrived long ahead of the buggy. Only the Americans were confused. With cool self-assuredness, the new boys demanded to be taken to the Head of the school. Susan, chairman of the reception committee, led them upstairs to Dean Whittlesey's office, since Mrs. Whittlesey could speak several foreign languages.

The three young men stood at stiff attention, clicking their heels with the military air of reporting to a superior officer. Politely, in cultured German, one of them stated, "We do not wish any misunderstanding. We are 100% Hitler Youth. The legation did not tell you this, we have learned. But it is imperative that you know. We are proud Nazis, held in this country against our will. We live only for the day we can return to the Fatherland." They all bowed, and waited for the Dean's reaction.

Dean Whittlesey gasped inside herself, but she managed to keep her face immobile. Quietly she said, "We were expecting refugees—homeless boys from the war area."

"Yes, we understand," said one. "That is why we speak up now."

Another added, "They showed us the letter about Sammy. But we too are now classified as refugees. We came to this country as exchange students, in the place of American boys who went to our homes and studied in Germany all summer. Now war has been declared and your government has frozen many ships and all passports. We just can't get home for awhile."

"My name is Karl," one boy said. "Otto and Fritz are financially sponsored at your school by the families of the boys whose places they took, as those boys must stay in Germany for awhile. I am the one to whom your school offered a scholarship. My parents can afford to pay my expenses here, but your government forbids arrangement of credit now."

Dean Whittlesey invited them to sit by her little fireplace until she returned. She sent refreshments up to them while she went out in the chill fall wind to the potato field to talk to the Principal, who was helping with the harvest to get some fresh air and exercise.

The Principal came in and told the boys that nothing could be done about the situation until she could call a meeting of the Board of Directors. In the meantime they were to consider themselves guests of the school. Classes were beginning tomorrow but they were free to roam around and get acquainted.

It was three days before the members of the Board could assemble for an emergency meeting. In joint session with the faculty, they went out on the hilltop and sat on blankets, with plenty of air and sunshine to keep their heads clear!

"The school will be accused of subversive interests. Parents will remove their children from the school. The Board members and faculty will be dubbed Nazis. These fanatical Hitler Youth will contaminate the minds of our American students."

So said all except three, who countered with, "Here is our chance to show three Nazis what democracy is. If we send them away, we will be helping them to remain Nazis. They have already been in this country for three months, but look at them. They are still steeped in Hitlerism.

No one has gone out of their way to help them to understand American ways. Here is a wonderful opportunity—right inside our own doors."

It was an all-afternoon session. But one by one we saw the chance to prove the worth of democracy to three impressionable boys from Hitler's Germany. When the sun was low in the sky, we took the final vote—it was unanimous to keep our Nazis.

As a safeguard, however, a period of probation was set. "You have two months in which to prove yourselves acceptable in our midst," the Dean told them in their own familiar tongue. "We want you to feel at home, and to try to be as happy as you can in an environment which is strange to you. You will be expected to live up to the few school rules, the same as for the rest of the students, and the day that one of you is found trying to win any of our students over to your Nazi creed all three of you will be shipped back to New York. Mr. Jackson, our history teacher, says he will give you ample opportunity to discuss Hitlerism out in the open, in history class and in general assembly, providing you courteously listen to the opposing arguments of the American students."

It was a "learn by doing" school, run by student government. There were no servants or hired men, except the farm manager. There was a cook, but she was a member of the staff. All the cleaning of classrooms, stairs, bathrooms, dormitories, and the kitchen was done by students. They took turns washing dishes, setting tables, feeding chickens and pigs, chopping or sawing wood, cleaning horse stalls, churning butter, and milking cows.

All of this was a bitter blow to Fritz, Karl, and Otto, for they not only came from homes with servants but they were unaccustomed to the thought of boys doing household chores. Besides, they were cultured and mature beyond their years; they were so well grounded in French, Greek, and Latin, and in mathematics, physics, and music that they were capable of teaching those subjects to the American students. And how could they submit to government by such immature, irresponsible, untrained savages? They themselves were only sixteen, yet they were already qualified to enter college. When twitted by one of our students as to why they had come to a high school if they were so smart, they scornfully replied they preferred a postgraduate course to entering an American university. Only Germany could give them a higher education worthy of superior intelligence.

In their first month with us they isolated themselves as much as possible. They huddled together at the outer edge of the gatherings by the big fireplace during assembly and at required evening sessions. They sat together at the table, they jabbered in German in secluded corners, they refused to attend any of the school entertainments, they insisted upon joint work jobs—if one was assigned kitchen duty, all three wanted to be in the kitchen; when one drew the task of sawing wood, the other two insisted upon sawing wood too. When the students were dancing, or skiing, or enjoying parties, Otto, Fritz, and Karl were engrossed in newspapers, news magazines, or radio news programs. They had been trained to spend six hours a day on current events, so they had no time for recreation. The frivolous activities of American youth disgusted them.

All the girls in the school were attractive; two, Nancy and Sue, were downright pretty and the popular ringleaders of almost everything. All of the girls were normal teenagers, eager to make a favorable impression on the opposite sex. When the German boys first arrived, the girls were delirious over such male handsomeness and polished manners. They fell over one another trying to attract attention. They discarded dungarees for feminine outfits, they finagled for strategic jobs. The American boys became "drips" compared with the tall, Aryan cavaliers.

The Germans met these overwhelming advances with amused courtesy at first, but gradually they grew deliberately aloof. They dodged the girls. They walked out on them. They talked in German in front of the girls and rudely laughed, making scornful faces which the girls resented.

The girls became embarrassed. Then angry. They went back to their jeans and moccasins or bare feet. Nancy and Susan sharpened their tongues and brought all their feminine wiles into line against the "enemy," and the other girls backed them up by ridiculing the guttural German language and poking obvious fun at everything the boys did. They pinned silly signs on the backs of the three boys; they made unnecessary noises during radio news broadcasts; they tormented the Germans with wisecracks all through work jobs. Most of these things were done subtly, behind the backs of us teachers, but we weren't exactly blind.

About the middle of the third month of the school term, not long after the boys had been told they were off probation, I noticed there was an unusual hubbub in the kitchen, and as I was on duty I thought I had better investigate. As I approached the big double sink on the opposite side of the kitchen from the girls, all three German boys stopped working and stared pleadingly at me. Their faces were red and sweaty from the steaming dish water, and they were in obvious misery.

"What's the matter, boys?" I asked. "Can't you make them hold their tongues? Give 'em good answers right back! That's what American kids like. They like a give-and-take argument."

"Please," begged Karl, with a beautiful pronunciation and accent I could never help but enjoy, "Is this a pot?" He held up a big crockery vegetable dish.

"Sure that's a pot," yelled Nancy across the big kitchen from her dish sink.

"And here's another," shrieked Sue, sliding across the linoleum with a metal milk pitcher and dropping it on top of the huge pile of pots and pans in the boys' sink.

"Pots and pans are only those containers in which food is cooked," I stated firmly, overwhelmed with sympathy for the three foreigners whom I had noticed seemed to have the whole student body nagging at them lately. I carried the questionable dishes back to the girls, and drew cheers from one side of the kitchen, and howls of objection from the other.

After the dishes were done, the three boys came to me with profuse thanks and assured me I was the only friend they had in the school. I was the only one with kind words for them, the only one who ever took their part. They broke down and told me they were homesick, out of their element, and unhappy.

Their rooms were in another building, and as soon as they left to study for the evening, I went to the Principal's office and demanded a meeting, immediately, of the whole school except the refugees. When I explained why, the Principal, who had been one of the first to urge that we keep the boys, was shocked. She had the student body called together at once. We met before the huge, walk-in, friendly fireplace—all except the three Nazis.

I called the students' attention to the kitchen scene of less than an hour ago, then asked them frankly, "Do you feel you are helping those Nazis to understand and love democracy? Do you think you are showing them Christian kindness? How many of you honestly believe that you have shown them a form of government and religious philosophy which they would consider worth exchanging for their familiar Nazi-ism?"

Not one hand went up. All eyes stared thoughtfully at the blazing six-foot logs in the fireplace. The only sound was the soft crackle of the fire.

Soon one of the girls grumbled, "But they don't cooperate with us."

"They talk German all the time," muttered a boy recently snubbed.

"They won't come to our parties," said Sue. "They say 'no' to everything. They even ridicule our school prayers. They never go to church with any of us."

"Do you think," suggested Dean Whittlesey, "that if you were stranded in Nazi Germany, and were miserably homesick, that you would care to go to parties? Would you want to spend hours doing things their way, like hanging over radio news programs? These boys aren't any more accustomed to our ways than you would be to theirs."

Some of the students looked up at the Principal to see what she thought. "They are truly homesick," she said, looking around at them all with appealing sympathy. "But they are such brave Nazi youth they aren't going to let you see it. They are putting on a big bluff."

After a pause, giving them time to contemplate these things, she added, "You know Karl is an only child. He would give anything to be home with his parents right now. If you want them to come to your parties, and go to movies with you, or dance with you, you must help them get over their homesickness by leading them into the adventure of experiencing American life in happier ways than by teasing and sarcasm. I am sure that the kinder you are to them the more frequently they will be tempted to talk to you in English. You'll have to find ways to show them how to enjoy youth and freedom. They just don't know how to do it. They never had this freedom before, which you have lived with since you were born."

She turned the meeting over to the student government, and the faculty sat back and listened. In a tumble of confessions and expressions of remorse, the students heaped condemnation upon themselves. They apologized to the faculty. Unanimously they voted to help our three Nazi boys, from now on, to appreciate democracy and Christianity. "May we make some fudge for them? Right now? And take it up to them? asked Sue. We all knew how those boys loved any kind of American chocolate candy.

The kitchen was abuzz at an unaccustomed hour. That meant poorly prepared lessons for the next day, but it was worth it. While the fudge was cooling, the whole gang of students crowded around the fireplace and worked over a friendly note more diligently than over any class assignment. Then every student signed it. Pete, the best-liked boy in the school, was chosen messenger. His face glowed, for he had been exceptionally sarcastic to Karl that afternoon, and now he could atone in person. At bedtime he delivered note and fudge to three puzzled German faces.

The next day both sides were mutually embarrassed by the sudden change in the atmosphere. But subtly, in the days that followed, the pendulum began to swing; perceptibly the fanaticism of the three Nazis slipped downward, away from that 100%.

Faculty and students had vainly tried to persuade the three boys to contribute to the school newspaper, for all of them expressed themselves so beautifully in written English. But the paper was an extra-curricular activity, which to Hitler Youth was a time-waster. Two days after the kitchen episode, however, Otto and Fritz marched mechanically into the Principal's office and offered to write regularly for the school paper if they could have a current-events column. We all but hugged them, for their occasional talks on world events were presented in a fair, unbiased manner, with a mature finesse which left students and faculty open-mouthed with fascination. And that afternoon Karl came in and offered to run a music column, and to contribute to book reports. His class papers on the Shakespearean plays had already been the talk of the school.

The square dance that wound up the pre-Christmas term found two of the German boys on the floor. Fritz and Otto didn't know many steps, and they were militarily stiff; but a ton of ice melted as the girls showed them how to dance. Fritz confided to Sue in the midst of the "Sailor's Joy" platter, "Karl didn't come because he's too shy. He's scared of girls."

Sue whispered to Nancy, Nancy whispered to Roger. The three of them slipped out into the silvery winter night and half ran, impeded by slipping and skidding in the snow-crusted, frozen road ruts, up to the boys' dormitory. They banged on Karl's door.

"Get dressed right away, Karl, or we'll break your door down. Put on your best clothes and come dance with us," said Roger.

"Who is 'we'?" asked Karl cautiously. "Who is in the hall with you?"

"We are," called Nancy. "Sue and I are here. Get dressed, Karl. We want to dance with you." Karl didn't answer, but they could hear him moving and rustling about the room.

Not many minutes later, in a small classroom off the living room dance floor, the two prettiest girls in the school, assisted by their usual Number One boy friend Roger, gave scared but bravely smiling Karl his first lesson in square dance steps. Soon Karl was out in the crowd, and by the end of the evening the Germans were so entertained by one another's indecorous antics they were obviously having more fun than anyone else in the school.

The three Nazis didn't miss another school party. In fact, the radio and *The New York Times* were partially supplanted from then on by the phonograph. There were times when the faculty thought they would lose their sanity if Fritz played the "Polish Polka" once more, yet everyone was so happy about the blossoming of those once-frozen, mechanized, youthful spirits that the boys could grind out the same record all day long if they wished to, and no one would say anything.

Their conversion was hardly begun. The three of them were invited to spend Christmas vacation in the homes of their various sponsors, so they were widely separated. They returned to the school a month later, full of intense discussion of what they had seen, both then and during the previous summer. Otto argued with some of our boys over the American roads they had traveled on. He was sure the excellent concrete highways over which he had been taken for rides were only "exhibition" roads—that they didn't go very far. He insisted there were not enough miles of good roads in this country to have any military value. Only Germany had wisely built roads of sufficient extent and durability to support tanks and trucks.

The grocery shelves in the stores he had been taken to were a marvelous false front, designed to keep up American morale. Such abundance was limited only to isolated areas, where they could be shown off to foreigners who must be impressed. It was pathetic to hear them try to find propaganda in every least, silly movie. They couldn't accept anything at face value. Even in the movie, "Gone With the Wind," they found propaganda aimed at the European situation. Our American students found the task of explaining doubly difficult when there wasn't anything to explain.

Near the end of January, the boys received notice from New York to be ready to leave at a moment's notice, as arrangements were being completed to ship them to Germany by way of California, Japan, and the Siberian railway. At that time, Germany and Russia were still at peace. But Fritz wrote in the school paper that week a few lines which later proved his skillful ability at news interpretation: "The role of Russia seems to be rather mysterious. German police are said to have taken possession of 200 miles of formerly Polish, now Russian, railroad, and thus to have obtained a common frontier with Rumania."

The order to be ready to leave threw the boys into a frenzy of excitement. Karl discovered that the handle of his suitcase was broken, and he nearly had apoplexy because no transportation was available at that instant to get his suitcase to the village to be repaired. The boys reverted to their old ways of jabbering in German in isolated corners. They spent long hours again listening to the radio. Once, when teased for not joining a gang going skiing out in the bright sunshine instead of huddling indoors, Fritz answered, "What is skiing? We go home. To die in front of guns." Their faces were white. For days there was no more Polish polka. Even the American students hadn't the heart for it.

The wait for word from New York stretched out into days, then weeks. Automatically the boys drifted back to more carefree activities. They deserted the radio even to sit by the fireplace and chew gum and gab with the girls. Nancy was an expert bubble blower, and the three Nazis became appreciative students of the idle art. Competition for the girls' favors flared up again, the stamping of feet to the Polish polka rocked the building after class and work hours.

In their school work, the boys were honor students in every subject. Having already graduated from high school, they didn't take a full load. Instead, they relieved Dean Whittlesey of some of her heavy schedule by tutoring French and Latin. Karl took over one of the music classes. The German boys were beginning to think for themselves. They were no longer the automatons who had to be told every least thing to do, who once obeyed orders like robots, and never relaxed like the normal, carefree ways of our American youngsters.

In the middle of winter all three boys celebrated their seventeenth birthdays, several days apart. There were cakes and candles, and so much singing and jolly teasing the boys beamed with pleasure. For each birthday the students took up a collection and bought the no-longer-too-proud-Aryans a new pair of shoes, which all badly needed by then. The birthday celebrations tightened friendships in both directions, and put a final end to the ice and the formality.

Fritz, Otto, and Karl now actually bubbled over with school spirit. They went out of their way to tackle the unattractive jobs. They teamed up with anyone who needed help. They joined the weekend skiing trips in the school truck. They danced gracefully, unhampered any longer by military precision. No longer were they identified only as "the three German boys," for each now was an individual personality.

Otto and Fritz plunged into dramatics with a fervor which brought flattering sighs from faculty and students, and two of them began poring over Hollywood magazines and dreaming out loud of taking that movie capital by storm. Otto as a leading man had the girls almost swooning at his feet. Fritz, we accidentally discovered, had a beautiful voice. One night we had a special song fiesta around the piano with Fritz as lead tenor. So eager was he to make up for lost time he even joined in singing with us the American patriotic songs. That was the beginning of many happy song fests with them, and to the pride and pleasure of the whole school, Fritz and Otto joined the choir in one of the village churches. Karl's voice didn't qualify, but he graciously attended services with us.

Events at Eastertime emphasized the change in our German boys, who were now less than 50% Hitler Youth. Another order came, just before vacation, stating that the boys must be ready to leave at any moment. When the message reached them, they and a group of students were in front of the fireplace, waxing their skis for the last time, as the sun was high and the snow was getting too soft. Not one of the boys moved. They frowned and just stared unhappily at the fire, in poignant silence. After a while they went on waxing their skis.

These Germans, once so eager to get home to the Fatherland, looked at one another and grumbled. They muttered vague things about hoping the plan would fall through again, or that the boat they were assigned to would sink before they had to leave the school. Suddenly, in little-boy fashion, Fritz said, "I bet you'll be glad to get rid of us." Then he noticed that the girls were crying. He whispered, "I'm sorry."

Reluctantly they put aside their skis. "We've got to pack," said Otto, "just in case. But there'll be a moon tonight. Let's go skiing tonight after supper if we can get permission."

The girls fluttered over them. Nancy ran to the kitchen to make some hot cocoa. A gang of students trailed them to their room, to brush suits, shine shoes, mend anything needing it, and to sew on buttons.

Sue had her sewing box under one arm, and clung to one of Fritz's arms with the other.

"If you stay in America," she said with a pleading whimper, "you can be of more use to your country after the war. Whether Germany wins or loses, you could help your Fatherland more by staying alive."

"Do you think so?" Fritz sighed. "Germany will win anyway!" he exclaimed, and tried to cheer her up with his gay laughter all the way to the dormitory, for much good-natured razzing had answered that taunt. One of the American boys flung at him, "Germany will win, if America stays out of it."

"Yeah, *if*," answered Otto in a prophetic tone.

This time the order from New York threw the boys into a fit of depression. A party had been planned for the evening before vacation; but now it was cancelled. Instead, everyone spent the last evening around the log fire, reminiscing, teasing, exchanging good wishes as if the farewell were already upon them. For who knew if they would be all together after the holiday? The Germans had been told to remain where they were for the Easter vacation in order to facilitate response to urgent orders. But when the Americans returned at the end of vacation they were as happy as the birds to find Otto, Karl, and Fritz exceedingly busy with farm chores.

By June, Hitler's enlightened youth were automatically accepting anything they came across in the American scene for just what it appeared to be, and they openly admitted they loved this rugged, free land. They were proud of their old barn clothes. They bragged about their manual skills and invited people to see how dexterously they handled the circular power saw and the hand saws. They loved the mountains and the woods; they loved their small room, which they themselves freshly wallpapered during the Easter vacation. They doted on the American girls, and strutted for their attention. They raved over movie favorites; they reveled in their free and easy companionship with the American boys, and seldom spent more than an hour a day on news broadcasts.

Karl now openly admired Roosevelt, and Churchill, and democracy. They gave credit to Hitler for unifying Germany and assuaging German pride, but they no longer had any use for the Nazi machine. They frankly preferred the American way of life. Hitler Youth was now but a blind alley to them, too fanatic, and they wanted no more of it. "Our eyes are open," Fritz dramatically stated. "We have seen and lived both sides." More than anything they had ever wanted in their lives, they now longed to go to American universities. With the help of Dean Whittlesey and their sponsors, Otto chose Yale, Karl selected Harvard, and Fritz was determined to go to Cornell. Since they had been honor students in both Germany and America, the universities accepted them, listing them as exchange students.

They participated in our school's graduation exercises with all the fervor of normal American high-school kids, and when the excitement was all over, one by one they went up to the Dean's office. Speaking deliberately, in English, Fritz, with tears in his eyes, said, "I want you to know that if America enters the war I hope I lose my right arm before I am called upon to shoot at an American boy."

Otto, alone with the Dean a few minutes later, huskily stammered, "I hope something happens to my eyesight if I ever kill an American at the front."

Karl awaited his turn outside the door, and watching the other two leave with hanging heads, he could hardly talk when he went in and confronted the Dean. But all three had planned this, and it was now his turn. Dean Whittlesey, having sons of her own, knew how to comfort him so that he could find his voice. Finally Karl mumbled, fighting to keep back the tears, "I don't want to go back to Germany the way it is now. I want with all my heart to stay here in this country and become an American citizen." He told her all three had lain awake nights, trying to concoct some way of evading return to Germany. "We thought of running away and changing our names, and getting jobs in the big cities, but we know our families would suffer from our mistakes. My mother would be thrown into a concentration camp."

Thus ended the school year of the three Nazi boys whom we invited to stay after they had strutted into Dean Whittlesey's office and declared themselves 100% Hitler Youth. They were guests at various homes during the summer, even visiting some of the school's students. Otto had the cherished wish granted of seeing the Grand Canyon.

By fall, Karl and Otto were back in Hitler's Reich. Fritz, having given up Cornell because of the uncertainty of his continued residence in this country, managed to stow himself away in a small college. But before the fall semester was half over, he was compelled to sail for Germany.

Letters from the three boys had been frequent and newsy all summer; they wrote to their classmates and to the school. But once they were back in Germany, the letters they had promised were few, brief, and obviously censored. Then a black, worrisome curtain of silence hid them from us, from right after Christmas until spring. We couldn't even tell if our letters were reaching them. Then, just as our orchard apple blossoms were scenting the mountain air, a pall fell over the school when news came that Otto had been killed in service.

Only a few weeks later, a letter came from Fritz's parents. He, too, had died at the front, for a cause he no longer believed in.

But Karl survived. As soon as the war was over, he found a way to get back to the United States. Today he is a citizen of our free country, and his children are native-born Americans. His dearest wish was granted, and we who had voted to keep those three Nazis couldn't have a finer reward.   END

The Ordeal of Aunt Phoebe

by Laurie Hillyer

Miss Phoebe Felicity Ames, landing at Logan Airport in Boston, glanced hopefully toward the group inside the gate, waiting to meet the passengers from the Chicago plane. Would young Felicity, her grandniece and namesake, be among them? Alas, no—and Miss Ames felt a disappointment whose intensity surprised her. "I wouldn't want you to meet me at Logan," she had written Felicity, "but I know you will want to hear all about the Family so I will take a taxi to Cambridge and, if convenient, I might perhaps spend the night."

As for saying she did not want Felicity to meet her, Miss Ames found that, the older one grew, the more prone one was to say, a shade wistfully, that one did not want what one really did.

Felicity was the apple of her aunt's eye, but the rest of the young generation of Ameses was shocking beyond words. There were so many divorces that one was unable to sort out who belonged to whom and Sarah Ames, one of Felicity's cousins, was always flying to Paris or Los Angeles or wherever, with young men whose only difference was in their names since each (according to the snapshots Sarah thoughtfully sent her parents) resembled an amiable caveman who had somehow acquired a guitar.

Felicity, who went to Radcliffe, was, nevertheless, mannerly, neat, friendly with old as well as young, and charming. She majored in English and was, in brief, the kind of Boston Ames a Boston Ames should be.

She met her aunt at the apartment door—ruffled (but neat) sand-gold hair, sand-colored slacks that matched her hair and a green-gage shirt that made her wide-apart hazel eyes look greener then they really were. Behind her was a pleasant-looking, non-hippie young man whose dark hair, Miss Ames noted with relief, was thick but, even his small sideburns, barbered.

"Aunt Phoebe! How nice," cried Felicity, who had evidently never received—or had forgotten—her aunt's note. "Aunt Phoebe, this is Peter Brett," she added after embraces. "He's been wanting to meet you."

"I've heard a lot about you, Miss Ames, from Fliss," said Peter, shaking hands. He picked up Miss Ames' bags which had been set down beside the elevator and brought them into the hall. "I've been wanting to meet you very much."

This was true, Felicity had sparked his curiosity. "My Aunt Phoebe is a vanishing type," she had said, "and determined to hold out until the end, I can tell you, before vanishing. Her creed is the Family."

"Family?" Peter had echoed.

"Yes. The Ames. Us. But, except for me, she is terribly shocked at our generation. You know that Boston limerick, Peter? My father says Aunt Phoebe wants it to go like this: 'Here's to good old Boston/ home of the sacred names/ where Cabots speak only to Lowells/ and Lowells speak only to Ames.'"

"How does it go, really?" asked Peter, having grown up in New York.

"The bean and the cod," explained Felicity, "God. There are quite a lot of Ameses for the Lowells to speak to," she added, "about sixty-two in the Boston telephone book, after all."

"Felicity and I are good friends," now said Miss Ames, with an affectionate glance toward her namesake, "in spite of the generation chasm, so called."

"Generation gap, darling," said Felicity, gently.

"Chasm is an almost synonymous and much more melodious word," Miss Ames explained.

Peter laughed. "It's *much* more melodious. The word 'gap' always makes me think of a kid who has lost all his front teeth. My mother has a horrible picture of me on her bureau like that."

He took Miss Ames' topcoat and hung it up, and they all sat down in the living room in comfortable chairs.

"Well, tell me all about the Family," said Felicity, "how are Mother and Dad? And has the latest Ames divorce gone through?"

Miss Ames looked momentarily stricken, nodded and veered to Felicity's parents who were not (yet) divorced and whom she had been visiting at their winter home in Arizona.

Peter, amused, watched the two Phoebe Felicitys, the elderly spinster and her twenty-year-old niece. They were both slender, tall and straight, with the kind of clear-cut profile associated with John Keats. Miss Ames wore black oxfords and a gray tailored suit and her straight gray hair was drawn into a decisive knot behind. Felicity was barefoot, with ruffled sand-gold hair, but Peter decided there was a resemblance and also a lot of affection between them.

Miss Ames turned courteously toward him in case he was thinking (which indeed was true) that she wished he were not there. "Are you also studying in Cambridge?" she asked him.

"No," said Peter, "I'm just here for the weekend. I'm an architect. I live in New York.

"Oh—New York," said Miss Ames. "Do you design skyscrapers?"

"In a way I do. My firm is interested in tearing down nineteenth century slums and replacing them with high-rise, low-cost flats."

"That's a very worthy cause. Still, I can't help hoping that all nineteenth century houses aren't going to be torn down. I live in one," said Miss Ames, "and I think it's quite nice, don't you, Felicity?"

"I think it's beautiful," said Felicity, "and I'd love to show it to Peter sometime. It's on Commonwealth Avenue in Boston, Peter. Tell him about it, Aunt Phoebe, while I make us some tea."

"You might ride back with me today if you'd care to," said Miss Ames, who saw that Felicity had forgotten her suggestion about spending the night. "What do you think of Cambridge, Peter?" she asked as Felicity disappeared into the kitchenette. Her calling him Peter was a crossing of the chasm. It would have been easier for her to have called him Mr. Brett. "As I drove past the Square and saw all those young people with wild streaming hair and battered floppy hats, I asked myself, *Is this Cambridge?* In Felicity's father's day, the boys wore neat plaid jackets and saddle shoes and had crew cuts and good manners."

"Well," said Peter cautiously, "the Harvard boys and girls can have charming manners still. There's a kind of movement, isn't there, against standardization and the status quo?" He felt relieved when Felicity returned with the tea.

"Lapsang Souchong," she said, cheerfully. "Your favorite, Aunt Phoebe. No cream and no sugar and medium strong, isn't that right? And here's some beautiful cinnamon toast— not a bit burned, either," she said, lifting an eyebrow toward Peter.

"Thank you. And now," said Miss Ames with a doting look toward her namesake, "we can settle down and you can tell us some of the interesting things an English major learns at college, Felicity."

"Right on, Felicity," said Peter. "Miss Ames," he added, "your niece can sound like a brain but, believe me, you've no idea how much there is she doesn't know."

Their eyes met across the teapot.

"I learn a great deal from Felicity," said Miss Ames. "I often wish my parents had sent me to college. Relatively few girls went in my time."

"You know a great deal, Aunt Phoebe," said Felicity. And thought, startled, *but does she, really? about what? Well,* she thought, *about loyalty.*

A pleasant feeling of camaraderie developed over the tea, after which Miss Ames, before leaving, went to the bathroom to freshen up. She glanced about the apartment on her way. It belonged to an Ames cousin. Felicity, who usually lived in a dormitory, was just there for the month. Things were in order in the kitchenette and hall. The bedroom door was closed. In the bathroom she approved the lemon soap and almond hand lotion and looked about for the row of embroidered guest towels, an adjunct to all Ames bathroom racks. Things seemed somewhat confused. Her glance fell on the bathroom door. She gasped and it was an audible gasp, she heard it. On the hook hung a gossamer nightgown, very feminine—what, she recognized, is called a shortie—and, over it, very masculine, a rumpled pair of blue and white pajamas. She could not direct her gaze away from the nightgown and the pajamas, much as she wanted to do just that. They had a casual look as if there were nothing odd about their being there.

She opened the door, closed it and returned to the living room, hoping no one would notice the shaking of her hands.

"Felicity," she said—she did not look at Peter—"I think we had better have our visit in Boston another time. I . . . " she floundered, ". . . don't know what shape the house will be in, after all. Another time will be better." As she glanced at Felicity, who was looking surprised and concerned, she felt tears rising. Getting command of herself, she said, "Would you please call me a taxi?"

Alone in her own room, Miss Ames sank down in the nearest chair and stared straight ahead of her, knowing this was the worst day of her life, which she had expected to be so happy. Felicity and this Peter living together. Not married. Living together. Betraying the Family like all the rest. Not Felicity. What should she do, what should she do? Should she call Arizona? Perhaps Roger, her nephew, Felicity's father, a lawyer, could . . . could . . . well, he could not do anything, of course, nobody could, and she abandoned the thought of calling Roger almost before it took shape. Moreover, she did not want to talk about this to anyone, the more people who knew about it, the more dreadful. Not *Felicity.* And she saw Felicity the adored, being cast out of Paradise (Boston and Cambridge) in a terrible snowstorm which was obliterating her and the baby she clasped, rolled in a blanket, in her arms. She abandoned this thought, too, as ridiculous, and yet . . . and yet . . . how would anyone brought up like Felicity know about what was called the Pill? She sat there, not moving, seeing with that inner eye, which her favorite poet so mistakenly called "the bliss of solitude," the hook on the bathroom door.

The telephone rang. She sat perfectly still and listened to its ringing. There was not a single person, not one, to whom she felt she could talk. The telephone went on ringing, in its stupid, inexorable way, demanding, insistently, that it be answered.

It rang on and on and finally Miss Ames, trained to respond to any legitimate summons, found herself almost automatically crossing the room and lifting the receiver.

"Aunt Phoebe?" It was the light and pleasant voice of Felicity's mother, whose odd name was Everard, shortened to Evvie. "Oh, I'm so glad we got you. Roger and I have been wanting to know that you were safely home."

"I'm here."

"Did you have a good flight? Did you have any trouble at O'Hare?"

"No more than usual." She then prodded herself to sound as if nothing were wrong. "It's very good of you, Evvie, to call."

"Well, we wanted to know. And we miss you already. Aunt Phoebe did you see Fliss?"

Miss Ames stiffened, wary. There was an oddly urgent note in the question. What now? I'm just back from seeing her," she said.

"How did she seem?"

"Why, the same as ever—a dear, dear child. Why?"

"Well, Aunt Phoebe—the oddest thing. Who do you think turned up just after you left? Sarah Ames, no less, with one of her swains, full of love and song. They were driving to Mexico and their Volkswagen had broken down and he left her here while he went back to the garage to get it fixed—they came in a taxi. I hardly recognized Sarah, she wears her hair all over her face in little curly *streaks*. But the point is, Aunt Phoebe, she said she had recently seen Fliss and a young man was living with her, there in that apartment. Sarah didn't seem to think there was anything strange about it, of course, but, Aunt Phoebe, there wasn't anyone living there, was there? My God! She said someone named Peter. Roger and I have been pacing the floor."

During this outpouring a resolution had formed and strengthened in the mind of Miss Ames. One of the interesting things in life, she had found in her long career, is that one's mind can astonish one, can take a stand the owner of that mind had never expected it would take. She found her mind determined to protect Felicity at all costs, even to the point, though she hoped this would not be necessary, of lying.

"Sarah," she said flatly, "is a perfect ass and always has been. I find it difficult, always, to remember she is an Ames. As for someone named Peter, he most certainly was there, Evvie, having tea. He lives in New York. A very gentlemanly young man. I liked him. We talked about poetry and he is flying back tonight to New York."

"He wasn't *staying* there? You're *sure?*"

Miss Ames took a deep breath, hoping it was not audible, across the miles. "Evvie, no one other than Sarah Ames would conclude that a young man who comes to tea expects to spend the night."

"He *wasn't* staying there, then—you're *sure?*"

"My dear Evvie, he was having tea. Peter Brett is an architect and lives in New York and was having tea with Felicity and spending the weekend," she said in firm ringing tones, "with a friend."

"There was nothing to make you think—?"

Now she must do it. *"Nothing."*

When the conversation ended, Miss Ames was relatively sure she had been successful. She herself then, like Felicity's parents, paced the floor.

"Peter, whatever happened to Aunt Phoebe," Felicity said, "leaving us suddenly like that? As if something suddenly upset her?"

"Well," Peter replied, slowly, "I think something *did*. I think she suddenly realized I was staying here with you, Fliss, and it *did* upset her. Hell."

"But how did she realize it? Everything was happy at first, she seemed to *like* you, what changed it?"

"I don't know, dear. E.S.P."

"E.S.P.? Oh. Maybe. The thing is, she wrote me she was coming and I forgot it—why did I ever? I'm awfully fond of her. And she's so *lonely*. And she builds me up in her mind, she sort of identifies with me, she sort of thinks I'm herself when young."

"But you *are* alike," said Peter, "in a curious way. Each in his own fashion."

When, the next day, Miss Ames found an envelope from Felicity in her mailbox—bright green ink, square letters, young, firm hand —she was afraid to open it. What would it say? What could it say? Perhaps Peter had a wife who wouldn't divorce him but didn't love him. Perhaps—might this be possible?—they really *were* married but for some reason didn't want it known. She slit the envelope neatly, unfolded the paper with the Cambridge heading and began to read.

Dearest Aunt Phoebe,

It was awfully nice seeing you and I was awfully glad to have you and Peter meet. We are trying an experiment which you will understand because you and I are friends and because you are always able to cross that impassable chasm.

The thing is, simply, Peter and I believe a promise is something sacred that has to be kept. This applies to a lot of things—the marriage service, for instance. How can people all over the place go on breaking that beautiful promise—until death do us part—to smash all of the time? We don't want to, we want to be sure. That's why Peter and I have tried really knowing each other as well as we possibly can, and being together night and day, until we are sure we can keep that promise until death do us part.

We hope we will see you often and Peter who has gone back to his high-rise low-cost flats in New York sends his love with mine.

Your friend,
Phoebe Felicity II

Miss Ames, having read this, had the bewildered feeling that Felicity had taken her by the hand and guided her gently along a path she had never expected to explore.

She then had one of those strange thoughts she had never expected to have—was it possible that she herself, and not Felicity, was mistaken? Had she condemned before she tried to understand? She read the letter again, slowly. Right or wrong—and Miss Ames could not *indeed* so suddenly be ready to concede that Felicity was right—Peter and Felicity had mapped out a course they *felt* was right. I *must do the impossible*, she said aloud. After all, that was the great secret of life and she had lived long enough to know it. Unless you realize it, you can't survive. You say to yourself, *I can't do it*. And you *do* it. You say to yourself, *it can't be done*, and you banish the thought as if it had never been. You say to the young, *I can't get over to your side of the chasm*. And you *get*. She had always been proud of holding out for her principles—but might it be a mistake sometimes, after all, to hold out?

She called a taxi. She was going to Felicity's apartment and the mystique which existed between them told her Felicity would be there. She might easily be in class, of course, but Miss Ames did not think she would be. Nor was she.

Felicity opened the door to her aunt and on her face was the startled and anxious expression of a child who has broken the rules and is determined to stand pat.

"Aunt Phoebe!" she exclaimed, and stood with the doorknob in her hand, waiting.

Miss Ames looked at her namesake, noted the apprehension in her face and realized one thing only—how much she loved her.

"Hello, Felicity," she said. "I thought I'd just run over in answer to your letter."

And she put her arms around her and kissed her hard.   END

Beyond Shadow Island

by Edward M. Holmes

I never thought, of course, that I would forget him or that I would especially care whether I did or not. Now sometimes, though, I wish I could, for there is something about the fellow that hangs on, that keeps coming back. Nights when a man cannot sleep because of the gale tearing at the eaves of the house or, strangely enough, just the opposite—when moonlight, unreal almost, breaks between light pillow humps of fog and shines silvery on the flat, calm surface of the water—times like that I keep hearing what he said—like on a record—or seeing him again, standing on the wharf here in Oak Harbor where I first met him, or on the storm-whipped rocks at the head of Shadow Island where I saw him last; and I guess I was the last one to see him, unless you choose to count Jeremiah, which I don't. He might have, though—counted Jeremiah, I mean. It would have been like him all right.

I was standing on the wharf that Sunday afternoon early in March, watching the high seas outside, when he drove into the parking lot in a station wagon so overloaded it almost scraped bottom. He walked down onto the wharf a reasonable distance from where I was standing, nodded, the way any stranger might, and, like me, looked out to the southeast. There was something to look at. We had had no storm—the gale had been somewhere else—but now, with no wind whatsoever, we were getting the surf. The spray didn't just fly; bits of it hung in the still air around every island, above every ledge, with the sun shining through it, bursting into rainbows, mixing the colors with the green of the spruces and the pink of the high rocks. He said something about it; "corona," he called it.

"Mhm," I said—or something like that.

"Means 'crown,' " he said, "only it's kind of different, more glorious sort of. You can't touch it. Like what you see around the sun in an eclipse."

"Well, Godsakes! The educated type," I thought. Not that I'm not used to them; it's just that most of them don't appear until the beginning of summer, same as dogfish. As for "corona," it made me think of cigars first; but I could see what he meant. Not too stupid at that. I've heard worse.

"I don't suppose it's any day to go out," he said.

"Out where?"

"To one of the islands."

"Not unless it was a matter of life and death," I said. He nodded.

"Which island you thinking of going to?" I asked.

"Shadow Island."

"Whatever you want to go out there for this time of year?"

"I bought it," he said.

Well sir, I give him a quick, sharp look, and he didn't seem to be out of his head. Besides, as such fellows go, he had talked sensibly enough. I knew these island men; we'd had several of them. I don't mean the ones that was born and raised on an island and now fish from it; they're the same as anyone else. I mean the ones that come from away, the city more often than not, and go out to one of these lonesome, sometimes almost naked spots where there ain't nothing but crows and mink. The astonishing thing is that some do really learn how to live there, learn how to stand it. It's even possible they like it.

"If you paid fifty cents, you was beat out of twenty-five," I said. He laughed. "They tell me there's a cabin on it."

"More or less," I said. "No one can put you ashore there for a couple—three days at the least."

"But you will when it flattens out?"

I nodded, or pushed my head forward like I was wearing a collar that hurt, meaning yes. "They tell me there is a lot of fellows has gone to Canada," I said.

He gave me a kind of amused look. "That's right. Two thousand of them," he said. "That's something I don't have to worry about, the draft. I got it behind me, all that."

He looked old enough, and worn enough so it could easily have been the truth.

"What you want to do, get away from it all?" I looked right at him when I asked that, but he didn't look back; he was staring out at some of them ledges, spray-hazed, between us and the outer islands.

"No," he says, "I don't. I want to get *to* it all."

I pulled a sharpened match out of my pocket, one I had left there after dinner, and did a little excavating around the molars.

"Any seals out there on Shadow Island?" he asks.

"Will be," I said, "when it warms up."

"Like to have some seals around," he said.

"Well, they're a friendly, sociable critter, like a dog. You ain't going out there alone?"

"Yes."

"That don't seem so good. Not that it's any of my business," I said. "Most of the fellows that take up an island, they have a woman with them. Now you take that island right out there . . . " I pointed— "Greenough's Island. Man and his wife been out there the last sixteen years, just them and the deer and the mink. And down east thirty-forty miles there's another outfit, fellow I heard about. Bought the island, built an airstrip, flies down there weekends from Boston with a tall, blond creature he's took an option on. Situation like that, I could see an island myself. But alone . . . "

"Women are pretty hard-headed, practical creatures," he says.

I wasn't going to dispute that, and we held a few seconds of silent communion over it, or maybe over something else—I ain't prepared to say what.

"You could at least take a dog. You got a dog?"

He shook his head.

I thought that one over a bit. "We got an extra up to our house, not quite young enough to be called a pup. Mongrel, of course. I don't know but the Old Lady 'n I'd just as soon you took him. He'd be company for you."

"Does he talk?" he asked.

I didn't say nothing for a moment.

"I'd like to take him if he doesn't talk."

Well, if that was the way he felt about it, I sure as hell wasn't going to say much.

"What's his name?" he asked, kind of grinning.

You couldn't help liking him when he grinned like that. "Jeremiah."

"How'd you come to name him that?"

"Old Lady done it. Been reading her Bible."

"Of course." He moved a few feet and set on one of Arch Lockey's lobster crates. Then: "The mainland could use a Jeremiah."

"So could you, this one," I said, "especially where you're moving out to that Godforsaken Shadow Island."

"Maybe that's the wrong name for it."

"Been named that—Shadow Island—as long as any can remember."

"Yeah, I suppose so."

We stayed there a while longer, staring like a couple of cussed idiots at them rainbow colors filtering through the sea haze. Finally I suggested he come up to the house, meet Jeremiah and the Old Lady, and see if we could persuade her to set us up a lunch. He told me his name was Frazier, Donald Frazier—something like that—and I noticed his station wagon carried a Colorado license plate. He was pleasant and sociable up to the house, and I could see he hit it off all right with the Old Lady and Jeremiah both. He rubbed Jeremiah behind the ears and praised up the Old Lady's cooking like he meant it. Of course the Old Lady asked him a batch of questions from time to time, but I never see a man who was so expert at dodging an answer and still not giving offense.

Hadn't he come a long ways from home?

"Well, yes, in a way you might say that."

After a time, she give up. She liked him though—I could see that—and I wasn't surprised when she told him he was welcome to stay with us until the seas should flatten out. He thanked us, said that was very kind and generous, but he had already taken a room in a motel back on Route One. He and Jeremiah would go back there and get used to each other, and he would telephone now and then to ask about the trip.

Four days later he and I unloaded his gear from the station wagon and put it aboard my boat. He had all the right things to survive a long time in the wilderness. I'll hand that to him. He had the tools, the clothes, the grub—practically everything he might need and not much he wouldn't. It took us almost an hour to get it aboard, an hour to run to Shadow Island, and another one to ferry it all ashore in the skiff from where I'd anchored my boat. I took him up through the woods and showed him the camp. It looked in hard shape but didn't seem to discourage him a bit. It still had a chimney, a door, and a couple of windows, and Frazier seemed to think there was nothing wrong with it that he couldn't fix. I offered to help him get his gear up there from where we had piled it above tide line on the rocks, but he said he and Jeremiah could do that all right.

"A hell of a lot of good Jeremiah will be," I said.

He laughed. "You'd be surprised: Jerry and I will get along first rate."

He asked how much he owed for the trip and paid me, and I shook hands with him and patted the dog a minute and wished them luck. "I'll stop in now and then when it's fit," I said.

"No need to do that."

"Well, I'll do it anyway," I said.

We had some soft days after that: the full moon came and went; then the wind pulled around to the northeast, and March, like it often does, roared itself out. The first day of it, I was out in that northeaster, where I had no license to be, except that I wanted to get in a couple-three hundred dollars' worth of traps before the storm stove them all up. And when I came in past Shadow Island, I see him and Jeremiah out on some of them great high rocks. The seas was getting over-grown by then, and white-lipped, three-four hundred yards to a stretch, and I had to look sharp at the wheel to keep one of them from breaking over the stern and filling her up. But I got a good sight of them once or twice, high there on Shadow Island Head, staring right into the wind's teeth. I waved once, and Frazier waved back.

A week later, after a northwester, when the seas had pretty much flat-tened out, I dropped anchor out there and rowed my skiff ashore to find out what was what. I hadn't gone far into the Shadow Island woods when I met Jeremiah, barking, and wagging his tail, and pranc-ing about, but of that Frazier fellow, outside the camp itself, there wasn't a trace. There was a plate, knife, and fork on the table, a frying pan unwashed, an open sleeping bag in the corner, and that was that.

The next Sunday I got Aaron Abram, Phil Dexter, and one or two others to go out there with me at low water. We circled the island in the woods, and circled it and circled it. We looked in the crevices around every rock; we searched in the tide pools; here and there we even took a good close look at a ledge.

"He must of slipped on one of them rocks in the storm," Aaron said. "There ain't no other explanation that makes sense."

"That's right. That's all it is," Phil said.

"Must be," I said.

But it wasn't all it was, not quite. Only I never told them the rest of it; if I had, it wouldn't have mattered to them in the least. That first day I went there after the storm, I found a piece of scratch paper beside the empty plate on a table in the camp, with words in pencil scribbled on it. Best as I can make out, it goes like this: *We looked deep into Walden Pond and drifted down the Mississippi we sought the prairie the desert the mountains until there was no more West with Taji soared beyond the sunset   with Fathers bathed in the blood of the unknown buck   now salt is on the briar rose near Ishmael's soft and dirge-like main and we seek the seal's wide spindrift gaze toward . . .*

It broke off, unfinished.

I don't, of course, make no sense out of it, although there are some that might. I set out to burn it in the stove once, but I couldn't do it, and tucked it behind the clock on the mantelpiece. And whether it is the words on the paper, or the way he looked, or what he said or didn't say—perhaps there are things that can't be said—I have no notion. I only know I can't forget, and that there are times I wish I could; there are dreams, nights when the wind roars at the caves, and I recall its singing in the rigging, or the moonlight breaks through the moving boughs of the tall spruces, throws living shadows on the waters, the bushes, the dried grass of the throbbing earth. Under the bed, the hound moans in his real world; and lying there, staring, I wait for sleep, waiting and praying maybe to forget, when every second of my life I know I won't.   END

Not Just a Summer Resident

by Trudi McCullough Osborne

The novelist Richard Table was a vain man, and among the things of which he was most vain was the beauty of his wife, though he he took pains to keep her from knowing this. He, himself, was no male counterpart of his wife's loveliness and therefore valued it the more. Despite thirteen busy years of marriage, she had retained a soft spareness of figure, and her patrician facial bones and an inner spirit lighting her expression gave increase to beauty with every passing year. She too was a writer, though her husband belittled her talent; he got away with it because he was such a mighty figure in the writing world. But her beauty he worshipped, even if he did it in secret as the follower of some forbidden sect might hide his devotions.

The Tables lived year round in one of those New Hampshire villages that in season burgeon with summer people. They cut a wide swath in the summer colony, Eleanor being loved and admired and Table being fawned upon and inspiring awe. But in the winter they more or less lived the normal life of the village, looking forward with the rest of Wreston to the weekly change of movie fare; shopping at the Greek's grocery; being one with the townsfolk and sharing with them morning coffee or rides to the station or facilities for digging themselves out of snowfalls. They met daily at the post office; kept each other's dogs during city absences; and felt the same concern over village zoning and tree plantings and taxes.

Richard Table often passed the time of day at the Fire Department or in making ritual calls at the hardware store or Softball League headquarters at the Legion. He was a friend of Willie Wyler, the town drunk, who spent most of his daylight hours on the curbstone of High Street. Though they never had raised a glass together, whenever Table took a trip he always sent postcards to Willie while he forgot to send them to others who would have expected and prized them. It was from Willie one could learn when the Tables were returning.

The great novelist took his role as townsman seriously. He had become a Wrestonite, not just a summer resident. When he visited Boston or New York, he frequented the best hotels and restaurants, but he would rather have taken a pratfall at the Ritz or at Pavillon than find that in Wreston, Jimmy Bronson, the village plumber, had become distant in his greetings.

His townsfolk Richard Table esteemed above all others, down to and including the middle-aged, hair-askew, hopelessly Raggedy Ann person of Mrs. Drought who was the Table's "help." Whether this attitude was an inversion of pride, a tribute to the gods or only productive of raw materials for his notebooks, it was of paramount importance to Table and it remained his chief vanity—beyond the pride in his work and his wife—to be accepted by ordinary people as one of them.

This being Richard Table, it followed as normally as Labor Day the Summer Season that when the county pruning crew showed up in front of his house and began lopping dead branches off trees overhanging the roadway, the novelist, whose writing was done largely at night, was out spending the time of day with the pruners. Before an hour had passed, he was handling traffic for the operation, waving a red flag to halt and pass through the bottleneck cars arriving from opposite directions.

By mid-morning he was allowed to take the hand at the buzzsaw. The crew had become Joe and Charley and "Rags" and Harry and "Feet" to him, and he was Dick, but Rags had an idea of who else this man might be. "Say, Dick, it says on your newspaper box there 'Table.' Are you that writer fellow, Richard Table?"

The novelist looked annoyed. "I guess so," he replied. "Rags, if one man tried to operate this saw by himself, could he do it? How would he go about it?"

Rags said no more on the subject of identity, but on the way home he told the crew who Table was. When they showed up the following morning they seemed even more pleased at the novelist's admiration of their skill and began shyly to press on him their own identities in terms of their greatest interests.

Charley, handling traffic that morning and having to give to it close attention, yet found occasion to tell Table, "I used to drive in the stock car races. I still go every Sunday of the season, but the wife made me quit driving last year after our fifth arrived."

Feet imparted, "I was one of those Walking Boys the shoe manufacturers hire to test out composition soles," and Harry—after several false starts—confided, "I'm getting married next month." In turn, Table told them that he had grown up on a farm, and he talked with devotion of lambing. They were a happy band, but there was not much more work to keep them together.

Unlike her husband, Eleanor Table wrote best in the mornings and as she presently was hard at work on an article nearly due, she had not witnessed the fellowship in front of the house on either day. She had a makeshift study off the kitchen where she could seclude herself, yet be not too far removed from her housewifely duties with their unyielding demands on time and of timing. The oven could be turned on or off, and the delivery boy or repair man admitted and her retreat accomplished with a minimum of diversion.

Accustomed to Eleanor's morning isolation, Table hadn't missed her presence, but he thought of her when Rags—the sweat saturating his shirt—asked, "Dick, is there some place we could get a drink of cold water?"

"Sure." Table's impulse was to fetch a jug of water for everybody, but he was reluctant to let go the rope he was holding, for this was the last limb to be felled. He knew Eleanor would be just near the source of supply in the kitchen. If they went for water themselves, they would see her. Might as well let them have a look at her, he thought in secret pride.

"My wife's in the kitchen. Just go on back and ask her for a drink. Any of you other fellows want one?"

When Rags returned, he gave Table a new and assessing look. It wasn't the usual look the novelist collected when he had displayed his wife, but the fall of the limb was too imminent to reflect on it. Then Charley went for a drink. He too reestimated Table upon his return and spoke to Harry and Feet, who went for water while Table happily assisted in the final sawing of branches, the loading and packing of gear. Joe was the last to make the trip to the kitchen and upon his reappearance the crew climbed aboard their truck, said they would be working out toward Wreston Junction that afternoon and bade hearty farewell to Table; too hearty, it suddenly occurred to him, almost as if they were sorry for him about something.

His novelist's imagination would not have taken long to figure it out, but almost before he had begun to think, Table had arrived at his own back door and entered the kitchen to be confronted by that offense to the eye that was Mrs. Drought. She stood at the sink doing a belated washing up. At her elbow were the glasses used by the crew. In her every feature, every property, every attitude, she was a travesty on beauty; a travesty even on homeliness. She was not old, but so unlovely.

"Did you see them—the men?"

"Yup."

"Give them water?"

"Yup."

"Oh, my God! Mrs. Table, where is she?"

"Inside." Agreeable but monosyllabic as ever, Mrs. Drought nodded toward the study.

"Eleanor!" Table burst in on his wife. "Come quick. We have to go someplace. Get your hat on."

"Get my hat on?" With Botticelli grace, Eleanor's neck curved toward him, lifting her head in wonderment. One hand rose to lips parted in astonishment as her mind groped its way back from abstraction.

"Yes, hurry." He didn't know quite why she had to have her hat on; her hair was a glory. But after a mistaken dose of Mrs. Drought, when the crew did see his wife she was to be not only a beauty but unmistakably the lady she was.

"But Richard, I'm writing!"

"Oh, bother your writing. This is important."

Eleanor's expression of amazement changed warningly; resentment, withdrawal, refusal lay just a finger snap away. "Well, so is this!"

Table quickly changed tack. "Come on, Eleanor, please. I'll read your manuscript for you tonight and correct your spelling."

An expression of craving, almost greed, appeared on Eleanor's lovely face. Her spelling was a sacrilege, and she once had been known to substitute the word "wax" for "paraffin" to avoid tracking down its double "ff's" in the dictionary. "You're not to touch the article though!"

"Of course not. That's not fair to you." He stretched out a hand to pull her from behind the desk.

"Why do we have to go now? Tell me that anyway."

"Some men. I've got to find some men who were working here."

"On our place?"

"No, on the road." He piloted her through the door toward the hall. "That highway tree pruning crew. Have to see them about something."

"Is anything wrong?"

"No, nothing's wrong." Table's tone was irritated and Eleanor asked no more as she loathed unpleasantness and knew that Table, when pushed beyond his willingness, could become malevolent. From the hall closet she snatched a small coolie style hat of crushable straw that she had used for the beach. She had picked it up in Portofino for a dollar.

"No, not that one!" and Table reached for an infinitely more expensive version of the same thing, by Bergdorf Goodman. Eleanor, further astounded, fell into aimless actions—refreshing her lipstick and searching her purse for keys—and Table shouting, "I'll get the car started," sped out the door.

The automobile he affected for village driving—though he kept a late model luxury car for trips farther afield—was a marvelously preserved classic, an open touring car of obscure origin. It took a bit of starting but thereafter progressed with regal locomotion.

Eleanor was waiting on the steps as he wheeled to a halt before the house. Without exchange between them, she got in; Table let out the clutch, turned left off his driveway and started for Wreston Junction. It was nearly noon.

Wreston Junction was not much more than a widening of the highway with a few streets parallel and behind it on either side. Sitting high in the ancient car, the Tables toured these streets slowly, Eleanor bemused and Table peering and listening intently as though the brilliant yellow truck with its buzz saw could escape the notice of any but the blind and deaf. He searched the same small area again, then reluctantly pulled in at Jake's Gas and Take Out Shack. All that was known in the Junction was known at Jake's.

"Yes, they was here," Jake informed Table. "Did some phoning and didn't buy lunch. Said their orders was changed and they was to go to one of the Springs for the afternoon."

Wreston itself was one of a constellation of villages of similar size and brilliance in Quincy County, the others of which all were named Springs, in one fashion or another: North Springs, South Springs, Mill Springs, Green Springs, and Springtown itself.

"Which Springs?" Table asked with what Jake took to be unseemly urgency.

"I can't recollect." And no amount of prodding or prompting aided his recollection.

Throughout the conversation, Eleanor had sat quietly unprotesting, but at its conclusion there were intimations that her hunger and her will were about to assert themselves. Table made a quick and tactical decision. "I'll take you to lunch," he said, "in Springtown."

Eleanor was enchanted. She thought fleetingly and guiltily of time passing and that she should be at work; but knowing that Table was going to read her manuscript and that would save her hours of ploughing through the dictionary, she relaxed happily and held on to her hat.

The car was lapping up the brief miles that separated the Springs hamlets. The selection of Springtown for lunch had made it necessary for them to pass through North Springs on the way, but it held no sign of a pruning truck and heavy equipment. Table pushed on toward Springtown and there—as if diligence ever brought reward—just inside the town limits he spotted the truck. It was unattended and work obviously had been suspended for the lunch hour, as ropes hung from trees and still uncut branches were piled before the buzz saw. But with his quarry assured, Table beamed at Eleanor and drove her on to their favorite restaurant.

He gave her two martinis, though he himself had only one, and watched and listened to her with fondness and amusement as she told him of her chagrin that morning when she couldn't find the word "surprise" in the dictionary.

"Richard, it is too shaming to be the way I am about spelling. I looked in two dictionaries and checked every word beginning with 'sup' before I just stumbled over it in the 'sur'." It was a sign—as it is with most married couples—that things were particularly well between them when they could discuss with each other their failings and faults rather than hide them.

Eleanor relinquished her martini glass for food. "I'm quite used to looking up words that have silent letters and too many consonants . . ."

"How do you spell that?"

"Oh hush, Richard! Do be serious. But to think that all my life I even pronounced it 'suprise'. It's humiliating!"

Though Eleanor never had known the purpose of the chase that engaged them, she had by now quite forgotten they had a purpose. Not so Table. Without conspicuous haste, he kept things moving. He paid the check, got Eleanor back to the car, regarded her for a moment with the heightened appreciation that anticipates the admiration of others, then headed the car toward the street where the pruning truck was parked. Men were at work now. He went around an extra block so he could approach the crew on their side of the street. He steered the car slowly and majestically toward them until, suddenly agitated, he briefly accelerated and then jerked it to a halt alongside the buzz saw. "Where's the other crew?" he shouted as if to usurpers, forgetting for once to honor and to make common cause with the common man.

"What other crew?"

"The one from Wreston."

"There isn't any crew from Wreston. We all work for the county."

"I mean the one that was working in Wreston this morning."

"How should I know?"

"Mill Springs," Table muttered to Eleanor as he threw the vehicle into gear. "Let's go to Mill Springs."

"Whatever for, Richard? I wish you'd tell me what this is all about."

"It's not about anything! I just want to drive around. Can't we take an afternoon to just drive around if we want to?"

His belligerent tone warned against reply, but the wind allowed

Eleanor to retort, safely unheard, "If 'we' want to? 'We'!" Her words were blown away and so, it seemed, was the New England country-side as stretches of its varied beauty, in succession, dropped behind the car's forward-thrusting hood. Again Eleanor held onto her hat and re-leased her grasp only as they pulled into and searched Mill Springs and then Green Springs, while Table listened intently and peered down vista and intersecting vista of shady streets.

There was only one place left, South Springs, and Table headed for it. He and Eleanor long since had ceased to communicate. She had not again condescended to ask his purpose, and he had only that in mind. He took the back road out of Green Springs and let the great car roar. Seven fast miles would see it done or not. But they had to be there, Table told himself. Jake had said "one of the Springs," and if Jake hadn't known he would have said nothing at all, and no amount of coaxing would have got a speculation out of him.

But Jake had known, and Table heard the buzz saw minutes before the yellow truck, dazzling as a festival float, loomed before them at the beginning of South Springs' main street. There in the road and immedi-ately recognizable stood Feet, red flag in hand, waving on the inter-mittent traffic. In one instant, Table's stubborn and angry face of the afternoon shucked off that mask for one of redressed pride and swift gaiety. "Eleanor, there they are!"

His announcement couldn't have been less necessary. Eleanor no more than he could have failed to sight the crew, and following the day's inexplicable chase she viewed them and approached them with eager expectancy, the while—and with unconscious femininity—as-suming her most engaging expression in preparation for an occurrence of importance, whatever unlikely form it might take.

"Feet," Table called as they advanced, and he let the roadster slow-march, with parade-ground pride, toward the red flag. "Hey, Feet!"

Feet, whose attention first had been caught by the ancient car, tried to wave it on, then raised his glance to the sound of his name and to the driver. "Dick! Hey guys, here's Dick."

One by one they straightened up from their postures of work on the ground or peered down from the limbs of the tree. Rags threw the buzz saw into idle. Thinking Table would pull up behind the truck, Eleanor grasped her handbag making ready to descend. So slowly were they going it seemed the car would stop of its own accord, but Table inched it on. As it crept past the men he made a fan-like wave with his arm, from low left to high right, and grinning with utter satisfaction sang out, "Hiya, fellows!" At the very top of his wave and when the car was at dead center before the crew, he added, "My wife and I are just out for a drive." And they rolled on.

Calls of fellowship and what could not have been other than a whistle followed them, but Eleanor's attention had swiveled and fastened on Table. For a mile or two, as the old car purred lion-like she regarded her husband with the same astonishment that had transfixed her when he burst into her study and told her to put on her hat. "But you didn't even talk to them!" finally broke from her. The wind blew it away.

Table, humming to himself, nodded and smiled at her inaudible words.

"I thought you had to see them about something!"

"What?" he bent toward her.

"I thought you had to see them about something. It was important!"

"I did. I saw them." He leaned back to the wheel, then exuberantly let a line or two of lyrics slip into the song he was humming.

That night after dinner he took Eleanor's manuscript and, with dispatch, corrected every misspelling in it. He even said, if rather absently—as he handed it back to her and his eyes encountered her beauty—that it wasn't bad.   END

Spring Thaw

by Kenneth Andler

Thaddeus Crosby was fourteen the very day he received the invitation. He was filling the woodbox in the farm kitchen when he saw the envelope lying on the table.

"There's a letter for you, Thad," his mother said. Beginning to prepare supper, she was energetically poking up the range fire with a lid lifter.

The boy turned over the envelope in his calloused hands, staring at it curiously. He fumbled open the letter and read it. Then without a word he handed it to his mother. She held it at arm's length to read.

"Why, that's fine, Thad," she said, an unnatural tightness in her voice. "You'll go, won't you?"

The boy, still silent, gazed out the open kitchen door at the New Hampshire mountains.

"No," he hoarsely replied at last. "I couldn't."

"Why, of course you could," his mother said earnestly, her voice rising. She went to him and put her arm around his shoulders. Standing hardly an inch taller than her son, she was all wiry determination.

"Father and Son Banquet!" Thad exclaimed, stiffening beneath her arm. "Why, heck, Ma, it was just a year ago today that Pa died."

"I know, I know," she said gently. "But the letter says that any boys without fathers to go with them can have a man be their father for that night."

"Aw," Thad replied, "I just couldn't do that."

"It'll do you good, Thad," Mrs. Crosby said with an air of finality as she moved over to the stove and became all business with the kettles and skillet. "It's not good for you never to go anywhere. You used to before . . ." Glancing at her son, she restrained herself with an effort from saying more.

Thad went out and began splitting wood in the yard, but he slowed down gradually and, driving his axe into the block, he stood lost in thought, staring off at the amethystine mountains soft in the May sunset. From the lower meadows the trilling of peepers rose into the crisp spring air.

Just a year ago he had come out here while the doctor sat at his father's bedside. He remembered just how the overturned tractor had looked off there in the side-hill field—the horrible mute evidence of the fatal accident. He recalled as though it were yesterday—could he ever forget it?—his mother coming to the kitchen door and the strange note of disbelief overriding the pain in her cry, "He's gone, Thad! He's gone!"

That's when the ice had begun to form about his heart. And when his mother's voice had died away in the farthest reaches of his brain, how the shrilling of the peepers in the evening air had risen up to engulf him.

Thad loosened the axe from the chopping block and absently ran his thumb along the blade. "It's the lonesomest sound in the world," he muttered.

Then the terrible gnawing thought which had possessed him for so long now, without any real basis in fact he sometimes realized, returned like a spectre—surely his father had wanted him to plough with the tractor that day. But he had gone to play ball in the village instead. It wouldn't have happened if . . . Thad fought it down as best he could and set a birch stick on the block.

He had been the man of the house for a year now. He was growing rugged, but he wasn't doing well in school although he used to get all A's. There was no time any more to play with the other boys, and he felt ill at ease in their company. He hardly ever left his own tiny village of Royden to go to the county seat of Oldsboro where the banquet was to be.

He just couldn't imagine getting up enough nerve to go to that meeting with all those men and boys from the whole county. And to have a man he didn't know for a "father!" Yet he desperately wanted to go—he couldn't tell why.

All winter he hadn't been anywhere. It might even be fun! Adventurous, like. Gosh, suppose he dared! Then as the picture of himself actually at the banquet flashed before him with terrifying vividness, he felt such a sinking in his stomach that he sat down upon the chopping block. Well, he thought, as the pang subsided, it's not for a week anyway.

As he continued to sit there, the yearning to go, like a kindled fire, flickered unquenched within him, blazing up now and then with a power he could not understand.

The sun was low as Thad pedaled his rickety bicycle toward Oldsboro on the day of the banquet. His cheeks shone from scrubbing, and his dark hair was neatly combed. He was ordinarily a rather good-looking boy with a broad, pleasant face and strong features, but right now there was a squint of determination about his dark blue eyes, and his mouth was set in a grim, level line.

This was going to be agony, he knew, but he guessed his mother was right. She usually was. It was a part of growing up, she had said. You had to face things, even though they tortured your very spirit.

"If you take hold of a thistle scared-like," she often said, "it will prick your fingers. But grab it firmly and it won't hurt you."

He wheeled along into the main part of Oldsboro, past the village green with the late afternoon shadows of tall elms lying long across the grass, past the Free Library, the County Court House, and down the half mile street to the South Church. Then his heart sank.

Gathered on the lawn in front of the church large groups of boys stood about, talking and skylarking. The building itself formed a background of imposing majesty with its brick, ivy-covered walls and white colonial spire, glowing in the sunset. The youngsters were so free and gay, the church so impressive and dignified, that Thad felt he could not possibly become a part of all this. He simply did not belong.

And how dressed up those boys were! Thad looked down at his dark trousers which were too short for him, at the tie which had been his father's and didn't seem right somehow, at his pull-over tan sweater so thin at the elbows. His knockabout work shoes, too, were quite unlike the well-shined oxfords those boys were wearing.

He fought down the panic which clamored for him to turn about and go home. Dismounting, he leaned his bike against a tree near the sidewalk. As he ambled toward the church with his clammy fists clenched in his trousers' pockets, he could see the boys turn to look at him, and he noticed with dismay that their conversation seemed to die down. It was borne in upon him poignantly that he was a farm boy, and poor; that his father was dead and here he was, so out of place, at this swell affair, a Father and Son Banquet. How could he have been crazy enough to let his mother talk him into coming?

But he kept plodding blindly ahead, and suddenly a dinner bell began clanging from the vestry. All the boys turned and moved toward the open doors where the fathers were standing.

A stocky, middle-aged man, with graying hair, pink cheeks and steel-rimmed glasses, Mr. Gibson, the Y.M.C.A. Secretary, his countenance beaming, came up to Thad, took him warmly by the hand and introduced him to his "father" for the evening, Alvin Wheeler.

Thad muttered a blurred, "Hello." He had seen Mr. Wheeler clerking in the hardware store—a tall, thin, sallow man who could turn on a smile and turn it off as one would operate an electric light.

The crowd of men and boys entered the large room filled with long tables on which the food, served family style, lay steaming. The hubbub of voices, the clatter of dishes, the bustling about of the church women who were "putting on the supper," the scraping of chairs being placed seemed perfect bedlam to Thad after his quiet farm kitchen. He stayed close to Mr. Wheeler and, looking up at him now and then, was rewarded by a flashing smile which disappeared as suddenly as it came.

Gradually everyone was seated, a hush seeped into the room and the minister said grace. It occurred to Thad as he saw them all pitch in to the meal that they were too busy to pay any attention to him, and he felt his tension easing. Suddenly he was hungry and he began to eat as though he hadn't eaten for a week, as indeed he hadn't, very much.

When the dinner was over and dishes removed, Mr. Gibson arose at the head table, rapping his water glass with a knife. As toastmaster and secretary of the county, he made some welcoming remarks. Various prominent citizens also spoke, somewhat at length. Then came the speech of the evening by a professional orator.

Thad became painfully aware that the other boys were getting bored and were looking at him curiously. As the speaker finally finished amidst synthetic applause, Thad anxiously assured himself that it was all over and that now he could sneak out of here fast for home.

Thad squirmed in his chair while Toastmaster Gibson launched into what appeared to be a conclusion to the program. Only half listening, Thad suddenly was startled to hear his own name and to see every eye upon him. Shaken to his boots, he strained for every word the man was saying.

"And this boy," the Toastmaster went on, "Thaddeus Crosby, who has been carrying on his mother's farm, has pedaled his bike seven miles, all the way down here from Royden, just to be with us tonight. How about a few words from you, Thad?"

The youngster felt the blood draining from his face and then come surging back to flush his neck and cheeks to the roots of his hair. This was worse than all the nightmares he had had this past week. Make a speech! It was impossible! Everyone was staring at him. He looked around frantically as though there might be a way to escape. But some vague advice about firmly grabbing a thistle raced through his confused mind.

Unaccountably, he found himself on his feet as though he were some- one else. He even heard himself talking, although his voice sounded strange to him.

"Well, gee," he began in a low tone, "I didn't know I'd have to make a speech. I never made one before. It gives me a shaky feeling all over. My knees are knocking together."

He looked down at them. They were knocking against each other, surely enough.

"And my stomach," he went on forcing a grin, and trying to speak up, "is full of birds or something. I never felt like this before. Do people always feel this way when they make a speech? I can't even see good. Everybody is just a blur out there. We don't have much going on up to Royden and all this seems like a mighty big thing to me around here."

Waves of friendly laughter and applause shook the room.

Thad picked up a tumbler of water with a trembling hand and gulped it down. Why, these people seemed to like him! They were laughing with him, not at him, he could see that. His vision cleared so he could see them all as individuals.

"I guess I ought to say one thing," Thad went on, his voice steadier now and sounding like his own, "and that is, you boys that have fathers ought to appreciate 'em. You don't think much about your father until you lose him and then it's too late. A father is mighty important to a boy. Mine died a year ago."

Thad's saying that made him catch his breath. He hadn't thought of mentioning any such thing. But somehow he wanted to talk, and it didn't seem to matter that he was speaking to a whole roomful of men and boys. He hadn't even told his mother how he felt, but had kept his feelings bottled up inside. Now he seemed to be bursting with things to say.

"You don't know how much work a father does until you try it yourself," Thad went on. "I've found out about that this last year. And with a father you feel more protected.

"Once I was out in a rowboat in the middle of Long Pond and it got to leaking and sank mighty fast. Instead of sitting there comfortable, fishing, I found myself in the water and had to start swimming. That's one way I felt when I lost my father. There were other ways . . . " His voice drifted off, but he began again with an effort.

"If your father dies, you feel awful bad to think of things he asked you to do that you never quite got around to. And you think of times when you wanted to tell him things to cheer him up and you hadn't said those things at all. You think of the times you might have shown him how much you cared for him and you hadn't done it. So everything gets to sticking in your head and you can't get it out. You even get to blaming yourself for—for all kinds of things."

Thad noticed with surprise that here and there a boy's lip was trembling, that Mr. Wheeler was blowing his nose, and that Mr. Gibson was removing his glasses and appeared to be polishing them with his handkerchief.

"Well," Thad concluded, "I guess that's all I've got to say so I'll sit down."

There was a long moment of complete silence, and then the room rocked with applause. The meeting broke up, and all the boys and their fathers, too, crowded around Thad, pounded him on the back and shook his hand.

Old Judge Tandy, who never spoke to anyone unless he had to, went out of his way to tell him gruffly, "Sonny, that's the only speech these folks will ever remember if they hear a thousand of 'em."

Thad tingled all over as he pedaled back toward home. He felt alive, as he hadn't felt for months. Why, everything, the whole world looked different now! People weren't hostile if you got to know them. They didn't look down on him; in fact they seemed to look up to him. And not only had he made a speech, of all things, but it had been quite a triumph. How brilliant seemed the stars and how beautiful the sickle moon above the Royden hills!

When he came to the brook in the Two Mile Woods, he dismounted from his bicycle and scrambled through some underbrush beside the plank bridge. Lying on his stomach, he drank deeply of the cold water. How freely the brook ran and how unlike the same stream when it was locked in winter ice not long ago!

Thad remembered the very day in March that the brook was freed. There had been a big rainstorm in the night and then the morning sun, amazingly warm, had worked a quick magic. The ice had disappeared, and the liberated water had sung a lilting song.

As Thad stood up, drying his mouth with the back of his hand, he had a strange feeling that he, too, had been thawed out, unfettered somehow, just like the brook.   **END**

You Get One Wish

by Richard S. Ullery

When Mrs. Bush, Dean Mortimer Owen's secretary, entered the inner office and announced that a young man named Llewellyn Griffith was waiting to see him, the dean swivelled his chair away from the ground-floor window that looked out on the campus beyond and told her to send in Mr. Griffith right away. He laid his report on the findings of the President's Advisory Committee aside, and awaited, with some eagerness, the appearance of his caller.

He was not acquainted with Llewellyn Griffith, but the name, obviously Welsh, stirred his imagination.

Dean Owen liked to describe himself as a Welshman. In any conversation he would, if at all possible, insert some remark about his Welsh lineage. With or without encouragement he was always ready to trace, in detail, his claimed descent from that Owen Glendower who made things so disagreeable for the English king in the fifteenth century. In the frequent and spirited arguments with faculty colleagues which help to lend spice to the daily doings of a college dean he was noted for his obstinacy, which he proudly attributed to what he chose to call his native Cambrian doggedness. However, there were those on campus who felt that his aggressive attitudes merely reflected his natural disposition, which some characterized as that of a thoroughgoing stinker.

He chose to ignore the fact that the first Owen in America, who had arrived about 1760, had espoused an English girl and that for six generations the Owens had been marrying into various families of French, English, German and Scottish descent. Dr. Haskell, chairman of the English department, a sturdy opponent of the dean in many campus controversies, had pointed out that from the time Owen's ancestor had come to this country from Llangerose or Glynncorreweg (the dean could not be sure which), the Welsh strain must have suffered considerable dilution.

Dr. Haskell had compared the strength of Welsh blood in Dean Owen's veins to that of a teaspoon of alcohol in a bucket of water. Pure jealousy, the dean had retorted, because of Haskell's inability to trace his own ancestry back beyond his grandparents. Dean Owen had been heard to imply that even in that tiny family tree only half its branches could be established with any degree of certainty. Many faculty members felt that this was going a bit too far, even for a person of Dean Owen's known propensities.   As a result, his wrangles with Dr. Haskell had become so vitriolic that Dean Owen often regarded with sympathy the historically unpopular attitude of Aaron Burr toward the activities of Alexander Hamilton.

No one in Dean Owen's circle of acquaintance was of Welsh descent. The prospect of meeting someone named Llewellyn Griffith excited him. Stanley, trudging his lonely way across darkest Africa, and learning that Livingstone was in the next village, must have felt much the same way.

The young man who entered the dean's office was rangy, red-haired and apparently about twenty-five years of age. Dean Owen thought it appropriate to greet him in Welsh.

"*Yn bur ganolig*," Llewellyn Griffith replied.

Unfortunately, the dean had gone as far as he could in the ancestral tongue. He had often thought of studying Welsh seriously, but had been unable to find anyone to teach him.

"Please sit down," he said. "What can I do for you?"

The young man pulled a chair close to the dean's desk. "*O Cymru deuais i'th weled, deuis fel y'th welwyn,*" he continued.

"Would you mind speaking English?" the dean asked. "My Welsh is a trifle rusty."

"Very well," Llewellyn Griffith said. "I was saying that I came from Wales to see you. You are in the direct line from the Mortimer Owen who came to this country two hundred years ago."

"Yes," the dean agreed. "How do you happen to know that?"

The young man paid no attention to the question. "The Owen family in Wales has died out," he said.

"I'm sorry to hear it," the dean said.

"So, you are also the oldest living direct descendant of Owen Glendower."

"Well," Dean Owen said, "I have often told people so, but I was never really sure. Thank you for bringing me the information, Mr. Griffith. Can I help you in any way?"

"No. But I am duty bound to do something for you."

"How is that?" the dean inquired.

"I am of the fortieth generation in direct line from Merlin," Llewellyn said.

"Merlin, the magician of King Arthur's court?" Dean Owen stared doubtfully at the young man. "I had never heard that he had children."

"The written histories don't mention him after his girl friend Vivian put a spell on him and imprisoned him under a rock," Llewellyn admitted. "But he was not quite so sequestered as you might think."

"But how could—who—you are joking, young man," the dean stammered.

"There was some scandal at the time, but things were hushed up. That was when the family name was changed to Griffith. Let's leave it at that," Llewellyn said. "Now, let me tell you why I am here."

"I should certainly like to know," Dean Owen said.

"Please don't keep interrupting," Llewellyn said, leaning back in his chair and putting his fingertips together.

"Owen Glendower died five hundred years ago," he said. "Because of his courageous fight for Wales against the English invaders, the head of the Griffith family of that time—Merlin's direct descendant, and my ancestor—vowed that he, and those who would succeed him as head of the family, would see to it that one wish would be granted to the eldest male in direct line from Owen Glendower in each generation, forever."

The dean leaned forward, fascinated. The telephone on his desk shrilled. "I can't talk to anyone now, Mrs. Bush," he said. "Go ahead, Mr. Griffith."

"There was some difficulty at first because, as you may know, after Owen Glendower's death all members of his family dropped their surname and became known as Owen—for security reasons. But the vow that was made has been faithfully kept in each generation. For example, the wish made by the Owen who came to this country two hundred years ago was that he could get to America."

Dean Owen's scalp crinkled. "Are you trying to tell me," he gasped, "that Merlin's powers have been passed down—"

"Of course," Llewellyn said impatiently. "You inherited your grey eyes, didn't you?"

"Well, yes," the dean agreed. "But I'm not sure that my ancestor who lived in Merlin's time had grey eyes—"

"Don't argue about details," Llewellyn ordered. He shifted his gaze from the window, and his eyes bored into Dean Owen's. "When your great-great-grandfather, or whatever he was, left Wales, there was considerable discussion in my family about who should next inherit the wish. Finally it was decided that it should be granted to the oldest Owen still living in Wales. Now, as I have told you, the last Owen over there directly descended from Owen Glendower has died. And so—"

"You mean," the dean broke in, "that the chance to have a wish granted now comes to me?"

"Naturally," Llewellyn said. "If it has taken you all this time to figure that out, it seems to me that the intelligence of the Owen family has sadly deteriorated—"

"I should like to improve my golf game," Dean Owen said wistfully.

"Let's not be frivolous," Llewellyn said sharply. "I could do that for you, of course. But I should hope that you'd wish for something of more magnitude than to excel in a sport invented by stupid Scots."

The dean, who had been striving for some years without success to play a golf course in less than 97 strokes, resented this aspersion against the royal and ancient game. But before he could retort, Llewellyn had engulfed him in a further flow of words.

"This trip has been difficult enough for me without your trying to be humorous," he complained. "I can grant you any one wish— within reason. I can't give you eternal life. Or turn you into an elephant or a donkey—although I must say that the latter might be appropriate."

The dean felt that it was time to end this nonsense. "All right, Mr. Griffith," he said. "I have work to do. Who put you up to coming here? Was it Dr. Haskell?"

"I do not know any Dr. Haskell. I have told you that I am here because I am under orders from the head of my family to do something for you." He hesitated a moment before continuing. "Something happened in my last assignment—it was not my fault—but things went wrong. I cannot afford to waste time or make any mistake in your case, or I shall suffer for it. Tell me what you would like to happen to you."

The young man must be mildly insane, the dean thought; probably I should humor him, until I can get him out of my office. "I don't know what to ask for," he said.

Llewellyn Griffith struck his fist on the desk. *"Diawl!"* he exclaimed. "A man who doesn't know what he wants out of life! How the Glendower line has degenerated! But—I am bound to help you. You have worked at this college a long time. Would you like to be its president?"

A shudder tremored Dean Owen's body. He recalled vividly the comment made by Shakespeare's Henry IV about the uneasiness of the head that wears a crown. "No indeed!" he replied with sincerity.

Llewellyn rolled his eyes despairingly. "There must be something you want! Have you no ambition at all?"

"Well, " the dean said, "I have always wanted to know the Welsh language as if it were my native tongue." If this were not merely the nonsense of a slightly crazed young man, he thought, how gratifying it would be, when Haskell makes some snide remark about my paucity of Welsh blood, to be able to come back at him with a vituperative retort delivered entirely in Welsh!

"Consider it done," Llewellyn said. "From now on it will be as though you had been born and brought up in Wales." He rose. "Goodbye, and may your granted wish bring you happiness," he said, in Welsh.

The dean stood up and extended his hand. "Thank you. It has been a pleasure to meet you," he said, also in Welsh.

When Llewellyn Griffith had left, Dean Owen stared for a little while out his window, half smiling at the recollection of the fantastic conversation with that somewhat addled young man. But he's certainly harmless, he thought, and squared himself up to his desk again.

He picked up the report on the findings of the President's Advisory Committee, which he was scheduled to present at the faculty meeting next day. This will be a crusher for Haskell, he mused; he'll have a minority report to make, but I'll swarm all over him. I'll take him down a few pegs tomorrow. He shoved the report into his pocket and picked up the phone.

"Who called me a few minutes ago?" he asked Mrs. Bush.

"What did you say, Dean?"

"I asked you, who wanted to talk with me?"

"I'm sorry, sir, I can't understand a word you're saying," Mrs. Bush answered. "Dean Owen, are you ill?"

At this point the dean realized that he had been speaking Welsh. He had understood what she was saying, but only Welsh phrases had sprung to his lips in reply. It was like that time in Quebec when he had tried to talk French with Canadians and had found to his horror that all knowledge of that language had deserted him. He struggled for English words. He thought of Thoreau's man, who heard a different drummer. Into his reeling brain flashed a terrifying vision. The faculty meeting tomorrow. Himself striving to put into words the report he was to make. Hopelessly groping and stammering. And that man Haskell giving his minority report with his customary fluency.

He groaned, dropped the telephone on his desk and clutched dizzily at his head.

The collective undertone gabble of the hundred or so faculty members attending the meeting began to fade when the president rapped with his gavel. The buzzing became muted in the seats immediately in front of the president's chair, and silence gradually overpowered the chatter, row by row, until the room was quiet.

Dean Owen, sitting in his usual place directly in front of the president, had not engaged in the customary pre-meeting conversations that had occupied his colleagues. He had purposely entered later than most, and had responded to greetings with only a nod or a slight wave. When seated, he appeared to be studying with great care the sheets of the committee report which he was scheduled to present, and with such apparent concentration that he seemed oblivious of what went on around him.

The truth was that he did not dare to talk with anyone. He had escaped from his office and his secretary the afternoon before by simulating a severe coughing spell, and had thus concealed from Mrs. Bush the awful fact that whatever he might have said would have had to come out in Welsh.

In his bachelor apartment, panicky and terrified, he had experimented and found that, while he could occasionally think of some English words, his speech was an uncontrollable garble of Welsh and English. He could understand English—he discovered that by turning on the television—but that was small consolation.

He thought again of the faculty meeting and the report he was to make. How could he do that in his present state? He could of course claim illness . . . nervously he picked up his report. To his surprise, he found that he could read it perfectly well. He spoke the first sentence aloud, and knew that his words were English. So the spell is faulty, he thought. He recalled that Llewellyn had mentioned having made a mistake in some previous assignment. "He certainly mixed up this one," he said aloud—and realized that he was speaking Welsh. "When I speak my thoughts it comes out Welsh—but when I *read* aloud it is English." I can present my report, he had mused. I can read it; but I must try not to speak with anyone at the meeting. Afterward I'll arrange a leave of absence. Maybe I can find Llewellyn, somehow. Anyway, if I practice constantly speaking and reading aloud, perhaps the spell will wear off.

So now he sat silently in the faculty meeting, half listening to the inevitable motion to omit the reading of the minutes of the last meeting; the report of the dean of students concerning the latest "manifestation of student unrest," and his deft parrying of a question from the floor as to which, if any, of the staff might have been involved in fermenting such manifestations; the reading of the academic standing committee's list of students who should be dropped from the rolls for "failing to maintain the scholastic standards required by the college," followed by a brief and disregarded protest from the director of athletics that some of his best boys were on that list; a question from the chairman of the philosophy department, who wondered if anyone had given any thought to upgrading the prestige of our campus lecture series, and pointing out that he had been unable to discover anyone on the schedule representing the very important field of philosophy, and a bristling reply from the chairman of the lecture committee, who stated that a great deal of thought had been given to the choice of lecturers, and that the omission of philosophers was because usually they were less than inspiring speakers—meaning, of course, no disrespect to anyone present.

The beehive buzz had gradually increased while these matters were discussed. Dean Owen, glancing up from his papers, glimpsed his ancient enemy, Dr. Haskell, leaning back to whisper to the people behind him and gesturing with a handful of sheets, which the dean knew to be the minority report which Dr. Haskell would present after Dean Owen had read the majority report.

"And now," the president said, as the chairman of the lecture committee, with a final venomous stare at the philosophy chairman, took his seat, "and now, the very important item on our agenda, the report on the findings of the President's Advisory Committee. Dean Owen."

Dean Owen rose, bowed silently to the president, and began to read.

"In view of the controversial nature of the subjects discussed, and the findings of the Committee, which were not unanimous, it was decided that two reports should be made. I will now read the majority report." As he read he realized joyfully that his rendition was quite normal, and the silence of his listeners showed that they were impressed. He finished and sat down.

Out of the hum and buzz that immediately arose, the voice of Dr. Haskell sounded stridently.

"Just a minute! Before I read the minority report, I must point out that some of the statements presented by Dean Owen do not at all coincide with my recollection of what occurred. To be frank, I am reluctantly forced to believe that the dean has colored and loaded parts of his report so as to put forward, most unfairly, some very unwarranted assumptions not shared by several other members of the committee, including myself. I would like to ask Dean Owen a few questions on these points."

"That would seem to be in order, if it will clarify matters," the president said. "Please proceed, Dr. Haskell."

Dr. Haskell asked his question. Dean Owen knew very well the answer he wished to make. He achieved what he hoped was a sarcastic and superior smile and made an intensely concentrated attempt to utter the English words. When he spoke, every one of the faculty turned toward him in amazement. Their comments surrounded his voice like a haze. "What's wrong? Is he sick? A stroke, perhaps?"

He broke off the flow of Welsh words. The president rose from his chair. "Are you all right, Dean Owen?"

Dizzy, his brain almost numbed by the failure of his tremendous effort, he answered, *"Na ganolig."* Then, from the blank, whirling vortex of his racked mind he managed to dredge up a translation. "Not—well," Dean Owen gasped.

The dean sat at home, reading English aloud, which he hoped would help to break the spell. It was the second week of his sick leave. When the phone rang, he reached for another book in which he had found the sentence, "I'm sorry, I cannot talk with you now." He had been using this phrase in answering the telephone; if he read it aloud, he could be sure of not breaking into Welsh. "I'm sorry, I cannot talk with you," he began, and was interrupted.

"You must. Llewellyn Griffith here."

Dean Owen gripped the phone and his heart pounded. "Where are you?" he demanded, not knowing whether he was speaking Welsh or English, and not caring.

"Penarth, in Wales," Llewellyn replied.

"I was never so glad to hear from anyone in my—"

"Let me talk. You have an elder cousin in America—I should have looked him up rather than you. The directions I received confused me. My family is sending my cousin Harlech to see him."

"What about me? Your spell has been a terrible thing—"

"I must recall the gift I made to you—it was of course a mistake."

"Good!" Dean Owen said. "Can you do it right now?"

"The spell is dissolved as of this moment."

"Hurray!" shouted the dean, happily conscious that he was no longer speaking Welsh. Captain John Smith, reprieved by Pocahontas, must have enjoyed similar emotions.

"I have been instructed to tell you that another gift will be made to you, to compensate for breaking your spell."

"No! That's not necessary!"

"My cousin Harlech will come to see you about that very soon."

"Look here!" Dean Owen expostulated. "I don't want another—"

"This call is costing a great deal of money, and my family insists that I pay for it—no expense account this time," Llewellyn said. "Goodbye."

Dean Owen sits in his ground-floor office again. Mrs. Bush enters and says, "There is a young man out there to see you, named Harlech Griffith."

An unpleasant prickle courses along the dean's spine. "I cannot see him," he says.

"He says it is very important and he'll wait all day if necessary. It's to do with your being a descendant of somebody named Owen Glendower."

Dean Owen rises and walks, almost runs, to the window and opens it. Mrs. Bush stares, bewildered, as he slides across the sill. He turns toward her as his feet touch the ground. "Tell him," Dean Owen says, "that he is mistaken. I'm not descended from Owen Glendower, and there's absolutely no relationship between me and any of the Glendower family."   END

Once upon a Time

by Marga Joerden

Through the summer evening, Theodore Crawford occupied a kitchen chair hidden away beneath a green curtain of beech leaves in his son's front yard. The murmur of a television program came from an open window where the rest of the family, except his granddaughter, Carole, spent their leisure time. The chair under the tree was Theodore's substitute for a rocking chair on a front porch where a man could have a ringside seat on the world. Darned nonsense sitting in the house watching shadow people and listening to canned voices. What could a man learn about life from that?

The quarter moon above had tipped like a silver ladle and poured milky light over the neighborhood. To be truthful, there really wasn't much doing on the Portsmouth street, but Theo (Robin had always called him Theo) steadfastly refused to give up and join the others.

A flood of light and the roar of a souped-up engine interrupted his musing. Tires shrieked as the car braked before the house. The car door on Carole's side rasped open, but the young man with her had simply vaulted over his door. He had left the motor running while they stopped on the sidewalk, his granddaughter turned, received a quick kiss, and the young man took a few running steps to leap into place behind the steering wheel. He blasted off.

The girl stood there until he was out of sight and the night still again, relaxed to silence from the noise of his going. When she turned toward the house, Theo called softly, "Not much of a kisser, is he?"

"He's just a friend."

"Same guy sparking a girl most of a year has something on his mind besides friendship. Or should have."

"Sparking," Carole mimicked. Her tone implied he was hopelessly old-fashioned.

"Words and ways might change," Theo defended, "but people go on pretty much the same."

"Granddad, I'm sorry," Carole parted the curtain of beech leaves and leaned in to give Theo a hug. She laughed, a tender little sound. "I guess courting in a buggy and courting in a hot-rod are not too different."

"The buggy was a good deal quieter," Theo answered, "and if the spooning couple lost their good sense, there was still the horse to get them home."

When Carole started towards the house, Theo watched her. She seemed glum, somehow, maybe just a bit despairing.

The racing stripes on the boy's car, applied with luminescent paint, had stood out clearly in the moonlight. Racing. It had been a man's way to prove himself, he supposed, since some ancient clan established foot races. As for Theo, he remembered the urge well!

Robin had said, yes, she'd ride to the church picnic in Theo's buggy so his folks could ride with her parents.

"Sugar doll," he whispered to himself as he helped her up onto the high, black, button-tufted seat. She wore a summer dress of white eyelet flounces, cinched at the waist with a blue ribbon. A white straw hat was tied over her blonde curls with ribbons, also of blue.

"We'll take the lead," Theo said. "Then the stirred-up dust won't settle on your dress."

Robin smiled, her blue eyes bright and expectant, and her skin glowed a little deeper pink.

Theo had curried his bay gelding until the horse was as glossed as fine satin and rippled with each step like liquid caramel. The day was hot, blue sky cloudless, greening grass and field daisies dew-washed. An occasional grasshopper whirred up under the clopping hooves.

In all his daydreams, Theo was debonair, polished and courteous, and his conversation brilliant. Now he couldn't remember a single one of his gay stories, so carefully rehearsed while he worked in the hay fields. The truth was, Theo could prove himself in any kind of contest—wrestling, shooting, racing—these were his natural bent, but the social graces were something else for a farm boy.

The approaching echo of a trotting horse came from behind. Miserable in his unwanted silence, Theo felt a kind of relief when Malachi Devers pulled alongside.

"Pretty girl you got there," Malachi called, holding even as they moved along the road.

"You bet!" Theo grinned. He glanced at Robin and she was blushing.

"Race you to the picnic grounds. Winner eats ice cream with your girl."

"You're on!" Theo cried.

At the same instant they snapped the reins over their horses' backs. Malachi pulled ahead.

"He—aaa!" Theo hollered, flicking the reins again. He leaned

forward, giving the gelding its head, and they raced into the wind.
His attention was all on the contest, holding his flying track, avoiding contact with Malachi's spinning wheel hub. They swayed dangerously over the ruts, bouncing and weaving in the mad dash forward.
When they had gained a small lead, Theo glanced at Robin. Pale,
she gripped the buggy side with one hand and held her hat, ribbons
untied and streaming, with the other. His heart leaped with excitement. "Come on! He—aaa!" he urged the gelding again. He could
hear Malachi just behind, choking in the dust roiled by their wheels.

Theo's buggy rocked through the gate, almost upset, and swung
triumphantly into the picnic grounds. Pulling back smartly on the
reins, he brought the equipage to a halt, but before he could dismount
and give Robin his hand, she had jumped out.

She turned, furious, one hand still holding her hat. "You young
hell-rake!" she spat at him, and flounced away.

Deflated, Theo moped about, nibbling disinterestedly on a chicken
leg. When he saw Robin some time later, perched on a boulder and
eating freezer ice cream with Malachi, he wandered off, leaving his
father and young stepmother to drive the buggy home.

In bed that night, Theo couldn't sleep. He fretted, throwing himself about, forgetting the loud squeak of his bedsprings. After a while
Josie, his stepmother, came to the door, her figure, distorted with late
pregnancy, silhouetted in moonlight from the window.

"Anything wrong, Theo?"

He was quiet a few seconds. Then, "Why'd she act that way? The
race was for her."

"Was it?"

"Well . . . at least to *show* her."

"Maybe she's looking for something more in you, Theo. Something
more grown-up."

Heat rushed up through him. "You mean I acted like a kid? I just
wanted to make her proud."

"Well, how do you suppose she felt, you risking your afternoon
with her for a race with Malachi? And how do you think it looks to
her when you have to show off every time she's around? Is that *all* you
have to show her, Theo? That you can always *beat* someone?"

Theo didn't answer, and Josie went back to bed. Josie was nearer
to his own age than his father's. He liked his stepmother and was willing
to consider what she said.

Several weeks later, on Saturday morning, Theo worked in the vegetable garden pulling weeds. He stopped just long enough to wipe
his face and drink a dipper of cool water. He tried to avoid thinking

about the dance that evening. Oh, he would be there, but he disciplined his mind from imagining himself gliding smoothly across the floor, Robin in his arms. He just knew his feet would get tangled up like last time when he was on the dance floor.

Substituting a look out over the valley for his daydreams, he had a pleasurable thought that some day part of this land would be his. The landscape shimmered in the sun. The sky stretched in indolent brilliance, cupping the gently swelling breast of a distant rise. "Robin's eyes are brighter than the sky above Strafford Blue Hills," he said aloud. The comparison delighted him. He smiled and went back to work.

Shortly before dusk, he bathed in Halfmoon Pond and dressed in the clean clothes he had stashed in nearby bushes. The white shirt had a small rip, and he told Josie about it when he went in. She turned from the black iron cookstove.

"I'm sorry, Theo. There's another one ironed, but a button's missing. You sit right here while I sew it on."

He ate while she sat across from him replacing the button with quick stitches. Josie had dark places beneath her eyes and she looked tired. When she rose, she moved with slow heaviness. Theo knew she was uneasy because her time was near and his father away brokering potatoes. She filled the dishpan with hot water from the stove.

"Maybe I should stay home, Josie. You'll be alone."

"Nonsense. You've earned a night of fun."

"Fun?" Theo snorted. "I can't even dance. My feet are tongue-tied."

She grinned at his expression.

"Theo, you've danced with me. I know you're not awkward." She rinsed the soapy dishes.

"With her I am."

"Shut your eyes and pretend it's your old stepmother."

He looked closely at her again. "I'd better not go. You don't look too good."

She turned and placed her hand on his. "I'm just tired. Going right to bed. You go to your dance."

When Theo arrived at the party, Robin was already on the floor, dancing with Malachi. Theo chose another partner and found he danced very well because his mind wasn't dwelling on it. He wanted desperately to ask Robin next, but he knew he would simply keel over if he stepped on one of her dainty slippers with his clodhopper feet. Finally, he saw her near the refreshment table and followed her there.

"Evening, Robin."

"Why, Theo! I didn't realize you were here. Are Josie and your father with you?"

"No. Papa's on a trip. Josie didn't think it proper to come since she's due . . ." He blushed and stammered, "I mean, most any day . . ."

Robin looked at him, her eyes politely asking what he meant, the corners of her mouth twitching suspiciously.

She's laughing at me! he thought, and grew even hotter. "You know—the baby."

"Oh, of course. Theo, will you tell Josie I plan to call tomorrow afternoon? And, now, you haven't danced with me."

Obediently, he led her to the floor. They were managing nicely when someone tapped Theo's shoulder. He missed a step and came down hard on Robin's foot. Her face reacted slightly, but he could see she didn't want to show the pain.

Furious, Theo whirled. Malachi was at his elbow. Theo grabbed him by the coat lapels, lifting him up on tiptoe. People quickly cleared frantically. Robin, having stepped back, moved forward again.

"Your dance, I believe," she said to Malachi.

Theo released the coat and watched Malachi dance off with Robin in his arms. Everyone was staring, and Theo stamped off the floor, the crowd opening before him. He made for the door, blind with anger. When he got home, Josie was still awake.

"I made a fool of myself again," he told her.

"Oh, Theo! What she needs to see is how sweet and helpful you can be. Like offering to miss the dance for me."

He went to sleep thinking, "She'll never know how I feel. Why do I have to act like a cocky idiot?"

When Theo awoke it was near noon, and Josie, her face pallid and drawn-looking, was calling him.

Panic erased all thought of sleep from his mind.

"It's the baby," she said, and even as she spoke, she winced with pain.

"I'll get Doc Reeves."

She shook her head. "No time."

"But I can't . . . "

"Of course you can, Theo. You have to."

As quickly as it had come, the panic ebbed. "All right, I'll be right there."

Most of the details of what happened next remained with Theo as flashing impressions blurred into a whole of incredulous awe. Josie instructed him as he sterilized thread and scissors to tie and cut the umbilical cord. Sometimes he gave Josie his hand to grasp as a pain hit, sometimes he blotted the perspiration which wet her face, or tilted a cup of water to moisten her dry lips. He placed sterile cloths in the basket to receive the infant.

But the actual moment of birth was no blur. He received the wet, warm, purplish-red lump of humanity in his hands as it emerged from the birth canal during a great thrust and groan. Quick, unexpected tears stung his eyes and a swell of emotion rose in his throat.

He felt a sudden exaltation and stared at his father's new son. As though by instinct, Theo's hands performed the required tasks. The baby started breathing. Its blue-gray eyes wonderingly searched its new environment. No bottom-whack was necessary.

"A boy," he said to Josie as he quickly wrapped the infant and placed it in the basket. "Looks fine. Breathing easily."

He turned back to the mother. The dark smudges beneath her eyes contrasted frighteningly with the pallor of her face. She lay quietly, inhaling and exhaling in deep gasps. After the ordeal was finished, Josie fell into exhausted sleep.

Theo worked in the room, cleaning and straightening. He wanted desperately to get the doctor here, to be sure the baby and mother were safe.

Before he finished, the infant began a fussy cry. Theo lifted the raucous bundle and carried him to the parlor to make him comfortable. An urgent knock sounded at the door, impatient, as though it were the second or third time. Then the door opened and Robin's worried voice called.

"Anybody home?"

He'd forgotten she was coming!

Before Theo could answer, Robin walked in. A series of emotions swept over him; a feeling of foolishness, standing there with the tiny child in his huge hands. Then embarrassment. Defensiveness. In an instant, a quick surge of pride replaced all the rest.

"Theo!" Robin cried. "The baby's here?"

"Just born," Theo answered.

"Is the doctor still with Josie?"

"Didn't have time to get him. Started too fast."

"Oh, heavens! And you handled it all by yourself! I'll stay so you can get Doctor Reeves."

Theo sighed with relief. "Would you, Robin? I was afraid of leaving them alone."

"Take my horse. She's all ready, and she's fast."

Theo couldn't speak his thanks. He handed the baby to Robin, stood there a moment, speechless, then ran out the door, untied Robin's filly, and leaped into the saddle. Cool wind tore at his hot, tired face as he sped over the countryside. It took a brisk twenty-minute ride to reach the doctor's house. Theo slid from the horse's back just as the door opened and Doc Reeves hurried out.

"Josie's baby?"

"Already here."   ·

"Everything all right?"

"Seems so with the baby. Josie—she doesn't look so good."

Doc Reeves nodded and mounted the horse his wife just then led from the barn. "No need you should keep up," he said. "That filly's tired. I'll be there when you get back." He turned his horse and urged it to a gallop.

Theo patted Robin's filly and praised her. He held sugar lumps in his palm for her to nibble before they started back. Now that the urgency was past, Theo let the horse plod along. The dramatic moments replayed themselves in his mind at an accelerated tempo. Finally, he came to the fast ride to the doctor's, hearing the loud echo as the flying hooves flashed over a wooden bridge, and the strange, muffled sound of galloping through a green tunnel of birch trees.

Suddenly, an impression broke through the rest, a moment just before leaving the house. There had been something new in the way Robin looked at him. He couldn't quite peg it, but if she usually seemed to be looking *down* at him, even in amusement, now she appeared to be looking *up* at him.

He was so tired he tucked the thought away to be examined later. He slumped in the saddle. With very little direction Robin's filly carried him home.

When he came into the house, everything seemed calm and ordered. Robin had used the time to straighten things and start some supper. Theo had forgotten to eat all day.

Doc Reeves came into the kitchen and sat down at the table with him.

"How's Josie?" Theo asked.

"Exhausted. But she'll be all right. She had a harder time because she worried about your father being away. Worried about you having such responsibility."

"I wouldn't have guessed. She seemed mighty brave."

"She's mighty proud of you, Theo, the way you took hold. That's all she talked about. Asked how a great big clumsy kid could be so gentle."

Theo's face and neck grew hot. He saw a flush and a smile come to Robin's face as she turned back to the stove to dish up a plate of boiled potatoes, cold ham shoulder, and creamed peas.

After the meal, they checked and found the baby and Josie sleeping. Doctor Reeves left and Robin went to the door. She said to Theo, "My folks'll be worried, I've been gone so long. Can you manage tonight? I'll be back first thing in the morning."

"I'm thankful you came, Robin. I'd forgotten you mentioned it last night." Memory of last night and how he had behaved made Theo suddenly redden, but it didn't really seem to matter now.

"I'll walk a ways with you," he offered.

The evening sky was tinged with shades of rose fading into gold. The mellow, wobbling coo of doves mourned the passing day. Theo led Robin's filly as they walked across the open quadrangle from the house, toward the dusky, moisture-scented coolness of the birch trees.

They didn't say much as they walked, but it was an easy, pleasant silence. They heard the leaves of the birches, closed and mingled above their heads, rustling softly in the evening breeze. The little brook running through the raspberry patch burbled and guzzled as it ran.

At the end of the farm road, Theo handed the reins to Robin and stepped close to help her mount. Her warm lips brushed his cheek.

"Oh, Robin!" Theo said.

"It's not Robin," Carole's soft voice answered. "It's me, Grandfather. You must have gone to sleep."

"I was just thinking. Called her name."

The moon had disappeared and the night had turned dark. The street was deserted and the television chatter turned off. In the quiet, a cricket fiddled and a bird chirped sleepily. Carole had lowered herself to the grass beside Theo's kitchen chair.

"I love him, Grandfather," she admitted, resting her head against his leg.

"He love you?"

"I think so. But we have to wait so long. At least another year." He heard muted anguish in her voice.

"He's a fine young man," Theo said.

A whispered, "I suppose."

"He cares a lot? He wants things right?"

She murmured assent, quieter than before.

"Then have faith, Granddaughter."

She sniffed a little and wiped at her tears.

In spite of the dark, he hooked a finger under her chin and lifted her face.

"Plenty of time later for real kisses."

Carole straightened her shoulders and tossed her hair. "Sometimes I'm afraid he's just a weak-minded idiot, vaulting over car doors and roaring around like a maniac. I want to talk about something important like life and marriage . . . and babies." She stood up, stretching her arms over her head to touch the curved branches which formed the beech alcove.

Theo smiled to himself, remembering his own showing-off when he wanted most in the world for Robin to know his true feelings.

"The time'll come. Unexpected, like. Something important happens. The masks fall away. Then you'll really see each other. Everything that follows," he paused for a long moment, then went on, "—sweeter than anything before . . ."

They shared a silent interval. Then Carole came closer.

"I love you, Grandfather," she said in a lilting whisper. She dropped a quick kiss on his forehead and ran back to the house.

You taught me that, Theo mentally reminded Robin. Nothing has ever equaled it, seeing for the first time the real face of that stranger you've given your heart to. He blew his nose. Then he muttered, "I'm as big a fool over her as I ever was!" He parted the beech-leaf curtain, crossed the dark lawn to the house, and went in to his lonely bed. END

Apple Harvest

by June Brown

Long as I can recollect, Newton Glendive has had his apple stand across the road to sell the drops and the extras he didn't carry into the village to market. Like as not he never even came out when a car stopped and honked. I allow the only reason he kept the stand was so on days when he couldn't find anything else to do he could set out at the stand and watch folks go by and no one could claim he was lazy. If he'd got real comfortable, he wouldn't even go back up to the barn to fetch more apples when he ran out. So considering all that, there was no reason why he should've up and acted so blamed ornery when I got my idea.

When Clay, he was my husband, passed on, I sold off most of the farm, but I still had a parcel of apple orchard left. It was right next to the house, and it didn't seem right to sell it and have some stranger owning what was under my nose. Besides, those apples had always been Clay's pride and joy. For the last five years I've always let the Belcher boys come in and pick the apples and sell them, seeing as how I didn't need the money and they did, and I couldn't pick them all, and they could. But this year the Belcher boys took themselves down to New York, so I was left holding the apples, you might say. I hated to see those apples just rot on the trees, so I set me to thinking. Then's when I got the idea.

More people stopped at Newton's than ever got apples, so why couldn't I sort of sop up the extras? I could pick enough apples every morning to get me through the day, and I could set down by the road and sell them and maybe work on my quilt some. So I made me a sign that said "Apples For Sale" which I fancied up some with some pretty little flowers around the edges. I always did have a good hand with paint, if I do say so.

I lugged out a sawhorse and set it down by the road and leaned the sign on it. I got out my old wicker chair from the barn. It didn't take me any time at all to pick a few bushels of Macs, and when I got them down to the road I set down real comfortable with my quilt. It was peaceful setting there, listening to the bees swarming in the trees, and smelling the sweet warm smell of my apples.

I didn't notice when Newton first came out—I was just resting my eyes when I heard him bellow like a cow that's just found out her calf's on the other side of the fence. I looked up and saw him starting across the road with his eyes bugging and his face all red and held back. He got about to the middle of the road and turned square around and went right back up to his stand. I let on I hadn't seen him, but I sure was wondering what got into him. Well, he finally just set down on the bench front of his stand and stared past me, not once looking me in the eye.

When a car stopped at his stand, he jumped up nice as pie and waited on the folks in it like they were the President and his wife. He set down after they left and nodded at me with a downright smirky look on his face. I kept on with my quilt that I was making out of Clay's old shirts; it was going together right pretty.

Next time a car came down my side of the road and stopped, I watched Newton out of the corner of my eye. He was half out of his chair the whole time. When the apples were bought, I said a mite louder than I needed, "You folks come back anytime." Newton slammed himself back onto the bench, and his face got all red again. I sort of chuckled, but I put my hand up to my mouth like I was coughing, on account of I really didn't want any hard feelings.

Things just went back and forth all that afternoon—Newton hopping around like a fancy waiter, or just half getting off the bench and turning red, and me talking extra loud and coughing. I meant to go in early because I'd been hankering for some good chicken and dumplings, but I decided to wait until Newton made on like he was closing up. I settled down real deep, glad the Good Lord had blessed me with a big comfortable setting-down place. Newton, though, he didn't look so easy. He kept shifting around on his bench, and I reckon with as little tail-bone padding as he was provided that setting got right trying for him after a spell.

Long about the time the frogs and crickets had taken up where the bees left off, I decided that my chickens had got to be fed, so I nodded at Newton, turned my sign around, and went back up to the house.

I didn't get back to the road till after dinner the next day, seeing as I had to put up some pickles. Why I keep putting up things I don't rightly know—the cellar's so plumb full I had taken to setting my jars right on the floor. When I started down to the road, I picked up my potted Christmas cactus. Thought it would pretty-up the saw-horse. Well, I right near dropped the pot when I looked over at Newton's stand. It had a fresh coat of the barn reddest paint you ever saw, and a sign big as life that said "Apples For Sale" in big black letters. He'd even drawn a picture of an apple on it. Course, I've got to admit his drawing's not so good as mine. There was Newton, setting right out in front on his best parlor easy chair, smirking to beat all.

I put my cactus on the sawhorse and turned my sign around, but I just didn't have the heart to pick up my quilt. I wouldn't want to let on to Newton, but everything across the road did look right nice. It made my little sign and sawhorse look a mite puny.

There weren't many cars that stopped on my side of the road that day, and Newton just kept puffing up so's I thought he'd come near to busting. I slunk back to the house early that evening while Newton was namby-pambying around some customers.

After supper I came onto my new idea. I went out to the barn where way off in a corner Clay had put our Anne's playhouse after she'd gone off and married. I tell you I never did so much grunting and straining ever as I did getting that playhouse out of the barn, but I got it out to where I could tie it behind the pickup, then I dragged it out to the road. I went back to the barn and got a can of paint left over from when I did the kitchen. It was as pretty a pink as a body'd ever hope to see. I painted me another sign, and after that I just flung myself in bed.

Next morning, early, I got myself down to the playhouse where I took the sign off the sawhorse and nailed it over the door. I nailed the new sign right over the top of it so it now said "Fresh Picked Apples For Sale." I took my cactus back to the house, picked a bunch of asters, and set them on the window sill of the playhouse. It looked so cute and perky I could've just stood and looked at it all day. Seems like I hardly got my chair inside the playhouse and myself set down to catch my breath when I saw Newton prancing down to his stand. I wish you'd seen his face when he saw my playhouse! If ever a man was struck dumb, it was Newton. His face came on just as grey as his hair; then it turned redder than a rooster wattle. He stood there with all the starch gone out of him. When he saw me, he sort of shook himself together and started shining apples till I expect he had nothing left but a bushel of cores.

I'd plain forgotten to pick any apples, so I stopped watching Newton and went back to the orchard. All the time I was picking I was thinking on how poorly Newton looked, and how no man likes to have a woman better him. Still and all, he'd acted so uppity over a coat of barn red paint and his new sign, I just couldn't have set and took it. I brooded a spell, then went down cellar to get some jars of the new pickles and my special watermelon rind preserves. I set them all in a box and fetched them right down to where Newton was still polishing apples. I let on like I was puffing from carrying them jars so he wouldn't see how backwards I was feeling.

"I brought you some of my pickles, Newton. Don't reckon you're inclined to put any up just for yourself." I made out as if that was some joke, and laughed it up for quite a bit. I'll say this for Newton, he didn't stop polishing, not for one minute.

"Well, I'll just leave the pickles here." I swear I don't know what came over me, but there I was just a-polishing an apple with my apron. When I caught on to what I was doing, I set that apple down quick.

"Place looks good, Newton."

"Ayeh."

"I always admired red."

"Well, it ain't pink."

Now I thought that was real nice, him allowing that my stand looked pretty too. I mighty near skipped back across the road, I was that relieved things were patched up. That just goes to show what a soft spot I've got in my head for Newton Glendive.

Next thing I knew was not only had he put "Extra Fresh" in front of his sign, but underneath he had a new sign that said "Watermelon Preserves and Pickles For Sale." I figured that was about the lowest a body could stoop.

I set and stewed all morning; and when I saw Newton sell a jar of my pickles, I had my mind all settled. I went out to the barn and painted me another sign. After that I got out my folding table and chairs and carried them alongside the playhouse. I lugged down a couple of jugs of cider the folks that bought the orchard had given me. While I spread my prettiest flowery cloth on the table I could see old Newton's ears prick up. He liked to bust when I nailed up the "Cold Cider For Sale" sign.

After a spell a car stopped and some folks got out to set around the table. Newton stood up like a man with a spell laid on him, and commenced eating out of a jar of my watermelon preserves sort of absent-minded like. He looked so trance-y, I was almost scared he'd hook his tonsils with his pocket knife every time he took a bite.

Things settled down real quiet after that. Customers were pretty evenly divided, but I noticed Newton lighting into the preserves every time I served up some cider. After a few days, he painted over the "Watermelon Preserves" part of his sign, so I figured he'd eaten himself clean out.

By the end of the week there just wasn't any fun left to getting out to the stand, what with Newton being no kind of company at all. I had a notion I'd outdone Newton a mite too much, and it had plain sapped the spirit out of him. I felt real poorly about that. I pondered over it for a spell; then I decided I just had to take steps. I finally hit onto my plan, and I tell you it was about the best thing I ever got onto. I hunted up Clay's old cane, tore up an old sheet and wrapped up my ankle real professional. I hobbled out to the stand late enough so's I was sure Newton would be out to see me limping up.

Well, he was real took back. He looked like he was turned around about what to do, but it didn't take him long to hightail it across the road. I told him how I'd had a fall. I carried on some about it being hard for a woman to run an apple stand. I let on that with a hurt ankle I'd probably just have to give up. I was so bent on convincing Newton that I plumb began to believe myself.

Newton said nothing for a spell. Then his face got all red and squinched up while he commenced talking a mile a minute. He came up with a right good arrangement.

He made me sit real comfortable-like and just tend to my quilt while he closed up his stand and lugged all his apples over to the playhouse. He looked terribly pleased with himself when he nailed up his new sign, "Newton Glendive, Manager" right over the playhouse door.

When the customers stopped for apples, Newton just plain took over. He swelled up like he was the only one with a mite of sense and know-how, and he got bossy right off.

It felt real nice to have a man around again.   END

The Magic Hat

by Earle Westcott

In every old family there is a storyteller, just as in every old family there is a story to tell. Our family is especially old and there are a number of stories, but there is only one storyteller now alive, and that would be Great-uncle Manny.

We are an old country family. By this I mean that we have lived here on the coast of Maine for over two hundred years, and among us there has never been a governor or Revolutionary War hero. We have survived from generation to generation passing on a legacy of not much more than a few stone-walled farms from son to son.

When the neighbors were buying their first automobiles, we were buying secondhand horses. When the great wars came along in succession like gaudy traveling carnivals, the neighbors took sides and argued, and their sons went off to be lieutenants in the infantry; but the sons of our family didn't care about that. We cared about the land and fishing, and about the stories old uncles told around the stove on chilly evenings. And when our own were taken away to be privates in the infantry, we put up with it the way we put up with potato worms or the whooping cough. After the wars pulled up their stakes and moved on, the neighbors' sons returned for a short time, only to leave again for the cities they had newly seen; but when we came back to the stone walls and marshland along the bare Atlantic, we came back to stay.

I am telling you nothing new. Great-uncle Manny would tell you the same thing, only he would tell it in a way that would make you feel special and part of the family even if you were a stranger—even if you were a neighbor. His stories are now disrupted by whiskey and melancholy, and he often wanders off into the past without taking you with him; but when I was a boy and he was in his prime, Great-uncle Manny could turn the night magic with his stories. My favorite was the one about his brother coming home from the Great War. I liked that one best because of the hat.

Wendell was a special case in the family because he managed to distinguish himself in the war. Great-uncle Manny says it was an accident, because we all have too much sense to risk our necks like that. All the same, Wendell was made a corporal and sent home with a citation for holding out during a gas attack. This was back when the army formed regiments made up entirely of men from the same region of the country. After the war they put a stop to it when they found whole counties stripped of their young men. It was like a forest fire that rolls out of the woods and lays waste one fellow's land and spares his neighbor's. The loss itself was bearable, but not the capriciousness of the loss.

The *Coastal Weekly Star* got hold of Wendell's citation and printed a front-page story before he even got home. Two neighbors' sons had died in the skirmish, and a committee was formed to welcome Wendell home. Great-grandmother Comstock told them that Wendell was coming in on the Friday train, and the Welcome Home Wendell Comstock Committee decorated the station with red, white and blue bunting, and the high school band practiced late Thursday evening.

The whole family and half the town turned out on Friday morning. With overall pockets stuffed with cherry bombs, Great-uncle Manny tussled with his school friends on the platform, carefully keeping Great-grandmother Comstock's notorious thimble at a safe distance. Manny was a celebrity among his friends, and he boasted about how his big brother had slaughtered an ever increasing number of cowardly Huns. Manny heard the whistle, and Councilman Wentworth motioned to the band, which struck up an enthusiastic "My Country, 'tis of Thee." Great-grandmother Comstock pulled a cotton hanky from the sleeve of her print dress and wiped her eyes as Great-grandfather Comstock rejoined her from in back of the ticket window where he and some of the other men had been celebrating the celebration. They all held their heads very high, and above the din Manny heard Councilman Wentworth tell one of the neighbors that when the Great War was over and victory had been seized, the world would have the fine boys from Maine to thank for its freedom.

Mothers grabbed their darting children and pulled them back from the rails and a terrier scampered across the tracks in front of the engine as it trembled to a halt. Stopping seemed to cause it great pain and steam coursed out from the mansized wheels, drowning out the band and causing the women to grab onto their bonnets. The men held themselves erect and forward, trying very hard not to blink, testing themselves against the force of air strong enough to rip the draped bunting. A nimble conductor hopped from a Pullman coach, placing a wooden stool beneath the iron steps at the very second the train stopped.

Manny heard the name of our town bellowed out importantly from inside the cars, and the first passenger, a salesman of some sort, stepped off. Then came Mrs. Buzzle, who had been visiting her chronically pregnant sister in Portsmouth, another salesman, a recruiting officer, and the mail sack, but no Wendell. Councilman Wentworth approached the officer and Great-grandfather Comstock joined him. They asked if there weren't another fellow, a soldier, on board. The officer told them that since there was a war on, there were plenty of soldiers on board. Manny looked up into the windows and he could plainly see other soldiers, but none of them looked like Wendell. He saw Great-grandmother Comstock talking to Mrs. Buzzle, and then both of them scanned the sleepy faces pressed against the windows. The band played on like a neglected gramophone.

The conductor drew his watch by the chain out from a flannel vest heavy with fastened buttons and bulging pockets. He stared at the watch as if he were trying to recognize some old friend in the face of a stranger. "All aboard," he said to himself, and then loudly, "All aboard," and swung down to pick up his wooden stool. Just as the engine rang two bells, Manny spied something between the cars on the other side of the tracks. A fellow all in khaki, bent beneath the khaki sack he carried over his shoulder, was moving rapidly away from the station. Manny darted between the wheels, scooting under the Pullman, and sprinted towards the escaping figure.

"Wendell!" he hollered, "Wendell, wait for me. It's me, Manny."

The figure turned and without dropping the sack stretched out a free arm. Manny ran into him and nearly knocked him over and hugged as hard as he could. Manny looked up and almost cried out. It was Wendell all right, but it looked like only half of him.

"Shut up, Manny," he said. "Let's get out of here before the train leaves and they get a look at us."

"Let me carry the sack," Manny said, "I'm bigger now. I could carry it easy."

"Not now, Manny. Come on."

Wendell was off again with Manny trailing along in wonder. Wendell began to wheeze a little from his heavy, broken run, while Manny trotted next to him, pleading to help with the sack. They reached the stand of elms that lined East Road just as Manny heard the train huffing and rattling. He looked back to see if they were being followed and saw the caboose clearing the railhead. The band had mercifully wound down, but the crowd still stood on the platform. Manny tried to make out the faces of his family, but he could only be sure of his mother's massive print dress, flapping in the breeze like the torn red, white and blue bunting.

Manny turned away and saw that Wendell was already some distance down the road. He was not running now, but walking gamely towards home. Manny raced up to him.

"The sack," said Manny, "let me carry the sack for you."

"No, Manny."

"Hey, how come you got off on the wrong side, Wendell?"

Wendell didn't seem to hear him.

"Huh, Wendell, how come you got off on the other side of the train?"

Wendell still didn't answer, and Manny felt as if he would bust apart from all the questions he had to ask. As they reached the dirt road that led down to the farm, he began to ask his brother about France and the Huns, and about the size of the boat he crossed over on, and how long it took to do it, and if Wendell had ever been in an airplane, and if it were true that the Germans ate little French children for lunch. In fact, he was so intent on his questions that it took him some time to notice that he was doing all the talking. He was chattering away and Wendell wasn't saying a thing.

Manny looked up at his brother's dusty, sweating face, which in his emaciated condition seemed all jaw and nose. Even the campaign hat looked too big for him, as if his head had shrunk since the hat was issued. The crown was indented perfectly in four places, and the stiff circling brim was starched and very military. In the oversized uniform, Wendell looked like a sack carrying a sack. His lean white wrists and neck stuck through the khaki material like tender shoots on a dirty potato. Very unimpressive. But the hat was something else again. Crisp and decisive, the head gear rightfully belonged to a valiant young officer leading his men over the top, or to a smart trooper executing a perfect salute, flicking his fingers to the brim and then cutting away cleanly. Manny noticed how the leather chin strap swayed under the weight of the unfastened brass buckle and brushed against Wendell's gaunt cheek. Manny wanted that hat.

"Can I try on your hat?" Manny asked defensively, because he expected either another "No" for an answer, or no answer at all, but Wendell took the hat from his head and plopped it over Manny's face. The inside smelled of sweat and that curious mothball smell of all military clothing. Manny righted the brim and saw his brother smiling at him. Wendell's teeth had gone bad.

The two of them continued towards the farmhouse, Wendell limping slightly, Manny keeping an eye out for a possible German ambush. He picked up a rifle from the roadside and every so often he would charge a suspicious-looking grove of spruce or climb to the top of a rock to scout the road ahead. Then he fell in next to his brother, broken branch over his shoulder, marching smartly down the road.

When they reached the unpainted, clapboard house, Wendell told Manny to run in and fetch him a shirt and pair of trousers. Nobody was back from town yet, and Manny bounded towards the empty house, filled with houndish pleasure of pleasing his big brother just back from whipping the Huns.

"Manny, Manny, for Christ's sake, hold up a minute."

"What?" Manny yelled, whirling around as he reached the front porch.

"You know the wall over behind the barn, the wall between the orchard and the pasture?"

"We got corn in that pasture now," said Manny helpfully, but he was sorry he said it when he saw that it did something terrible to his brother's face.

"You know the wall anyway. The wall's still there, right? You get my clothes and bring them over around to that wall."

"Hey, Wendell, what color shirt do you want?"

Wendell just looked at Manny for a second, and Manny knew that he must have said something stupid again. You had to watch what you were saying around these war heroes. The least little thing seemed to make them fly off the handle.

"You just bring any one you want, okay Manny?"

Manny nodded and then he bolted through the screen door. He pounded up the stairs, holding the big hat down on his head as it revolved around his ears and tried to leap over the banister. He reached the cedar chest at the end of the hall and slid into it on his knees. He fumbled with the tricky latch that only a woman with fingernails could open properly. He slammed his fist down on the polished, knotty top and tugged at the pretty nickel lock. Manny couldn't let Wendell down, not now, so he grabbed the hat from his head and scraped the latch with the prong of the brass buckle. Click, and she opened, and Manny threw up the lid and dug into the cedar-smelling, cool and folded garments until he found the things that Wendell used to wear. Great-grandmother Comstock put them there right after Wendell had left for the war.

Manny found a pair of dungarees and the red shirt with the cowboy stitching around the pockets that he remembered was Wendell's favorite. Leaving the cedar chest lid wide open, Manny threw the clothing over his shoulder, put on his hat, and ran down the stairs to the porch. Nobody was coming down the road yet, but Manny thought he heard a squeaking wagon axle and tramping hoofs. He raced out behind the barn to the stone wall by the orchard.

Wendell was stripped to the waist, all white and bone and sinew, digging a trench next to the wall with the manure spade. His back was covered with sweat, and the methodical, almost mechanical motion

of his digging kept Manny from saying anything. Manny laid the clothing over the wall and kept his mouth shut. Wendell jammed the spade into
the black earth, tearing up clumps of dirt, veined by white webs of
grass and ivy roots which caused the shovel to snag and then gave
way with the popping sound of a dozen rotten shoe laces. A little deeper
and wet grey sand came up without the troublesome roots so that
the digging went easier and quickly. When the hole was about three
feet deep, Wendell pulled himself up and straightened his back, placing both hands at the base of his spine. He took a deep breath and coughed
a short, ugly cough, holding his clenched fist tight against his mouth.
His cheeks turned pink and full, and then slackened like a sail bereft
of a breeze. Then he rolled the khaki sack into the trench with his
foot. The sack thumped on the bottom of the hole, and Manny heard
a fantastic metal clank of what he thought sure to be guns and bay-
onets and possibly even a German helmet with a spike on the top.

"Wendell, what's in there?" Manny whispered. "What ya got in
there?"

But Wendell was like a deaf old man. He sat on the stone wall and
picked up his red shirt. He traced the fancy cowboy stitching with his
finger and looked at it for a while before he put it on. It was too big
for him. Then he pulled off his khakis and threw them into the hole.

"Wendell," cried Manny, "how come you're doing that? What's
going on?"

Wendell pulled up the dungarees and fastened them. Then he took
the hat from Manny's head and tossed that into the hole too. This was
too much for Manny, who had been standing there helplessly while
his crazy brother had thrown away a whole sack full of treasures.
Manny leaped into the hole after his hat. He put it on and scrambled
out and over the stone wall.

"No, Wendell, please, not the Rough Rider hat, too! Let me keep it,
please," Manny begged as he backed away from his brother, clutching
the hat to his head, ready to spring away if he had to.

Wendell shivered in the hot sun and looked over Manny's shoulder
towards the farm.

"Okay, Manny. You keep the hat."

When Great-uncle Manny reached this part of the story, his eyes would
blaze like the fire you could see darting through the grate of his black
kitchen stove. The story got longer every time he told it, but he always
told it the same way. He was funny and relaxed when he started, stretching in the pine rocker by the stove, sipping whiskey and spring

water from his tin cup, but by the time he finished, Great-uncle Manny became a different person. He was like a magician or an Indian medicine man, and I sensed his familiarity with secrets that no one else could ever dream of.

"But he let you keep the hat, right, Uncle Manny?" I asked on cue.

"He sure did. Wendell looked right through me, and then he says, 'You keep the hat, but keep it out of my sight. I don't want it around, any of it,' and he turned back and filled in that cussed hole and for the rest of his days he'd never speak of it."

I asked Great-uncle Manny one time why he never dug up the sack. He told me, peering over imaginary glasses and guessing my intentions, that it wouldn't be the proper thing to do, that it would be like disturbing his brother's grave. The thought of that sack still buried out there in the night by the old wall made my skin crawl, and I moved closer to the stove. The kitchen was hot near the fire and drafty around the walls and corners. Common utensils and familiar faces became objects glowing uncertainly in the uneven light. The tea kettle was a trembling hive out of which swarmed a cloud of hornets, and Aunt Catherine in her shawl by the pantry door was a sorceress, a gypsy who carried off children. A wood fire burns like memory, causing shadows to appear more distinct and real than the objects which cast them. Perhaps this is why our memories are so active during an evening around a wood fire; perhaps that is why we always remember such evenings.

"You still got the hat, don't you, Uncle Manny?"

"I sure do. It's up in the cedar chest this minute."

"Can I go up and try it on?"

"You leave your Uncle Manny's things alone," the shadow of my mother would say.

"That's all right, Ellen, the boy can't harm it none. You go right up there and put it on if you like."

And off I would fly, out of the bubble of kitchen light, through the dusky parlor and up the stairs to the cedar chest. I slid into it on my knees and fumbled with the scratched nickel latch and threw open the lid and dug down deep into the cool and cedar-smelling past. The hat was as starched and stiff as ever, and I smelled the old sweat around the headband, but now the hat smelled of cedar, too. I put it on and fastened the brass buckle on the chin strap, and then I crawled along the dark hallway to the window. I pressed my nose to the freezing pane. The glass became clouded with my breath and I wiped it clear with my hand.

Outside in the snow I saw a German creeping up from the stone wall. His face was masked against the wind, and, hunched over in his heavy battle gear like a black tree stump, he slipped behind the far side of the barn. I waited, watching the corner of the barn closest to the house. He was trying to catch me off my guard. I waited, and he emerged near and in my sights. He stepped out into the open, and I could see the metal spike on his helmet shine in the brittle white cold of moonlight.   END

Uncle George's Mysterious Fortune

by Patrick J. Leonard

For as long as I can remember, a never-failing topic of conversation in our family and our village was the source of my Great-uncle George's wealth.

The family, and everyone in town, knew Uncle George, and his father and grandfather before him; and all of them had eked out only a bare existence working on the old Leonard Cape Cod farm, sometimes lobstering and fishing, but never making much money.

In fact, there was no indication of wealth until one day, way back in 1904, when Uncle George suddenly bought the Miller place, and hired carpenters, masons, plumbers, and painters, then purchased the finest surrey with a fringe on top ever seen on the Cape, a beautiful little mare, and some of the finest prize-winning livestock in the area. He got everything shipshape, hired the two Tooters, father and son, to look after things, and just settled back to spend his life sitting around the farm or the Town Hall, or walking his acres to watch the Tooters. He sailed his sloop around on aimless little day trips and in general began living the carefree life of a person of considerable wealth— with not one hint from him or anyone else where all the money had come from.

Every single one of his purchases he paid for in cold cash. Old Cy Schofield, the town banker, told his cronies that Uncle George came in one day just before he started spending all the money and planked down $25,000 and said he wanted to open an account. Old Cy was completely flabbergasted, checked and double-checked to make sure the money was not counterfeit, and at first a bit gently but later pressing hard, tried to force Uncle George to tell where he got the money. Blustering, Old Cy backed down when Uncle George allowed that he probably could find a bank somewhere else handy to town where the banker would not be so consarned nosy.

People started treating Uncle George with quite a lot of deference and respect once the news got around (which it did quicker than a squall hitting town), and in a short time, although he was only twenty-seven at the time, no one aside from his immediate family

called him "George" anymore. He became "Mr. Leonard" almost overnight, and everyone listened to him with real attention.

One can hardly imagine the speculation that went on in our small town
about Uncle George's sudden prosperity. Old Cy, Captain Beacham, Doc
Caldwell, Lawyer Folger, men who in another age would be termed the
wise men of the village, got their heads together night after night in the
back of Doc Caldwell's Drug Store and talked it over.

They reasoned that none of the Leonards ever had any money; so
Uncle George could not have obtained his wealth from the Leonards.
Us Leonards could have told them that! Everyone knew that Uncle
George had worked around the old homestead, gone fishing, was on a
couple of voyages up to the coast of Maine in old Capt. Tobias Starks'
Rosanna, the same sloop which old Captain Toby sold in 1902. We all
knew that Uncle George and a rather shiftless fellow named Jose who
was always getting into scrapes—no one knew his last name but his
father came from "the islands" and married the Tolliver girl, the one
who had spells—left town in 1902 and went to work in a shipyard in
East Boston. After a couple of weeks the work petered out in the shipyard and Uncle George and Jose came home. This trip, and the jaunts
with Captain Toby in the *Rosanna*, and a couple of trips to Boston on
the Old Colony Line train were the only times Uncle George had ever
left town, and he was always back the same day—so where did he get
the money?

As far as anyone could figure it out, there was only one answer—
BURIED TREASURE! Everyone had heard the stories of the pirates,
and Matilda Page at the library did a lot of research on this angle.
She became convinced that Captain Kidd only buried a portion of his
treasure on Gardiner's Island, and on his way to Boston must have
buried the rest of it on Dead Neck, a long sandbar off Waquoit Bay
and that somehow Uncle George, known to spend idle days out there,
must have found it, gone to Boston with it, and sold it to jewelers.

This made a great deal of sense to Lawyer Folger. He said that Uncle George, even if he was a Leonard, would be smart enough to keep
his mouth shut when he found the treasure and would certainly go
to Boston and sell it at some of the jewelry stores there. He even
made some enquiries in Boston, but learned nothing, and said that
Uncle George must have sworn the jewelry stores to secrecy, and what
would keep wise jewelers quiet was the knowledge that Uncle George
must have a good amount more for sale. And if they talked, he would
sell his jewels elsewhere. This only made the stories grow and grow.
Other men spent hours digging on Dead Neck, but got only seashells
for their pains.

Quite a few of the local boys started to try to follow Uncle George around as unobtrusively as possible, hoping he would visit his treasure trove. Uncle George speedily became aware of this surveillance and took a perverse joy in leading them on many a wild-goose chase. He particularly delighted in having shiftless Jose, who had played pranks on him in the past, follow him around, and once he dropped a "map" which Jose retrieved, and then spent hours digging on Moose Hillock, a rocky ridge in the center of Ellen swamp. The holes Jose dug are still there. The older Sanderson boy and Teddie Talbot nearly drowned one night when they saw Uncle George stealthily sneak out of his house, hurry down to the pier, get into his sailboat, and take off towards Woods Hole. They started after him in a leaky old yawl which they had to beach off Falmouth as it started to founder, and when they were walking up the beach, they heard Uncle George jeering at them from the shadows offshore.

After a few months of this, the boys (and some of the older citizens too!) tried a new tack. On some pretext or other, a shindig would be held at someone's house and Uncle George would, of course, be one of the guests. Hard cider and all kinds of liquor would soon start to flow, but Uncle George could hold his own with the most hardened topers, and they never got a bit of information out of him. Eventually they gave up in complete frustration on parties as they proved so expensive. There was never a party at Uncle George's although he got many a hint.

Years and years went by. The novelty wore off, but the question was still in everyone's mind. Where *did* he get all the money—the cuss never worked. Uncle George got fatter, blander, ran for Selectman and then Town Clerk, and held the Town Clerk's job for over 30 years. He never married, although every spinster and widow within miles was especially nice to him. Most of his fatness must have been caused by the many luscious pies and other goodies the hopefuls baked for him.

Uncle George, ever jovial, continued on his placid way. Only one strange thing happened, and this was in his later years. When Old Jose, who had become the town soak, was on his deathbed, he sent for Uncle George. This was just before World War II. No one was surprised at Old Jose's request, as Uncle George was always ready with a cash donation for Jose when no one would hire him and he was "on the town."

Uncle George entered the sickroom at Widow Looby's boarding house, where most of the town's indigents lived. Old Jose had been there for the past couple of years, since his wife died. Only Sairey

Tompkins, the visiting nurse, was in the room. Old Jose was in a coma. Sairey told Uncle George that the end was near, that Old Jose would not last the night out, that he kept slipping in and out of comas and any sudden excitement would surely kill Old Jose, so Uncle George would have to be careful.

After a while, Old Jose came out of his torpor. Seeing Uncle George, he said, "George, I am a dead man. Tell me something. Where did you get all the money?"

Uncle George glanced at Sairey, who busied herself tidying up something in the corner, and kept looking at her without saying anything until he caught her eye and motioned her to leave the room. Sairey was all ears (the Tompkinses always did have large ears but this is not what I mean) and she hated to leave, but she walked out and closed the door softly after her. About a minute later, Uncle George jerked the door open so quickly that the doorknob nearly took off one of Sairey's ears, the one she had at the keyhole.

Well, he sent her packing and stood in the doorway until Sairey walked down the hall and down the stairs, rubbing her ear all the time and trying unsuccessfully to look dignified.

Uncle George carefully closed the door. About five minutes went by with only the low rumble of his voice, and then there was a great loud yell from Old Jose and a big thump on the floor.

Sairey rushed back to the room and there was Old Jose, tangled in his ankle-length nightgown, stark dead on the floor beside the bed. Uncle George was standing over him and told Sairey that as he was talking the old man suddenly yelled, tried to climb out of bed, and dropped dead. Young Doc Potter (Old Doc Caldwell had died years before) was called, pronounced Jose dead, and Josh Powers, the undertaker, came to take the body away.

Then it was found that there was no money to bury Jose, so Uncle George bought a pine coffin, a lot at the Old Windmill Cemetery, and a headstone. Not many people came to the burial, on sort of a middling-poor fall day, but Uncle George was there. Josh Powers said later that he saw Uncle George laughing as Josh was shoveling the dirt on the pine coffin, but of course no one ever did believe Josh. Right now, knowing what I know—I believe it.

A few more years went by. Uncle George got older and fatter, and then one morning one of the Tooters, the third generation to work for him, came down to the village and announced that he had found Uncle George dead in his bed. Uncle George had been fine the night before, sitting in front of a big fieldstone fireplace, drinking hard cider and rum, and reading the *Cape Cod Gazette;* then he'd gone to bed, and died peacefully in his sleep.

Well, I am telling you, the family really went through his house with a fine-tooth comb even while Josh Powers and his men were groaning and tugging to carry Uncle George out. Search as we could, we did not find any treasure. The next thing we knew, a lawyer from a big law firm in Boston, that none of us had ever heard anything about, drove down and told the family that his firm had been handling Uncle George's affairs for over fifty years. He told us that, long before his time, Uncle George came into the law office, told the men who were the partners in the firm at that time that he had come into a lot of money, that he was just a country boy, and asked them to handle the money for him.

The lawyer, a lanky, youngish fellow, then got all of us Leonards together in the big room where Uncle George had spent his last evening. Standing in front of the fieldstone fireplace, he read Uncle George's will. Uncle George had remembered all of us Leonards equally in his will—the babies and the gray beards sharing just the same—so we all got something; but as there were so many of us, each only got a few hundred dollars. Still, this was a few hundred dollars more than we had, so we were happy.

After the lawyer read the paper out, there was a pause. Cousin Ellen was the first to speak. She said, "Tell us something, did Uncle George ever let on to you fellows just where he got his money?"

The lawyer laughed and reached into his briefcase, saying that Uncle George had once told him someone would ask that and that Uncle George had prepared the whole story so that finally everyone would be satisfied. He took out an old envelope, and on it we could see, in Uncle George's familiar big square letters:

HOW I GOT THE MONEY

The lawyer asked if he could open the envelope and read what was inside of it, and of course we all yelled "yes" as loud as we could. He slit the envelope carefully and deliberately, with a letter opener, and then began to read the letter, which ran, as near as I can remember, like this:

"In October of 1902 Jose the Portygee and I went up to Boston and got jobs at the shipyard where the McKay clippers used to be built in East Boston. We roomed at a house nearby for a week or so, then found a room at a house owned by the widow of an old sea captain. She was all alone in the world and quite lonesome, and she and Jose hit it off from the start. Nights when I was up in bed I could hear them laughing and giggling and carrying on down below. We were only there three or four days and then most everyone got their walking papers at the shipyard, and as Jose and I were the last men hired, we were let go. When we told the widow we were leaving, she carried on something terrible and clung to Jose, and the last thing we saw was her crying away as we walked down Border Street towards Maverick Square to get the trolley to take us to the South Station where we got the train and headed home.

"On the way home, Jose kept looking at me and laughing. I could not figure out what was wrong, he was always playing tricks on me—dowsed me once with a bucket of icy seawater in January off Portland in the *Rosanna*.

"Finally, just before we got in to the station at home, I got mad and asked him what was the story. 'Remember the old widow?' he says. 'While you were up in bed, she and I had a grand time downstairs, and I told her that I was going to marry her some day.'

" 'What has that to do with your laughing at me?,' I asked.

"Jose answered, slapping his knee and bursting out laughing again, 'When she asked me what my name was and where I lived, I gave her YOUR name and address,' and he went wild laughing again.

"Well, this did not seem funny to me at all, and I told him that if I ever heard any more about it I would fix him good, and I shook him and told him he had played a dirty trick on the poor widow, and then I sort of forgot about it.

"Well, a couple of months or more went by and one day I got a letter from some lawyer in Boston. He said that the old widow had got sick and died, but before she did, she changed her will and rather than leave all her money to some museum or something up there, she had left it all to me. I kept my mouth shut, figuring it was one of Jose's tricks, but got to thinking about it and went up to Boston and found out that it *was* all true.

"I got some smart Yankee lawyers to handle the money for me, and whenever I got a bit short, sent for some. And I made up my mind I would never tell a soul until I was dead."   END

The Flying Lynnds

by Bartlett Gould

It was Saturday, and Eileen was staying with her mother for a couple of days. I had the house to myself. After taking my time about getting up and shaving, I went downstairs in pajamas and bathrobe, set the percolator going, prepared a couple of eggs for scrambling and put an English muffin on to toast.

Only then did I go to the front door to pick up the *News*. A two-column headline at the lower left-hand corner caught my eye:

"FLYING LYNNDS" MEET DEATH
IN MOUNTAIN CRASH

I went through the story slowly while polishing off the eggs and muffin. A group of Boy Scouts had been hiking up near Mt. Madison and one of them had become separated from the others. It is no joke to be lost in the White Mountains in late fall, and search parties were organized at once. To make it worse, the weather was turning bad.

Apparently (the paper went on to say) Jack and Kit Lynnd in their farmhouse in Sellers Falls heard the news broadcast and, without bothering to telephone for advice or permission, had hauled out an old plane they had restored to flying condition and taken off from a stretch of pasture land back of their home. Ellsworth Turner, a neighbor, reported he had gone over while they were warming their engine and Jack had told him they were going to try to locate the missing boy. When reporters wanted to know why, in view of the lowering ceiling, he had not tried to dissuade them from the attempt, Turner had shrugged and said: "The Lynnds weren't folks you argue with."

As it turned out, the lost youngster demonstrated good sense and the benefit of his Scout training. Refusing to panic, he spent an uncomfortable night on the mountain but made his way down safely the next day.

Jack and Kit Lynnd were not so fortunate. The weather caught up with them, and they plowed directly into a mountainside.

Youngsters have their heroes. Nowadays it could be Neil Armstrong, Bobby Orr or maybe some rock singer. But when I was a kid the ones on my pedestal were Lindbergh, Roscoe Turner, Jimmy Doolittle— and the Flying Lynnds.

The newspaper noted that the element of mystery surrounding the Lynnds' life had extended into their death. So far as anyone knew, neither one had flown since 1933. Their licenses had expired long ago. For that matter, their plane wasn't licensed either. It was an antique, restored, possibly to safe flying condition, but who could tell? No FAA examiner had been invited to inspect it. The flight itself was regarded as a gallant but futile gesture; it was late afternoon and they could not hope to see the missing boy except for that one shot in a hundred thousand that he would be in the open waving his shirt at the time they happened to pass directly over.

An inside page featured a photo dug out of the files and labeled *The Flying Lynnds and their transatlantic plane.* Actually, the Bellanca in the picture was not the one in which they flew the Atlantic, but who would know or care? It was part of the long dead past. There was a brief outline of their career, concluding with the transatlantic flight of 1933. They had crossed the ocean safely, but landed far short of the distance mark they had been trying to establish. After this flight, the Lynnds had severed their ties with aviation and gone into seclusion. With other and livelier things for the public to concern itself with, the Lynnds were soon forgotten.

The newspaper wound up with: "The reasons for the Lynnds' abrupt withdrawal from the aviation scene were, and remain, an enigma. The Lynnds would never discuss it. Now, no one will ever know."

I poured myself another cup of coffee. The newspaper was wrong. One person *did* know.

Me.

My job consists of traveling New England trying to convince school officials that Moore and Graham textbooks are better than those turned out by the competition. About a month ago I was driving home through New Hampshire. The day was bright and the sky was blue. It was still early fall, but here and there some maple leaves had begun their change to vivid yellow. Ahead of schedule, and with no particular reason to hurry home, I got off the superhighway and cruised leisurely down a series of secondary and back roads, relaxing and enjoying the scenery.

Just past Sellers Falls I passed a small farmhouse, white, with a red barn out back that could have used a coat of paint. All this I took in at a glance as I sailed past, but I also glimpsed two other things that made me slow down, then pull over. One was the name on the mailbox: LYNND. The other was the tip of an airplane wing sticking out of the barn door opening.

For a few moments I sat thinking. Lynnd is an unusual name, and although I hadn't thought about them for years I knew that Jack and

Kit were supposed to be living somewhere in New Hampshire. That airplane wing decided me. I got out and strolled back.

The house was even smaller than it first appeared. The shrubbery had
been clipped, but not for a long time, and the cement walk leading to
the front door had split open in a few places and grass was leaking
up through the cracks.

There was no one outside. I have the normal reluctance to butt in
where I haven't been invited, but the barn door was open and the airplane in view. There couldn't be anything too private about it. So
I sauntered up, stopping maybe a dozen feet away.

It was an ancient single-engine high-wing monoplane, beautifully
restored. Colored blue and white, the fabric shone as though it had
received ten coats of dope and a hand-rubbed finish. I remembered all
the Lynnds' planes had been blue and white.

"What do you want?"

Startled, I swung around to see a man of medium height, but so slender he seemed taller. He was dressed in brown slacks, loafers, a tweed
jacket and a white turtleneck shirt. His hair was gray but still abun-
dant. He had a small, carefully clipped mustache and his face was lean
and wrinkled. He was in his late sixties, at least, but as a kid I had
pored over his picture too often to be mistaken, even after forty years.
It was Jack Lynnd.

"My name's Clayton Stone," I told him. "I was just driving by and
saw your plane and figured no one would mind if I looked it over.
A Fairchild "24", isn't it?"

His eyes softened a little. "Yes. It was a complete wreck when my
wife and I picked it up some years back."

"Mind if I take a closer look?"

"Go ahead." So I walked around the ship in a state of enchant-
ment. The workmanship was superb.

The back door of the house opened and Kit Lynnd came out. Only
a bit shorter than her husband, she was dressed in black slacks and dark
blue pullover. Her hair was probably dyed, as it showed no gray.
Forty years ago she had been considered very attractive; some of it remained. Her skin was wrinkled and a bit leathery, but she had kept her
figure. Her nose was too sharp and prominent, but it lent strength
to her face. I remembered the talk that used to go around, that when it
came to flying Kit had a smoother hand on the stick than Jack, and it
was her drive more than his that kept them going.

Her cold, suspicious eyes stared at me.

"Kit, this gentleman just stopped to take a look at the Fairchild.
This is my wife, Mr. . . . what did you say your name was?"

"Clayton Stone. How do you do?"

She nodded but said nothing.

"Mr. Lynnd was telling me you two rebuilt this from a basket case," I went on. "I've never seen a cleaner job."

Her expression lost some of its hostility. "Thank you. Do you fly?"

"I used to, a little. But I couldn't get by the eye exam during the war, and can't afford to put in as much time as I'd like on my own."

They made no answer. I glanced at the long stretch of pasture behind the barn.

"Seems to me there's room enough there to take off," I ventured. "Ever try it?"

There was a brief silence, then Jack said noncommittally, "That would be against regulations. It's not licensed."

I was reasonably sure they had made at least one or two trial flights in that Fairchild, and equally sure they were not about to admit it.

I prepared to leave, but hesitated. The memories of forty years ago were too strong to allow me to walk away without paying my respects to their great days.

"You're the 'Flying Lynnds' of course," I said. They nodded without expression.

"You may laugh, but when I was a kid you were a couple of gods to me. I had a scrapbook full of your pictures, and when you were overdue on that Atlantic flight I remember sneaking upstairs to my bedroom to pray for you. Really."

I'm not sure just what reaction I expected, but I certainly was not prepared for the one I got. They stared at me, stony-faced, for about fifteen seconds. It seemed like minutes.

"I suppose we ought to thank you," said Kit finally. "But those days are past. We don't dwell on them"

After that, there was no point in tarrying. I stumbled awkwardly through another thanks for letting me look at their plane, they nodded, and I walked to my car and drove off.

On the way home I mulled over the encounter and wondered what in the world could be eating that couple. While we had been talking it had crossed my mind to ask them why, in view of their evident love for aircraft, they had retired so early, figuring that after all those years they would not mind my mentioning it. Now I was profoundly grateful I'd kept that question to myself.

Our public library isn't the greatest in the world, but due to a sizable bequest from Mrs. Berriman Huffman, we do have a large vault kept at the proper temperature and humidity for storing documents. The bequest was mainly to make sure that the papers of the late Mr.

Huffman—owner of the largest factory in our city and mayor for three terms—were preserved for posterity. However, the vault also contains a complete file of the Boston newspapers for many years back.

So the following Saturday, having nothing better to do and being driven by a combination of curiosity and nostalgia, I dropped in, requisitioned the papers and addressed myself to the business of reviewing the career of Jack and Kit Lynnd.

Jack had apparently been bitten by the flying bug about the time of Lindbergh's New York-Paris flight, scraped up the money to learn to fly and started up a small airport in western Massachusetts. One of his first pupils was a young, attractive and ambitious girl named Katherine Corwin. He married her.

Came the Depression and the couple discovered that a small town airport in 1930 was about as profitable as selling swimming trunks to the Eskimos. Casting around for something better, they entered a few regional air races and were expert enough to pick up some cash. Then Kit started doing parachute jumps, and they found out that one woman performer was worth three men any day. The newspapers began calling them "The Flying Lynnds."

Late in 1930 they made a try for an endurance record but developed engine trouble and had to come down. Following this they obtained backing to enter the 1931 Bendix race, and were actually in the lead when forced down four hundred miles short of Cleveland. They tried the following year and again did not finish, but the husband-and-wife combination drew much more sympathetic attention than the one who came in first.

In 1932 they set a new speed record from Montreal to Daytona Beach. This brought them a cash prize and enough extra from endorsements and personal appearances to finance a new Bellanca and make a few shrewd investments in real estate.

Early in 1933 they fitted the Bellanca with extra fuel tanks and announced they were going to try for a transatlantic distance record.

By 1933 the Atlantic had been flown a number of times, but the ocean was still as wide and the water as cold and deep as it ever was. Public interest in the Lynnds' attempt was greater than anyone born since 1940 would believe.

Like many another ocean flyer of that era, they elected to start from Old Orchard Beach, Maine. They got off shortly after sunrise one morning in early June and were seen five hours later over Nova Scotia. There was no actual word from the plane; radio was extra weight and neither Jack nor Kit were experienced operators anyway. They carried fuel for forty-two hours—enough, with luck, to reach Baghdad.

There followed long hours of silence during which the Flying Lynnds were not reported. Eventually it became certain that their fuel was exhausted, and it was assumed there were now two more victims of the North Atlantic.

Then came the gratifying news that the Bellanca was down in a remote section of Ireland. They had landed on a small, soggy pasture and nosed over, breaking the propeller and landing gear. The Lynnds were uninjured, although too shaken and weary to give a coherent account of their trip. They spoke vaguely of storms, compass trouble and strong head winds.

Previously, the Lynnds had followed a policy of being accommodating to the media. Now they turned surly and refused to pose for pictures or give interviews. When they left their hotel and were, of course, immediately surrounded by reporters, they pushed their way through without speaking. Jack finally went so far as to take a poke at one persistent radio newscaster. After that the Lynnds remained in their rooms.

The reporters did not take this treatment lying down. Being popular heroes, the news accounts had to handle the Lynnds gingerly; but before long it was suggested that their flight, from the standpoint of its announced objective, was far from a shining success. Ships at sea reported conditions no worse than usual over the North Atlantic, and the Weather Bureau would not confirm the existence of any gale winds along their course. An expert had examined their damaged plane and insisted the compass was perfectly okay.

A nationally syndicated New York columnist wrote a sharply critical piece claiming it was obvious that the Lynnds had botched their navigation, become lost and wandered over the ocean for hours, and were now taking out their humiliation on the press.

The Lynnds made no attempt to reply. They sold their Bellanca to an English pilot, who wanted it for a flight to Australia, and took the first boat home. Their meals were served to them in their stateroom.

After their arrival they remained silent to all questions, and when a few well-meaning acquaintances proposed to give them a welcoming banquet, the Lynnds squelched the idea with scant courtesy.

Within a few weeks they had bought a house in New Hampshire and moved in, presumably to live on their investment income. By that time their actions had ceased to be newsworthy, and the Lynnds quickly faded from public view.

That was the story. My eyes were tired, and I leaned back in my chair and shut them while I tried to think. I had hoped to solve a riddle, but the answer seemed as far away as ever.

Review the facts: the Lynnds had embarked on a transatlantic flight with their usual verve and customary concern for publicity values. They arrived morose and silent.

Flying had been their preoccupation, their passion, and their life. Immersed completely in the world of cloud and sky, they had abruptly forsaken it.

What had happened during those forty-two hours in the air?

At least some trace of the old love still lingered: witness the restored antique in the barn.

I have a stubborn streak. Making a separate pile of those papers covering the final two months I began going through them again, carefully. I skipped nothing. And this time an item on another page caught my eye. It was a small item, with no apparent connection to the Lynnds, but when I read it my stomach tightened as though I had been thrust into freezing water. All at once it became clear what had happened over the Atlantic. It was as simple as the meshing of two gears.

I had to be sure, which meant checking the papers even more painstakingly than before. The library closes at eight o'clock and the librarian was casting impatient glances at the clock before I was through. I was tired and hungry, but I knew I had the answer. It made me just a little bit sick.

It was about two in the afternoon of the next day—Sunday—when I pulled up in front of the small white farmhouse with the red barn. The sky was overcast and it was raining, tiny drops not much more than a heavy mist, but enough to soak the grass and keep the trees dripping.

They must have seen me drive up, for Jack Lynnd answered my knock immediately. He stood with eyebrows raised but did not invite me in.

"There's something I have to say to you and Mrs. Lynnd," I told him.

He shrugged slightly and led me through a short hallway and into a sitting room. The furniture looked worn. There was a TV over against the wall, a few magazines scattered around and on the mantlepiece an old-fashioned pendulum clock and a picture taken many years ago of Jack and Kit standing beside a three-place open biplane, vintage 1929.

Kit was sitting on a rocking chair by the window, a magazine on her lap. She stared at me with recognition but not cordiality. I glanced around and selected a chair.

"May I sit down?"

They nodded, and after I had settled myself Jack took a seat on the faded divan. They eyed me with a sort of expectant wariness but did not speak. I waited a moment, then said quietly:

"Do you remember a boy named Paul Lawten?"

It was obvious to me that they did. They made no answer, but their faces were the color of an old newspaper.

"Paul was born the same year I was," I told them. "Later on his mother and dad were killed in an auto accident. In 1933 he was living with his grandmother, in Connecticut. From all accounts a lively, happy sort of kid.

"Nearby was a river where Paul used to fool around on a raft, even though the current was strong. So when he turned up missing one day and a couple of neighbors said they'd seen him heading for the river, it was thought likely he'd drowned.

"They never located his body, but the hope that he might turn up somewhere else died out when the days went by with no word of him. But the truth was, Paul hadn't gone to the river.

"Now a 12-year-old kid is not important, as those things are measured. The newspapers didn't waste much space on Paul when he was first missing, and in a few days they stopped mentioning him altogether. But I read enough about him to get a pretty fair picture.

"Paul was a good deal like me. He built model airplanes. He mowed lawns and did odd chores for pocket money, which he used to buy aviation magazines and flying books. Now and then he would save up enough for a five-minute hop with some barnstormer. Anyone who could get a plane off the ground was a hero to him. The greatest, of course, were those supermen who flew the oceans and broke the records. He would have traded his chance of Heaven any day to make a flight like that.

"Probably a million kids felt the same way. Paul was different; he had the spirit to try. On his own, he hitchhiked to Old Orchard Beach.

"The way your Bellanca was designed, the pilot and copilot sat up front. Directly behind was that extra gas tank you had installed. Only a few inches between the tank and the fuselage, but enough for Paul to get through. And as the Bellanca was tied down in the soft sand above the high water mark—with no one on guard—it was easy for him to crawl in back during the night, and hide.

"The Bellanca would be a little tail-heavy, but not enough to be noticeable with full tanks.

"Paul would be afraid you'd turn back if you discovered him, so it was probably several hours before he got around to crawling out from behind the tank. It must have been a shock, but maybe you weren't too unhappy at first. All the more publicity, to have a stowaway aboard.

"However, it turned out that neither one of you was capable of doing a decent job of dead reckoning. God knows how much time you lost due to navigation error, but it must have been a lot. You began to panic. The sight of miles of cold dark waves, when you're lost and running low on gas, can be pretty grim.

"Ordinarily Paul's extra weight wouldn't make more than a few miles difference, even in a flight of forty hours. But you ran into icing. It builds up awfully fast, and about all you could do was to go down and hope for a warmer layer of air near the surface. I imagine by the time you got to within a few feet of the water the ice had started to melt, but you were still too heavy to hold your altitude. A hundred pounds became pretty important.

"So you got rid of that extra weight, managed to hold your altitude long enough for the ice to melt, and made it across to Ireland."

They sat as motionless as two cast-off puppets, their eyes hollow and unreadable. There was no sound save the ticking of the clock.

I stood up and slipped on my raincoat.

"I drove up here," I told them, "because I wanted you to know there was someone who stayed awake last night imagining how the kid felt when he realized what was going to happen to him.

"Remember, you were gods to Paul. I know, because I felt the same way once."

Jack turned his head toward Kit, and for several seconds she looked directly at him, her face as unreadable as the markings on a worn gravestone. Then, almost imperceptibly, she shook her head. Jack got up and moved toward me. He stopped about four feet away and flexed his hands once, as though preparing to sail into me.

"What kind of a two-bit clown are you? Ever hear of the word coincidence? During the summer of '33 there must have been at least fifty kids drowned in the United States. In some cases, like this Paul you're talking about, they didn't find the body. But nothing to do with us.

"Forty years later you put two and two together and get seventeen, and have the brass to burst in here and insult us with your nutty notions. I'm not as young or tough as I used to be, but—get out of this house before I throw you out!"

I turned and went through the hallway and into the fresh air, shutting the door quietly behind me. I splashed my way to the car and drove home with no noise but the engine, the hiss of tires on wet pavement and the monotonous scraping of the wipers reminding me of the pendulum clock on the mantlepiece.

And for company the realization, forcing its way in like cold water seeping through the seams of a pressure tank: it *could* have been coincidence.

By the time I arrived home, I could think calmly and was beginning to suspect I'd make a terrible mistake. What in the name of God had possessed me, to go charging up to Sellers Falls, and sound off on the flimsy evidence I had? No evidence at all, really — just a hunch. Apparently I had so identified with Paul Lawten that my imagination had run away with me.

I had been hoodwinked by my own fantasy.

Wait . . . how about the expression on the faces of Jack and Kit Lynnd when I'd first mentioned Paul's name? Was that fantasy?

It was not. I had been right the first time.

A few weeks later I picked up the phone and obtained the Lynnds' number from Information. I dialed it.

"Mr. Lynnd?" I said. "Clayton Stone. You've probably heard the news. There's a twelve-year-old kid lost in the mountains. Why don't you take that Fairchild of yours and try to locate him?"

Then I hung up.   END

Gunther's Song

by Alvin S. Fick

Nobody knows for sure where Aunt Marsha went. But there isn't a soul in Perryville who does not recall why she left, even though it happened so long ago hardly anyone talks about it any more.

I was eleven and I remember it had been unusually hot and dry for so early in the summer. I'm sure I was eleven because it was the first summer on my newspaper route. The *Perryville Clarion* lowered the age minimum for me, no doubt because Dad contributed an occasional poem to the editorial page.

We were sitting on the porch after supper, maybe an hour before sunset. Mom and my little sister Katy were in the swing, Dad was in the big rocker with the *Clarion* in one hand and a cigar in the other. He sat with his back to the Jenner's yard, not because he didn't get along with them, but so it would be convenient to flick ashes over the railing into the flower bed. Aunt Marsha was sitting by me on the steps.

"Warren," said Dad, "why don't you get out the hose and sprinkle the lawn."

In a few minutes I had the grass looking like somebody's sequined green evening gown. The gentle hiss of the water leaving the hose nozzle seemed to stir the birds in the trees along the sidewalk into one more sleepy goodnight song. Three blocks away over on Elm Street I heard the last trolley of the evening go by. It stopped once at the corner of Clancy Avenue, probably to let old man Pringle off. He always worked late at his grocery store putting stock on the shelves.

I gave the flower bed by the porch a very elaborate watering. It was pleasant to be near the gentle undertones of conversation and to smell the fragance of the cigar smoke. I gave a little flick of the hose to send a few drops toward Aunt Marsha who was still sitting on the steps with her elbows on her knees and her chin cupped in her hands. She laughed at me, and I remember how the evening sun gleamed on her long chestnut hair.

Mom gave me that "Now Warren" look so I had to stop.

I guess it was about this time that both Aunt Marsha and I heard the sound of music faintly, almost as a footnote to the rustle of the water leaving the hose and splashing on the sidewalk in front of the steps. I guess I always communicated better with Aunt Marsha than anybody I know. She just looked at me, and I knew she wanted the hose turned off as much as I did so we could listen to whatever it was coming down the street making music.

By the time I had coiled the hose and hung it on the rack on the driveway side of the house, we could see a man walking east a half block away. When he was opposite the house he must have seen all of us sitting there for he crossed the street. He had been walking briskly but now his steps were slowed, almost as if he were tentatively extending a handshake to someone who might rebuff him. He was playing a mouth organ. Over his shoulder was a wide strap from which hung a brown canvas bag, not very different in size or shape from my newspaper bag.

As he came nearer he stopped playing, and from the corner of our lot to the gate at the end of our sidewalk his progress was especially slow. When he reached the gate he stopped, slipped the bag from his shoulder and began again to play his harmonica.

How can I describe its sound? I wonder what wild things were trapped in him, what joys that could come out in such unnameable music. Beside me I heard Aunt Marsha give a quick little intake of breath.

We listened as the man played. Not once did he put together in sequence any two notes which sounded familiar; it was as if he had come from another world and brought with him the music of the stars he had passed on his journey. When his song was ended it did not seem that he had stopped playing; rather the notes drifted off until I rubbed my eyes to see if he still stood there, or had been spirited off and was now finishing the melody as he walked over the horizon.

We sat in stunned silence. Even Mom, who used the word tramp for anybody who looked different and came into town on foot, seemed mesmerized.

"That was lovely," said Aunt Marsha.

"Can't we ask him to sit with us a while and have a glass of lemonade?" she added. Quickly, before Mom could answer, Aunt Marsha stood up and walked to the door, her hands smoothing the folds of her dress against her slenderness as she went.

Simple manners dictated the course of events. Aunt Marsha had spoken—out of some emotion that brought a flush to her cheeks—loudly enough for the man to hear.

Dad motioned me down off the steps. When I got to the gate and opened it the man did not step inside but reached into his pocket and handed me a card. I burned to look at it but instead dropped my hand to my side and carried it to my father.

He read it aloud to my mother.

"I am a deaf mute. I am looking for work."

I could see my mother tense and stiffen on the swing seat. She put her arm around Katy in a gesture which made me go all cold inside.

"Common decency, Mary," my father said, "common decency. But I better speak to Marsha first." He got up from his chair and went into the house.

Meanwhile, the man stood by the gate, and I noticed he had already picked up his bag and had slung it over his shoulder.

Aunt Marsha came out of the house in a minute carrying a half pitcher of lemonade left over from supper, and Dad was right behind her with a tray with some glasses on it. Aunt Marsha looked a little pale but her head was high. She took a glass from the tray, filled it and carried it out to the gate. She stood there very straight and I thought looking quite lovely while the man slowly emptied the glass.

In a town the size of Perryville little happens that is not common knowledge in a matter of hours. I have often wondered why with this effective grapevine communication we felt we needed the small daily paper—unless it was to be able to hold Pringle's Grocery to the prices listed in his weekly ad. Most of the old ladies around town liked the *Clarion* and kept scrapbooks in which they pasted recipes and accounts of births, weddings and funerals—bulging and frayed big books which they pulled out of the bureau drawer to read during long winter evenings. Even Mom kept a scrapbook, although hers was not so large. Mainly she saved Dad's poems and clippings of his occasional letters in the "Vox Pop" column.

Nearly a week later, during which time very little had been said at home about the stranger who had wandered into Perryville and who apparently had wandered right out, I saw someone kneeling in the flower bed beside the Dawson house over on Elm Street. I had finally mastered the art of rolling the *Clarion* into a tight tube, and was beginning to develop a degree of finesse and accuracy in delivering it to the front porches directly from the seat of my bicycle while in motion. Just as I swung my arm in an arc and tossed the paper, one of Dawson's three cats ducked under the fence and I swerved to miss it.

The *Clarion* came to rest on the porch roof, much to my consternation. I couldn't leave it there. Old Man Dawson owned half the town, was on the board of directors at the bank, and one phone call from him to the *Clarion* would cost me my job.

I figured my only chance was to enlist the aid of the man working among the flowers. For the first time I looked closely and saw the same faded blue shirt, the yellow hair just curling over the edge of the collar, the cord trousers. It was the harmonica man.

He was completely absorbed in his weeding chore, and was not aware of my presence, so I waited until he finished the row of marigolds and stood up to stretch. He was tall, and his strong-looking face had been turned a nut brown color by the sun. I was surprised to see how young he looked—much younger than he had seemed in the long evening shadows a week ago, certainly younger than my father. He wiped his hand on his pants leg. I was pleased that his grin and his hand-shake were both warm.

I was momentarily paralyzed by the thought that I did not know how to communicate with a deaf person. Finally I tugged at his sleeve and led him around to the front of the house. When I pointed to the porch roof, he took from his pocket a small pad and a stub of pencil. He wrote on the pad and handed it to me.

"Ladder in carriage house," it read. "*Talk* to me. I can read your lips. My name is Gunther."

"I'm Warren Tucker," I said. His eyes brightened when I told him I remembered him from a week ago, and that I liked his harmonica playing. He had underlined the word talk on the slip of paper. He watched my face intently, and I felt that my words were like rain falling on parched earth.

We brought the ladder out together and leaned it against the edge of the porch roof. I stepped aside, certain that Gunther would insist that I stay off the ladder, just as my father would do. But he grinned and waved me to go up and retrieve the paper. If I hadn't liked him before I would have liked him for that. After I thanked him we put away the ladder. I couldn't wait to get back on my bike to finish my route, and to carry home the word of my discovery.

At supper that night we were having dessert before I found a lull in the conversation so I could deliver my bolt of news.

"Gunther is still in town."

Only Aunt Marsha reacted. I watched her over the top of my glass of milk as the color rose in her cheeks.

"Who's Gunther?" my mother asked.

"Gunther who, or who Gunther?" my father asked.

Right then Katy asked for more cake. For Aunt Marsha's sake I was glad she did.

"Gunther who plays the mouth organ, that's who," I said.

That night we did not sit on the porch, but all of us stayed in the house to listen to Aunt Marsha run through her Sunday music on the piano. She had studied music at Juilliard for a couple of years, but aside from playing the organ for the Methodist church services, she had not made use of her training. She played for us at home, and we liked to hear her, especially Dad. Sometimes he would sit and watch her while she played. He would have a look in his eyes which helped you understand why he brought her home to live with us after their parents died. I hardly remember Grandma and Grandpa Tucker at all. Aunt Marsha took a job in the office of the broom factory in Perryville, and she helped out so much in the house that there was little reason for Mom to find fault with the arrangement.

By Saturday I guess everybody in town knew that there was a deaf mute working on the Dawson estate on Elm Street. There was not as much clucking as there might have been had Mrs. Dawson been living when Gunther was hired. In her shrewish way she had gone through a succession of gardeners and groundskeepers, no matter how skilled and conscientious they had been in maintaining the fifteen acres of estate. But even she could not have criticized the manner in which Gunther worked.

Dawson took little interest in the gardens, lawns and wooded trails while Mrs. Dawson lived, but under Gunther's loving hands the place bloomed and sparkled so that Dawson himself began to stroll about the grounds, thumbs hooked in the armholes of his vest.

I saw Gunther often, and during the daytime while old man Dawson was down at his broom factory office I would go over to visit my new friend. He used up many little pads responding to my boyish prattle, teaching me about plants and the small animals and birds which abounded in the wooded part of the Dawson estate. We kept the visits rather clandestine so that no word ever got back to Dawson. I felt no guilt because Gunther told me how little Dawson paid him in addition to his living quarters over the carriage house.

Of course I rambled on about my mother and father; I told him hilarious tales of the scrapes Katy got into; I took over my baseball gum cards to show him—and sometimes I talked to him about Aunt Marsha. Even then, I thought he listened ever more attentively with his eyes when I spoke of her. Now I am sure that he lived for those hours when a small boy made him a part of the family he no longer had.

Only Aunt Marsha knew how often I visited Gunther but even she did not know how fond of him I had become. Who else knew how to whittle a wooden whistle? Who could play strange and haunting songs on the mouth organ that caused a hush in the woods, followed by a torrential chorus from the birds? Who else could know what I said when I merely mouthed the words, not uttering any sound?

Over the weeks my boldness grew until I finally urged him to come to church services on a Sunday late in August.

"You can read the pastor's lips when he preaches the sermon," I said.

"I will come," he wrote on his note pad.

When we filed into church that morning Gunther was already there, sitting in a pew next to the organ and choir loft, which seemed a little strange to me. I thought that because of his shyness he would seek a seat in a darker corner in the back of the church.

Aunt Marsha was already on her bench at the organ and began to play while the church was filling. As soon as the first notes rolled from the pipe organ I saw Gunther reach out and lay his hand on the dark wood paneling enclosing the choir loft. My father saw it too, gave me a knowing look and nudged Mom with his elbow. Gunther was listening to the organ.

Gunther's plain, worn work clothes were a contrast to the business suits, ties and female finery which filled the pews. I was relieved and a little proud that Dad went over and shook Gunther's hand when we filed out on to the sidewalk after the service. We had to wait until Aunt Marsha finished the recessional and had hung her choir robe in the church parlor before we could leave for home. Off to one side, his cap crushed in his large brown hands, Gunther also waited. When Aunt Marsha came down the steps she saw him, her hand raised as if in salute, then moving to touch her throat lightly.

Gunther bowed in an Old World manner which seemed appropriate to the occasion, and handed her something. It was a small piece of paper which Aunt Marsha looked at for a moment. She reached out and touched his arm. Over the breeze stirring the leaves overhead in the maples I could hear her talking to him, although I could not distinguish the words. How sad, I thought, that he cannot hear her beautiful voice.

Aunt Marsha joined us. She and I looked back as we turned the corner. Gunther still stood by the steps, his hand raised in goodby.

"I have asked Gunther to come and visit us some evening this week," Aunt Marsha said.

"He's so strange," my mother said.

"He's lonely," Aunt Marsha answered.

"He's a bit younger than you, Marsha," my father said. He said it gently, but the look of pain on her face must have made him wish the words unspoken.

"Warren told me how old Gunther is," Aunt Marsha said. "When I'm 87 and he's 80 it won't make a bit of difference."

Mom's pursed lips said more than five minutes of talk could have.

Gunther came over on Thursday night just before Labor Day. I had delivered a note from Aunt Marsha which she let me read. It was a simple but nice invitation told in that ungushy but warm way she had of putting words together.

It was a wonderful night. Aunt Marsha played the piano with Gunther standing beside her, his hand on the wood. He was an absorbed audience, watching each of us as we spoke. I was elated because I had learned so many of his mannerisms and expressions that I was able to help convey some of his feeling and responses without the use of his pad.

Aunt Marsha and Gunther took a picnic lunch on the trolley out to Crescent Park on Monday.

Gossip has always been a prime commodity in Perryville. Drop a shoe in one end of town and the folks in the other end will know within a half hour whether it was a left or a right. Not that Aunt Marsha cared—or Gunther, for that matter—what the people of Perryville thought. I take that back, at least a little of it. She cared to the extent that the talk might bring down upon the rest of us in the family a degree of discomfort, and I know now that Gunther must have held the same concern for her.

None of us expected that within three weeks Aunt Marsha would lose her job at the broom factory, or that Gunther would stop in at the house that same evening, his brown canvas bag over his shoulder, to say good-by. I have since that day given thanks to whatever instinct it is that small boys sometimes have which makes them absent themselves from adult activities at critical times. I know only that Gunther and Aunt Marsha were alone in the living room for what seemed like a long time, and I only got to wave at him as he walked down the sidewalk.

Aunt Marsha did not leave her room during the rest of the evening. Two days later when I came home from school with Katy in tow, Mom was sitting in the kitchen wringing her hands. When Dad got home he let me read the note Aunt Marsha had left on the kitchen table while Mom was down at Pringle's for groceries.

Aunt Marsha had gone to search for Gunther.

The next three months were empty and strange. School held my mind and burned up my daytime hours, but the evenings were long and the house sepulchral. Only an occasional card came from Aunt Marsha to give a hint of her agonizing quest. I say it was three months because it was almost that to the day when Aunt Marsha returned. Maybe I should say more than three months; maybe I should say a thousand years. It seemed that long, and even after she returned things were not the same.

I think she had done all her grieving before she came home. When I opened the door to her knock she stood there with her suitcase, looking drained and tired.

Dad laid his paper on the floor beside his chair and came over to her. He took her suitcase and put his arm around her shoulders.

"I couldn't find him," was all she said.

Wounds have a way of killing us or healing into scars which don't hurt much when we are busy during the day. At least Aunt Marsha went on doing her hurting in her own way, and keeping it pretty much to herself. Rather than look around for another job she asked Mom and Dad if they would permit her to give piano lessons in the house. Her bedroom on the first floor was large enough to hold the piano so the door could be closed while fingers which itched to clutch a hockey stick labored up and down on the scale.

Pastor Humes came and pleaded so eloquently with Aunt Marsha to come back as organist at the Methodist church that she finally agreed. It was a decision to make through courage, probably wrenched from her more by her love of music than churchly devotion.

Next May, long after we had again fallen into a familiar pattern of life, the kind of thing happened which brings the pink of new pain to an old hurt we think has healed.

My father discovered on the editorial page of the *Clarion* a poem he had not written himself. Although he was in no way disturbed by the competition—to hear him tell it—he was intrigued because the poet had not given his name. It read,

> *Today I stood on the rolling crest*
> *Of a field the morning sun had blessed;*
> *To feel the west wind and see it pass,*
> *To seek the truth from whispering grass.*

"Hey, that's pretty good," Dad said after he read it aloud to us. "Mary, you should put that in your scrapbook, even though I didn't write it."

Aunt Marsha said nothing, but I thought she looked a little pale. Before I went to bed she took me aside in the kitchen.

"Could you speak to the editor of the *Clarion* tomorrow when you pick up your papers?" she asked me. Then she showed me the slip of paper Gunther had handed her that day in front of the church. It was a brief little poem whose construction and gentleness, Aunt Marsha said, were similar to the one in the *Clarion*. I couldn't see this myself, but I would do anything for Aunt Marsha.

"Well," said white-haired Mr. Deller at the *Clarion*, "all there was with that poem was a note which said the sender wanted to remain anonymous. You know what that means, son? It means I couldn't tell you if I knew. I guess there's no harm in saying what little I do know. The note didn't have a name on it anyway, only the letter G.''

He wouldn't tell me the postmark, even though I swore it was a life-and-death matter.

"When you are eleven, there's no such thing as a life-and-death matter."

"I'm twelve now," I told him.

After that, whenever there was an unsigned poem on the editorial page I brought home an extra copy for Aunt Marsha, who I am sure had started a small scrapbook herself.

It was nearly three years later that something happened which everybody still remembers but few ever mention. Of course, I would remember it better than most, and even after thirty years it comes to mind with pureness and clarity.

It was summer again in Perryville, the end of June and school.

Along about this time of year the service in the Methodist church used to begin to pall on me. Through the open windows you could hear the robins calling as they wormed the lawn between the church and the manse, and high in the trees along the street the orioles were caroling.

Pastor Humes had just received the offering up front from the ushers and had returned to the red plush-covered chair next to the pulpit where he sat to muster up his religious forces prior to the sermon. During this respite, Aunt Marsha always gave the congregation a short organ recital, a treat they seemed to enjoy, although Dad thought its Juilliard-based quality may have been a little lost on them.

I had nearly dozed off when I heard strains of music foreign to the Methodist pipe organ. Through the open window came a strange and haunting melody. One would not think that such a small instrument as a mouth organ could fill so large a room with its vaulted ceiling. Perhaps the breeze was just right; maybe the angle of the tilted glass amplified the sound.

The hidden player went on, the song unknown to all of us, yet in its longing, lonely notes there was a pull and a universality which composers spend lifetimes trying to arrange into music. From the first chords I had been watching Aunt Marsha. She had turned toward the window, her hand at her throat in a characteristic gesture, her eyes shining. She turned to the keyboard and from the organ came a plaintive, soft music, a gentle counterpart to the beseeching song streaming in from the window. The duet went on, the organ answering but always subdued.

At last Aunt Marsha stopped playing. She sensed the finish of the song and seemed to want the paean of longing and joy streaming through the window to stand alone in the quiet hall. She stood, removed her choir robe and folded and hung it over the loft railing. She stepped out of the loft and started down the aisle.

When she walked by our pew, my Dad stood up. Then everybody in the church rose as she walked toward the door at the back. I saw she was crying and smiling at the same time, but then so were some other people.

Nobody knows for sure where Aunt Marsha went, but all of us in Perryville know why she left.   END

The Price of Antiques

by Edmund Curley

When Josh Abbott was younger, new in town, and just starting out in the antique business he got word that he should make contact with Bernard J. Russell, foremost junk dealer in the area.

"Go and see him," Joe, the barber, advised solemnly, "he'll fix you up with anything you might want. No trouble for him; he's got more stuff from the past than you'll see in the next ten years."

Josh had received a good haircut. It was a beautiful spring day, and when he stepped from the barber shop a cool, grass-scented breeze tingled his freshly clipped neck. Everything was just right so he took the advice.

Josh was not well acquainted with Noank's streets but he knew the shore road below the village and it was near the end of this that Bernard Russell lived.

"Look for a high hedge at the corner," Joe had told him; "That'll be Jones' place hiding behind it. When you get there, step into the middle of the street and look up. You'll see an old garage on a high slope behind Jones' house. Jones owns it but he lets Russell rent it for an antique a month. Just walk up the driveway and poke around till he comes out."

Josh smiled at the instructions.

"Just poke around, huh. I shouldn't ring or knock?"

"No!" The exclamation was immediate.

"No, don't do that. Just poke around a bit. He'll see you."

Joe's demeanor had changed remarkably in those brief seconds and Josh tried to identify the range of expressions that had crossed his face. Was it panic that he had seen or fright, carefully masked and levered down to caution?

"He'll see you, and he'll come out," Joe repeated as Josh left the shop.

When he stood before the dilapidated garage Josh wondered whether he had made a mistake. The lower half of the building was locked tight and curtains, a different pattern for each of the four windows, hid any signs of residence on the floor above. But he had come and it would be senseless to throw away an opportunity. Antiques were hard to come by in a town where everyone knew their value and seemed to begrudge anyone who considered them in terms of profit. Carefully, he picked his way over discarded lumber, broken tools, and shreds of fishing nets until he reached the side of the building. A screen door banged at the rear and he looked up. Nobody. But there was the sound of movement in the grass where the back of the garage leaned against the slope.

Josh hopped some fencing materials and peered around back. A few yards from the garage stood a man, about fifty years old, pot-bellied, in a dirty T-shirt and overalls. The sun glinted off his metal-rimmed spectacles as he adjusted them before stooping in the grass.

Josh was about to call out but almost immediately the man rose holding a black and white cat by the scruff of its neck. The cat wriggled in protest, but the man's grip was sure and with his other hand he tugged at a rusty metal plate leaning on the grassy slope. The plate resembled a section from an old boiler, but it swung wide with a raspy squawk as the man pulled.

Immediately, the cat screeched and swung its hind legs in a desperate try for escape, but the man held it at arm's length until he was ready. Then with a practiced snap of his wrist he flung the cat into the dark hole the plate had covered and slammed it shut again.

Josh stood transfixed. Seconds passed as the pot-bellied man gazed at the iron door and Josh stared at him. Gradually, Josh realized that he was listening for more sounds from the cat but there was nothing. Then, unnerved by his position, he pressed back around the corner and wiped his palm over the perspiration that had suddenly burst from his forehead.

"What the hell . . ." he muttered at the end of a long exhalation from his tightened chest. And he inched back a few steps before turning to the safety of the garage front. He was still trying to regain his equilibrium when the man who had disposed of the cat stepped into view. He threaded his way effortlessly through the junk and came up to Josh. He was smiling and again adjusting his glasses.

"Afternoon," he said, "can I he'p ya?"

"I . . . uh, I'm in antiques," Josh answered, hoping his voice was calm, "and down at the barber shop they told me you might have some things I could look at."

"And what's yer interest?" His voice was kindly. "I've got a lot of things ya know."

Why the devil had he thrown the cat in that hole, Josh wondered. Did he kill it? Maybe there's a well in there.

"D'ya have any preferences?" His tone was calm, even pleasant.

"No, just . . . general."

"More like for buyin' later on, eh? C'mon then and have a look. Most of my stuff's inside."

The man turned and led the way to a door on the other side of the building—a typical proprietor leading a customer to his wares.

Maybe it's some sort of a storage cellar, Josh mused, and maybe there are mice there that he wants the cat to kill.

"My name's Josh Abbott," he offered to the other's back as they reached the door.

"Bernard J. Russell." He motioned for Josh to enter first.

Inside it was dark but as soon as his eyes had registered the change, Josh gaped. The entire place was crammed with incredible pieces and they all looked brand new. For a moment he suspected something wrong: the gleaming metal, polished wood, and sparkling china lining shelves, hanging from rafters, and stacked in every corner made too sharp a contrast with the cement floor and unfinished walls. Were they reproductions? He looked again and saw that they were not.

A mahogany washstand at his elbow held a large crockery washbasin to fit the original piece. The basin was filled with polished "glassies" that appeared to be new. Josh stared at the mound of giant marbles and their transparent interiors frozen in beautiful spirals of red, green, and blue porcelain. A choice one caught his eye and he plucked it from the pile. A silver rabbit crouched in the center of the glass. He put it back. Another held a golden rooster. They weren't fakes; nobody made these anymore.

They were in such good condition! He peered closely. No scratches, no nicks or slivers missing. Nineteenth-century boys had not played with these.

The washstand was complete, too—a small shelf for toiletries, another shelf for soap and brushes, even the towel racks, polished like new, of course. There was a crockery pitcher that matched the bowl and a slop jar.

"The whole bathroom's right here," Josh muttered.

"Yep," Russell had heard him. .

"Well, why don't ya look around. I got somethin' to 'tend to."

Josh turned to an old wingback piled with antimacassars. They were like new, they *were* new, finely crocheted in a variety of designs. There must have been three dozen of them.

A shelf at chin level was lined with bone dishes, a whole set, one for each member of the family; all the same pattern and, yes, there on a higher shelf was the complete dinner set. There were dishes everywhere and . . . A row of cup plates caught his attention. He stepped closer. Cup plates—the tiny dishes used for setting teacups on after the tea had been "saucered" for cooling. They were of Sandwich glass.

"My God," Josh whispered, his gaze roving about the room.

A sturdily made brush harrow leaned against the far wall. There was a snow roller beside that, its six feet of wood looking as though it had never been used. A box of horse clogs—a whole box—was on the floor in front of the roller, and that was a pung running back into the shadows.

There were several stoves about—two dignified parlor pieces with nickel trim and a cluster of small tin footstoves. Nearby were other metal goods; brass warming pans, iron lawn dogs, and some handsome fire trumpets.

Josh let his eyes feast voraciously. He moved here and there, quickly, stopping only long enough to touch an object here, another there, as if it were a dream and everything was soon to vanish. There was a patent rocker, sand shakers, mustache cups, shaving mugs, and even a shipmaster's symptom book. He found the book by a window and as he put it back, chanced to glance through the dusty panes to the yard behind the garage.

He froze. The iron door in the slopeside was open again and Mr. Russell was bent forward retrieving something from it now. He turned, balancing a coach lamp in one arm while with the other he swung the iron plate closed. But just before it closed there was a hint of something still within, something not proper for rational vision, a glimpse of misshapenness shambling backward from the light, cratered eyes, and a mouth quivering like . . . Josh squinted against the sunlight's trick and looked again. The door was closed, but even if it were open, there was, of course, nothing.

Mr. Russell approached the garage, and Josh slipped from the window to greet him at the door.

"Find anythin' special?" the proprietor asked as he set the gleaming coach lamp on the floor and stood up adjusting his spectacles.

"Everything you have is special," Josh blurted. "I've never seen antiques in finer condition, and some of the articles you have are . . . extraordinary. Where did you ever manage to get them?"

There was a twinkle, not unpleasant, in the man's eyes.

"That's my secret," he answered, "but if you're ever in the markit for somethin' specific, you let me know 'n I'll git it for ya."

"Yes," Josh hesitated, "I imagine you could."

"Jist give me a day's notice, that's all," Russell continued, "I don't charge much."

The next time Josh stopped at the barber shop he made it a point
to thank Joe for the tip about Bernard J. Russell.

"Think nothing of it. When you're starting a business you need
all the connections you can get and Mr. Russell's the one for you."

"But there is something strange about him, Joe," Josh had intended to probe, to mention the episode with the cat and a short while later
the antique lamp taken from inside the slope . . . almost as if in barter.

The barber's reaction cut him short.

"Nothing unusual about Mr. Russell. He's a businessman and a
good one. I'll bet if you talked prices, his were fair."

"Yes, but . . ."

"No 'buts', son. He's a fine man. Lived here all his life and never
bothered anyone."

"But the cats!" Josh insisted loudly, not realizing he had used the
plural until Joe was answering him.

"You know about them, eh? Well, keep it under your hat. Nobody pries in Noank and talking about that is prying. It's just his way."

Josh was aghast. Grisly phantoms tumbled across his mind. If it was
a question of cats, of something that went on often. . . ? Then what
about the other thing, that unnameable thing he'd thought he'd seen?
What about that?

"Son," Joe called without turning from the cash register as Josh was
about to leave.

"Yes?"

"Don't bother about it. It'd be best."

Josh went out without answering and never returned to the barber shop. It was not that he had taken to disliking Joe, merely that
he acquired a small store the following week, not in Noank but in
neighboring Mystic. All in all, he judged it was the best site he could
hope for. The price had been right, and Mystic had a guaranteed summer tourist trade drawn to her seaport and museum. He had a good
chance with antiques now and there was never reason to drive extra
miles down the coast to Noank.

That is, not until the day the dealer from New York sized up Josh's
stock and broached a possibility. The dealer needed ties with antique
people outside the city. "To fulfill particular requests" was how he'd
put it. He told Josh that if he could contact him when he needed particular pieces and could count on Josh to provide him with a good
number of them, their commerce could be constant and profitable.

"There are a lot of collectors in the city," he said, "and they come to
me when they're looking for something difficult. I need good sources
of supply."

Josh had never been quite able to erase his mind's picture of Bernard J. Russell's garage, and, as the New York dealer spoke, that memory overcame all reservations.

"I think I may have a good source of supply," he said.

Josh and the dealer hunched over the shop counter as the New Yorker pencilled off items on a scratch pad.

"Why don't I try you out with this one?" he said, "It's a real stickler."

"A church stick?" Josh questioned.

"Yes. A very old item—from colonial days, I believe. It's a light stick which the tithing men used to awaken sleepers in church. On one end is a rabbit's foot and on the other a foxtail. At least, that's how this collector describes it."

After the dealer had left Josh closed up and drove the shore road to Noank. It was a clear day with the sun beaming off the water, and he felt a warm assurance of impending prosperity. He had been foolish not to have gone back to Russell's before. After all, he and the Noanker were in the same business. He would simply state his need and ask whether Russell could fill it. If he could, then they would decide on a fair price, and he could contact New York accordingly. Straightforward barter in the best Yankee tradition.

"A church stick, is it," "Bernard J. Russell's eyes twinkled behind his freshly adjusted spectacles. "That's a bit diffrint but I'm sure I kin git one," he smiled.

"One day's notice?" Josh questioned, hardly believing his good fortune.

"Yep." A nod. The spectacles slid forward and Bernard J. Russell bobbed his head slightly to arrest their progress. The bobbing brought his face close to Josh's where he held it intimately. He tapped a forefinger gently at his nosepiece, and his eyes gleamed responsively.

". . . if you'll bring me a cat, that is."   END

The Collaborators

by Eleanor Boylan

Kenneth Newhouse drove west along the Concord Turnpike reading his mail. His rationale for this risky procedure was threefold: the pike was newly widened and satin-smooth; his last class at Boston University dismissed at three o'clock so he was always ahead of the rush; and, alas, there was little in his mail of late to warrant more than a glance at its contents.

On this lovely fall Monday he did indeed have the pike to himself but the mail was duller than usual. Slowing before the traffic light at Spy Pond he reached for the only thing worth looking at, the Tilsboro Book Catalogue. This at least was always fun. "See what $1.95 will buy! *Weird Sexual Practices of the Aborigines* (reduced from $25.00)." As he lifted the catalogue, an overlooked pink envelope ornamented with daisies revealed itself.

A horn behind him blared and he proceeded past the light, reaching for the letter. In a small, neat hand it had been addressed to him in care of his agent in New York and from thence forwarded to Boston University. A royalty check? Had some dear, lovely amateur group dug up one of his plays? . . . He turned the envelope over and felt a slight constriction in his throat at sight of the name.

Mrs. Grace Woodgate Turner

Newhouse drove almost to the Lexington line without attempting to analyze his feelings. At the big, empty parking lot of St. Camillus' Church on the outskirts of Arlington he pulled off the turnpike, stopped the car and opened the letter.

Dear Mr. Newhouse:

I sure hope you remember me, Lee Woodgate's sister Grace. Lee brought you to my house a few times when you and he were writing plays together. That's what I'm getting in touch with you about.

Please, Mr. Newhouse, will you write to Lee and try to patch things up? I don't know what you two quarrelled about but I do know that Lee hasn't had a bit of luck with his writing since that last play you did together. He's in New York (I'll put the address on the back of this letter) but when you write be sure not to mention that I asked you to. He'll deny that he's unhappy or hard-up but don't you be fooled.

The last few lines said something about how she knew he wouldn't be sorry. Newhouse dropped the letter face down on the seat beside him and started the car. He reached into his pocket for a pencil and began to scribble on the letter's backside. By the time he'd reached Concord Center he'd finished, and driving down Monument Street he read what he'd written. Ten minutes later he was at his typewriter assuring his daughter over his shoulder that he'd be back from the post office in time for supper. He wrote:

Concord, Mass.
Oct. 25

Dear Lee:

I'm going to begin this letter by betraying a confidence: in this morning's mail I received, among other appeals for charity, a letter from your sister Grace begging me to write to you. She requested that I not mention her part in the proposed peace negotiations. By now, I have no doubt the poor lady envisions us huddled over a first act together.

I remember your sister well; a very pleasant person whose feelings I wouldn't hurt for the world. So I shall write her and say I've gotten in touch with you. There, of course, my obligation ends, since I would rather be keelhauled than ever again collaborate with you on so much as a telegram.

Are you still writing those awful plays with the words "THIS IS A PROTEST AGAINST RACIAL DISCRIMINATION!" screaming between every line? The last one I heard about got as far as New Haven. Cheer up, the next one may reach Boston. I may even be asked to review it; in which case I shall say the following:

"Lee Woodgate, once the most amiable, perceptive and witty of black writers, has become a self-conscious, preachy bore. From his eminence as a brilliant satirist he has skidded to the crowded arena of placard-bearers who, should you challenge what their signs read, hit you on the head with them. Mr. Woodgate was my collaborator for eight years. I was 'aware' that my hair was brown, my daughter's hair yellow and my father's gray. I never needed to be told by Congress what honest men are told by their conscience—that all men are created equal. Together Mr. Woodgate and I wrote (some said) funny plays about real people. Now he writes dull sermons about ancient vices. He is no longer a first-rate playwright; he is a third-rate crusader."

Well, so much for my potential review. It will be read with approval by thousands who admired you before you commenced your tedious canting. As for myself, I haven't even *thought* of starting a play. I find teaching at Boston University very stimulating, and after so many years of collaboration it's refreshing to work alone. I'm a new man—a whole man— not half a team bickering over our hero's motives. Thankfully, that's all in the past. Deo gracias.

By the way, one thing does occur to me and since I'm writing I may as well ask: for some time now I've been trying to remember the name of a

certain perfume that we both remarked on one night in Mimi Lake's
dressing room during the run of, I think, *The Silent Waterfall*. It was very
subtle and aromatic and Mimi said she got it in Madrid and told us the
name. If you recall it (you never used to forget anything) will you jot it on
a postcard?

Yours
Ken

Newhouse was, after all, late for supper. From the post office he
drove over to Wayside, the Nathaniel Hawthorne home on Route 2A,
and sat in his car across from the lovely weathered house, staring at it
dreamily.

Four days later he again pulled into the parking lot of St. Camillus' Church (telling himself he was *not* superstititious) and opened
a letter.

New York
Oct. 29

Dear Ken:

"Gratias" is spelled with a *t*; Latin, not Spanish. The bit about "col-
laborating on a telegram" is good. Perhaps "cablegram" would be even
funnier since they are usually *more* restricted as to words. Rather than
"crusader" I'd prefer "pamphleteer." It's more appropriate and you get
the alliteration. Leave out the adjectives—they're implied. Now listen to
it: "He's no longer a playwright, he's a pamphleteer." Much stronger.

The perfume episode took place during the run of *Things That Are
Caesar's* and your exact words on the occasion were: "If I ever fall in love
again I would like to give her that scent." Do you mean to tell me—though
you probably did *not* mean to—that in your dotage you have toppled?
You must be sixty-seven or eight if you're an hour. I'm amazed that your
poisonous disposition hasn't curdled every gland you possess. As I
recall, you were going to "devote yourself to your motherless daughter"
or words to that effect. What *does* Jenny think of your autumnal romance?
I hope she isn't too mortified. She must be marriageable age herself by
now. Well, the name of that Spanish stuff was "Carmen's Rose." Good
Luck.

My sister Grace is very tiresome. I have an extremely busy schedule and
can scarcely afford the time even for this letter. For the past year I've
been doing intensive research in preparation for a play (hopefully three
acts and in poetry) on the horrors of slavery. You, being basically a super-
ficial person, are incapable of appreciating a man's development to the
point where the burning issues of his day are of more importance to him
than a set of good reviews in the morning newspapers. I too am a new man,
conscious of a great cause and, like yourself, still giddy from the pleasures of working in solitude.

What on earth are you doing in Concord, Massachusetts? The question
is rhetorical.

Lee

Newhouse reached into the back of his car, grasped the handle of his portable typewriter and heaved it over the seat. He moved from beneath the wheel, placed the machine on his knees and started to type rapidly.

Dear Harriet Beecher Stowe:

Rhetorical, my eye! You're consumed with curiosity. If you had bothered to *read* my letter instead of editing it, you'd have noticed that I mentioned teaching at Boston University. Concord is not far from Boston, as you may have learned during that underprivileged childhood you've lately been bleating about, and, happily, Jenny lives here.

She was married last year to a young law student at Harvard and his parents gave them a pretty house not far from "the rude bridge that arched the flood." When I came up here for this teaching job they prevailed on me to stay with them and I've become more and more enamored of the area. I haunt the landmarks; spend hours in the Emerson Museum, swim in Walden Pond (spoiled, of course, but still rather lovely when you're in the middle of it in a rowboat) and walk in Thoreau's woods. Now, there was a man for your burning issues! And it wouldn't take him three acts, all in poetry. Are you INSANE? I should like to hear Thoreau's comment on, say, the bomb threat . . . "The best bomb shelter is a good conscience." (Never mind Thoreau—that's damn good Newhouse!)

Well, among the landmarks that I visit most frequently is the Nathaniel Hawthorne home called Wayside, a huge, rambling old love of a place where he wrote most of his books. And this brings me to the point . . .

You're right, I'm in love. Utterly and inarticulately. And she is young and I am old and the thing is ripe for your raucous ridicule. (I defy you to improve on *that* alliteration.) I'm telling you because I dare tell no one else, least of all the girl herself, and it occurred to me that if I could read a few well-turned phrases of scorn in your familiar style—your *old* familiar style—it might bring me to my senses sufficiently enough to pry me away from her. I simply cannot make myself stop seeing her and it is becoming increasingly imperative that I do. It's just possible that your gibes may turn the trick. Let me give you something to work on:

Her name is Margaret Mulqueen and she is dark-haired and very tall—taller than I—with impossibly blue eyes and milky Gaelic skin. To put it simply, she is the most beautiful woman I have ever seen, though scarcely a woman, being only nineteen and a student at a small Catholic college near here. She worked this past summer, and still does on weekends, as a guide at Wayside, and Nathaniel stares down upon her from his portrait as if he saw the ghost of Alice Pyncheon moving about his house telling tourists that in this room he did so and at that desk he wrote such.

I took her "tour" the first time I visited Wayside. She was very sweet to an old man, spoke a little louder and paused on the stairs to allow me to take breath. Evidently, she considers me as old as you do. I am only sixty-three. She has a most exquisite voice. I went back the next day to hear it again and this time I talked to her for a little while on the lawn. I told her I was a Hawthorne devotee—God forgive me—and she was instantly excited and pleased. It seems that she has steeped herself in his work. She came to Wayside to take a routine summer job and began dutifully reading Hawthorne to make her "tour" more interesting. The books and house have gradually obsessed her till she can think of almost nothing else. This kind old gentleman who spoke to her on the lawn and who also admires Hawthorne is the first person who seems to understand and sympathize . . . Oh, she is so tearingly, unconsciously beautiful . . . I would risk my life to catch one glimpse of her face.

Is this sufficient? Surely by now you are calling me ten kinds of a fool. Put it in writing—by the next mail if possible.

Ken

Newhouse mailed the letter on his way back to the house, where a note informed him that Jenny and husband were at a cocktail party and he'd find cold cuts in the refrigerator. He made a sandwich and a drink, got into his car and drove back along the turnpike to Route 128. There he headed north toward Salem.

A reply lay on his desk two days later. He restrained himself from tearing it open, sped up the turnpike at three o'clock and coasted into his usual spot in the church parking lot. Making a mental note to find out what St. Camillus' claim to sanctity was, he opened the letter.

Dear Ken:

Your letter reeked with advancing senility but in most respects was amusing and well expressed. The incongruous spectacle of an Irish-Catholic Alice Pyncheon wandering about a museum reciting a spiel for a salary has a nice element of surrealistic farce.

As for your pitiful quandary I have only one suggestion: take this milkmaid out to dinner, spend a complete evening in her company and note how soon the "obsession" will wear thin as she has you dancing your poor old bandy legs off till the small hours . . . But for God's sake leave me alone! The distractions this week have been endless, and tonight I must travel with a delegation to Rye Beach, New Hampshire. We plan to confront a prominent resort proprietor who has been refusing to register Blacks.

Lee

Restraining himself only because Jenny was having a dinner party that evening, Newhouse wrote not a line till next morning. He opened his first class with a surprise quiz and during it sat at his desk writing furiously in longhand, ignoring the outraged faces before him.

Dear Lee:

An old and once valued friend asks for your help in a personal crisis and you go to New Hampshire. Why don't you go to hell? I understand the proprietor there will register anyone.

Your suggestion is useless. I've taken Margaret to dinner any number of times. There is never any dancing or mention of dancing. We talk about her, about me, and always, in the end . . . about her fantasies. It's almost frightening. She seems to identify with Marianne or Alice or Zenobia, depending on her mood. I tell you, Lee, this girl is definitely fey . . . possibly a little mad. And I am so bewitched that I would follow her to Bedlam.

It is a weird coincidence that she lives in Salem where, of course, the House of the Seven Gables is located. There isn't a cranny of that spooky old place that she doesn't know as well as her own home. Her family consists of a father and some brothers. Mother dead. I am not regarded with favor by the father and brothers who seem plebeian and suspicious. One evening last week her father had the gall to ask me how old I am. Margaret was distressed and mortified and when I met her for lunch next day I could tell she'd been crying. I said: "Margaret, does your family object because we're friends?" She said: "Yes. And father wants me to leave my job at Wayside. He thinks I dream and pretend too much." Which, of course, she does. But if they are brutal to her, God knows what she might do . . .

Until this week I've considered myself reasonably safe. I have not made love to her and have been content with her presence. I am content no longer. And I know she would marry me for I have been smarter than a lover, I have been a listener. I've never smiled at her fantasies nor discouraged . . .

Write quickly, Lee! Be your most devastating self!

Ken

He mailed the letter between classes, and before starting home that afternoon walked a block down Commonwealth Avenue to the university library. There *A Complete Compendium of Christian Saints* informed him that Camillus de Lellis was a sixteenth-century French saint noted for his healing of the sick. Newhouse gave a strangled laugh and was frowned at by the librarian.

A few days later, a Saturday, he spent the entire day at Wayside, driving to the university in the evening to get his mail. It was quite dark when he pulled into the parking lot of the church, and he switched on the ceiling light of the car to read the letter.

My dear Donatello:

Your faun's ears are rapidly growing into those of a jackass. I have almost stopped laughing. You're obviously a crazy old fool and could do serious harm to this girl, your daughter and yourself—in that order of importance.

But I'm convinced that she'll never have you. In fact, a direct proposal of marriage might frighten her out of that dream world and back to her senses. Be warned of the look of horror on her face as you go shakily down on one knee.

Lee

Jenny's husband studied for an exam that night and Newhouse sat on the porch with her till quite late. She was in a reminiscent mood and wanted to talk about her mother. They recalled the lovely, clear things, and he embellished what she only faintly remembered. She may have wept a little; it was too dark to tell. The fragrance from the gardens of the old Buttrick estate across the road was heavenly. Shortly after midnight Newhouse typed a single page:

Dear Lee:

Bravo! Your letters have given me the same glow of pleasure and admiration that your work used to! The subtlety of your allusions! The glint of your wit! The strength of your barbs! Oh, Lee, when will you realize that you— you, *yourself*—are more of an asset to your race than all the delegations that ever marched on the puny white bigots in boresome resorts!

Can you tell that I'm in high spirits? Margaret and I are to be married on Thursday. It will be very quiet, just Jenny and her husband. The father and brothers are behaving badly but I'll not let that spoil my happiness.

And I won't bother you again. Best of luck with the play, and most affectionate regards!

Ken

Three days later Newhouse arrived at the university at eight in the morning, two hours before his first class, and hung about while the mail was being distributed. He seized the envelope and, with a mental apology to St. Camillus, tore it open.

Ken:

I'm flying to Boston to prevent you from making a fool of yourself. When I get through with this nymph she will never speak to you again, and you will never speak to me.

Lee

He tore down the hall and dove into a phone booth. Western Union was infuriatingly slow to answer, but finally a lackadaisical voice asked for his message. He dictated it carefully:

Lee: Brace yourself. Margaret Mulqueen and aging suitor exist only on paper. Can't get past first act. Forgive trick. Desperate for your help. Fine drama department here to do play if turns out well. Was dying to write you but too proud when sister's letter came. Praise be St. Camillus who heals all. Will explain. Wire or call me at Jenny's when to expect you.

Jenny said afterwards she couldn't make head nor tail of a telegram that was phoned in late that afternoon; but then, her father had always had a lot of nutty friends so she took it down exactly as the operator gave it to her:

Ken: Knew it all the time. Or did I? Arrive Boston 10:18 tonight. Thanks for compliments on letters. However consider sister's letter my real masterpiece.

END

Second Time Around

by Newlin B. Wildes

The case came up for trial in Winston County Court early that December, and it was said that nobody—judge, attorneys, certainly not the jury panel—wanted any part of it. It was very cold that day, and the prisoner, as he was brought into the courtroom, had on a dark herringbone overcoat with raglan sleeves, apparently a Burberry, and a handsome gray Homburg hat worn at a distinguished angle.

An attendant took the coat and hat and the prisoner sat down in the cage, looking very much like a chairman of the board about to call his meeting to order. He had gray hair, almost white, a little long and brushed close to his well-shaped head. His face was square, stern, with the confidence that sometimes comes from power, authority, and, although age was beginning to loosen the flesh around his mouth and his jaw, the line of the lips was firm and the blue eyes were searching clear under craggy white brows.

His gray suit was so well cut as to be unobtrusive, his tie a dark solid blue over a white shirt. His left shoe, seen as he casually crossed his legs, had the dull gleam of recent boning. He looked out over the courtroom calmly, not seeming very interested, but as if he were there visiting, perhaps getting material for a book. Instead of being on trial for his life.

Judge James C. Whittaker glanced at the prisoner almost nervously. Judge Whittaker was young enough, thirty-five or thereabouts, to be the prisoner's son. He had achieved his judgeship at an early age by shifting political allegiance at a crucial time, and because he was tired of the poorly paid trivia of country law, wanting a quiet and safe spot so that he could be with his family and could, from time to time, do some fishing and hunting. Winston County was in Vermont, and Shireton, where court was being held, was a small town, a village actually, settled comfortably among the high, wooded hills and open fields that give the state its quiet and rural charm. Except that, with this trial, Judge Whittaker felt that things might not remain quiet and removed. Already the courtroom was crowded, and there was a reporter from a big city daily, with doubtless more to come.

Judge Whittaker sighed. He was a short, round-faced, sandy-haired young man, seeming at times too immature for his judge's robe. He had a sound enough knowledge of the legal aspects of his position, but was inclined to allow certain leeways and freedoms in testimony and procedure, if he felt that it furthered a good and fair trial. He was the sort of man who enjoyed reading to his children before they went to bed, who released most of the fish that he caught, and who cut his own firewood, alone and deep in the winter forest. Now he called the two attorneys to his bench, ready to get on with a trial for which he had no stomach.

"Let's not drag this thing out," he said, almost pleadingly, and Lew Searner, assistant district attorney for the state, shrugged. "You can count on me," he said. "I've only got two or three witnesses, and they'll be short. It's a cut and dried case. First degree, premeditated."

He looked at Ken Pollard, attorney for the defense, and tried to be very casual and confident. Searner was a young assistant, using the state as a stepping stone to private practice, and perhaps a little in awe of Ken Pollard.

Pollard smiled briefly. He was sixty or thereabouts, short, big-shouldered, his sandy hair a tight bristle, his eyes dark and his face completely expressionless. He had been born and brought up in Vermont, had practiced in the area all his life, and did not hurry.

"Don't want to hold you up too much," he said, "just want to bring out a few things. Just a few simple things."

Judge Whittaker looked at him, half questioning, then turned away. The formal opening of the case took place and then Whittaker nodded to Lew Searner. Searner walked slowly over to the jury box, unsmiling, stern. He was tall, with wavy black hair and a cleft in his chin. At one time he had thought of becoming an actor. Now he put both hands on the rail, looked first at the jury foreman, then up and down the two rows. The twelve people in the box watched him, fascinated, perhaps a little nervously. It was the first jury duty for most of them.

They had been carefully picked, especially by Ken Pollard. Five were women. Pollard would have liked two more, but had to settle. Three were wives of retired men; two were from the farm. The farmers' wives were large-bosomed women with what Ken Pollard hoped were gentle faces. Three of the men were elderly, new to the area, and in the first blush, Ken Pollard hoped, of loving the rural life. There were no farmers. It had been easy for Ken to avoid them—they had obligations, stock, milking to do. He didn't want farmers. The remaining four included a small shop owner, the proprietor of the local riding stable, a clerk from the Inn, and an artist who never sold any pictures. The area was full of those. Lew Searner spoke impressively.

"Ladies and gentlemen," he began, "I am going to prove to you, prove without the shadow of a doubt, that this defendant, this John Lee Adams, the man you see across this room, did willfully and with premeditation shoot and murder his neighbor and part-time employee, Barton Webb of East Cordon. That the defendant shot Webb in cold blood and then gave himself up to the police. I'm not going to *tell* you what happened on that afternoon of June 23. I'm going to let the people who were there, who actually saw and watched what happened, I'm going to let them tell you."

He turned dramatically. "Call Augie Racker to the stand," he said.

Augie Racker got up from his chair, took three steps forward, realized that he still had his cap in his hands, started back, thought better of it, stuffed the cap in his pocket, smiled sheepishly, and stumbled as he climbed to the witness chair. He was narrow-shouldered, stooped, his hair long, greasy, and cowlicked. His teeth, in the nervous smile, were gone or blackened. He had shaved close and cut himself. His suit was a greenish black, padded lumpily at the shoulders, and had evidently not been worn for some time. He was sworn in, and had some difficulty remembering his right hand from his left.

Lew Searner smiled at him. "Don't be nervous, Augie," he said, "just tell us the truth. You worked for Bart Webb—right?"

Augie's voice came out high falsetto, and he cleared his throat and tried again. "That's right," he said. "Hired man. Three years. Lived on the place."

"Why don't you just tell us what you saw on the afternoon of June 23, the day Bart was murdered."

"Exception," Ken Pollard said.

"Granted," Judge Whittaker said, "strike the 'murdered.' "

Searner shrugged. "Go ahead, Augie," he said. Augie's eyes showed their whites, but he was beginning to enjoy himself.

"We was hayin' up to Adams'," he began, "up on the hill. It was about two o'clock an' Bart he was workin' the side delivery rake, windrowin' up in the big field down below the main house. I was gettin' the baler set. It was a hot day, a little breeze, good for hayin'." Augie looked around, wet his lips. The jury watched him.

"Go on," Searner prompted. "What happened?"

"Well," Augie said, "I dunno. Bart was a-rakin' an' well, there was this dog of Adams', kind of a collie type, I guess. Black an' white with them kind of yellow eyes, and a fresh young dog. White tip to his tail. An' well, it got runnin' at the wheels on the rake, bitin' at the rubber tires, barkin' some, and well, Bart he yelled at him a few times, but the dog kept chasin', barkin.'

"I could see Bart gettin' kind of mad, he's quick with animals you know, real quick, short-tempered, and then the dog got in the way of the tractor an' Bart he had to stop. That annoyed him some, I guess, an' he tried to chase the dog away and it would go a little an' then set down. Bart he got back up on the tractor an' then the dog came back an' started after the rig again an' Bart went around two times an' then he stopped an' got off an' well, then he booted the dog once or twice. A couple of times." Augie stopped.

"Then what happened?" Searner prompted again. Augie looked at John Lee Adams in the prisoner's cage. His greasy head of hair went down and he examined his hands.

"Well," he said, still not looking up, "well, I guess the dog he yelped some, quite some, an' then—then this Mr. Adams he come down over the hill, runnin'. Never did see him move so fast." Augie glanced at Adams again, and Adams watched him, expressionless.

"So," Augie went on, "Mr. Adams he ketches up with the dog, an' gets a hold of him, the dog wasn't movin' too fast, fact he was draggin' some, an' Mr. Adams he holds the dog's head in his hands a minute or two, lookin' at him, an' then Mr. Adams he looks up at Bart. Bart's back on the tractor seat now, kind of waitin', an Mr. Adams he says something to Bart an' I don't hear what it is 'cause I'm off there a ways on the baler.

"Then Mr. Adams puts the dog's head down, very careful, an' goes over to Bart on the tractor an' takes this flat little gun out of his pocket an' shoots Bart three, mebbe four times. Bart, he falls off the tractor an' Mr. Adams pays no attention to him, just goes an' picks the dog up in his arms an' starts on up the hill, runnin' an' stumblin' some 'cause the dog ain't too little, weighin' mebbe forty-fifty pounds. When he gets up the hill a ways I go over to Bart an' he's lyin' there, seemin' about dead." Augie stopped, wiping his face.

Lew Searner let the silence stand, sink in. "Then what did you do, Augie?" he asked finally.

"Then I heard Mr. Adams' car start, the big one, he's got two, an' I run off down the hill to Prescott's—I sure wasn't goin' up there to Adams' house—an' the Prescotts they called the State Police an' the doctor an' all, an' then Al Prescott he went on back to the field with me an' Bart was dead all right. Lyin' there. After a while the State Police come an', well, that was that."

Lew Searner nodded, very slowly. "That'll be all, Augie," he said. "Thank you. Now call—"

"Wait a minute," Judge Whittaker said. "Ken, do you have any questions?"

Ken Pollard got up stiffly, carefully. "Augie," he said, as if he had known the witness for a long time, "just how many times did Bart Webb kick this dog of Mr. Adams', of the defendant? You said 'once or twice'—was that all?"

Augie twisted his head. "Well," he said, "once or twice. Three or four times, mebbe."

Ken Pollard stood there, looking at the witness. "Augie—" he said finally, warningly.

Augie Racker had his cap in his hands, looking down at it. "Augie," Ken Pollard said, almost gently, "didn't Bart Webb get real mad and kick that dog half a dozen times, and then stomp it? Didn't he? Come on, Augie."

Augie twisted the cap some more. Then his head came up. "Well," he said, half defiantly, "well, Bart he was quick with animals. Mebbe he did get pretty rough with the dog. I guess he did."

"And the dog howled some, didn't it, Augie? Yelped and howled so Mr. Adams heard way up in the house on the hill and came running? Isn't that right, Augie? Didn't the dog cry something terrible?"

Augie Racker nodded slowly. "Yes," he said, "I guess it did."

Ken Pollard turned. "That's all, Augie," he said. He sat down. The jury shifted uneasily, the women looking at each other. John Lee Adams sat motionless in the prisoner's cage.

Three other witnesses were called by Lew Searner. Al Prescott, who had come up the hill with Augie, said that Bart Webb seemed to be dead when he got there. The State Police Captain, who had reached the scene very quickly, said, "No, the first call we got was from this Mr. Adams, the defendant. Said he had shot a man. Called at two forty-one. Prescott called some later." The medical examiner testified that Bart Webb had been shot four times with a foreign automatic. Ken Pollard didn't question them. He sat hunched at counsel's table, drawing idly on a pad, face expressionless.

At the end of the second day, the prosecution rested. Lew Searner told the jury that he had proved premeditated murder in the first degree. The jury stared back at him. On the third morning, Ken Pollard took over.

He moved out from his table unhurried, quietly purposeful, his face brown, seamed, and kindly, his suit rumpled. "Call Dr. Robbins to the stand, please," he requested.

Dr. Robbins was sworn in. He was about forty, powerful, with very keen eyes, strong wrists, brisk movements. "Dr. Robbins," Ken Pollard said, "you're a veterinarian, aren't you?" Robbins nodded. "And you were in your office the afternoon of June 23, weren't you?" Robbins said that he had been.

"And the defendant, John Lee Adams, came to your hospital that afternoon about three o'clock?" Robbins said that he had.

"Will you tell us what happened, please," Pollard requested.

"Well," Robbins said carefully, "he had this dog with him, a border collie. It was in bad shape."

"How bad?" Pollard inquired.

"Most of its ribs were stove in, splintered, so that they were piercing some internal organs. Both hind legs were broken at the hips, compound fractures." The jury stirred uneasily.

"Could the animal walk?" Pollard asked. Robbins shook his head.

"Hell, no," he said, "Mr. Adams carried it in. It was almost dead."

"What did Mr. Adams say to you?"

"He asked me to make every effort to save the dog's life. I told him after further examination, that there wasn't a thing I could do. Lungs, kidneys, and so forth were ruptured, and I felt that nothing could save the dog."

"And Mr. Adams said?"

"He asked me if I thought the dog should be put to sleep. I said I did think so. Then I did what he asked."

Ken Pollard walked a step or two, slowly, head down. "Did Mr. Adams say what had happened to the animal?"

"He said a man working for him, Bart Webb, had kicked the dog."

"And did you feel that the dog's wounds were made that way, by kicking, stomping?"

Robbins nodded. "I did. Every indication pointed to it."

Ken Pollard moved thoughtfully. Then, "Dr. Robbins, have you ever been called to Bart Webb's farm in the past?"

Robbins said, somewhat reluctantly, that he had been.

"And what were you called for?" Ken Pollard pursed.

The veterinarian shifted on the stand. "Well," he said, "the last time, month or so ago, was for a horse Webb owned."

"What was the matter?"

"The animal had apparently been beaten around the head with a heavy club or instrument of some sort," Robbins said.

"And did Webb say how that had happened?"

The doctor's face showed no emotion. "He said he had had to trim the animal up a bit to get it to mind," he said.

"Thank you, Doctor," Ken Pollard said. He turned away, then back to the witness. "Oh," he said, "one more thing. After you had done what Mr. Adams asked, put his dog to sleep, did he leave the body with you?"

"No," Dr. Robbins said, "He wanted to take it back with him. I helped him put it in his car."

"That's all. Thank you, Doctor," Pollard said. He walked over and looked at the jury. Then he shook his head, sadly, and went back towards his table. "Please call the defendant, Mr. John Lee Adams," he said.

Lew Searner got up quickly, sensing, apparently, what Pollard was about to do, and wanting to delay it until the impact of Robbins' testimony had lessened. "Like to request a recess," he said.

Judge Whittaker called the two attorneys to his bench for a whispered conference. Then, "I can see no reason for it," he said finally. "We have a lot of time ahead of us today. Request denied."

John Lee Adams came out of the cage and up to the witness stand. The courtroom was dead silent. The defendant was a tall man and had some difficulty getting his legs adjusted in the witness chair. No one smiled. No one moved. Ken Pollard asked the witness his name, for the record.

"And your business?"

"I retired, three years ago," Adams said.

"And before that?"

"I was vice president for sales and merchandising for General Supply, food manufacturers."

"That is a competitive business, Mr. Adams?"

Adams allowed himself a shadow of a smile. "Very," he said.

"And required a lot of traveling, being away from your home a great deal?"

"More than half the time," Adams said.

"So that you did not see as much of your family as most men?"

Adams hesitated. "I saw very little of them," he said.

"Your family consisted of?"

"My wife and two sons."

"Are any of them with you now, here on your farm?"

The witness shook his head. "My wife and I were divorced five years ago. I haven't seen my sons since that time."

"How old are your sons?"

"Twenty-nine and thirty-one this year," the witness said.

"And may I ask you just why you don't see them any more?"

The witness shifted slightly in the chair. There was still no expression on his face. The jury watched him intently.

"I was divorced for mental cruelty," he said finally. "The boys sided with their mother. They were right. I was sharp, very demanding, insistent that they do things the way I wanted them done. I couldn't seem to realize that they had problems of their own, that they weren't part of my business organization. Towards the end, I was tired. I did not contest the divorce."

Ken Pollard nodded, walked a step or two, looking at the floor. "So," he said finally, "when you retired, you came up to this farm alone. Is that right?"

"That is correct," the witness said. Lew Searner got up.

"Your Honor," he said, "I don't see what all this has to do—"

Judge Whittaker held up his hand. "The witness will proceed," he said. Ken Pollard nodded.

"You have help in your house here?" he inquired.

The witness shook his head. "A cleaning woman, once a week," he said.

"No cook, no maid, no man for the grounds?"

"No," Adams said, "I take care of myself quite well."

"But you must be able to afford help," Lew Pollard insisted, "you must have a substantial income, a pension and so forth. Isn't that so?"

"I have a reasonably good income," the witness admitted, "but well, I have other uses for it."

"Such as?" Ken Pollard asked.

The witness twisted in the chair. "The divorce settlement was, well, quite large," he said uncomfortably.

"And you didn't fight that settlement?"

"I requested it," the witness said.

Ken Pollard paced the floor for seconds, head down. "So you live by yourself, work by yourself outdoors. Don't you get lonely?"

John Lee Adams hesitated. His eyes were straight ahead, but he did not seem to be looking at anything in the room. He seemed to be looking through it and beyond it. "I had the dog," he said. "I had Bennie."

There was not a sound, not a move. Ken Pollard stood with a hand on the jury rail. He nodded slowly. "So you had the dog, Bennie," he said, "the dog that died. When and where did you get him?"

"I got him out of a barn about two and a half years ago. He was two months old. He was very undernourished, weak. Jim Robbins here helped me get him back in shape, feed him correctly, vitamins and so forth."

"And he was with you most of the time since you got him?"

"He was with me all the time," John Lee Adams said, "We walked the woods and fields together, we hunted woodchucks, we fished, he rode everywhere in the car with me, he slept beside my bed. We did everything together, everything. Perhaps I spoiled him, but he would do anything that I asked him to do. At any time."

"Why do you say that you spoiled him?" Ken Pollard asked.

The witness raised his head, taking a deep breath. "I don't think I really spoiled him," he said. "I tried to understand him, to realize why he did what he did, to see his point of view. If he was wrong about something, I corrected him. He seemed to understand. In three days, for example, he would stay well back from a stream where I was fishing—things like that."

"You took a lot of trouble with him, didn't you?" Ken Pollard said.

The witness shook his head. "No," he said, "not too much. I couldn't take too much trouble with him. You see," the witness raised his head and his voice was very quiet, "you see, this was sort of the second time around for me. I'd alienated my first family by not being understanding with them, not looking at their point of view, not seeing them as individuals. I wasn't going to make that mistake again." He allowed himself just a shred of smile.

"You may think that a dog isn't much of a second family. Maybe you're right, maybe wrong. I don't know. I only know that this dog thought I was God, that I could do no wrong. And, more important perhaps, that I was his friend, that I would stand beside him at all and at any times, that I would never let him down. He came to me when he was hurt. He called me when he was happy. He was part of me. When he died, part of me died. That was all."

The big man stopped talking. Again there was that silence. Ken Pollard waved a hand in dismissal. "Thank you, Mr. Adams," he said.

Lew Searner got up quickly. "But you did shoot and kill Bart Webb, didn't you?" he said.

John Lee Adams nodded. "Oh, yes," he said.

The summations by the prosecution and the defense were short. Lew Searner told the jury that he had proved John Lee Adams had shot and killed Bart Webb with premeditation. "He had the gun with him when he came down the hill," he said, "person doesn't carry a gun unless he plans to use it. And he admits he shot Webb—says so himself. I ask for a first degree verdict."

The jury looked at him, emotionless, the faces of the women going slowly red. Ken Pollard rose, coming moderately over to the jury.

"I'm not going to say much to you," he said. "You've heard the story—both sides of it. All I'm going to remind you is that about the only thing this Mr. Adams, this defendant, had going for him, or with him, was this dog, this Bennie. That was about all he had left to take care of, to have take care of him. And when he heard and saw this friend, this companion of his, being maltreated, being killed by Bart Webb, well, it was part of him being killed. So you can say he acted in self-defense, if you want to. Yes, I think you can say he acted in self-defense. That's the way I'd feel about it. And thank you."

It was some two hours later, about three o'clock that afternoon, that the foreman knocked from inside the jury room. The bailiff, Joe Peterson, told Judge Whittaker that a verdict had been reached. The crowd came back, scrambling for places, the reporters stayed by the door to be close to the telephones. Judge Whittaker took his robed place on the bench and the defendant, John Lee Adams, was brought in. He still had that calm, removed, remote look, as if these matters did not really concern him, that he was not involved.

Judge Whittaker asked if the jury had reached a verdict, and the foreman said that it had.

"And what," Judge Whittaker said, "is your verdict?"

"We find the defendant," the foreman said, "we find him guilty of manslaughter. And we request clemency."

There was a quick burst of applause from the crowd and Judge Whittaker stopped that. The faces of the women jurors were pink and they smiled happily at the crowd. John Lee Adams sat in the prisoner's cage and did not smile, change position, or show any emotion whatsoever. He did shake hands with Ken Pollard, who came over and said something to him very low.

On the steps outside the courthouse, Lew Searner said, "Whittaker will give him a year or so, and he'll be free in two months. You did a good job, Ken."

Ken Pollard nodded. "Maybe so," he said, "maybe so. But I don't think Adams cares. I guess it's too late for that. You don't get a third time around, not often. Too many ghosts." He walked off down the street, a little stiffly as usual. END

The Tree with a Birth Certificate

by Lester C. Boyd

If my grandfather was alive, he wouldn't have been disgraced by what Uncle Juniper did.

The rest of the family was, though, all except my grandmother, of course. She still goes into the parlor every day to dust him off. None of my uncles or aunts go in the parlor at all. They all say they can't stand to see Uncle Juniper leer at them.

I don't think it's a leer. It's kind of a happy smile.

Anyway, all they ever say is, why didn't he go out West or someplace if he wanted to make a fool of himself, instead of doing it right here at home where the whole town would know about it.

I guess they never liked Uncle Juniper very much anyway, even if he was their own brother, because when Grandpa died he left some money in a trust fund so he wouldn't ever have to work. This made the rest of the family jealous because *they* all had to work for everything they got. Grandpa left them the farm, but my Uncle Carl always said that being left the farm was like being sentenced to a treadmill.

Grandpa always said that the rest of the family were only drones. He felt none of them would ever contribute anything particular to the store of human knowledge. So they could take care of themselves.

They used to say that the only thing Uncle Juniper would ever contribute was some new kind of nuttiness. But Grandpa was right, I think, because none of my other uncles or aunts could ever think of things like Uncle Juniper could. That's what he used to do, think of things. He was an inventor, not the kind that invents things, but the kind that thinks of things to invent.

Once I asked Grandpa why he wouldn't let Uncle Juniper tell people about his ideas and Grandpa said it's for his own good—nobody would understand him because he didn't have a profit motive.

Sometimes my uncles and aunts would say, if he's so smart, why doesn't he think of something that will make us all rich and we can all move someplace that doesn't smell like a cow barn, but Grandpa just laughed and said they could live in places that smelled like worse things than cow barns. They said they couldn't think of any.

One of the things Uncle Juniper liked to do was sit and watch grass and flowers and things grow. I guess he couldn't really see them grow because they grow so slow, but he could watch them and he always knew they were growing because they were bigger when he stopped watching them than they were when he started. Sometimes, like when he watched trees grow, it took a long time though.

One day while he was watching a tree he began to wonder why people couldn't grow the same as trees do. He said if trees and grass and things can get their nourishment from the soil, why couldn't people? He said that maybe eating was just a habit people got into, like smoking, and when they got started they couldn't stop. He said probably nobody had ever tried to get nourishment from the soil, so if somebody would stand in the ground long enough and get fertilized and watered and everything, maybe he would get nourished. Then people wouldn't have to eat any more, and they wouldn't have to work. It was kind of funny he thought of that because he never worked anyway, but I guess he was just thinking of other people who have to work to get money to buy food.

Anyway, he decided to try it; but when he told the rest of the family about it, they all laughed and said he was crazy and tried to talk him out of it. He said he was going to do it anyway because he was over twenty-one and he didn't have to do what they told him because he had the trust fund Grandpa had left him, and he didn't have to depend on them.

They all said just because you are over twenty-one and financially independent doesn't mean you have to be crazy, does it? They said if you go standing in the ground trying to grow like a tree it will disgrace the whole family. My Aunt Mary said the next thing you know you'll be trying to fly through the air like a bird, but Uncle Juniper said, now who's crazy, everybody knows that people can't fly. He had her there, all right.

After a while, when they saw they couldn't talk him out of it, they all said, oh, for heaven's sake, if you've got to do it go out behind the barn where at least nobody can see you from the road. The only thing my grandmother said was for him to wipe his feet when he came back in the house for supper if he was going to stand in the dirt.

He said you'll see. After a while I'll be getting my nourishment from the soil and I won't have to come in the house at all, and Aunt Emma said, ha, you'll be getting your nourishment at the happy house if the authorities ever find out about this.

So Uncle Juniper got some fertilizer from the barn and some good, rich loam and dug a hole out behind the barn where he'd get a lot of sun and put the fertilizer and loam in the hole. And every day after that he'd go out and take off his shoes and socks and stand in it. I used to go out every day and talk to him but the rest of the family kind of ignored him and made believe he wasn't there. Except my grandmother, who told him he had to stop using natural fertilizer because it was noticeable in the house when he came in. I don't think she understood him either, but at least she was nice to him.

Anyway, one night he didn't come in for supper and my grandmother sent me out to get him. He said he didn't want any supper. He said he wasn't hungry and he thought it was because he was beginning to get his nourishment from the soil. Then Grandma went out to try and get him to go in because she said he would catch his death of cold out in the night air.

I think the rest of the family wished he would catch his death of cold because they said, oh, for heaven's sake, let him stay there if he wants to, he'll come in when he gets hungry. After a while Grandma said all right, but get him a blanket in case it gets cold, and she told Uncle Juniper to be sure and come in if he got hungry because she'd leave some supper on the back of the stove. We had beef stew and dumplings for supper that night, which was one of his favorites.

But he didn't come in all night, and the next morning Uncle Carl and Uncle Fred tried to pick him up and carry him in. They couldn't. That's when they found out he was really rooted.

After that there was a big argument. Nobody knew what to do about it. Grandma wanted to bring him out a bowl of oatmeal and a cup of cocoa, which is what Uncle Juniper always had for breakfast, but he said he wasn't hungry because of all the nourishment he was getting from the soil, but if she wanted to sprinkle some of that patented plant food around him, he said that would be all right. Grandma always said the patented plant food she used on her flower garden was the reason she had such a good garden.

Aunt Mary said, oh, for heaven's sake, patented plant food! The next thing you know he'll want a beehive next to him so he can be cross-pollinated, but Grandma told her not to talk like that in front of children and mixed company. After a while Grandma said, well, I'm going to call the doctor, and Aunt Mary and Aunt Emma said, ye gods, if the doctor comes, tell him Juniper's adopted, will you?

The doctor came and looked at Uncle Juniper and took his temperature and everything and said, there's nothing wrong with him that I can see. Grandma said, I know there's nothing wrong with him, and the doctor said, why did you call me? I want him moved into the house, Grandma answered.

The doctor said he couldn't help her there because he wasn't a tree doctor, and he didn't know anything about transplanting a tree, and it didn't seem to him that Uncle Juniper would flourish in the house anyway. So Grandma called the tree doctor and the tree doctor came and looked Uncle Juniper over and said, what do you want me to do? Grandma said, move him in the house, and the tree doctor said, move him in the house, are you crazy? You can't transplant this time of year. Besides, he said, he's in a nice sunny spot with good soil and drainage and he'd be much better off there than in the house.

Grandma started to cry and Uncle Fred said, look, Ma, there's no need to cry about it. He said he and Uncle Carl would pull him up if she wanted and take him over to the mental hospital at Fallsberg; but Grandma said no, he's not crazy, just rooted, and she didn't want him in a mental hospital with a lot of crazy people. So Uncle Fred and Uncle Carl said, all right, let him rot in the ground for all we care, we've got to get the hay in.

Grandma cried some more, but Uncle Juniper said he was all right and didn't want to go in the house anyway and after a while she stopped.

After that Uncle Juniper was happy just standing there for the rest of the summer. The only thing was that Grandma and me and the hired man used to have to take care of him because the rest of the family wouldn't go near him. We used to have to water him and put on the plant food and keep the birds off; not that Uncle Juniper didn't like the birds, but Grandma was afraid they'd peck at him looking for insects. My Aunt Mary wanted to build a big fence around him so nobody could see him, but Grandma said, no, how would you like to have somebody build a big fence around you? Aunt Mary said, if I was rooted like him, I'd insist on it. She got the maddest because she was trying to get married at the time and she was afraid nobody would marry her if they found out she had a brother who was rooted. She said if I ever told any of the other kids about it, she'd kill me—and I guess she would have too.

Another trouble was when Uncle Juniper wanted to be moved. The tree doctor would have to come and do it. He'd dig a new hole and put fertilizer and stuff in it and then he would dig up Uncle Juniper and bind his roots in burlap and move him to the new place. One time they found that he had such a long tap root they were afraid to dig him up any more, so they had to leave him where he was. It was lucky he was in a good place out near the pasture spring where there were some nice maples and elms around to keep him company.

When the cold weather came, Grandma used to worry that he would be cold, but by that time Uncle Juniper was growing a nice, thick coat of bark and he seemed to be warm enough.

Then one day some surveyors from the state came along, and they told the family that Uncle Juniper was right where a new expressway was going and he would have to be moved because he was right where he would be on the white line. Grandma said, no, you can't move him because his tap root is too long. The tree doctor said so. So the state surveyors said they didn't know anything about a tap root, all they knew was that they weren't going to change the course of a six-lane highway because of some nut who thought he was a tree. They said if the family didn't get him out of there by the time the bulldozers came through, they would have to cut him down.

Aunt Mary said if the state backs down on this one, I'll never vote Republican again, and Uncle Fred said it looked like the family might get its money's worth out of their taxes for a change. I think they would have been glad if the state did cut Uncle Juniper down.

But Grandma said she wouldn't stand for it, so she went out and hired a lawyer, and the lawyer went to court to get a judge to get out an injunction for the state to leave Uncle Juniper alone. The people from the state said we don't have to leave him alone because we took him by eminent domain, and the law says if we take property by eminent domain we can cut down trees on it. But Grandma's lawyer said, you do not own him because you can't take people by eminent domain. What is this, the pre-Civil War South or something?

They said he is not people.

Grandma's lawyer said, oh no, what do you think this is, and he showed them Uncle Juniper's birth certificate.

So instead of cutting him down the state built a rotary around him. Uncle Juniper was happy in the rotary. While they were building the road, he had a lot of company because the men who were working used to sit in his shade and eat their lunches. Then, when they finished the road, they made a kind of a park around him with flowers and grass and things, and they put in tables and benches, and people used to stop there for picnics. About the only time he wasn't happy was when somebody tried to carve his initials on him. They arrested the man for defacing public property.

One time my uncles and aunts got together and decided that they should have Uncle Juniper's trust fund as long as he wasn't using it. They said Grandpa's will said they should split it up if anything happened to Uncle Juniper, and there wasn't any question, they said, that something had happened to him. The probate judge said they were only supposed to get the money if Uncle Juniper died, and since he was still alive it was still his. Uncle Carl said, boy, that's great, some trees live for hundreds of years.

But they didn't have to wait that long. What finally killed Uncle Juniper was the exhaust fumes. Grandma noticed he was looking kind of wilted one day just after a Fourth of July weekend when there was a lot of traffic. The tree doctor came and looked at him and said it was the carbon monoxide from the cars that made him sick. He said there was a temperature inversion over the weekend and it held the poison gases close to the ground. The doctor gave Uncle Juniper some shots and loosened the soil around his roots and had a highway crew hose down his leaves to wash off the poison, gave him special plant food and everything.

But Uncle Juniper just got worse and worse, and finally so bad the doctor sat up all night with him. But it didn't do any good. He died the next day.

Grandma said, well, we just can't let the poor soul stand there, we got to do something about him. So she made my Uncle Fred and Uncle Carl take the pick-up truck and the big cross-cut saw and go out and get him. They cut him off real close to the ground because that's what Grandma told them to do. But when they got him home they didn't know what to do with him.

My Uncle Fred said maybe we can haul him down to the lumber yard and have him sawed up into boards to fix the shed where it needed fixing, but Grandma said, no, it was a horrible idea, fixing the shed with your own brother.

My Aunt Emma said why don't we cremate him in the fireplace and Grandma said perish the thought.

After a while Grandma called Mr. Shields who carves monuments for the graveyard and asked him if he could carve a life-size statue from a tree trunk, and he said sure, do you want me to get the tree trunk for you. Grandma said, no, I already got one.

So she got a picture of Uncle Juniper before he got rooted and made my Uncle Carl drive her over to the monument works. Mr. Shields said, it's a nice piece of wood all right. Grandma said, can you make him smile like in the picture? And Mr. Shields said, sure, I'll give you a call when it's ready.

A couple of weeks later he called up, so we went over and got it. It looked just like Uncle Juniper before he got rooted, and it had a nice, happy smile. Grandma said it was lovely and she cried a little bit. Aunt Mary and Aunt Emma cried too.

Grandma gave the statue a coat of clear varnish and put it in the parlor right next to where she keeps Grandpa's coffin plate. She dusts it every day.

After that, my uncles and aunts went to the probate judge again to tell them that Uncle Juniper was dead and could they have the trust fund now, and the judge asked them if they had a death certificate. They said, no, they didn't, but he was dead all right. The judge said, well, if you haven't got a death certificate he's not dead as far as this court is concerned, and he told them that if they wanted, they could file a claim and if Uncle Juniper didn't show up in seven years they could have the money.

So they don't go in the parlor any more. They all said it wouldn't be so bad if he didn't have that triumphant smile on his face as if he knew they were trying to get his trust fund and they couldn't, but I don't think it's triumphant. I think it's just happy.

I think the whole trouble is they never understood Uncle Juniper.

                                                                    END

I Can Show You Morning

by Linda Triegel

Emma stood in the middle of the empty room and tried not to remember. But the sunlight came in the window and shone on the worn spot on the wooden floor that had been under Gideon's rocking chair, and it shone on the desk where he wrote down the sermons he had thought out sitting in the rocker, and it shone on the faded wallpaper that Gideon had refused to have replaced because it was the same pattern his mother had hung in their home in Concord. Emma couldn't help but remember.

The house was very still. Motes of dust in the shaft of sunlight danced merrily, but in ghostly silence. Emma closed her eyes and, hearing nothing and seeing nothing, imagined herself suspended in space, floating far above this earth in which she no longer felt at home. Then a horse whinnied and she heard the jingle of harness as it shook its mane to clear the flies away.

They were waiting for her. They kept a respectful distance until she was ready to leave, but they were waiting nevertheless. Old Eleazer Hanks, Gideon's hired man, had fetched the new minister and his wife, who were waiting to move into the Parsonage—into her home. Then Eleazer would drive her to Cook's Corners to meet the stage-coach to Pittsfield. When she was ready.

Emma sighed. She was as ready as she would ever be. Oh, my God, my Saviour! Why did it have to happen like this, why? With no warning, no preparation, swept from life and happiness to loneliness and old age before her time in the swift second of a frightened horse's kick. Why?

No use demanding why, they told her. It was God's will. His will be done. Amen. Emma could understand that the Lord might have need of Gideon, but did He have to take him so soon? They'd been married scarce ten years. And what was the good of leaving her behind? She was nothing without him, no earthly use at all. Alone, she was only a burden on the parish. The deacons had asked her, out of courtesy, to stay, but she had elected to go home, to be a burden on her mother instead. Oh, why?

Emma stepped out of the door and turned to lock it behind her. Then she remembered that it was no longer her house to lock, and took the key out again. She walked down the path, feeling the spring breeze on her cheek as she went. Bits of white blossom from the crab apple tree in the meadow sailed by her on the breeze. The wind caught at her shawl. It tugged at her, as if to pull her back up the path, but she did not heed it.

The new minister stood beside the wagon, his wife meekly at his side and their belongings piled neatly around them. He was a tall, stern-looking man with a habit of raising his chin when he spoke. It gave him an air of arrogance. Emma thought he would never reach his congregation, as Gideon had done with the sheer force of love and hope in his message.

He cleared his throat noisily. "Ah . . . madam, I . . . "

Emma interrupted. "The house is yours, Reverend Kingman." She drew herself up to her full height, which was not considerable at any time, raised her candid blue eyes to his, handed him the key.

Mrs. Kingman stepped hesitantly forward, and took Emma's hand. In an almost inaudible whisper, she said, "Thank you so much, Mrs. Wilkes. We shall take good care of your house."

Emma smiled briefly. "I hope you will be as happy in it as we were."

Mrs. Kingman gave Emma's hand an understanding squeeze. The Reverend cleared his throat again.

"Hrrumph! Yes. That is as the Lord may see fit! Now, madam, if I may assist you . . . ?"

Eleazer looked on somnolently as the Reverend handed Emma up onto the seat beside him. Then he flicked the reins and the sorrel mare started off down the road. Emma did not look back.

"Drive around over the River Road, Zed."

Eleazer flicked the reins again, and the mare obligingly turned right at the fork, onto the dirt road that skirted the town. It twisted and turned under drooping willows, following the river to come out above Cook's Corners. It was longer, but it did not go past the church.

Eleazer maintained his silence and Emma was glad to be left in peace. That was all she wanted now, to be left in peace.

"The Corners" was what folks called the juncture of the local farm roads with the main pike road from Worcester and Boston. Mr. Jamison had his General Store there, and appeared to be expecting a shipment on the morning's coach, for he had opened his door earlier than was his custom. There were already several ladies mulling over the neatly piled bolts of gingham and calico, and sifting demerara sugar experimentally through their fingers.

Along the far side of the pike road ran a stone wall, over which grew wild grape vines in profusion. In season, and even out, it was a favorite meeting place of the young people of the town, for whom gathering the wild grapes was as heady an experience as drinking the wine made from them. This morning, there was only one young man and two girls there. But when Emma saw who the young man was, she was surprised that the girls were only two.

The schoolmaster, Andrew MacKenzie, was naturally an object of some importance to the local young people. Being also young and unmarried and blessed—cursed, Emma substituted—with a gypsy-like brand of good looks and merry black eyes, he was even more naturally the object of the adoration of his female pupils. Some of them had been known to repeat the eighth grade three times just for the privilege of seeing him every morning.

This was not to say that Mr. MacKenzie's fancy encompassed only the younger belles. Emma had often seen him after Sunday service, rambling through the churchyard and reciting the epitaphs in the tombstones for the amusement of damsels of eighteen and nineteen, who were denied his company on weekdays. Later, he would stroll with a whole gaggle of them—that was the only way to describe such silly geese—down to the millpond, where he read them lectures in the mysteries of botany. At least, that was what the girls said he did. Gideon had been fond of Andrew, but Emma privately thought that the accomplishments in which the schoolmaster excelled were not such as the young people of the county would be wise to emulate.

Eleazer helped Emma down from the wagon and, since her other belongings had gone on ahead of her, hauled only a single battered portmanteau out of the back. She thanked him, and said good-bye; she preferred to wait alone. Eleazer shuffled a bit, then put his hat back on and went away, leaving Emma seated primly on the wooden bench outside Mr. Jamison's store.

She had not been there long when the schoolmaster saw her and raised his black brows in mild astonishment. With a wave of his hand as charming as it was casual, he dismissed his companions and sauntered over to Emma. He took off his wide-brimmed hat and, in the manner of the rural swains, held it awkwardly in front of him and touched his lanky forelock to her.

"Good morning to you, Mrs. Preacher, ma'am!"

Emma eyed him accusingly. "Why do you talk to me like that, Andrew MacKenzie? I know perfectly well you speak civilly to everyone else!"

"Well, ma'am," replied Mr. MacKenzie upon reflection, "I reckon you always look at me so proud and lady-like, you make me feel like a regular country bumpkin!"

Emma frowned. She tried always to be lady-like, but Andrew Mac-Kenzie made it sound like no virtue at all.

"And what brings you out so early on this fine morning, ma'am?"

"The eight o'clock coach brings me, Mr. MacKenzie, and takes me. I am going . . . away."

The sparkle in the schoolmaster's dark eyes concentrated itself into a piercing glance. He put his foot up on the bench and, leaning closer to her, looked Emma full in the face.

"Why?"

But at that moment, two of the ladies who had been turning Mr. Jamison's dry goods upside down, stepped out of the store.

"Good gracious!"

"Emma!"

Mr. MacKenzie took his foot off the bench and straightened himself. The ladies swooped down on Emma like hawks on a baby chick, and pinned her small person between their decidedly more ample figures. Emma, caught between Mr. MacKenzie's unexpected question and the sudden flurry on both sides of her, turned rosy red with confusion.

"Why . . . why, Mrs. Larabee! Mrs. Bradford!"

Mrs. Larabee espied the portmanteau resting innocently at Emma's feet.

"Emma, dear! You aren't leaving? Why, you never breathed a word!"

Emma stiffened, and belatedly regained some of her composure. "Yes, I did, Maria. I said to you, last Sunday after service, that I was going home to Pittsfield."

"But Emma," observed Mrs. Bradford, not unkindly, "you also said that you did not expect to go before the end of the month."

Emma lowered her eyes. "Yes. I'm sorry, Eliza. I misled you. But I . . . I couldn't bear to say good-bye, you see . . . "

"I beg your pardons, ladies," interrrupted Mr. MacKenzie, "but I perceive that the coach has arrived. It will not wait overlong. Mrs. Wilkes, if you please . . . ?"

Emma took Andrew's outstretched hand and looked up at him gratefully. He interposed himself neatly between Emma and the ladies and sheltered her from their cosseting, as he dexterously led her to the coach, which was just then pulling to a dusty stop. The driver, a rosy individual with a red silk sash wrapped incongruously around his homespun middle, jumped down, shouting "Cook's Corners, five minutes!" Mr. Jamison arrived to claim his shipment from Worcester, and Emma found herself inside the coach, her portmanteau thrown up on top with the rest of the baggage. Then Andrew got in after her and closed the door behind him.

Settling himself into the corner opposite her, he caught her eye and grinned. "Did I fail to inform you, Mrs. Wilkes? I myself am bound for Northampton!"

The driver shaved the edge off the announced five minutes, and soon the coach was rattling down the pike, leaving two open-mouthed ladies abandoned at The Corners.

"Well!" said Mrs. Larabee.

"Well," said Mrs. Bradford, "it's a pity, that's what it is."

The coach bumped its way over the rutted turnpike, and lurched sideways several times to avoid passing riders, carts and cattle. Emma felt more than her body being shaken and jarred and tossed this way and that on the hard leather seat. There was only one other passenger in the coach, a mild-looking man with spectacles and an open copy of a newspaper in front of him; but he folded his paper and left them at the next stop. Emma did not even notice that he had gone, but continued to search her befogged mind for the answer to the question that plagued her still.

Why?

Andrew stretched his legs across the aisle and rested his big feet on her side of the coach. He had his hat pulled down over his eyes and was whistling a little tune. Emma watched him, but then it occurred to her that he must also be watching her from under that ridiculous hat, and she turned her head away.

"Lovely morning," he said suddenly.

Startled, Emma looked out of the window. It *was* a lovely day! The sun shone brightly and flecked the surface of a passing duck pond with gold. Patchwork fields, seamed by stone fences, were embroidered with thick patches of dandelions and wild clover. The scent of fresh clover, of flowering buckwheat, meadowsweet and lilac filled the air. The world looked fresh and young and happy, and the realization of it struck Emma like a glow. Why—she had not even noticed that spring had come around again, just as it did every year! Somehow, she had not thought it would. Gideon had always given a special prayer of thanks for spring days. God is life, he said, and as we love God, so we must be glad of His gift of new life.

From over their heads came a muffled shout.

"Oak Hill! Five minutes!"

Three ladies and a young married couple got on at Oak Hill. Andrew elected to remove himself to make more room for them in the coach, and he joined the driver on his perch. The married couple settled into a corner and became immediately absorbed in themselves. Of the three single ladies, two regarded Emma suspiciously, but the youngest, a girl of about fifteen, smiled. Emma smiled back, but made no move to introduce herself to the newcomers.

Emma was glad to be relieved of Mr. MacKenzie's discomforting presence. He made her feel—well, guilty was the only way to describe it, as if she were doing him some injustice. Absurd! Did he not see that she wanted merely to be left alone? Was that so selfish of her? Apart from that one tormenting question he had flung at her back at Cook's Corners, he had said nothing to indicate that he understood, or was even aware of, what she had been through. Oh, Gideon, she thought, scowling, whatever did you see in that man!

Emma would have liked to shut out the world and to drift to Pittsfield on a puff of blown dandelion, but the coach springs creaked, and the wooden wheels jarred over every pebble in the roadway. And it was impossible to ignore her fellow passengers.

The two older ladies appeared to be sisters, and the younger one their niece. They were en route to Northampton also. This Emma collected from the remarks of the more vocal of the two ladies to the other. The talkative lady had a good deal to say to the girl, too, and the purple plumes on her bonnet danced with the motions of her head as she scowled and scolded.

"Louisa, don't fidget!"

"Louisa, mind your cloak. It's dragging on that dirty floor!"

"Louisa, stop looking out the window!"

Louisa rebelled at this last. "But Aunt, where am I to look, then?"

"Louisa, don't be impertinent!"

The quiet lady, with an anxious glance at the other passengers, was moved to intercede, and enquired plaintively, "Really, Marilla, what harm. . . ?"

"Martha!!"

Martha and Marilla. Goodness, thought Emma, what a pair! She could imagine Gideon poking gentle fun at them in that way of his, neither condemning nor ridiculing, but putting them nicely in their proper perspective. Oh, but that poor child! Emma guessed by Marilla's stony countenance that she was unmarried, and by Martha's black costume that she was a widow. But what a pair to bring up a child! There would be little laughter in poor Louisa's life, except what she could find in it for herself.

Emma sat up. Laughter! That had gone the way of her springs. Could *she* ever laugh again? But imagine ending her days like Marilla, whose disused smile must be by now rusted into immobility, or worse, like Martha, too timid and spiritless to dare to smile, much less to laugh!

"Belchertown! One hour for dinner!"

Directly the coach had stopped, the door opened and Andrew MacKenzie appeared before it. Oddly enough, the sight of his sparkling eyes sent a flood of relief through Emma.

"Mrs. Wilkes, your dinner waits for you."

Marilla eyed Emma suspiciously as she stepped out of the coach, grasping as she did so the arm of a man who was not, from all appearances, her husband. Once out, Emma looked up at Andrew in perplexity. He held up a basket that looked remarkably like a picnic lunch.

"Bought it from the driver," he confessed, "for the price of a pint of strong ale. His wife packed it."

Emma took the hamper and feeling the weight of it, said, "It seems you had the better bargain."

"Not at all," Mr. MacKenzie assured her, "my worthy homespun friend tells me he would far rather pass the dinner hour over a cheerful glass in the good company of Mr. Gilbert's tavern than to suffer the same fare he receives at home for nothing. Or as he himself would put it, 'Fair exchange is no robbery!' "

The schoolmaster and the preacher's widow made their way to a sheltered spot near a small, still pond away from the roadway. They sat on the grass and unpacked the lunch. Andrew sat by the water and leaned over to watch the millions of tiny creatures moving about in it. His posture reminded Emma strongly of Gideon. Gideon had always noticed the smallest things in life, while Emma saw only Gideon, through the rosy mist of a love so complete that no other life existed for her. She had not thought then that she would have to find a life without him.

Presently Andrew said, conversationally, "How did you get on with your companions in travel?"

Much to his astonishment, Emma almost laughed, before she caught herself and said only, in a conspiratorial whisper, "Oh, Andrew, they're so funny! Martha is such a timid little mouse, and Marilla watches her like an owl—her eyebrows dart together, like this—and those feathers on her hat . . . !" She stopped abruptly.

"Go on."

Emma shook her head. "I guess it wasn't as funny as I thought."

They finished the lunch, which Andrew claimed accounted in no small part for the driver's girth, being rich and plentiful as it was. Emma agreed, but she had scarcely tasted it. She cleaned her hands delicately on the pocket handkerchief Andrew lent her, while he poked a clump of grass with a chicken bone.

"Whatever are you doing?"

"Shhh! Watch."

There was a rustling movement from within the grass; presently a tiny black nose appeared from within and twitched ecstatically at the whiff of unaccustomed meat. In a moment, Andrew held a small brown mouse in his hand.

"'Wee, sleekit, cowrin' timorous beastie!'"

Emma leaned over to touch the tiny creature. "But there is no 'panic' in his little breast. How tame he is!"

"Why should he not be?" Andrew asked, and finished the verse:

> *Still thou art blest, compared wi' me;*
> *The present only toucheth thee:*
> *But och! I backward cast my e'e*
> *On prospects drear!*
> *An' forward, though I canna see,*
> *I guess an' fear!*

Emma looked up. Was he reproaching her? But there was nothing on his face. He opened his hand and let the mouse go; it scurried off again into the grass. Andrew seemed reluctant to move himself yet awhile, however.

"Why are you going to Northampton?" Emma asked.

He grinned. "Why, I'm goin' a-co'tin', Mrs. Preacher, ma'am!"

She quickly let that one go. "Oh! I thought you might have family there."

"No. No family."

Andrew looked up at the sky and continued in a conversational tone, "My Ma died when I was eleven. Of the cholera. My two younger sisters went with her, and a year later, my father finally gave up trying to get along without them, and followed. He thought he was leaving enough money behind to get me through school, but the creditors took it all, and they sent me to an orphanage . . . Emma, wait!"

Emma had jumped to her feet, her face flushed, blue eyes darkened with tears on the brink of spilling over, as fresh pain seared through her. She almost screamed the question at him:

"Why do you tell me this?"

Then, "What are you trying to do to me?"

Her hands formed hard fists, tense with wanting to beat against something, and when Andrew stood up and took her in his arms, they hit against his chest. Emma burst into the tears that had been held back for weeks.

"I'm sorry, Emma, but you must see it was the only way!"

His voice was gentle, but her brain could not take in the words.

"Sometimes," he was saying, "to get a stream back into its proper course, you have to explode it out of the wrong one."

He held her tighter and spoke to her in the voice that was most truly part of him. "Emma dear, it's the wrong way ye've been runnin': d'ye think Gideon woulda thanked ye for it? D'ye think he wanted ye never to smile again, never to love again? Gideon's gone, lass, ye canna go wi' 'im."

Emma broke away, but had not the will to run from him. Andrew went on, "I didn't tell you all that about me for naught, Emma. I've learnt from it, I think. I've learnt that you can't run away from life, as you are trying to run away from it, from your friends and from your home. I've learnt that spring will come every year, whether you will it or no, and that it's best to welcome it. And I've learnt that what the Psalm says is true, that weeping may endure for the night, but joy cometh in the morning. Emma—come and look at the morning with me."

After what seemed like long hours, Emma's tears dried themselves up. She felt strangely depleted, as if all the bad humours in her had been washed out. She heard a thrush suddenly begin to sing. She heard the rustle of leaves over her head. People talking. Fresh horses shaking their manes impatiently. The coach driver's voice bellowing for his passengers, so that they might go on with their journey. And from within herself, she heard the echo of that Psalm: *Oh Lord, thou hast brought up my soul from the grave; thou hast kept me alive . . .*

When they arrived in Northampton, Andrew waited with her until the coach was ready to go on again. Then he handed her up and, closing the door behind her, reached in and took her hand.

"God be with you, Mrs. Wilkes," he said as he let her go.

"God is always with me, Mr. MacKenzie. In one form or another."

The driver cracked his whip and the coach lurched out of the yard, scattering dust and clatter and little boys in its wake. Andrew stood calm in the midst of the confusion and when Emma looked back, he took off his hat and waved it in the air. Emma smiled.   **END**

Hey You Down There!

by Harold Rolseth

Calvin Spender drained his coffee cup and wiped his mouth with the back of his hand. He belched loudly and then proceeded to fill a corncob pipe with coarsely shredded tobacco. He scratched a match across the top of the table and, holding it to his pipe, he sucked noisily until billows of acrid smoke poured from his mouth.

Dora Spender sat across the table from her husband, her breakfast scarcely touched. She coughed lightly, and then, as no frown appeared on Calvin's brow, she said, "Are you going to dig in the well this morning, Calvin?"

Calvin fixed his small red-rimmed eyes upon her, and, as if she had not spoken, said, "Git going at the chores right away. You're going to be hauling up dirt."

"Yes, Calvin," Dora whispered.

Calvin cleared his throat, and the action caused his Adam's apple to move convulsively under the loose red folds of skin on his neck. He rose from the table and went out the kitchen door, kicking viciously at the tawny cat which had been lying on the doorstep.

Dora gazed after him and wondered for the thousandth time what it was that Calvin reminded her of. It was not some other person. It was something else. Sometimes it seemed as though the answer was about to spring to her mind, as just now when Calvin had cleared his throat. But always it stopped just short of her consciousness. It was disturbing to know with such certainty that Calvin looked like something other than himself and yet not know what that something was. Someday though, Dora knew, the answer would come to her. She rose hurriedly from the table and set about her chores.

Halfway between the house and the barn, a doughnut-shaped mound of earth surrounded a hole. Calvin went to the edge of the hole and stared down into it distastefully. Only necessity could have forced him to undertake this task, but it was either this digging or the hauling of barrels and barrels of water each day from Nord Fisher's farm a half mile down the road.

Calvin's herd of scrub cattle was small, but the amount of water it consumed was astonishing. For two weeks now, ever since his well had gone dry, Calvin had been hauling water, and the disagreeable chore was becoming more unpleasant by Nord's clumsy hints that some form of payment for the water would not be amiss.

Several feet back from the edge of the hole Calvin had driven a heavy iron stake into the ground, and to this was attached a crude rope ladder. The rope ladder had become necessary when the hole had had become too deep for any wooden ladder Calvin owned.

Calvin hoped desperately that he would not have to go much deeper. He estimated that he was now down fifty or sixty feet, a common depth for many wells in the area. His greatest fear was that he would hit a strata of rock which would call for the services of a well-drilling outfit. For such a venture both his funds and his credit rating were far too low.

Calvin picked up a bucket to which was attached a long rope and lowered it into the hole. It was Dora's back-breaking task to haul the bucket up hand over hand after Calvin had filled it from the bottom of the hole.

With a mumbled curse Calvin emptied his pipe and started down the rope ladder. By the time he got to the bottom of the hole and had filled the bucket, Dora should be there to haul it up. If she weren't, she would hear about it.

From the house Dora saw Calvin prepare to enter the well, and she worked with desperate haste to complete her chores. She reached the hole just as a muffled shout from below indicated that the bucket was full.

Summoning all her strength, Dora hauled the bucket up. She emptied it and then lowered it into the hole again. While she waited for the second bucketload, she examined the contents of the first. She was disappointed to find it had only the normal moistness of underground earth. No water seeped from it.

In her own fashion, Dora was deeply religious and at each tenth bucket she pulled up she murmured an urgent prayer that it would contain more water in it than earth. She had settled at praying at every tenth bucketload because she did not believe it in good taste to pester God with every bucket. Also, she varied the wording of each prayer, feeling that God must become bored with the same petition repeated over and over.

On this particular morning as she lowered the bucket for its tenth loading, she prayed, "Please, God, let something happen this time . . . let something really and truly happen so I won't have to haul up any more dirt."

Something happened almost immediately. As the rope slackened in her hands indicating that the bucket had reached the bottom, a scream of sheer terror came up from the hole, and the rope ladder jerked violently. Whimpering sounds of mortal fear sounded faintly, and the ladder grew taut with heavy strain.

Dora fell to her knees and peered down into the darkness. "Calvin," she called, "are you all right? What is it?"

Then with startling suddenness Calvin appeared, literally shooting out of the hole. At first Dora was not sure it was Calvin. The peeled redness of his face was gone; now it was a yellowish green. He was trembling violently and had trouble breathing.

It must be a heart attack Dora thought, and tried mightily to suppress the surge of joy that swept over her.

Calvin lay upon the ground panting. Finally he gained control of himself. Under ordinary circumstances Calvin did not converse with Dora, but now he seemed eager to talk. "You know what happened down there?" he said in a shaky voice. "You know what happened? The complete bottom dropped right out of that hole. All of a sudden it went, and there I was, standing on nothing but air. If I hadn't grabbed aholt of the last rung of the ladder . . . Why, that hole must be a thousand feet the way the bottom dropped out of it!"

Calvin babbled on, but Dora did not listen. She was filled with awe at the remarkable way in which her prayer had been answered. If the hole had no more bottom, there would be no more dirt to haul.

When Calvin had regained his strength, he crept to the edge of the hole and peered down.

"What are you going to do, Calvin?" Dora asked timidly.

"Do? I'm going to find out how far down that hole goes. Get the flashlight from the kitchen."

Dora hurried off. When she returned, Calvin had a large ball of binder twine he had gotten from the tool shed.

He tied the flashlight securely to the end of the line, switched it on, and lowered it into the hole. He paid out the line for about a hundred feet and then stopped. The light was only a feeble glimmer down below and revealed nothing. Calvin lowered the light another hundred feet and this time it was only a twinkling speck as it swung at the end of the line. Calvin released another long length of twine and another and now the light was no longer visible, and the large ball of twine had shrunk to a small tangle.

"Almost a full thousand feet," he whispered in awe. "And no bottom yet. Might as well pull it up."

But the line did not come up with Calvin's pull. It stretched and grew taut, but it did not yield to his tugging.

"Must be caught on something," Calvin muttered, and gave the line a sharp jerk. In response there was a downward jerk that almost tore the line from his hands.

"Hey," yelled Calvin. "The line . . . it jerked!"

"But, Calvin," Dora protested.

"Don't Calvin me. I tell you there's something on this line."

He gave another tug; again the line was almost pulled from his hands. He tied it to the stake and sat down to ponder the matter.

"It don't make sense," he said, more to himself than to Dora. "What could be down underground a good thousand feet?"

Tentatively he reached over and pulled lightly on the line. This time there was no response, and rapidly he began hauling it up. When the end of the line came into view, there was no flashlight attached to it. Instead, there was a small white pouch of a leatherlike substance.

Calvin opened the pouch with trembling fingers and shook into his palm a bar of yellow metal and a folded piece of parchment. The bar of metal was not large but seemed heavy for its size. Calvin got out his jacknife and scratched the point of the blade across the metal. The blade bit into it easily.

"Gold," said Calvin, his voice shaky. "Must be a whole pound of it— just for a measly flashlight. They must be crazy down there."

He thrust the gold bar into his pocket and opened the small piece of parchment. One side was closely covered with a fine script. Calvin turned it this way and that and then tossed it on the ground.

"Foreigners," he said. "No wonder they ain't got any sense. But it's plain they need flashlights."

"But, Calvin," said Dora. "How could they get down there? There ain't any mines in this part of the country."

"Ain't you ever heard of them secret government projects?" asked Calvin scornfully. "This must be one of them. Now I'm going to town and get me a load of flashlights. They must need them bad. Now mind you watch that hole good. Don't let no one go near it."

Calvin strode to the battered pickup which was standing near the barn, and a minute later was rattling down the highway toward Harmony Junction.

Dora picked up the bit of parchment which Calvin had thrown away. She could make nothing of the writing on it. It was all very strange. If it were some secret government undertaking, why would foreigners be engaged in it? And why would they need flashlights so urgently as to pay a fortune for one?

Suddenly it occurred to her that possibly the people down below didn't know there were English-speaking people up above. She hurried into the house and rummaged through Calvin's rickety desk for paper and pencil. In her search she found a small ragged dictionary, and she took this with her to the kitchen table. Spelling did not come easy to Dora.

Her note was a series of questions. Why were they down there? Who were they? Why did they pay so much for an old flashlight?

As she started for the well it occurred to her that possibly the people down there might be hungry. She went back to the kitchen and wrapped a loaf of bread and a fair-sized piece of ham in a clean dish towel. She added a postscript to her note apologizing for the fact that she had nothing better to offer them. Then the thought came to her that, since the people down below were obviously foreigners and possibly not too well versed in English, the small dictionary might be of help to them in answering her note. She wrapped the dictionary with the food in the towel.

It took Dora a long while to lower the bucket, but finally the twine grew slack in her hands, and she knew the bucket had reached the bottom. She waited a few moments and then tugged the line gently. The line held firm below, and Dora seated herself on the pile of soil to wait.

The warm sunlight felt good on her back, and it was pleasant to sit and do nothing. She had no fear that Calvin would return soon. She knew that nothing on earth . . . or under it . . . could keep Calvin from visiting a number of taverns once he was in town, and that with each tavern visited time would become more and more meaningless to him. She doubted that he would return before morning.

After a half hour Dora gave the line a questioning tug, but it did not yield. She did not mind. It was seldom that she had time to idle away. Usually when Calvin went to town, he burdened her with chores to be done during his absence, coupling each order with a threat of what awaited her should his instructions not be carried out.

Dora waited another half hour before giving the line another tug. This time there was a sharp answering jerk, and Dora began hauling the bucket upward. It seemed much heavier now, and twice she had to pause for a rest. When the bucket reached the surface, she saw why it was heavier.

"My goodness," she murmured as she viewed the dozen or so yellow metal bars in the bucket. "They must be real hungry down there."

A sheet of the strange parchment was also in the bucket, and Dora picked it out expecting to see the strange script of the first note.

"Well, I declare," she said when she saw that the note was in English. It was in the same print as the dictionary, and each letter had been made with meticulous care.

She read the note slowly, shaping each word with her lips as she read.

Your language is barbaric, but the crude code book you sent down made it easy for our scholars to decipher it. We, too, wonder about you. How have you overcome the problem of living in the deadly light? Our legends tell of a race living on the surface, but intelligent reasoning has forced us to ridicule these old tales until now. We would still doubt that you are surface dwellers except for the fact that our instruments show without question that the opening above us leads to the deadly light.

The clumsy death ray which you sent us indicates that your scientific development is very low. Other than an artifact of another race it has no value to us. We sent gold as a courtesy payment only.

The food you call bread is not acceptable to our digestive systems, but the ham is beyond price. It is obviously the flesh of some creature, and we will exchange a double weight of gold for all that you can send us. Send more immediately. Also send a concise history of your race and arrange for your best scientists, such as they are, to communicate with us.

Glar, the Master

"Land sakes," said Dora. "Real bossy they are. I've a good mind not to send them anything. I don't dast send them more ham. Calvin would notice if any more is gone."

Dora took the gold bars to her petunia bed beside the house and buried them in the loose, black soil. She paid no heed to the sound of a car coming down the highway at high speed until it passed the house and wild squawking sounded above the roar of the motor. She hurried around to the front of the house, knowing already what had happened. She stared in dismay at the four white leghorns which lay along the road. Now Calvin would charge her with negligence and beat her into unconsciousness.

Fear sharpened her wits. Perhaps if she could dispose of the bodies Calvin would think foxes had gotten them. Hastily she gathered up the dead chickens and the feathers which lay scattered about. When she was finished, there was no evidence of the disaster.

She carried the chickens to the back of the house wondering how she could dispose of them. Suddenly, as she glanced toward the hole, the answer came to her.

An hour later the four chickens were dressed and neatly cut up. Ignoring the other instructions in the note, she sent the bulky parcel of chicken down into the hole.

She sat down again to enjoy the luxury of doing nothing. When she finally picked up the line, there was an immediate response from below. The bucket was exceedingly heavy this time, and she was fearful that the line might break. She was dizzy with fatigue when she finally hauled the bucket over to the edge of the hole. This time there were several dozen bars of gold in it and a brief note in the same precise lettering as before.

Our scientists are of the opinion that the flesh you sent down is that of a creature you call chicken. This is the supreme food. Never have we eaten anything so delicious. To show our appreciation we are sending you a bonus payment. Your code book indicates that there is a larger creature similar to chicken called turkey. Send us turkey immediately. I repeat, send us turkey immediately.

Glar, the Master

"Land sakes," gasped Dora. "They must have et that chicken raw. Now where in tarnation would I get a turkey?"

She buried the gold bars in another part of her petunia bed.

Calvin returned about ten o'clock the next morning. His eyes were bloodshot, and his face was a mottled red. The loose skin on his neck hung lower than usual and more than ever he reminded Dora of something which eluded her.

Calvin stepped down from the pick-up, and Dora cringed, but he seemed too tired and preoccupied to bother with her. He surveyed the hole glumly, then got back into the truck and backed it to the edge of the mound of earth. On the back of the truck was a winch with a large drum of steel cable.

"Fix me something to eat," he ordered Dora.

Dora hurried into the house and began preparing ham and eggs. Each moment she expected Calvin to come in and demand to know, with a few blows, what was holding up his meal. But Calvin seemed very busy in the vicinity of the hole. When Dora went out to call him to eat, she found he had done a surprising amount of work. He had attached an oil drum to the steel rod which rested across the hole. Stakes driven into the ground on each side of the hole held the rod in place.

"Your breakfast is ready, Calvin," said Dora.

"Shut up," Calvin answered.

The winch was driven by an electric motor, and Calvin ran a cable from the motor to an electric outlet on the yard lightpost.

From the cab he took some boxes and placed them in the oil drum.

"A whole hundred of them," he chuckled, more to himself than to Dora. "Fifty-nine cents apiece. Peanuts . . . one bar of gold will buy thousands."

Calvin threw the switch which controlled the winch, and with sickening force Dora suddenly realized the terrible thing that would soon happen. The creatures down below had no use or regard for flashlights.

Down went the oil drum, the cable screeching shrilly as it passed over the rod above the hole. Calvin got an oil can from the truck and applied oil generously to the rod and the cable.

In a very short while the cable went slack and Calvin stopped the winch.

"I'll give them an hour to load up the gold," he said and went to the kitchen for his delayed breakfast.

Dora was practically in a state of shock. What would happen when the flashlights came back up with an insulting note in English was too horrible to contemplate. Calvin would learn about the gold she had received and very likely kill her.

Calvin ate his breakfast leisurely. Dora busied herself with household tasks, trying with all her might to cast out of her mind the terrible thing which was soon to happen.

Finally Calvin glanced at the wall clock, yawned widely, and tapped out his pipe. Ignoring Dora he went out to the hole. In spite of her terrible fear Dora could not resist following him. It was as if some power outside herself forced her to go.

The winch was already reeling in the cable when she got to the hole. It seemed only seconds before the oil drum was up. The grin on Calvin's face was broad as he reached out over the hole and dragged the oil drum to the edge. A look of utter disbelief replaced the grin as he looked into the drum. His Adam's apple seemed to vibrate, and once again part of Dora's mind tried to recall what it was that Calvin reminded her of.

Calvin was making flat, bawling sounds like a lost calf. He hauled the drum out of the hole and dumped its contents on the ground. The flashlights, many of them dented and with lenses broken, made a sizeable pile.

With a tremendous kick Calvin sent flashlights flying in all directions. One, with a note attached, landed at Dora's feet. Either Calvin was so blinded by rage that he didn't see it, or he assumed it was written in the same unreadable script as the first note.

"You down there," he screamed into the hole. "You filthy swine.

I'll fix you. I'll make you sorry you ever double-crossed me. I'll . . .
I'll . . ."

He dashed for the house, and Dora hastily snatched up the note.

You are even more stupid than we thought, she read. *Your clumsy death rays are useless to us. We informed you of this. We want turkey. Send us turkey immediately.*

Glar, the Master

She crumbled the note swiftly as Calvin came from the house with his double-barreled shotgun. For a moment Dora thought that he knew everything and was about to kill her.

Please, Calvin," she said.

"Shut up," Calvin said. "You saw me work the winch. Can you?"

"Why, yes, but what . . . ?"

"Listen, you stupid cow. I'm going down there and fix those dirty foreigners. You send me down and bring me up." He seized Dora by the shoulder. "And if you mess things, I'll fix you too. I'll really and truly fix you."

Dora nodded dumbly.

Calvin put his gun in the oil drum and pushed it to the center of the hole. Then, hanging on to the cable, he carefully lowered himself into the drum.

"Give me just one hour to run those dirty rats down, then bring me back up," he said.

Dora threw the switch and the oil drum went down. When the cable slackened, she stopped the winch. She spent most of the hour praying that Calvin would not find the people down below and become a murderer.

Exactly an hour later Dora started the oil drum upward. The motor labored mightily as though under a tremendous strain, and the cable seemed stretched almost to the breaking point.

Dora gasped when the oil drum came into view. Calvin was not in it. She shut off the motor and hastened to the drum, half expecting to find Calvin crouching down inside. But Calvin was not there. Instead there were scores of gold bars and on top of them a sheet of the familiar white parchment.

'Land sakes," Dora said, as she took in a full view of the drum's contents. She had no idea of the value of the treasure upon which she gazed. She only knew it must be immense. Carefully, she reached down and picked out the note, which she read in her slow, precise manner.

Not even the exquisite flavor of the chicken compares to the incomparable goodness of the live turkey you sent down to us. We must confess that our concept of turkey was quite different, but this is of no consequence. So delectable was the turkey that we are again sending you a bonus payment. We implore you to send us more turkey immediately.

Glar, the Master

Dora read the note a second time to make sure she understood it fully. "Well, I declare," she said in considerable wonder. "I declare."   END

One Road to the Stars

by Lorna Beers

O n the sixth of March, John Fairfield was driving through freezing slush on Hickory Road in the Green Mountains. A loose end of chain struck against the fender with each turn of the wheel, as against a gong. The sun, sinking toward the western ridges, flooded the slopes and the valley below with wine-colored light.

He had come from New York for his grandfather's funeral. He had not seen his grandfather for ten years, nor the solitary mountain farm where he had lived alone. It was the old man's choice to live there alone. Still, John Fairfield's conscience hurt, for he carried from that house the memory of bare poverty.

Neither had he seen his Uncle Gideon and Aunt Grace for a decade. They had looked small and lean as they sat, silent, at the services. They slipped away, "not putting themselves forward." He thought "Life's picked them clean." Perhaps it was to lighten a shadow of guilt that he was driving through the ruts of the early thaw.

He turned by the orchard and drove over the cracking ice into the yard. It was now dusk and he saw the yellow lamplight through the window. Uncle Gideon opened the door. Behind him the flame wavered in the draft.

"Well, John, so it's you! Didn't expect to see you again. Mind your step. Mighty slick."

John Fairfield came stamping onto the porch, rattling the zinc tub that hung on a nail against the porch wall.

The flame threw a circle of light on the table, but beyond that glow were shadows. Dimly he saw the stove with a red gash of fire along the open draft, the woodbox piled high with birch sticks, the old dog, the silvery thread of water running ceaselessly from a pipe into the soapstone sink.

Aunt Grace put her hands on his shoulders. "You've grown to a fine man, John." She did not ask him why he had not come before, for she had delicate feelings and was not happy to put someone in the wrong. Moreover, in her dignity she had got along well without her city relations—all those rich folks.

Supper was early in snow season. She had put down a ladle to greet him, and now she picked it up again and dipped into an iron

pot, filling the extra plate. There was a tranquil silence, like the silence
of nature. John Fairfield wondered if he should have come. He tried
to make talk. "When I go to work I pass a little shop where they have
Vermont Winesaps. Fifteen cents apiece."

Gideon looked up. "Don't get any such price here. Lucky if I get
a dollar a bushel. Don't have Winesaps, though."

They talked about apples. "Mostly McIntosh around here. Don't
favor them myself, but they turn a red that takes folks' eyes. Folks
like apples red." He mopped the last of his biscuit in syrup, pushed
back his chair, and took the lantern from its peg. He went creaking down
the cellar stairs and could be heard moving about below. The draft
sent the flame smoking against the chimney.

Aunt Grace sat with her hands folded on the table. Her nephew looked
at those hands and thought of the zinc tub on the porch.

"Aunt Grace, would you like to have an electric washing machine?"

"Well, John, it wouldn't be no use to me. The electricity doesn't
come within a mile of us. They wouldn't put them poles all the way
to this slope for the mite we'd use."

"Isn't there anything you'd like, Aunt Grace?"

"I don't spend much time wanting things."

"Don't you have any wishes?"

"Oh, wishes. Yes, I can say I do."

"What do you wish for?"

She looked at him wide-eyed, abstracted. "To see the ocean again
where I grew up near Portsmouth, to see them little sandpipers walking
along near the lapping tide, making tracks like bits of thread in the
wet sand." She mused. "There's a poem about a sandpiper. I've
liked that poem from girlhood on. Sometimes when Gideon's outside and can't hear, I say that poem aloud. Then I see the clouds low
over the water, and that little bird making peeping sounds, and it
seems we're alone in the world, that little bird and me."

Gideon came from the cellar with his lantern and a splint basket
of apples. "I've brung a sampling. Now," setting the basket on the
table, turning the lantern wick low and blowing out the flame, "that
Astrakhan has no business lasting like that, but I stowed a few in
the sawdust near the ice. There's ice in the root cellar ain't melted in
my memory. Astrakhan's dying out, but I grafted a branch on a wild
apple root. Wrong way to do, they say, but I did that forty years ago,
and now that Astrakhan has a display of red to one side, and the wild
tree has a display of green to the other. Same with that strawberry
apple. Grew off a wild root. Getting a little mealy now, but after
the first frost it has a taste of honey."

They tasted apples. "Yes," Gideon said, "I hate to see the old kinds go. I've got two Wolf Rivers and a Gravenstein down the slope. Got a Snow Apple and a Maiden's Blush that's come along on a wild root. No, I don't get any money out of them. Gracie likes them and neighbors come to fetch a few. No, I do it for the apples' sake. I hate to see them go."

"That's so, he does," Grace said. "Why, last spring a nor'easter broke the old Striped Spy, and I saw him out grafting to a root beyond the barn. Who do you think's going to eat them apples, Gideon? Not you. You'll be up on the hill before ever they bear."

"Mebbe so," he said."Mebbe so."

John Fairfield had never known one could talk so long about apples. The wheezy clock on the shelf struck nine.

"We'd better be going to bed, seeing I'm hanging tomorrow."

"Gideon! You're not!" She stood, dish towel and plate in her hand, looking at him with dismay.

"Well now, Gracie, I am. Eli, or no Eli."

"Not by yourself, you ain't, surely? You ain't fit for such work. Not no more."

Gideon said with stubborn finality, "Thaw, freeze, tap the trees."

John Fairfield looked from the one to the other. "Who's Eli?"

"Eli? Why Eli's come for twenty years for the sugaring. Takes his vacation so he can. Sap got a few days ahead of him, but he'll be along."

"What do you have to pay help like that up here?"

"Pay? Pay Eli? Why, Eli wouldn't take no money. Two, three cans of syrup, mebbe."

Grace turned and said solemnly, "He comes for the joy of it."

Every night, after the fire was banked, wind, snow, or moonshine, Gideon stepped beyond the porch to look at the weather. John went with him, and Grace, pulling a shawl around her. The air was clear and the stars shot out spars of light.

Grace stood, her arms folded, her face turned upward. "Seems you could reach up and touch one. Yes, that's how close they are. In the day you would never know they were there. Then comes night and they shine in all their glory." She stretched her hand toward the sky. "That's how near we are."

A long howl came from the hemlock spinney on the hill and was answered by a call as eerie. The dog quivered and his hair bristled.

"What's that?"

"Timber wolf. They're coming back. Saw two, three the other night out beyond the barn."

The bedroom was cold and tendrils of draft stole through the floor cracks and around the windows. John Fairfield lay under a feather quilt and had a hot stone at his feet. There was no curtain on the window and he watched the bare lilacs move silently before the pane. He slept and woke thinking he heard an orchestra, but it was the wind humming down the slope.

He thought about Aunt Grace. Those hands, that tub. That cold cellar from which she fetched every potato, every apple. He wanted to transform her life, to put a furnace in that dark hole, to see a row of "utilities" along the kitchen wall, a bathroom with gushing hot water. He wanted to give her a television set to bring the world in.

In his indignation he sat up. "It's a disgrace, this poverty in these hills! It's a national scandal how these people live. I doubt Uncle Gideon sees two thousand dollars a year and that is poverty by definition."

The wind piped at the corners of the barn. A mouse gnawed in the wainscot. He crawled under the feather quilt again and slept.

He was awakened by the rattle of the stove lids. It was still dark, but Uncle Gideon was making the fire. There was the slap-slap of batter as Aunt Grace beat up the buckwheat cakes.

John Fairfield, wrapped in the quilt, looked into the kitchen. "Uncle Gideon, this hanging. I'll stay today and help you." Uncle Gideon smiled, meaning, "Don't reckon you'll be much use, but it's your choosing."

Thus it was that at sunrise John rode with his uncle up the hill. He wore old clothes that smelled of barn. He sat on the bobsled among the buckets as the ancient tractor spluttered and left cleat marks in the snow.

The sugaring road wound here and there through the bush. Uncle Gideon scanned each tree, seeing the old wounds, finding the cracks in the bark where the new growth was. He looked at the branches above, to which the sap was rising, and artfully made the tap with his auger. John Fairfield fetched the buckets from the bobsled, set the spouts and hung the pails. After an hour he was trembling with fatigue, but the old man went steadily from tree to tree. He had a faint smile and now and then he looked after his nephew stumbling through the soft snow and over bare patches where fallen branches among last autumn's leaves laid traps for his dragging feet.

The sky was deep blue and bowling clouds raced from east to west. The tops of the maples were rosy with swelling buds. Bluejays kited among the bare boughs and one swooped low as Uncle Gideon turned his auger and pecked him on the head. Ruefully he pulled off his cap and rubbed the place.

"What you so mad about?" He followed the bird with his eyes. "Thinks it's his sugarbush, that's what. Scrapping birds, them jays. Mighty pretty, though. Well, guess it's your woods as much as mine."

They ate their lunch sitting on a log near the sugar house. The snow was melted in patches and small lavender butterflies fluttered over the lichens. "Where do they come from?"

"Well, now, I've often wondered. Them first taps now—they'll be around the leaks near the spouts. They come from nowhere. An hour of spring and there they are."

The next day John Fairfield drove back to New York. He wrote several letters to his Aunt Grace. He wanted to send her something to make her life easier, but he could think of nothing that was right. Money? They had drawn themselves up with offended pride when he said he would like to "help" them. They did not know they were poor. In the end he sent nothing at all. Gradually his memory of them faded to a mere statistic in the national disgrace, and then they slipped from his consciousness entirely, until one morning in the following December.

He walked as usual from his office to meet friends who lunched casually together. He was tired. He was depressed. It was a gray day with spits of sleet, and the sidewalks were gluey with a scum of oily soot.

Deep in melancholy thought, he stepped off the curb to cross the street when a taxi stopped with squealing brakes and the driver shouted, "Why in hell don't you look where you're going?"

His dignity shattered, John Fairfield sprang backwards onto the sidewalk. He had been insulted, and he felt a fool. Burning red, he glanced at the people milling about at the curb's edge, but they were aware of nothing except what passed in their own heads. "Enemies," he thought. "To me. To one another."

A row of overflowing trash cans edged the sidewalk and he took the inner wall, shouldering sideways against the crowd. He passed the sunken steps of the fancy grocery store, and pausing for free passage, he looked down, as into a cellar. The apples were a red pyramid in the window. "Vermont Winesaps. Fifteen Cents," and he saw as if he were before him, Uncle Gideon and his splint basket of apples. He saw the stove, the guttering wick, the silvery thread of water.

John Fairfield went down a step and stood a moment with closed eyes, remembering the sweet breath of apples. He opened the shop door and bought one apple, then turned back toward his office leaving his casual friends to lunch without him.

From his window he saw a terrain of roofs shrouded in mist and smoke. Here, above the city, the sleet had fallen as light snow. He put the apple on his desk and sat before it. A half hour before, he was heavy with a carefully hidden despair, whose origins he did not understand. He had left this despair in the murky streets below, and he was far away in the hills watching Uncle Gideon polish an Astrakhan apple against the breast of his flannel shirt.

How old was Uncle Gideon when he grafted a bough of Striped Spy on a wild root? Seventy? Aunt Grace said, "You'll be up on the hill before it bears." There was tenderness in her voice and she was smiling.

"Mebbe so," he said. "Mebbe so."

Who was it said, "If I knew I was to die tomorrow, I'd plant an apple tree today?" Luther? Yes, Luther. Great souls acted like that.

The evening after the bucket-hanging, while Gideon milked the cow, Aunt Grace recited "The Sandpiper" for him, standing straight, as she had done long ago at Recitation Hour in the little white schoolhouse near Portsmouth. The child, the bird, the leaden, white-flecked sea— how she evoked it all, her heart's desire.

He leaned forward, resting his forehead on his hands.

The stars bristled and the wind started a hundred violins over the cold mowings. The long call of the timber wolf was like a racial memory of danger. So had been the peeping of the bird at the sea's edge. Danger at the very heart of things, accepted, embraced. "Thou, little sandpiper and I."

What strength, what peace she had, standing there, her roughened hands folded. Where had it come from? "That's how near we are," she said.

He mused. Saint Francis took a vow of poverty. He went about with bare feet, with a beggar's bowl. Can you have it both ways? Must you have an innocence of desire? Why in hell don't you look where you're going?

Uncle Gideon talked to the birds. "Guess it's your woods as much as mine." He had put down his auger and walked to the bobsled for the bag of cracked corn.

"Give me again O Nature your primal sanities." Who said that? Can you have it both ways? They are custodians of something precious, and I am the one who is poor in everything that is finally worthwhile.

He reached for his overcoat to go out and do the only thing he could think to do—buy something for Aunt Grace and Uncle Gideon. Snow was falling in the streets now and the walks were slippery with gray slush. He went down the steps toward the pyramid of apples. On the shop door in flaking gold letters was printed, "Gift Baskets Delivered to Hotels and Steamers."

He had a box made up with Christmas wrappings, of Smyrna pulled figs and Swiss chocolates, such luxuries as Aunt Grace could never have seen. Leaning on the counter, he wrote a note to tuck among the glacéed Australian apricots. "Merry Christmas," he wrote. He paused and stood looking toward the street where dim figures jostled, bent against the blowing snow. He turned and wrote quickly as if it were an act of folly, "Could you use an extra hand sugaring this March? If you can, like Eli, I'll come for the joy of it."   END

Summer of Snakes

by Betty Gulick

Five summers ago snakes came from the hills to High Valley because of the drought. I was twelve years old that year, and Betsy was five.

The summer began like every summer I can remember. The day after school let out we left for High Valley Farm with plans to stay till school began in the fall. That year I was big enough to do most of the things that Dad would have done, like taking off shutters, mowing the side lawn, chopping wood for the fireplace fire. I was the man of the family, Mom said.

With the first chores over, we quickly eased into summer. Soon it was like we never lived anywhere else. By the first of July all of my cousins—four boys and six girls—had arrived. On the Fourth of July, like a family of Sherpas, Mom, my uncles and aunts and all of us kids carried our food and fireworks up the steep path through the woods to the Fourth of July Rock, the highest part of our land. It overlooks the valley way below. Before it got dark we fellows climbed around on he face of the cliff, Bill leading the way. He climbed to some places none of the rest of us dared follow. Bill is my oldest cousin, two years older than I, and, oddly enough, still the one I like best.

After dark we shot off our sky-rockets. We watched them explode and fall down over the valley like a fountain of fireflies. We toasted marshmallows and sang songs around the big bonfire. That was the last bonfire we had that summer. It was already getting too dry in the woods.

Scooped out like a saucer, High Valley Farm is closed in on three sides by hills. It's sort of a family farm that Grandfather Todd bought years ago to get his family out of Boston in the summer. The only farm animal we have now is Jim, a horse that is blind in one eye and walks down the road at a slant. Aunt Izzy, who never got married, takes care of him. In the center of the farm are the Big House, where Aunt Izzy lives, and the barn. There's an orchard and blueberry field up behind them. Uncle William, Uncle Walter and my father built their own houses up the other slope—not too near or too far from each other. On Saturday nights, if the report from Aunt Mabel to Uncle Will wasn't good, we could hear Bill yell when he got the strap. And Mom would say things like: "Will's too harsh with that child." I hated Uncle Will for his meanness. I still do. I never told Bill we could hear him.

Uncle Will's house is farthest away from ours up the slope. Uncle Walt's house is halfway down and off to one side. Our house is the smallest. You can see through the knotholes from one room to another. It was meant to be temporary, till my Dad could build something else. But he died, so it's all we have and we're darn glad to have it—just like it is. My uncles commute to High Valley on weekends. The rest of the time my aunts are alone with their kids, just like Mom. She would have been lonely up there without my two aunts.

On Saturdays Mom often took Betsy and me into town. We'd have supper, go to a movie—things like that. Going home, Betsy would fall asleep in the back seat of the car and Mom would talk to me in the dark. She'd remind me of things about Dad so I wouldn't forget, like the time I was five and my tricycle ran away down the driveway with me on it. Dad yelled for me to hang on. He ran down the lawn beside me, leaped the hedge and lifted me off seconds before the bike crashed in the street. Betsy doesn't remember him at all. She was just a year old when he died.

"Your father was a fine, brave man," Mom would say. "You get more like him every day."

I wished she wouldn't talk like that. She doesn't so much anymore . . .

That summer we did all the old things and some that were new. Bill invented a game we called Guerrilla War, which we played in the woods. You had to get to a goal without being seen by the enemy. If they saw you, they'd call you by name and yell: "You're dead!"

Bill, George, Philip and I repaired the tree house in the large pine back of our house. We spent a lot of time clearing the brush away from the edge of the brook where it widened out into the swimming hole. We fixed the dam and built a platform, too, to dive off of. It was neat. And we kept thinking: what luck, all the good weather. It hadn't rained since we'd come.

"Let's make the girls pay for their swims." said Bill when we'd fixed everything up. "We've done all the work."

"Swell," I replied. "Let's charge five cents a swim."

"Aw, that's too much," said George. "We don't own the brook."

"I was thinking of something else, not money," Bill remarked. And he grinned in a funny way.

"Like what?" I asked.

"Like having them pull their bathing suits down."

"Heck! What do you want them to do *that* for?" asked Phil.

"Look, stupid," said Bill. "If you don't know, I'm not going to tell you." And he didn't.

"I think we ought to get a penny a swim at least," I said, "for all the work we've done."

"Okay," agreed Bill. "We can charge both."

The next time the girls came down for a swim, Bill told them the rules: a penny, strip to the waist, and don't tell the grown-ups. The girls all agreed, except George's sister Marty. She was fourteen-and-a-half that summer, the oldest of all my cousins. She said she'd think about it.

The next day was pretty hot for High Valley. All the girls showed up for a swim, including Marty. They lined up, gave their pennies to Bill, pulled their bathing suits down to their waists, counted to ten and jumped in. Marty was last. I felt sort of funny about the whole business, but I looked just the same. When I saw Marty, somehow I knew it was she whom Bill had wanted to see all along. Above her belly she curved suddenly out, round and smooth, like soft baby chicks. I wanted to cuddle them both in my hands, stroke them, hold them next to my face. I still think of them . . . Anyway, Marty counted to ten real fast, gave a toss of her head and jumped in. That went on every day, although when Bill forgot to collect pennies, no one said beans.

By the end of July the upper well had run dry, one of the two wells that fed our house and Uncle Will's. Uncle Walt's well seemed to be doing okay. The grass had burned off, and I didn't need to mow the side lawn anymore. No fires were allowed out of doors anywhere. Swims took the place of baths. And then we began to see snakes all over the place.

"It's happened before," said Mom. "They're driven by thirst, poor things. They don't want to hurt people, but they'll strike if they're frightened. So watch where you step." She told Betsy and me to stay out of tall grass, and she wouldn't let us go barefoot.

Uncle Will found a nest of copper-heads back of his pump house. He and Bill burned them out. Bill said one got away. Aunt Izzy, who walks with a cane, beat a rattlesnake to death near the Big House. She skinned it and stretched the skin on a board to dry in the sun. Then she mounted the skin on a fancy board and hung it over the fireplace in the Big House. Mom said she shouldn't have killed it; rattlesnakes give fair warning.

One day I heard Betsy scream. She was playing on the side lawn, where the grass was short. I ran out of the house with my baseball bat. I beat the snake to death, as it tried to get away. It looked like a copperhead, but after I'd killed it I could see it was only a milk snake. I felt bad about that. The markings are the same, but copperheads have poison glands at the base of their skulls, and their heads are shaped like a wedge. Mom said I should have looked carefully before killing it. And I should have.

That same week I saw a black snake in the pit under our bathroom window. It's damp down in there where the pipes enter the house from the wells. I yelled to Betsy and Mom to come watch. The snake had a lump in the middle. Slowly, the lump began moving toward its head and finally the snake disgorged a frog all flattened out and dead. Then the snake slithered away under the house.

But the biggest black snake I ever saw—Big Black Sambo we called him—liked to lie in the sun on the stone wall near the barn. We let him be. Black snakes ate the mice in the barn, Aunt Izzy said, and kept the rattlers away. When Sambo was sunning himself, we'd play follow-the-leader up in the rafters of the barn and jump in the hay. It drove Aunt Izzy wild. She said it spoiled the hay. We didn't believe her. She's a sourpuss and never likes to see anybody have a good time. If we saw her coming, we'd hide in the hay. One time she was so mad she nearly got Philip with the pitchfork. It pricked his leg. He screamed.

Aunt Izzy yelled: "Get out of here, every damn one of you kids. And stay out!" Bill, George, Philip and I came sneaking out from under the hay. We left on the double. Aunt Izzy's face was so red and her eyes so wild, I was scared. She'd gotten Bill in the arm, too. It was bleeding. He said it was nothing. I think Aunt Izzy was crazy that day with the heat, the sunshine or something. I never went back. Bill did.

I was getting ready for bed when I heard Mom scream. I came running. It was nearly dark outside. Mom was staring at the floor, but I heard the rustling on the straw matting before I saw it. A black snake again. My heart started pounding. "I'll get my bat," I whispered, as though it might hear.

"No. Don't hurt it," said Mom. "See, it's leaving. My screaming must have scared it. Let's see where it goes." It slithered away into the kitchen. We followed at a safe distance behind. On the back door it went onto the screened porch. It disappeared under the old ice box. "It must have come up the drip-hole in the floor," said Mom. "We'll have to plug that up in the morning. Come to think of it, melting ice is a good source of water. That snake is wiser than we are." After that it was my job to empty the tray of water under the ice box.

By now we were all pretty sick of sunshine and snakes. There's something brooding and cruel about sunshine that never lets up. Night after night the sun would go down like a huge egg yolk that

broke on the edge of the hill and splattered all over the sky. Red
sky at night may be sailors' delight, but it wasn't mine. Every night a
whippoorwill whipped its brain out—and mine. I had a hard time
getting to sleep. I'd think about how nice it was to hear rain pat-
tering on the roof. Sometimes at night I'd hear dry leaves rustling and
think it was rain. I even prayed for rain.

By the middle of August no one was allowed to draw water from the
old well beside the Big House without special permission from Aunt
Izzy. It was hard to believe that when I was thirsty I couldn't let down
the bucket and draw up the coldest, clearest water in the world and
drink as much as I wanted. And the swimming hole got so low it wasn't
fun anymore.

After a lot of coaxing, Mom finally let me go to Mineral Falls with
the other fellows. It meant a long walk through the woods. She was
afraid we'd come across snakes. But there's a nice, deep pool at the
bottom of the falls, and we needed a decent swim for a change.

Bill led the way. We made a lot of noise as we went through the
woods. We saw no snakes at all. When we reached the top of the falls,
we saw that it, too, had been greatly changed by the drought. Instead of a great waterfall, plunging down and breaking on the boulders below, it was a swift, shallow stream with bare rock showing in
places. Part way down, just at the point where the brook really be-
comes the steep waterfall, a large rock showed. It was right in the
center and divided the stream into two falls. But the pool was still
there, deep and clear, and that was what we had come for.

"I'm going down on the other side for a change," said Bill. He
rock-hopped across the stream. This was something we'd never been
able to do before.

"Not me," replied George. He and Phil started down the way we
always went.

"Wait for me!" I called to Bill. I started across after him. One
minute I was leaping from rock to rock, the next I was on my bottom, heading for the boulders below. I may have screamed. I don't
know. I didn't have time to think. I just slid fast. By a fluke I landed
on the large rock with the water going past me on either side. I sat
there, frozen with fright, too scared to think, to move, to know what
to do.

"Stay still," Bill yelled. "I'll come and get you." He walked down
beside the stream till he was just across from me. He was not very
far away, but it seemed an impossible distance to me. He sat down and
calmly took off his sneakers. Barefooted, he made his way over to me.
"You're okay," he said. "I got over here. We'll both get back." I nod-

ded, sick with fear, unable to look at the pool and the boulders below. Bill told me exactly where to put my feet, he held my hand, and we made it. It took me a while to get un-scared. We went skinny-dipping then in the cold water. But the day had been spoiled, and so had the seat of my pants, which made Mom sore. I didn't tell her exactly what had happened—just that I fell. And no one seemed braver or grander to me than my cousin Bill.

Then, what we dreaded most, happened. It was the weekend. Mom turned on the kitchen faucet, there was a sputtering sound, and no water came out. "That's funny," she said. "I just heard Uncle Will's pump going. There has to be water for it to go. There must be a break in the pipe somewhere below the pump house. Will you go look?" she asked me. "It shouldn't be hard to find. This is serious. I hate to think of wasting a drop these days. Maybe Uncle Will could do something. Lucky he's here today."

I started up the road, inspecting the pipe all the way. Our house and Uncle Will's were hitched to the two wells by a long system of pipes that ran above ground. I could find no break in the pipe along the road. Then I followed the pipe into the woods to the pump house and around to the back where the pipe divides into two. At that point each pipe has its own valve to control the separate water supplies. Water comes down to us by gravity, but Uncle Will's has to be pumped part way back up the slope. I looked at our valve. I could hardly believe what I saw. It was turned almost all the way off. Now, that valve has to be turned with a wrench. Someone had deliberately turned it off!

I heard a noise and looked up just in time to see Bill disappearing behind a tree. It was like Guerrilla War! But this was no game, and I didn't yell: "Bill, you're dead." Our eyes met for an instant. I looked away, but not before I saw the mocking smile on his face and the wrench in his hand. Bill! Bill had turned off our water, so *they* could have it all. Maybe he'd turned the valve more than he meant to this time. Maybe that's why the pressure had been getting so low . . .

I walked slowly back to the house. "Well," said Mom, "what did you find?"

"Our valve's turned almost all the way off." I didn't look her in the eyes.

"Turned off! she cried. "Why who would do a thing like that?" She didn't need me to tell her. "I'm going right up to see Uncle Will. This is outrageous! Did you see anyone?"

"Just a snake," I lied.

"You stay here with Betsy," she said. "I'll be back soon."

It seemed like an awful long time she was gone. I knew I should have told her I'd seen Bill. It would have made it easier for her, maybe. But Bill was my friend. He'd saved my life. . . . But there was Mom all alone against that whole family of robbers, robbers of water! Why hadn't I challenged Bill? Had it out with him there in the woods? He wouldn't have hurt me. I knew that. But I was afraid of that mocking smile. Afraid.

When Mom returned, her lips were pressed tightly together, her face was quite red. "They're lower than snakes," she said. "They *meant* to harm us!" I'd never seen her so mad. "You didn't tell me you saw Bill!"

"I didn't want to snitch on him," I told her.

"Well, *he* snitched on *you*," she said. "He told me you saw him. I must say I'm not very proud of you. They never would have done such a thing if your father were alive . . . Well, we're going home. I'm not going to fight with them again. I don't have the stomach or strength for it."

"Oh, Mom, do we *have* to?" I cried. "It's not fair!"

"Fair?" she said. "Of course it's not fair. A lot of things in this world aren't fair. But there's no help for it. Your Uncle Will told me quite bluntly there are seven of them and three of us. If anyone has to go home, it should be us, he said. So we're going. I told him to leave our valve alone for twenty-four hours, and we'd be gone. Now," she said, "please get me the wrench. I'm going to turn our valve on again. We'll get things cleaned up around here and start packing."

"Want me to come with you, Mom?"

"No," she answered. "I don't." Then she put her arm around me. "I'm sorry. I shouldn't be angry with *you*. I'm just . . . disappointed, that's all. Well, all right. Come along if you want to."

She led the way. She turned on the valve. It was stiff, so I was some help. We started back on the path. She went first. I heard her gasp, give a cry of surprise or pain.

"I've been bitten, she said. "On the ankle." And we watched the copperhead slither off in the brush.

"I'll kill him!" I yelled and started after him.

"No," said Mom. "It's too late now. We need to take care of my bite. Quickly. Come along."

I followed her back to the house. It wasn't fair! Mom was the only one who didn't want to kill snakes. When we got back to the house Betsy was sitting on the porch waiting for us. "Get a knife. Your penknife will do," Mom said to me. "Hold it in the flame on the stove for a few minutes. Then bring it here. I don't want to move around any more than I have to. Hurry!"

When I got back she had her sock off, and I could see the two fang marks on her ankle. "Betsy," she said, "go get the first aid kit." Betsy ran off. "Now," she said, "I can't reach my ankle, so you'll have to suck out the poison for me."

"Oh, Mom, I can't. I'm afraid . . ."

"It doesn't matter to be afraid," she said. "It's what you do when you are that counts." She took the knife and made two quick cuts like she was playing tic-tac-toe on her skin. Blood started pouring out. "Do you want me to die?" she asked. "Don't swallow any of it. Just suck hard and spit it all out." She leaned back on the step and closed her eyes.

I knelt on the ground in front of her and put my lips to her ankle. The taste of blood and poison mixed in my mouth. I sucked and spit, sucked and spit . . . Finally, she said, "I guess that's enough." Before I had time to throw up, she added: "Now run and ask Auntie Blanche to drive me to town. I should see a doctor. Hurry!" She turned to Betsy. "Give me the bandage." I ran.

Betsy held my hand as we watched the car disappear down the road. Mom smiled and waved. She looked awful pale. Betsy started to cry. "Mommy won't die, will she? Mommy won't die!" she wailed.

"She'll be okay," I said. "I sucked all the poison out, didn't I ? Don't cry, Betsy. Don't cry."

But there was this crying inside me. It wasn't for Mom. And not for me. It was on account of how changed everything seemed to be . . .

END